WINSTON GRAHAM

Ross Poldark

A NOVEL OF CORNWALL

1783–1787

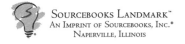
SOURCEBOOKS LANDMARK™
AN IMPRINT OF SOURCEBOOKS, INC.®
NAPERVILLE, ILLINOIS

Published by Sourcebooks Landmark, an imprint of Sourcebooks, Inc.
P.O. Box 4410, Naperville, Illinois 60567-4410
(630) 961-3900
Fax: (630) 961-2168
www.sourcebooks.com

Originally published in London by Werner Laurie Ltd., 1945

Library of Congress Cataloging-in-Publication Data

Graham, Winston.
  Ross Poldark : a novel of Cornwall, 1783-1787 / Winston Graham.
      p. cm.
  1. Poldark, Ross (Fictitious character)--Fiction. 2. Cornwall (England : County)--
Fiction. I. Title.
  PR6013.R24R67 2009
  823'.914--dc22

                        2009029763

                Printed and bound in the United States of America
                VP 10 9 8 7 6 5 4 3 2 1

CONTENTS

PROLOGUE

1

Joshua Poldark died in March 1783. In February of that year, feeling that his tenure was becoming short, he sent for his brother from Trenwith.

Charles came lolloping over on his great roan horse one cold grey afternoon, and Prudie Paynter, lank-haired and dark-faced and fat, showed him straight into the bedroom where Joshua lay possed up with pillows and cushions in the big box bed. Charles looked askance round the room with his small watery blue eyes at the disorder and the dirt, then lifted his coat-tails and subsided upon a wicker chair, which creaked under his weight.

"Well, Joshua."

"Well, Charles."

"This is a bad business."

"Bad indeed."

"When will you be about again, d'you think?"

"There's no telling. I fancy the churchyard will have a strong pull."

Charles thrust out his bottom lip. He would have discounted the remark if he had not had word to the contrary. He hiccupped a little—riding always gave him the wind these days—and was heartily reassuring.

"Nonsense, man. The gout in the legs never killed nobody. It is when it gets up to the head that it is dangerous."

"Choake tells me different, that there is other cause for the swelling. For once I misdoubt if the old fool is not right. Though in God's truth, by all appearance it is you that should be lying here, since I am but half your size."

Charles glanced down at the landscape of black embroidered waistcoat spreading away from under his chin.

"Mine is healthy flesh. Every man puts on weight in his middle years. I would not wish to be a yard of pump water like Cousin William-Alfred."

Joshua lifted an ironical eyebrow but said no more, and there was silence. The brothers had had little to say to each other for many years, and at this, their last meeting, small talk was not easy to find. Charles, the elder and more prosperous, who had come in for the family house and lands and most of the mining interests, head of the family and a respected figure in the county, had never quite been able to get away from a suspicion that his younger brother despised him. Joshua had always been a thorn in his flesh. Joshua had never been content to do the things expected of him: enter the Church or the Army or marry properly and leave Charles to run the district himself.

Not that Charles minded a few lapses, but there were limits and Joshua had overstepped them. The fact that he had been behaving himself for the last few years did not score out old grievances.

As for Joshua, a man with a cynical mind and few illusions, he had no complaint against life or against his brother. He had lived one to the limit and ignored the other. There was some truth in his reply to Charles's next comment of, "Why man, you're young enough yet. Two years junior to me, and I'm fit and well. Aarf!"

Joshua said: "Two years in age, maybe, but you've only lived half as fast."

Charles sucked the ebony tip of his cane and looked sidelong about the room from under heavy lids. "This damned war not settled yet. Prices soaring. Wheat seven and eight shillings a bushel. Butter ninepence a pound. Wish the copper price was the same. We're thinking of cutting a new level at Grambler. Eighty fathom. Maybe it will defray the initial outlay, though I doubt it. Been doing much with your fields this year?"

"It was about the war that I wanted to see you," said Joshua, struggling a little farther up the pillows and gasping for breath. "It must be only a matter of months now before the provisional peace is confirmed. Then Ross will be home and maybe I shall not be here to greet him. You're me brother, though we've never hit it off so well. I want to tell you how things are and to leave you to look after things till he gets back."

Charles took the cane from his mouth and smiled defensively. He looked as if he had been asked for a loan.

"I've not much time, y' know."

'It won't take much of your time. I've little or nothing to leave. There's a copy of my will on the table beside you. Read it at your leisure. Pearce has the original."

Charles groped with his clumsy swollen hand and picked up a piece of parchment from the rickety three-legged table behind him.

"When did you last hear from him?" he asked. "What's to be done if he doesn't come back?"

"The estate will go to Verity. Sell if there are any purchasers; it will fetch little. That's down in the will. Verity will have my share in Grambler too, since she is the only one of your family who has been over since Ross left."

Joshua wiped his nose on the soiled sheet. "But Ross will come back. I've heard from him since the fighting ceased."

"There's many hazards yet."

"I've a feeling," said Joshua. "A conviction. Care to take a wager? Settle when we meet. There'll be some sort of currency in the next world."

Charles stared again at the sallow lined face which had once been so handsome. He was a little relieved that Joshua's request was no more than this, but slow to relax his caution. And irreverence on a deathbed struck him as reckless and uncalled for.

"Cousin William-Alfred was visiting us the other day. He enquired for you."

Joshua pulled a face.

"I told him how ill you was," Charles went on. "He suggested that though you might not wish to call in the Revd. Mr. Odgers, maybe you would like a spiritual consolation from one of your own family."

"Meaning him."

"Well, he's the only one in orders now Betty's husband's gone."

"I want none of them," said Joshua. "Though no doubt it was kindly meant. But if he thought it would do me good to confess my sins, did he think I should rather tell secrets to one of my own blood? No, I'd rather talk to Odgers, half-starved little hornywink though he is. But I want none of them."

"If you change your mind," said Charles, "send Jud over with a message. Aarf!"

Joshua grunted. "I shall know soon enough. But even if there was something in it with all their pomp and praying, should I ask 'em in at this hour? I've lived my life, and by God I've enjoyed it! There's no merit to go snivelling now.

"I'm not sorry for myself and I don't want anyone else to be. What's coming I'll take. That's all."

There was silence in the room. Outside the wind thrust and stirred about the slate and stone.

"Time I was off," said Charles. "These Paynters are letting your place get into a rare mess. Why don't you get someone reliable?"

"I'm too old to swap donkeys. Leave that to Ross. He'll soon put things to rights."
Charles belched disbelievingly. He had no high opinion of Ross's abilities.

"He's in New York now," said Joshua. "Tart of the garrison. He's quite
recovered from his wound. It was lucky he escaped the Yorktown siege. A
captain now, you know. Still in the 62nd Foot. I've mislaid his letter, else I'd
show it you."

"Francis is a great help to me these days," said Charles. "So would Ross have been
to you if he was home instead of cousing around after Frenchmen and Colonials."

"There was one other thing," said Joshua. "D'you see or hear anything of
Elizabeth Chynoweth these days?"

After a heavy meal questions took time to transmit themselves to Charles's
brain, and where his brother was concerned they needed an examination for
hidden motives. "Who is that?" he said clumsily.

"Jonathan Chynoweth's daughter. You know her. A thin, fair child."

"Well, what of it?" said Charles.

"I was asking if you'd seen her. Ross always mentions her. A pretty little thing.
He's counting on her being here when he comes back, and I think it a suitable
arrangement. An early marriage will steady him down, and she couldn't find a
decenter man, though I say it as shouldn't, being his sire. Two good old families.
If I'd been on my feet I should have gone over to see Jonathan at Christmas to
fix it up. We did talk of it before, but he said wait till Ross came back."

"Time I was going," said Charles, creaking to his feet. "I hope the boy will
settle down when he returns, whether he marries or no. He was keeping bad
company that he should never have got into."

"D'you see the Chynoweths now?" Joshua refused to be side-tracked by refer-
ences to his own shortcomings. "I'm cut off from the world here, and Prudie has
no ear for anything but scandal in Sawle."

"Oh, we catch sight of 'em from time to time. Verity and Francis saw them at
a party in Truro this summer—" Charles peered though the window. "Rot me
if it isn't Choake. Well, now you'll have more company, and I thought you said
no one ever came to see you. I must be on my way."

"He's only come quizzing to see how much faster his pills are finishing me off.
That or his politics. As if I care whether Fox is in his earth or hunting Tory chickens."

"Have it as you please." For one of his bulk Charles moved quickly, picking
up hat and gauntlet gloves and making ready to be gone. At the last he stood
awkwardly by the bed, wondering how best to take his leave, while the clip-clop
of a horse's hoofs went past the window.

"Tell him I don't want to see him," said Joshua irritably. "Tell him to give his potions to his silly wife."

"Calm yourself," said Charles. "Aunt Agatha sent her love, mustn's forget that; and she said you was to take hot beer and sugar and eggs. She says that will cure you."

Joshua's irritation lifted.

"Aunt Agatha's a wise old turnip. Tell her I'll do as she says. And—and tell her I'll save her a place beside me." He began to cough.

"God b' w' ye," said Charles hurriedly, and sidled out of the room.

Joshua was left alone.

He had spent many hours alone since Ross went, but they had not seemed to matter until he took to his bed a month ago. Now they were beginning to depress him and fill his mind with fancies. An out-of-doors man to whom impulse all his days had meant action, this painful, gloomy, bedridden life was no life at all. He had nothing to do with his time except think over the past, and the past was not always the most elegant subject matter.

He kept thinking of Grace, his long-dead wife. She had been his mascot. While she lived all had gone well. The mine he opened and called after her brought rich results; this house, begun in pride and hope, had been built; two strong sons. His own indiscretions behind him, he had settled down, promising to rival Charles in more ways than one; he had built this house with the idea that his own branch of the family of Poldark should become rooted no less securely than the main Trenwith tree.

With Grace had gone all his luck. The house half built, the mine had petered out, and with Grace's death, his incentive to expend money and labour on either. The building had been finished off anyhow, though much remained unrealized. Then Wheal Vanity had closed down also and little Claude Anthony had died.

…He could hear Dr. Choake and his brother talking at the front door: his brother's dusky thickened tenor. Choake's voice, deep and slow and pompous. Anger and impotence welled up in Joshua. What the devil did they mean droning away on his doorstep, no doubt discussing him and nodding their heads together and saying, well, after all, what else could one expect. He tugged at the bell beside his bed and waited, fuming, for the flip-flop of Prudie's slippers.

She came at last, ungainly and indistinct in the doorway. Joshua peered at her shortsightedly in the fading light.

"Bring candles, woman. D'you want me to die in the dark? And tell those two old men to be gone."

Prudie hunched herself like a bird of ill omen. "Dr. Choake and Mister Charles, you're meaning, an?"

"Who else?"

She went out, and Joshua fumed again, while there was the sound of a muttered conversation not far from his door. He looked around for his stick, determined to make one more effort to get up and walk out to them. But then the voices were raised again in farewells, and a horse could be heard moving away across the cobbles and towards the stream.

That was Charles. Now for Choake…

There was a loud rap of a riding crop on his door and the surgeon came in.

Thomas Choake was a Bodmin man who had practised in London, had married a brewer's daughter, and returned to his native county to buy a small estate near Sawle. He was a tall clumsy man with a booming voice, thatch-grey eyebrows, and an impatient mouth. Among the smaller gentry his London experience stood him in good stead; they felt he was abreast of up-to-date physical ideas. He was surgeon to several of the mines in the district, and with the knife had the same neck-or-nothing approach that he had on the hunting field.

Joshua thought him a humbug and had several times considered calling in Dr. Pryce from Redruth. Only the fact that he had no more faith in Dr. Pryce prevented him.

"Well, well," said Dr. Choake. "So we've been having visitors, eh? We'll feel better, no doubt, for our brother's visit."

"I've got some business off my hands," said Joshua. "That was the purpose of inviting him."

Dr. Choake felt for the invalid's pulse with heavy fingers. "Cough," he said. Joshua grudgingly obeyed.

"Our condition is much the same," said the surgeon. "The distemper has not increased. Have we been taking the pills?"

"Charles is twice my size. Why don't you doctor him?"

"You are ill, Mr. Poldark. Your brother is not. I do not prescribe unless called upon to do so." Choake lifted back the bedclothes and began to prod his patient's swollen leg.

"Great mountain of a fellow," grumbled Joshua. *"He'll* never see his feet again."

"Oh, come; your brother is not out of the common. I well remember when I was in London—"

"Uff!"

"Did that hurt?"

"No," said Joshua.

Choake prodded again to make sure. "There is a distinct abatement in the condition of our left leg. There is still too much water in both. If we could get the heart to pump it away. I well remember when I was in London being called in to the victim of a tavern brawl in Westminster. He had quarrelled with an Italian Jew, who drew a dagger and thrust it up to the hilt into my patient's belly. But so thick was the protective fat that I found the knife point had not even pierced the bowel. A sizeable fellow. Let me see, did I bleed you when I was last here?"

"You did."

"I think we might leave it this time. Our heart is inclined to be excitable. Control the choler, Mr. Poldark. An even temper helps the body to secrete the proper juices."

"Tell me," said Joshua. "Do you see anything of the Chynoweths? The Chynoweths of Cusgarne, y'know. I asked my brother, but he returned an evasive answer."

"The Chynoweths? I see them from time to time. I think they are in health. I am not, of course, their physician and we do not call on each other socially."

No, thought Joshua. Mrs. Chynoweth will have a care for that. "I smell something shifty in Charles," he said shrewdly. "Do you see Elizabeth?"

"The daughter? She is about."

"There was an understanding as to her between myself and her father."

"Indeed. I had not heard of it."

Joshua pushed himself up the pillows. His conscience had begun to prick him. It was late in the day for the growth of this long-dormant faculty, but he was fond of Ross, and in the long hours of his illness he had begun to wonder whether he should not have done more to keep his son's interests warm.

"I think maybe I'll send Jud over tomorrow," he muttered. "I'll ask Jonathan to come and see me."

"I doubt if Mr. Chynoweth will be free; it's the Quarter Sessions this week. Ah, that's a welcome sight!"

Prudie Paynter came lumbering in with two candles. The yellow light showed up her sweaty red face with its draping of black hair.

"Ad your physic, 'ave you?" she asked in a throaty whisper.

Joshua turned irritably on the doctor. "I've told you before, Choake; pills I'll swallow, God help me, but draughts and potions I'll not face."

"I well remember," Choake said ponderously, "when I was practising in Bodmin as a young man, one of my patients, an elderly gentleman who suffered much from strangury and stone—"

"Don't stand there, Prudie," snapped Joshua to his servant. "Get out."

Prudie stopped scratching and reluctantly left the room.

"So you think I'm on the mend, eh?" Joshua said before the physician could go on. "How long before I'm up and about?"

"Hm, hm. A slight abatement, I said. Great care yet awhile. We'll have you on your feet before Ross returns. Take my prescriptions regular and you will find they will set you up—"

"How's your wife?" Joshua asked maliciously.

Again interrupted, Choake frowned. "Well enough, thank you." The fact that the fluffy lisping Polly, though only half his age, had added no family to the dowry she brought was a standing grievance against her. So long as she was unfruitful he had no influence to dissuade women from buying motherwort and other less respectable brews from travelling gypsies.

2

The doctor had gone and Joshua was once more alone—alone this time until morning. He might, by pulling persistently on the bell cord, call a reluctant Jud or Prudie until such time as they went to bed, but after that there was no one, and before that they were showing signs of deafness as his illness became more clear. He knew they spent most of each evening drinking, and once they reached a certain stage, nothing at all would move them. But he hadn't the energy to round on them as in the old days.

It would have been different if Ross had been here. For once Charles was right but only partly right. It was he, Joshua, who had encouraged Ross to go away. He had no belief in keeping boys at home as additional lackeys. Let them find their own stirrups. Besides, it would have been undignified to have his son brought up in court for being party to an assault upon excise men, with its associated charges of brandy running and the rest. Not that Cornish magistrates would have convicted, but the question of gaming debts might have been raised.

No, it was Grace who should have been here, Grace who had been snatched from him thirteen years back.

Well, now he was alone and would soon be joining his wife. It did not occur to him to feel surprise that the other women in his life scarcely touched his thoughts. They had been creatures of a pleasant exciting game, the more mettle-some the better, but no sooner broken in than forgotten.

The candles were guttering in the draught from under the door. The wind was rising. Jud had said there was a ground swell this morning; after a quiet cold spell they were returning to rain and storm.

He felt he would like one more look at the sea, which even now was licking at the rocks behind the house. He had no sentimental notions about the sea; he had no regard for its dangers or its beauties; to him it was a close acquaintance whose every virtue and failing, every smile and tantrum he had come to understand.

The land too. Was the Long Field ploughed? Whether Ross married or not there would be little enough to live on without the land.

With a decent wife to manage things… Elizabeth was an only child; a rare virtue worth bearing in mind. The Chynoweths were a bit poverty-stricken, but there would be something. Must go and see Jonathan and fix things up. "Look here, Jonathan," he would say. "Ross won't have much money, but there's the land, and that always counts in the long run—"

Joshua dozed. He thought he was out walking round the edge of the Long Field with the sea on his right and a strong wind pressing against his shoulder. A bright sun warmed his back and the air tasted like wine from a cold cellar. The tide was out on Hendrawna Beach, and the sun drew streaky reflections in the wet sand. The Long Field had not only been ploughed but was already sown and sprouting.

He skirted the field until he reached the furthest tip of Damsel Point where the low cliff climbed in ledges and boulders down to the sea. The water surged and eddied, changing colour on the shelves of dripping rocks.

With some special purpose in mind he climbed down the rocks until the cold sea suddenly surged about his knees, sending pain through his legs unpleasantly like the pain he had felt from the swelling these last few months. But it did not stop him, and he let himself slip into the water until it was up to his neck. Then he struck out from the shore. He was full of joy at being in the sea again after a lapse of two years. He breathed out his pleasure in long, cool gasps, allowed the water to lap close against his eyes. Lethargy crept up his limbs. With the sound of the waves in his ears and heart he allowed himself to drift and sink into cool, feathery darkness.

Joshua slept. Outside, the last trailing patterns of daylight moved quietly out of the sky and left the house and the trees and the stream and the cliffs in darkness. The wind freshened, blowing steadily and strongly from the west, searching among the ruined mine sheds on the hill, rustling the tops of the sheltered apple trees, lifting a corner of loose thatch on one of the barns, blowing a spatter of cold rain in through a broken shutter of the library where two rats nosed with cautious jerky scraping movements among the lumber and the dust. The stream hissed and bubbled in the darkness, and above it a long-unmended gate swung whee-tap on its hangings. In the kitchen, Jud Paynter unstoppered a second jar of gin and Prudie threw a fresh log on the fire.

"Wind's rising, blast it," said Jud. "Always there's wind. Always when you don't want it there's wind."

"We'll need more wood 'fore morning," said Prudie.

"Use this stool," said Jud. "The wood's 'ard, twill smoulder."

"Give me a drink, you black worm," said Prudie.

"Wait on yourself," said Jud.

Joshua slept.

BOOK ONE

OCTOBER 1783–APRIL 1785

CHAPTER ONE

1

IT WAS WINDY. THE PALE AFTERNOON SKY WAS SHREDDED WITH CLOUDS, THE road, grown dustier and more uneven in the last hour, was scattered with blown and rustling leaves.

There were five people in the coach; a thin clerkly man with a pinched face and a shiny suit, and his wife, fat as her husband was thin, and holding to her breast a confused bundle of pink and white draperies from one end of which pouted the creased and overheated features of a young baby. The other travellers were men, both young, one a clergyman of about thirty-five, the other some years his junior.

Almost since the coach left St. Austell there had been silence inside it. The child slept soundly despite the jolting of the vehicle and the rattle of the windows and the clank of the swingle bars; nor had the stops wakened it. From time to time the elderly couple exchanged remarks in undertones, but the thin husband was unwilling to talk, a little overawed by the superior class in which he found himself. The younger of the two men had been reading a book throughout the journey, the elder had watched the passing countryside, one hand holding back the faded dusty brown velvet curtain.

This was a small spare man, severe in clerical black, wearing his own hair scraped back and curled above and behind the ears. The cloth he wore was of fine quality and his stockings were of silk. His was a long, keen, humourless, thin-lipped face, vital and hard. The little clerk knew the face but could not name it.

The clergyman was in much the same position over the other occupant of the coach. A half-dozen times his glance had rested on the thick unpowdered hair opposite, and on the face of his fellow traveller.

When they were not more than fifteen minutes out of Truro and the horses had slowed to a walking pace up the stiff hill, the other man looked up from his book and their eyes met.

"You'll pardon me, sir," said the clergyman in a sharp, vigorous voice. "Your features are familiar, but I find it hard to recall where we have met. Was it in Oxford?"

The young man was tall and thin and big-boned, with a scar on his cheek. He wore a double-breasted riding coat cut away short in front to show the waistcoat and the stout breeches, both of a lighter brown. His hair, which had a hint of copper in its darkness, was brushed back and tied at the back with brown ribbon.

"You're the Revd. Dr. Halse, aren't you?" he said.

The little clerk, who had been following this exchange, made an expressive face at his wife. Rector of Towerdreth, Curate of St. Erme, Headmaster of Truro Grammar School, high burgess of the town and late mayor, Dr. Halse was a personage. It explained his bearing.

"You know me, then," said Dr. Halse with a gracious air. "I usually have a memory for faces."

"You have had many pupils."

"Ah, that explains it. Maturity changes a face. And—hm. Let me see... is it Hawkey?"

"Poldark."

The clergyman's eyes narrowed in an effort of remembrance. "Francis, is it? I thought—"

"Ross. You will remember my cousin more clearly. He stayed on. I felt, quite wrongly, that at thirteen my education had gone far enough."

Recognition came. "Ross Poldark. Well, well. You've changed. I remember now," said Dr. Halse with a glint of cold humour. "You were insubordinate. I had to thrash you at frequent intervals, and then you ran way."

"Yes." Poldark turned the page of his book. "A bad business. And your ankles as sore as my buttocks."

Two small pink spots came to the clergyman's cheeks. He stared a moment at Ross and then turned to look out of the window.

The little clerk had heard of the Poldarks, had heard of Joshua, from whom, they said, in the fifties and sixties no pretty woman married or unmarried was safe. This must be his son. An unusual face with its strongly set cheekbones, wide mouth, and large, strong white teeth. The eyes were a very clear blue-grey under the heavy lids which gave a number of the Poldarks that deceptively sleepy look.

Dr. Halse was returning to the attack.

"Francis, I suppose, is well? Is he married?"

"Not when I last heard, sir. I've been in America some time."

"Dear me. A deplorable mistake, the fighting. I was against it throughout. Did you see much of the war?"

"I was in it."

They had reached the top of the hill at last and the driver was slackening his bearing reins at the descent before him.

Dr. Halse wrinkled his sharp nose. "You are a Tory?"

"A soldier."

"Well, it was not the fault of the soldiers that we lost. England's heart was not in it. We have a derelict old man on the throne. He'll not last much longer. The Prince has different views."

The road in the steepest part of the hill was deeply rutted, and the coach jolted and swayed dangerously. The baby began to cry. They reached the bottom and the man beside the driver blew a blast on his horn. They turned into St. Austell Street. It was a Tuesday afternoon and there were few people about the shops. Two half-naked urchins ran the length of the street begging for a copper, but gave up the chase as the coach swayed into the mud of St. Clement's Street. With much creaking and shouting they rounded the sharp corner, crossed the river by the narrow bridge, jolted over granite cobbles, turned and twisted again, and at last drew up before the Red Lion Inn.

In the bustle that followed, the Revd. Dr. Halse got out first with a stiff word of farewell and was gone, stepping briskly between the puddles of rainwater and horse urine to the other side of the narrow street. Poldark rose to follow, and the clerk saw for the first time that he was lame.

"Can I help you, sir?" he offered, putting down his belongings.

The young man refused with thanks and, handed out from the outside by a postboy, climbed down.

2

When Ross left the coach rain was beginning to fall, a thin fine rain blowing before the wind, which was gusty and uncertain here in the hollow of the hills.

He gazed about him and sniffed. All this was so familiar, quite as truly a coming home as when he would reach his own house. This narrow cobbled street with the streamlet of water bubbling down it, the close-built squat houses with their bow windows and lace curtains, many of them partly screening faces which were watching the arrival of the coach, even the cries of the postboys seemed to have taken on a different and more familiar note.

Truro in the old days had been the centre of "life" for him and his family. A port and a coinage town, *the* shopping centre and a meeting place of fashion, the town had grown rapidly in the last few years, new and stately houses having sprung up among the disorderly huddle of old ones to mark its adoption as a winter and town residency by some of the oldest and most powerful families in Cornwall. The new aristocracy too were leaving their mark: the Lemons, the Treworthys, the Warleggans, families which had pushed their way up from humble beginnings on the crest of the new industries.

A strange town. He felt it more on his return. A secretive, important little town, clustering in the fold of the hills astride and about its many streams, almost surrounded by running water and linked to the rest of the world by fords, by bridges, and by stepping-stones. Miasma and the other fevers were always rife.

…There was no sign of Jud.

He limped into the inn.

"My man was to meet me," he said. "Paynter is his name. Jud Paynter of Nampara."

The landlord peered at him shortsightedly. "Oh, Jud Paynter. Yes, we know him well, sir. But we have not seen him today. You say he was to meet you here? Boy, go and ascertain if Paynter—you know him?—if Paynter is in the stables or has been here today."

Ross ordered a glass of brandy and by the time it came the boy was back to say that Mr. Paynter had not been seen that day.

"The arrangement was quite definite. It doesn't matter. You have a saddle horse I can hire?"

The landlord rubbed the end of his long nose. "Well, we have a mare that was left here three days gone. In fact, we held it in lieu of a debt. I don't think there could be any objection to loaning her if you could give me some reference."

"My name is Poldark. I am a nephew to Mr. Charles Poldark of Trenwith."

"Dear, dear, yes; I should have recognized you, Mr. Poldark. I'll have the mare saddled for you at once."

"No, wait. There's some daylight yet. Have her ready in an hour."

Out in the street again, Ross turned down the narrow slit of Church Lane. At the end he bore right and, after passing the school where his education had come to an ungracious end, he stopped before a door on which was printed: "Nat. G. Pearce. Notary and Commissioner of Oaths." He pulled at the bell for some time before a pimply woman admitted him.

"Mr. Pearce bean't well today," she said. "I'll see if he'll see you."

She climbed the wooden stairs, and after an interval called down an invitation over the worm-eaten banisters. He groped a way up and was shown into a parlour.

Mr. Nathanial Pearce was sitting in an easy chair in front of a large fire with one leg tied in bandages propped upon another chair. He was a big man with a big face, coloured a light plum purple from overeating.

"Oh, now this is a surprise, I do exclaim, Mr. Poldark. How pleasant. You'll forgive me if I don't rise; the old trouble; each attack seems worse than the last. Take a seat."

Ross grasped a moist hand and chose a chair as far from the fire as was polite. Insufferably hot in here and the air was old and stale.

"You'll remember," he said, "I wrote you I was returning this week."

"Oh yes, Mr.—er—Captain Poldark; it had slipped my memory for the moment; how nice to call in on your way home." Mr. Pearce adjusted his bob-wig which, in the way of his profession, had a high frontlet and a long bag at the back tied in the middle. "I am desolate here, Captain Poldark; my daughter offers me no company; she has become converted to some Methodist way of belief, and is out almost every night at a prayer meeting. She talks so much of God that it quite embarrasses me. You must have a glass of canary."

"My stay is to be short," said Ross. It certainly must, he thought, or I shall sweal away. "I am anxious to be home again but thought I'd see you on my way. Your letter did not reach me until a fortnight before we sailed from New York."

"Dear, dear, such a delay; what a blow it would be; and you have been wounded; is it severe?"

Ross eased his leg. "I see from your letter that my father died in March. Who has administered the estate since then, my uncle or you?"

Mr. Pearce absently scratched the ruffles on his chest. "I know you would wish me to be frank with you."

"Of course."

"Well, when we came to go into his affairs, Mr.—er—Captain Poldark, it did not seem that he had left much for either of us to administer."

A slow smile crept over Ross's mouth; it made him look younger, less intractable.

"Everything was naturally left to you. I'll give you a copy of the will before you go; should you predecease him, then to his niece Verity. Aside from the actual property there is little to come in for. Ouch, this thing is twinging most damnably!"

"I have never looked on my father as a wealthy man. I asked, though, and was anxious to know, for a special reason. He was buried at Sawle?"

The lawyer stopped scratching and eyed the other man shrewdly. "You're thinking of settling at Nampara now, Captain Poldark?"

"I am."

"Any time I can do any business for you, only too pleased. I should say," Mr. Pearce hastened on as the young man rose. "I should say that you may find your property a little neglected."

Ross turned.

"I have not ridden over myself," said Mr. Pearce; "this leg, you know; most distressing, and me not yet two and fifty; but my clerk has been out. Your father was in failing health for some time and things are not kept just so neat and tidy as you'd like when the master's not about, are they? Nor's your uncle so young as he used to be. Is Paynter meeting you with a horse?"

"He was to have done so but has not turned up."

"Then, my dear sir, why not stay the night with us? My daughter will be home from her praying in time to cook me a bite of supper. We have pork; I know we have pork; and an excellent bed; yes, it would suit me well."

Ross took out a handkerchief and mopped his face.

"It's very kind of you. I feel that, being so near my home today, I should prefer to reach it."

Mr. Pearce sighed and struggled into a more upright position. "Then give me a hand, will you? I'll get you a copy of the will, so's you may take it home and read it at your leisure."

CHAPTER TWO

1

Dinner was in progress at Trenwith House.

It would normally have been over by this time; when Charles Poldark and his family dined alone, the meal seldom took more than two hours, but this was a special occasion. And because of the guests the meal was taking place in the hall in the centre of the house, a room too large and draughty when the family had only itself to victual.

There were ten people sitting at the long narrow oak table. At the head was Charles himself, with his daughter Verity on his left. On his right was Elizabeth Chynoweth and next to her Francis, his son. Beyond them were Mr. and Mrs. Chynoweth, Elizabeth's parents, and at the foot of the table Aunt Agatha crumbled soft food and munched it between her toothless jaws. Up the other side Cousin William-Alfred was in conversation with Dr. and Mrs. Choake.

The fish, the poultry, and the meat dishes were finished, and Charles had just called for the sweets. At all meals he was troubled with wind, which made female guests an embarrassment.

"Damme," he said, in a silence of repletion which had fallen on the company, "I don't know why you two doves don't get married tomorrow instead of waiting for a month for more. Aarf! What d'you lack? Are you afraid you'll change your minds?"

"For my part I would take your advice," said Francis. "But it is Elizabeth's day as well as mine."

"One short month is little enough," said Mrs. Chynoweth, fumbling at the locket on the handsome encrusted lace of her dress. Her fine looks were marred by a long and acquisitive nose; on first seeing her one felt a sense of shock at so much beauty spoiled.

"How can one expect *me* to prepare, let alone the poor child? In one's daughter one lives one's own wedding day over afresh. I only wish that our preparations could be more extensive." She glanced at her husband.

"What did she say?" asked Aunt Agatha.

"Well, there it is," said Charles Poldark. "There it is. I suppose we must be patient since they are. Well, I give you a toast. To the happy pair!"

"You've toasted that three times already," objected Francis.

"No matter. Four is a luckier number."

"But I cannot drink with you."

"Hush, boy! That's unimportant."

Amid some laughter the toast was drunk. As the glasses clattered back upon the table, lights were brought. Then the housekeeper, Mrs. Tabb, arrived with the apple tarts, the plum cake, and the jellies.

"Now," said Charles, flourishing his knife and fork over the largest apple tart. "I hope this will prove as tasty as it looks. Where's the cream? Oh, there. Put it on for me, Verity, my dear."

"I'm sorry," said Elizabeth, breaking her silence. "But I'm quite unable to eat anything more."

Elizabeth Chynoweth was slighter than her mother had ever been, and there was in her face the beauty which her mother had missed. As the yellow light from the candles pushed the darkness back and up towards the high-raftered ceiling, the fine clear whiteness of her took one's attention among the shadows of the room and against the sombre wood of the high-backed chair.

"Nonsense, child," said Charles. "You're thin as a wraith. Must get some blood into you."

"Indeed, I—"

"Dear Mr. Poldark," said Mrs. Chynoweth mincingly, "to look at her you would not credit how obstinate she can be. For twenty years I have been trying to make her eat, but she just turns away from the choicest food. Perhaps you'll be able to coax her, Francis."

"I am very satisfied with her as she is," said Francis.

"Yes yes," said his father. "But a little food… Damme, that does no one any harm. A wife needs to be strong and well."

"Oh, she is really very strong," Mrs. Chynoweth hastened on. "You would be surprised at that too. It is the breed, nothing more than the breed. Was I not frail as a girl, Jonathan?"

"Yes, my pet," said Jonathan.

"Hark, how the wind's rising!" said Aunt Agatha, crumbling her cake.

"That is something I cannot understand," said Dr. Choake. "How your aunt, though deaf, Mr. Poldark, is always sensible to the sounds of nature."

"I believe she imagines it half the time."

"That I do not!" said Aunt Agatha. "How dare you, Charles!"

"Was that someone at the door?" Verity interposed.

Tabb was out of the room, but Mrs. Tabb had heard nothing. The candles flickered in the draught, and the red damask curtains over the long windows moved as if a hand were stirring them.

"Expecting someone, my dear?" asked Mrs. Chynoweth.

Verity did not blush. She had little of her brother's good looks, being small and dark and sallow with the large mouth which came to some of the Poldarks.

"I expect it is the cowshed door," said Charles, taking a swill of port. "Tabb was to have looked to it yesterday but he rode with me into St. Ann's. I'll thrash young Bartle for not attending to his work."

"They do thay," lisped Mrs. Choake to Mrs. Chynoweth, "they do thay as how that the Prince is living at an outrageous wate. I was weading in the *Mercury* as how Mr. Fox had pwomised him an income of one hundred thousand pounds a year, and now that he is in power he is hard put to it to wedeem his pwomith."

"It would seem unlikely," said Mr. Chynoweth, "that that would worry Mr. Fox unduly." A smallish man with a silky white beard, his was a defensive pomposity, adopted to hide the fact that he had never in his life made up his mind about anything. His wife had married him when she was eighteen and he thirty-one. Both Jonathan and his income had lost ground since then.

"And what's wrong with Mr. Fox, I'm asking you?" Dr Choake said deeply from under his eyebrows.

Mr. Chynoweth pursed his lips. "I should have considered that plain."

"Opinions differ, sir. I may say, that if I—"

The surgeon broke off as his wife took the rare liberty of treading on his toe. Today was the first time the Choakes and the Chynoweths had met socially; to her it seemed folly to begin a political wrangle with these still influential gentlefolk.

Thomas Choake was turning ungratefully to squash Polly with a look, but she was saved the worst of his spleen. This time there could be no mistake that someone was knocking on the outer door. Mrs. Tabb set down the tray of tarts and went to the door.

The wind made the curtains billow, and the candles dripped grease down their silver sconces.

"God help me!" said the housekeeper as if she had seen a ghost.

2

Ross came into a company quite unprepared for his arrival. When his figure showed in the doorway, one after another of those at the table broke into words of surprise. Elizabeth and Francis and Verity and Dr. Choake were on their feet; Charles lay back grunting and inert from shock. Cousin William-Alfred polished his steel spectacles, while Aunt Agatha plucked at his sleeve mumbling, "What is it? What's to do? The meal isn't over."

Ross screwed up his eyes until they grew used to the light. Trenwith House was almost on his way home, and he had not thought to intrude on a party.

First to greet him was Verity. She ran across and put her arms round his neck. "Why, Ross dear! Fancy now!" was all she could find to say.

"Verity!" He gave her a hug. And then he saw Elizabeth.

"Stap me," said Charles. "So you're back at last, boy. You're late for dinner, but we've some apple tart left."

"Did they lame us, Ross?" said Dr. Choake. "A pox on the whole war. It was ill-starred. Thank God it's over."

Francis, after a short hesitation, came quickly round the table and grasped the other man's hand. "It's good to see you back, Ross! We've missed you."

"It's good to be back," said Ross. "To see you all and—"

The colour of the eyes under the same heavy lids was the only mark of cousinship. Francis was compact, slim, and neat, with the fresh complexion and clear features of handsome youth. He looked what he was, carefree, easygoing, self-confident, a young man who has never known what it was to be in danger or short of money, or to pit his strength against another man's except in games or horseplay. Someone at school had christened them "the fair Poldark and the dark Poldark." They had always been good friends, which was surprising, since their fathers had not.

"This is a solemn occasion," said Cousin William-Alfred, his bony hands grasping the back of his chair. "A family reunion in more than name. I trust you're not seriously wounded, Ross. That scar is a considerable disfigurement."

"Oh, that," said Ross. "That would be of no moment if I didn't limp like Jago's donkey."

He went round the table greeting the others. Mrs. Chynoweth welcomed him coldly, extending a hand from a distance.

"Do tell us," lisped Polly Choake, "do tell us thome of your experwiences, Captain Poldark, how we lost the war, what these Amewicans are like, and —"

"Very like us, ma'am. That's why we lost it." He had reached Elizabeth.

"Well, Ross," she said softly.

His eyes feasted on her face. "This is most opportune. I couldn't have wished it different."

"I could," she said. "Oh, Ross, I could."

"And what are you going to do now, my lad?" asked Charles. "It's high time you settled down. Property don't look after itself, and you can't trust hirelings. Your father could have done with you this last year and more—"

"I almost called to see you tonight," Ross said to Elizabeth, "but left it for tomorrow. Self-restraint is rewarded."

"I must explain. I wrote you, but—"

"Why," said Aunt Agatha, "Lord damn me if it isn't Ross! Come here, boy! I thought you was gone to make one of the blest above."

Reluctantly Ross walked down the table to greet his great-aunt. Elizabeth stayed where she was, holding the back of her chair so that her knuckles were whiter even than her face.

Ross kissed Aunt Agatha's whiskery cheek. Into her ear he said: "I'm glad to see, Aunt, that you're still one of the blest below."

She chuckled with delight, showing her pale brownish-pink gums. "Not so blest, maybe. But I wouldn't want to be changing just yet."

The conversation became general, everyone questioning Ross as to when he had landed, what he had done and seen while away.

"Elizabeth," said Mrs. Chynoweth, "fetch me my wrap from upstairs, will you? I am a little chilly."

"Yes, Mother." She turned and walked away, tall and virginal, groped with her hand for the oak banister.

"That fellow Paynter is a rogue," said Charles, wiping his hands down the sides of his breeches. "If I was you I should throw him out and get a reliable man."

Ross was watching Elizabeth going up the stairs. "He was my father's friend."

Charles shrugged in some annoyance. "You won't find the house in a good state of repair."

"It wasn't when I left."

"Well, it's worse now. I haven't been over for some time. You know what your father used to say about coming in the other direction: 'It is too far to walk and not far enough to ride.'"

"Eat this, Ross," said Verity, bringing a piled plate to him. "And sit here."

Ross thanked her and took the seat offered him between Aunt Agatha and Mr. Chynoweth. He would have preferred to be beside Elizabeth, but that would have to wait. He was surprised to find Elizabeth here. She and her mother and father had never once been to Nampara in the two years he had known her. Two or three times he glanced up as he ate to see if she was returning.

Verity was helping Mrs. Tabb to carry out some of the used dishes; Francis stood plucking at his lip by the front door; the others were back in their chairs. A silence had fallen on the company.

"It is no easy countryside to which you return," said Mr. Chynoweth, pulling at his beard.

"Discontent is rife. Taxes are high, wages have fallen. The country is exhausted from its many wars; and now the Whigs are in. I can think of no worse a prospect."

"Had the Whigs been in before," said Dr. Choake, refusing to be tactful, "none of this need have happened."

Ross looked across at Francis. "I've interrupted a party. Is it in celebration of the peace or in honour of the next war?"

Thus he forced the explanation they had hesitated to give.

"No," said Francis. "I—er—The position is—"

"We are celebrating something far different," said Charles, motioning for his glass to be filled again. "Francis is to be married. That is what we're celebrating."

"To be married," said Ross, slicing his food. "Well, well; and who—"

"To Elizabeth," said Mrs. Chynoweth.

There was silence.

Ross put down his knife. "To—"

"To my daughter."

"Can I get you something to drink?" Verity whispered to Elizabeth, who had just reached the bottom of the stairs.

"No, no... Please no."

"Oh," said Ross. "To... Elizabeth."

"We are very happy," said Mrs. Chynoweth, "that our two ancient families are to be united. Very happy and very proud. I am sure, Ross, that you will join with us in wishing Francis and Elizabeth all happiness in their union."

Walking very carefully, Elizabeth came over to Mrs. Chynoweth.

"Your wrap, Mama."

"Thank you, my dear."

Ross went on with his meal.

"I don't know what your opinion is," said Charles heartily after a pause, "but for myself I am attached to this port. It was run over from Cherbourg in the autumn of '79. When I tasted a sample I said to meself, it is too good to be repeated; I'll buy the lot. Nor has it been repeated; nor has it." He put down his hands to ease his great paunch against the table.

"I s'pose you'll be settling down now, Ross, eh?" said Aunt Agatha, a wrinkled hand on his sleeve. "How about a little wife for you, eh? That's what we've to find next!"

Ross looked across at Dr. Choake.

"You attended my father?"

Dr. Choake nodded.

"Did he suffer much?"

"At the end. But the time was short."

"It was strange that he should fail so quickly."

"Nothing could be done. It was a dropsical condition that was beyond the power of man to allay."

"I rode over," said Cousin William-Alfred, "to see him twice. But I regret that he was not—hm—in the mood to make the most of such spiritual comfort as I could offer. It was to me a personal sorrow that I could be of so little help to one of my own blood."

"You must have some of this apple tart, Ross," said Verity in an undertone behind him, glancing at the veins in his neck. "I made it myself this afternoon."

"I mustn't stop. I called here only for a few minutes and to rest my horse, which is lame."

"Oh, but there's no need to go tonight. I have told Mrs. Tabb to prepare a room. Your horse may stumble in the dark and throw you."

Ross looked up at Verity and smiled. In this company no private word could pass between them.

Now Francis, and to a lesser degree his father, joined in the argument. But Francis was constrained, his father half-hearted, and Ross determined.

Charles said: "Well, have it as you wish, boy. I would not fancy arriving at Nampara tonight. It will be cold and wet and perhaps no welcome. Pour some more spirit into you to keep out the chill."

Ross did as he was urged, drinking three glasses in succession. With the fourth he got to his feet.

"To Elizabeth," he said slowly, "and to Francis... May they find happiness together."

The toast was drunk more quietly than the others. Elizabeth was still standing behind her mother's chair; Francis had at last moved from the door to put a hand beneath her arm.

In the silence which followed, Mrs. Choake said:

"How nithe it must be to be home again. I never go away, even a little way, without feeling that gwatified to be back. What are the Amewican colonies like, Captain Poldark? They thay as how even the thun does not wise and thet in the thame way in foreign parts."

Polly Choake's inanity seemed to relieve the tension, and talk broke out again while Ross finished his meal. There was more than one there conscious of relief that he had taken the news so quietly.

Ross, however, was not staying, and presently took his leave.

"You'll come over in a day or two, will you not?" said Francis, a rush of affection in his voice. "We've heard nothing so far, nothing but the barest details of your experiences or how you were wounded or of your journey home. Elizabeth will be returning home tomorrow. We plan to be married in a month. If you want my help at Nampara, send a message over; you know I shall be pleased to come. Why, it's like old times seeing you back again! We feared for your life, did we not, Elizabeth?"

"Yes," said Elizabeth.

Ross picked up his hat. They were standing together at the door, waiting for Tabb to bring round Ross's mare. He had refused the loan of a fresh horse for the last three miles.

"He'll be here now, that's if he can handle her. I warned him to be careful."

Francis opened the door. The wind blew in a few spots of rain. He went out tactfully to see if Tabb had come.

Ross said: "I hope my mistimed resurrection hasn't cast a cloud over your evening."

The light from indoors threw a shaft across her face, showed up the grey eyes. The shadows had spread to her face and she looked ill.

"I'm so happy that you're back, Ross. I had feared, we had all feared—What can you think of me?"

"Two years is a long time, isn't it? Too long perhaps."

"Elizabeth," said Mrs. Chynoweth. "Take care the night air does not catch you."

"No, Mama."

"Goodbye." He took her hand.

Francis came back. "He's here now. Did you buy the mare? She's a handsome creature but very ill tempered."

"Ill usage makes the sweetest of us vicious," said Ross. "Has the rain stopped?"

"Not quite. You know your way?"

Ross showed his teeth. "Every stone. Has it changed?"

"Nothing to mislead you. Do not cross the Mellingey by the bridge: the middle plank is rotten."

"So it was when I left."

"Do not forget," said Francis. "We expect you back here soon. Verity will want to see more of you. If she can spare the time, we will ride over tomorrow."

But only the wind and the rain answered him and the clatter of hoofs as the mare sidestepped resentfully down the drive.

3

Darkness had fallen by now, though a patch of fading light glimmered in the west. The wind blew more strongly, and the soft rain beat in flurries about his head.

His was not an easy face to read, and you couldn't have told that in the last half hour he had suffered the worst knock of his life. Except that he no longer whistled into the wind or talked to his irritable mare, there was nothing to show.

At an early age he had caught from his father a view of things which took very little for granted, but in his dealings with Elizabeth Chynoweth, he had fallen into the sort of trap such an outlook might have helped him to avoid. They had been in love since she was sixteen and he barely twenty. When his own high-spirited misadventures caught up with him, he had thought his father's solution of a commission in the Army a good idea while the trouble blew over. He had gone away eager for fresh experience and sure of the one circumstance of his return which would really matter.

No doubt was in his own mind, and he had looked for none in hers.

After he had been riding for a time, the lights of Grambler Mine showed up ahead. This was the mine round which the varying fortunes of the main Poldark family centred. On its vagaries depended not merely the prosperity of Charles Poldark and his family but the subsistence level of some three hundred miners and their families scattered in huts and cottages about the parish. To them the mine was a benevolent Moloch to whom they fed their children at an early age and from whom they took their daily bread.

He saw swinging lights approaching and drew into the side of the track to let a mule train pass, with the panniers of copper ore slung on either side of the animals' backs. One of the men in charge peered up at him suspiciously, then shouted a greeting. It was Mark Daniel.

The main buildings of the mine were all about him now, most of them huddled together and indeterminate, but here and there the sturdy scaffolding of headgear and the big stonebuilt engine houses stood out. Yellow lights showed in the arched upper windows of the engine houses, warm and mysterious against the low night sky. He passed close beside one of them and heard the rattle and clang of the great draught bob pumping water up from the lowest places of the earth.

There were miners in groups and a number of lanterns. Several men peered up at the figure on the horse, but although several said good night he thought that none of these recognized him.

Then a bell rang in one of the engine houses, a not unmellow note; it was the time for changing "cores"; that was why there were so many men about. They were assembling to go down. Other men now would be on their way up, climbing ant-like a hundred fathoms of rickety ladders, sweat-covered and stained with rusty markings of the mineral rock or the black fumes of blasting powder. It would take them half an hour or more to come to the surface carrying their tools, and all the way they would be splashed and drenched with water from the leaky pumps. On reaching grass many would have a three- or four-mile walk through the wind and rain.

He moved on. Now and then the feeling within him was so strong that he could have been physically sick.

The Mellingey was forded, and horse and rider began wearily to climb the narrow track towards the last clump of fir trees. Ross took a deep breath of the air, which was heavy with rain and impregnated with the smell of the sea. He fancied he could hear the waves breaking. At the top of the rise the mare, all her ill nature gone, stumbled again and almost fell, so Ross awkwardly got down and began to walk. At first he could hardly put his foot to the ground, but he welcomed this pain in his ankle, which occupied thoughts that would have been elsewhere.

In the coppice it was pitch black, and he had to feel his way along a path which had become part overgrown. At the other side the ruined buildings of

Wheal Maiden greeted him—a mine which had been played out for forty years; as a boy he had fought and scrambled about the derelict windlass and the horse whim, had explored the shallow adit that ran through the hill and came out near the stream.

Now he felt he was really home; in a moment he would be on his own land. This afternoon he had been filled with pleasure at the prospect, but now nothing seemed to matter. He could only be glad that his journey was done and that he might lie down and rest.

In the cup of the valley the air was still. The trickle and bubble of Mellingey stream had been lost, but now it came to his ears again like the mutterings of a thin old woman. An owl hooted and swung silently before his face in the dark. Water dripped from the rim of his hat. There ahead in the soft and sighing darkness was the solid line of Nampara House.

It struck him as smaller than he remembered, lower and more squat; it straggled like a row of workmen's cottages. There was no light to be seen. At the lilac tree, now grown so big as to overshadow the windows behind it, he tethered the mare and rapped with his riding whip on the front door.

There had been heavy rain here; water was trickling from the roof in several places and forming pools on the sandy overgrown path. He thrust open the door; it went creaking back, pushing a heap of refuse before it, and he peered into the low, irregularly beamed hall.

Only the darkness greeted him, an intenser darkness which made the night seem grey.

"Jud!" he called. "Jud!"

The mare outside whinnied and stamped; something scuttled beside the wainscot. Then he saw eyes. They were lambent, green-gold, stared at him unwinkingly from the back of the hall.

He limped into the house, feeling leaves and dirt underfoot. He fingered his way round the panels to the right until he came to the door leading into the parlour. He lifted the latch and went in.

At once there was a scuffling and rustling and the sound of animals disturbed. His foot slid on something slimy on the floor, and in putting out his hand he knocked over a candlestick. He retrieved it, set the candle back in its socket, groped for his flint and steel. After two or three attempts, the spark caught and he lit the candle.

This was the largest room in the house. It was half panelled with dark mahogany, and in the far corner was a great broad fireplace half the width of the room, recessed and built round with low settles. This was the room the family had always lived in, large enough and airy enough for the rowdiest company on the hottest days, yet with warm corners and cosy furniture to cheat the draughts of winter. But all that was changed. The fireplace was empty and hens roosted on the settles. The floor was filthy with old straw and droppings. From the bracket of a candle sconce a cockerel viewed him with a liverish eye. On one of the window seats were two dead chickens.

Opening out of the hall on the left was Joshua's bedroom, and he next tried this. Signs of life: clothing which had never belonged to his father, filthy old petticoats, a battered three-cornered hat, a jar without stopper from which he sniffed gin. But the box bed was closed and the three captive thrushes in the cage before the shuttered window could tell him nothing of the couple he looked for.

At the farther end of the room was another door leading into that part of the house which had never been finished, but he did not go in. The place to look was in the bedroom upstairs at the back of the house where Jud and Prudie always slept.

He turned back to the door, and there stopped and listened. A peculiar sound had come to his ears. The fowls had settled down, and silence, like a parted curtain, was falling back upon the house. He thought he heard a creak on the shallow stairs, but when he peered out with the candle held high, he could see nothing.

This was not the sound he was listening for, nor the movement of rats, nor the faint hissing of the stream outside, nor the crackle of charred paper under his boot.

He looked up at the ceiling, but the beams and floorboards were sound. Something rubbed itself against his leg. It was the cat whose bright eyes he had seen earlier: his father's kitten, Tabitha Bethia, but grown into a big grey animal and leprously patched with mange. She seemed to recognize him, and he put down his hand gratefully to her enquiring whiskers.

Then the sound came again, and this time he caught its direction. He strode over to the box bed and slid back the doors. A powerful smell of stale sweat and gin; he thrust in the candle. Dead drunk and locked in each other's arms were Jud and Prudie Paynter. The woman was in a long flannel nightgown, her mouth was open and her varicosed legs asprawl. Jud had not succeeded in getting properly undressed, but snored by her side in his breeches and leggings.

Ross stared at them for some moments.

Then he withdrew and put the candlestick on the great low chest near the bed. He walked out of the room and made his way round to the stables at the east end of the house. Here he found a wooden pail and took it to the pump. This he filled, carried it round the house, through the hall, and into the bedroom. He tipped the water into the bed.

He went out again. A few stars were showing in the west, but the wind was freshening. In the stables, he noted, there were only two half-starved horses. Ramoth; yes, one was still Ramoth. The horse had been twelve years old and half blind from cataract when he left.

He carried the second bucket round, through the hall, across the bedroom, and tipped it into the bed.

The mare whinnied at his second passing. She preferred even his company to the darkness and unfamiliarity of the garden.

When he brought the third bucket, Jud was groaning and muttering and his bald head was in the opening of the box door. Ross allowed him this bucket to himself.

By the time he returned with the fourth, the man had climbed out of the bed and was trying to shake the streaming water from his clothing. Prudie was only just stirring, so Ross devoted the water to her. Jud began to curse and groped for his jack knife. Ross hit him on the side of the head and knocked him down. Then he went for another supply.

At his fifth appearance there was more intelligence in the eyes of the servant, though he was still on the ground. At sight of him Jud began to curse and sweat and threaten. But after a moment a look of puzzlement crept across his face.

"... Dear life!... Is it you, Mister Ross?"

"From the grave," said Ross. "And there's a horse to be seen to. Up, before I kill you." By the collar of his shirt he lifted the man to his feet and thrust him forward towards the door.

CHAPTER THREE

1

A WET OCTOBER EVENING IS DEPRESSING, BUT IT DRAPES SOME SOFT SHADOWS on the rough edges of ruin and decay. Not so the light of morning.

Even at the height of his mining, Joshua had always had a few fields under care, the house had been clean and homely, well furnished, and well stocked considering the district. After a tour which lasted from eight until ten, Ross called the Paynters out of the house and stood with legs apart looking at them. They shuffled and were uneasy under his gaze.

Jud was four inches the shorter of the two. He was a man in the early fifties to whom bow legs gave a look of horsiness and bulldog strength. During the last ten years satirical nature had tonsured his head like a friar. He had lived in this district all his life, first as a tributer at Grambler Mine, then at Wheal Grace, where Joshua took to him in spite of his weaknesses.

Prudie Jud had picked up at Bedruthan ten years ago. Their first meeting was one of the things that Jud held his tongue about even in his cups. They had never married, but she had taken his name as a matter of course. She was now forty, six feet in height, with lank Spanish hair incurably lousy; and wide shouldered, with a powerful body which bulged everywhere it aesthetically shouldn't.

"You're tired after a hard morning's work," said Ross.

Jud looked at him uneasily from under hairless brows. With Joshua he had always had to mind his Ps and Qs, but of Ross he had never been at all afraid. A harum-scarum, highly strung, lanky youngster—there was nothing in him to fear. But two years of soldiering had changed the boy.

"Tes as clean as a new-scrubbed place can be," said Jud on a grudging note. "We been at un for two hour solid. Splinters I got in me and from the old floor, drat un. Blood-poisoned I shall be maybe. Runs from your and to your arm, it do. Up yer veins, and then *phit*—ye're dead."

Ross turned his sleepy but unquiet eyes on Prudie. "Your wife has not suffered from her wetting? As well not to forget the feel and taste of water. Very little is used in gaol."

Jud looked up sharply. "Who says gaol? Prudie an't going to gaol. What she done?"

"No more than you have. A pity you can't share the same cell."

Prudie sniggered. "You will 'ave yer jest."

"The jest," said Ross, "was yours last night and for fifty nights before."

"You can't get neither of us convicted fur bein' a bit tiddley," said Jud. "Tedn't law. Tedn't right. Tedn't just. Tedn't sense. Tedn't friendly. Leave alone all we've done for you."

"You were my father's personal servant. When he died, you were left in a position of trust. Well, you may have a guinea for every field you find that isn't choked with weed and lying fallow, the same for a barn or a stable that is not falling down for need of a timely repair. Even the apples in the orchard are mouldering amongst the dead leaves for lack of someone to gather them—"

"Twur a poor summer for frewt. Down come the apples rottin' away wi' wasps in un. Shockin' twas. You can't do nothing to an apple when thur's a drane in un. Not except kill the drane and eat the apple, an' thur's a limit t'what two bodies can eat."

"Twas a nice chanst I didn' swaller one of they wasps," said Prudie. "Thur was I munching away as clever as you like. Then sharp, just as I has me teeth in un, I hears a 'vuzz-vuzz.' And, my ivers, there 'e is! You can't see the front end, but the back end is there wavin' about like a lamb's tail, all 'is legs a-going and striped like a flag. If I 'adn't just urd—"

"Get one of they in yer ozle," said Jud gloomily. "Out come their sting an' *phit*—ye're dead."

"Lazy in everything," said Ross, "but the search for excuses. Like two old pigs in their sty and as slow to move from their own patch of filth."

Prudie picked up her apron and began to dab her nose.

Ross warmed to his theme. He had learned abuse from a master and had added to it while away. Also he knew his listeners. "I suspect it must be easy to convert good stock into cheap gin," he ended. "Men have been hanged for less."

"We thought—twas rumoured—" Jud sucked his gums in hesitation. "Folks said—"

"That I was dead? Who said it?"

"Twas common belief," Prudie said sombrely.

"Yet I find it only near my own home. Did you begin the story?"

"No, no; tedn't true. Not by no means. 'Tis we you should thank for giving the lie to such a story. Nail it, I says. Nail it to the bud, I says. I've got the firmest faith, I says; and Prudie can bear me forth. Did we b'lieve such a wicked lie, Prudie?"

"Dear life, no!" said Prudie.

"My uncle has always thought you wastrels and parasites. I think I can arrange for your case to come before him."

They stood there on shifty feet, half resentful, half alarmed. He had no understanding of their difficulties and they had no words to explain. Any guilt they might have felt was long since overgrown by these explanations which they could not frame. Their feeling now was one of outrage at being so harshly attacked. Everything had been done, or left undone, for a very good reason.

"We've only four pairs of 'ands," said Jud.

Ross's sense of humour was not working or he might have been undone by this remark.

"There is much gaol fever this year," he said. "A lack of cheap gin will not be your only hardship."

He turned and left them to their fears.

2

In the gloom of the Red Lion Stables he had thought his hired mare had a damaged fetlock, but the light of day showed the lameness to be no more than the result of a very bad shoeing. The mare had an open flat foot, and the shoe was fitted too short and too close.

He rode into Truro next day on the almost blind Ramoth to see if he could do business with the landlord of the Red Lion.

The landlord was a little doubtful whether enough time had passed to give him the right to dispose of his surety; but legality was never Ross's strong point, and he had his way.

While in the town he drew a bill on Pascoe's Bank and spent some of his slender capital on two young oxen which he arranged for Jud to collect. If the fields were to be worked at all, there must be an outlay upon working animals.

With some smaller things slung over his saddle he arrived back shortly after one and found Verity waiting for him. For a sudden leaping moment he thought it was Elizabeth.

"You did not come to visit me, Cousin," she said, "so I must wait on you. That I have now been doing for forty odd minutes."

He bent and kissed her cheek. "You should have sent word. I have been to Truro. Jud will have told you."

"Yes. He offered me a garden chair but I was afraid to sit on it lest it collapse under my weight. Oh, Ross, your poor house!"

He glanced up towards the building. The conservatory was smothered with giant convolvulus, which had swept over it, flowered, and was beginning to rot.

"It can be put right."

"I am ashamed," she said, "that we have not been over, that I have not been over more often. These Paynters—"

"You've been busy."

"Oh, we have. Only now that the crops are in have we time to look round. But that is no excuse."

He glanced down at her as she stood beside him. She, at least, had not changed, with her trim little figure and untidy hair and big generous mouth. She had walked over from Trenwith in her working dress with no hat and her dove grey cloak pulled carelessly about her shoulders.

They began to walk round to the stables. "I have just bought a mare," he said. "You must see her. Old Squire is beyond recall and big Ramoth has not eyes to avoid the stones and ruts."

"Tell me about your wound," she said. "Does it pain you much now? When was it done?"

"Oh, long ago. At the James River. It is nothing."

She glanced at him. "You were always one to hide your hurt, were you not?"

"This is the mare," he said. "I have just paid five and twenty guineas for her. A great bargain, don't you think?"

She hesitated. "Does *she* not limp too? Francis was saying… And that right leg, which she holds—"

"Will get better more quickly than mine. I wish you could heal any injury by a change of shoes."

"What is her name?"

"No one knows. I am waiting for you to christen her."

Verity pushed back her hair and frowned with one eyebrow. "Hm… I should call her Darkie."

"For any reason?"

"She has that pretty black streak. And also it is a tribute to her new owner."

He laughed and began to unsaddle Ramoth and rub him down, while his cousin leaned against the stable door and chattered. Her father often complained that she was "lacking in the graces," meaning that she was incapable of the flowery but agreeable small talk which added so much to the savour of life. But with Ross she was never tongue-tied.

He asked her to dinner, but she refused. "I must go soon. I have far more to see to now that Father is not so nimble."

"And enjoy it, I suppose. Walk with me as far as the sea first. It may be days before you come again."

She did not argue, for it was pleasant to her to have her company sought. They set off linking as they had done as children, but this way his lameness was too noticeable and he loosed her arm and put his long bony hand on her shoulder.

The nearest way of reaching the sea from the house was to climb a stone wall and drop down upon Hendrawna Beach, but today they climbed the Long Field behind the house and walked the way Joshua had walked in his dream.

"My dear, you'd have some hard work to get things shaped up," Verity said, looking about her. "You must have help."

"There is all winter to spend."

She tried to read his expression. "You're not thinking of going away again, Ross?"

"Very quickly if I had money or were not lame; but the two together—"

"Shall you keep Jud and Prudie?"

"They have agreed to work without wages. I shall keep them until some of the gin is sweated out of them. And also this morning I've taken a boy named Carter, who called asking for work. Do you know him?"

"Carter? One of Connie Carter's children from Grambler?"

"I think so. He has been at Grambler, but the underground work was too heavy. There's not enough air in the sixty-fathom level to clear the blasting powder, and he says he started coughing black phlegm in the mornings. So he has to have outdoor work."

"Oh, that will be Jim, her eldest. His father died young."

"Well, I can't afford to pay invalids, but he seems an acceptable boy. He's starting tomorrow at six."

They reached the edge of the cliff where they were seventy or eighty feet above the sea. On the left the cliffs slipped down to the inlet of Nampara Cove, then rose again more steeply towards Sawle. Looking east, upon Hendrawna Beach, the sea was very calm today: a smoky grey with here and there patches of violet and living, moving green. The waves were shadows, snakes under a quilt, creeping in almost unseen until they emerged in milky ripples at the water's edge.

The gentle sea breeze moved against his face, barely touching his hair. The tide was going out. As they looked, the green of the sea quickened and stirred under the crouching clouds.

He had not slept well last night. Seen from this side with the pale blue-grey eyes half lidded, and the scar showing white on the brown cheek, his whole face had a strange disquiet. Verity looked away and abruptly said: "You would be surprised to learn—to learn about Francis and Elizabeth—"

"I had no option on the girl."

"It was strange," she went on haltingly, "the way it happened. Francis had scarcely seen her until this summer past. They met at the Pascoes. Then he could—could talk of nothing else. Naturally I told him you had been friendly with her. But she had already told him that."

"Kind of her—"

"Ross… I'm certain sure that neither of them wished to do anything unfair. It was just one of the things that happen. You do not argue with the clouds or the rain or the lightning. Well, this was like that. It came from outside them. I know Francis and he couldn't help himself."

"How prices have risen since I went away," said Ross. "I paid three and three a yard for Holland linen today. All my shirts have been eaten by the moths."

"And then," said Verity, "there was the rumour of your having been killed. I do not know how it came about, but I think it was the Paynters who stood most to gain."

"Not more than Francis."

"No," said Verity. "But it was not he."

Ross kept his tortured eyes on the sea. "That was not a pretty thought," he said after a moment.

She pressed his arm. "I wish I could help you, my dear. Will you not come over often? Why d'you not have dinner with us every day? My cooking is better than Prudie's."

He shook his head. "I must find my own way out of this. When are they to be married?"

"November the first."

"So soon? I thought it was to be more than a month."

"They decided last night."

"Oh. I see…"

"It is to be at Trenwith, for that suits us all best. Cusgarne is nearly falling down and full of draughts and leaks. Elizabeth and her mother and father are coming in their carriage in the morning."

She chattered on, aware that Ross was hardly attending but anxious to help him over this difficult period. Presently she was silent and followed his example in staring out to sea.

"If," she said, "if I were sure not to get in your way this winter, I would come over when I could. If—"

"That," he said, "would help more than anything."

They began to walk back towards the house. He did not see how red she had gone, flushing up to the roots of her hair.

So it was to be November the first, less than a fortnight forward.

He went a little way with his cousin, and when they parted he stood at the edge of the pine copse and saw her walking quickly and sturdily in the direction of Grambler. The smoke and steam from the mine was drifting in a cloud across the desolate rubble-scarred moorland towards Trenwith.

3

Beyond the rising ground which made up the southeastern rib of Nampara Combe was a hollow in which lay a cluster of cottages known as Mellin.

It was Poldark land, and in these six cottages, built in the form of a friendly right-angle so that everyone could the more easily watch everyone else's comings and goings, lived the Triggses, the Clemmows, the Martins, the Daniels, and the Viguses. Here Ross went in search of cheap labour.

The Poldarks had always been on good terms with their tenants. Distinction of class was not absent; it was understood so clearly that nobody needed to emphasize it; but, in districts where life centred round the nearest mine, polite convention was not allowed to stand in the way of common sense. The small landowners with their long pedigrees and short purses were accepted as a part of the land they owned.

On his way to the Martins, Ross had to pass three of the cottages, before the door of the first of which Joe Triggs sat sunning himself and smoking. Triggs was a miner in the mid-fifties, crippled with rheumatism and supported by his aunt, who made a bare living fishjousting in Sawle. It did not seem that he had moved since Ross went away twenty-eight months ago. England had lost an empire in the west; she had secured her grip upon an empire in the east; she had fought single-handed against the Americans, the French, the Dutch, the Spaniards, and Hyder Ali of Mysore. Governments, fleets, and nations had grappled, had risen, and been overthrown. Balloons had ascended in France, the *Royal George* had turned on her beam ends at Spithead, and Chatham's son had taken his first Cabinet office. But for Joe Triggs nothing had changed. Except that this knee or that shoulder was more or less painful, each day was so like the last that they merged into an unchanging pattern and slipped away unmarked.

While talking to the old man, Ross's eyes were straying over the rest of the cottages. The one next to this had been empty since the whole family had died of the smallpox, in '79, and it had now lost part of its roof; the one beyond, the Clemmows', looked little better. What could one expect? Eli the younger and brighter had gone off to some lackey's job in Truro, leaving only Reuben.

The three cottages of the opposite angle were all in good repair. The Martins and the Daniels were his particular friends. And Nick Vigus looked after his cottage, for all that he was a slippery rogue.

At the Martin cottage Mrs. Zacky Martin, flat-faced and bespectacled and cheerful, showed him into the single dark room downstairs with its floor of well-trodden earth on which three naked babies rolled and crowed. There were two new faces since Ross left, making eleven in all, and Mrs. Martin was pregnant again. Four boys were already underground at Grambler, and the eldest daughter, Jinny, was a spaller at the mine. The three next youngest children, aged five and upwards, were just the sort of cheap labour Ross needed for clearing his fields.

This sunny morning, with the sights and sounds and smells of his own land about him, the war of which he had been a part seemed unsubstantial and far off. He wondered if the real world was that one in which men fought for policies and principles and died or lived gloriously—or more often miserably—for the sake of an abstract word like patriotism or independence, or if reality belonged to the humble people and the common land.

It seemed that nothing would stop Mrs. Zacky talking; but just then her daughter Jinny came back from her shift at the mine. She seemed out of breath and about to say something when she pushed open the half door of the cottage, but on seeing Ross she came forward and curtsied awkwardly and was tongue-tied.

"My eldest," said Mrs. Zacky, folding her arms across her wide bosom. "Seventeen a month gone. What's to do, child? Have ee forgotten Mister Ross?"

"No, Mother. No, sur. Tedn't that at all." She went to the wall, untied her apron, and pulled off her big linen bonnet.

"She's a fine girl," said Ross, inspecting her absently. "You should be proud of her."

Jinny blushed.

Mrs. Zacky was staring at her daughter. "Is it that Reuben that's been playing you up again?"

A shadow fell across the door, and Ross saw the tall figure of Reuben Clemmow striding towards his cottage. He still wore his damp blue miner's drill coat and trousers, the old hard hat with its candle stuck to the front by clay, and he carried four excavating tools, one of them a heavy iron jumper used for boring.

"He follow me every day," said the girl with tears of annoyance in her eyes. "Bothering me to walk wi' him; and when I walk he says nothing but only looks. Why don't he leave me alone!"

"There now, don't take on so," said her mother. "Go tell they three young imps to come in if they d' want anything t' eat."

Ross saw his opportunity to leave, and got up as the girl ran from the hut and called out in a shrill clear voice to three of the Martin children who were working in a potato patch.

"He's a prime worry to we," said Mrs. Martin. "He d' follow her everywhere. Zacky's warned 'im twice."

"He keeps his cottage in an uncommon bad state. You must find the stench very poor when the wind is that way."

"Oh, we don't creen nothing 'bout that. It is the maid we're consarned for."

Ross could see Reuben Clemmow standing at his cottage door watching Jinny, following her with his small pale eyes and his disconcerting stare. The Clemmows had always been a trouble to the neighbourhood. Father and Mother Clemmow had been dead some years. Father Clemmow had been a deaf mute and had fits; children had made fun of him because of his twisted mouth and the gobbling noises he made. Mother Clemmow had been all right to look at, but there had been something rotten about her; she was not a woman content with the ordinary human sins of copulation and drunkenness. He remembered seeing her publicly whipped in Truro market for selling poisonous abortion powders. The two Clemmows had been in and out of trouble for years, but Eli had always seemed the more difficult.

"Has he given trouble while I have been away?"

"Reuben? Naw. 'Cept that he scat in Nick Vigus's head one day last winter when he was tormenting of him. But we hold no blame to him fur that, for I could do it myself oftentimes."

He thought: by returning to the simple life of the peasant one did not escape. In his case he exchanged the care of his company of infantry for this implicit concern for the welfare of people living on his land. He might not be a squire in the fullest sense, but the responsibilities did not deter him.

"Do you think he means harm to Jinny?"

"That we can't tell," said Mrs. Zacky. "If he was to do anything, he'd never get into no court o' law. But he's worrying for a mother, my dear, as you'll acknowledge."

Reuben Clemmow saw that he in his turn was being watched. He stared blankly at the two people in the doorway of the other cottage, then he turned and entered his own cottage, slamming the doors behind him.

Jinny and the three children were returning. Ross looked at the girl with more interest. Neat and trim she was; a pretty little thing. Those good brown eyes, the pale skin slightly freckled across the nose, the thick auburn hair, there would be plenty of admirers among the young men of the district. Little wonder that she turned up her nose at Reuben, who was nearly forty and weak in the head.

"If Reuben gives further trouble," Ross said, "send up a message to me and I'll come and talk to him."

"Thank ee, sur. We'd be in your debt. Maybe if you spoke to him 'e'd take some account of it."

4

On his way home Ross passed the engine house of Wheal Grace, that mine from which had come all his father's prosperity and into which it had all returned. It stood on the hill on the opposite side of the valley from Wheal Maiden, and, known as Trevorgie Mine, had been worked in primitive fashion centuries ago, Joshua having used some of the early working and rechristened the venture after his wife. Ross thought he would look over it, for any concern was better than moping the days away.

The next afternoon he put on a suit of his father's mining clothes and was about to leave the house, followed by mutterings from Prudie about rotten planks and foul air, when he saw a horseman riding down the valley and knew it to be Francis.

He was on a fine roan horse and was dressed in a fashionable manner, with buff-coloured breeches, a yellow waistcoat, and a narrow-waisted coat of dark brown velvet with a high collar.

He reined up before Ross, and the horse reared at the check.

"Hey, Rufus, quiet boy! Well, well, Ross." He dismounted, his face smiling and friendly. "*Quiet,* boy! Well, what's this? Are you on tribute at Grambler?"

"No, I have a mind to examine Grace."

Francis raised his eyebrows. "She was an old strumpet. You don't hope to re-start her?"

"Even strumpets have their uses. I'm taking a stock of what I own, whether it is worthless or of value."

Francis coloured slightly. "Sensible enough. Perhaps you can wait an hour."

"Come down with me," Ross suggested. "But perhaps you no longer care for such adventure—in that attire."

Francis's flush became deeper. "Of course I'll come," he said shortly. "Give me an old suit of your father's."

"There's no need. I'll go another day."

Francis handed his horse to Jud, who had just come down from the field. "We can talk on the way. It will be of interest to me."

They went indoors, and Ross searched among such of his father's belongings as the Paynters had not sold. When suitable things had been found, Francis stripped off his fine clothes and put them on.

They left the house, and to overcome the restraint Ross forced himself to talk of his experiences in America, where he had been sent as a raw ensign after only a month with his regiment in Ireland; of those hectic first three months under Lord Cornwallis when almost all the fighting he had seen had taken place, of the advance towards Portsmouth and the sudden attack by the French while they were crossing the James River, of the routing of Lafayette; of a musket ball in the ankle and his being drafted to New York as a result, so escaping the siege of Yorktown; of a bayonet cut in the face during a local skirmish while the articles of the preliminary peace were being signed.

They reached the mine and the engine house, and Ross poked about among the tall gorse for some minutes; then he went over to his cousin, who was peering down the shaft.

"How deep did they drive it?" Francis asked.

"No more than thirty fathoms, I believe; and most of that will be under water. But I have heard my father say that most of the old Trevorgie working drained itself."

"We have begun an eighty-fathom level at Grambler, and it promises big things. How long since this ladder was used?"

"Ten years, I suppose. Shelter me, will you."

The strong breeze hindered the lighting of the hempen candles. With one candle in the front of each hard hat they began to descend the ladder. Francis would have gone first, but Ross stopped him.

"Wait. I'll try it out."

The first dozen rungs seemed stout enough, and Francis began to follow. This was a fairly wide shaft, the ladder nailed to the side and supported with wooden platforms at intervals. Some of the pumping gear was still in position, but farther down it had fallen away. As they left the daylight, the strong dank smell of stagnant water rose to meet them.

The first level was reached without incident. By the smoky flickering light on his hat, Ross peered into the narrow opening of the tunnel; he decided to try for the next level. He called this up to the man above him and they went on down. Once Francis dislodged a stone, and it clattered on the next platform and fell with a sleek plop into the unseen water below.

Now the rungs began to prove treacherous. Several had to be missed altogether, and then one gave just as Ross put his full weight on it. His foot caught in the next rung, which was sound.

"If ever I open a mine," he called up, his voice echoing round the confined space, "I shall put iron ladders down the main shaft."

"When times are better, we intend to do that at Grambler. Bartle's father was lost that way."

Ross's feet went cold. He bent his head to peer at the dark, oily water which barred his way. The height of the water had dropped during the last months, for all round him the walls were covered with green slime. His breath rose steamily to join the smoke from the candle. Beside him, some two feet deep in water, was the opening of the second level. This was the lowest part of the old Trevorgie Mine.

He took two more steps down until the water was above his knees, then stepped off the ladder into the tunnel.

"Faugh! what a stench," came from Francis. "I wonder how many unwanted brats have been dropped down here."

"I think," said Ross, "that this level runs east under the valley in the direction of Mingoose."

He moved off into the tunnel. A splash behind him told him that Francis was off the ladder and following.

The walls here were streaming with brown and green stained water, and in some places the roof was so low that they had to bend to get through. The air was foul and dank, and once or twice the candles flickered as if about to go out. Francis caught up with his cousin where the tunnel widened into a cavern. Ross was peering at the wall where an excavation had been begun.

"See this," Ross said, pointing. "See this streak of tin showing between the mundic. They chose their level wrong. We know how big the jumps have been at Grambler."

Francis wet his finger in the water and rubbed the rock where the faint dark mottling of tin showed.

"And what then? You haven't seen our cost sheets at Grambler since you returned? The profits have a shy fancy to leap to the wrong side of the ledger."

"At Grambler," said Ross, "you have driven too deep. Those engines were costing a fortune when I left."

"They do not burn coal," said Francis. "They eat it as a donkey would eat strawberries. 'Munch,' and they're braying for more."

"Here a small engine would do. This level is workable even without pumping."

"Don't forget it is the autumn."

Ross turned and stared down at the black, foul water above his knees, then looked again at the roof. Francis was right. They had only been able to come this far because of the dryness of the summer. The water was rising now. In another few days, perhaps even hours, it would not be possible to get back.

"Ross," said the other man. "You heard, did you not, that I was to be married next week?"

Ross gave up his peering and straightened. He was about three inches taller than his cousin. "Verity told me."

"Um. She said too that you didn't wish to attend the wedding."

"Oh… it isn't that in so many words. But with one thing and another… My house is like the Sack of Carthage. Besides, I was never one for ceremonies. Let us go on a little. I wonder if it might not be possible to unwater all these old workings by means of an adit driven from the low ground beyond Marasanvose."

After a few seconds Francis followed his cousin.

The flickering light of the two candles bobbed about, throwing back the darkness here and there, drawing smoky shadows to follow and casting odd grotesque reflections on the bottle-dark water.

Soon the tunnel contracted until it became egg-shaped, about four feet six inches high and not above three feet across at the widest part. It had in fact been cut just big enough to allow the passage of a man pushing a wheelbarrow and bending his head over it. The water came to just below the widest part of the egg, and here the walls were worn smooth with the rubbing of long-forgotten elbows.

Francis began to feel the need of air, the need to straighten his bent back, the weight of thousands of tons of rock above his head.

"You must, of course, come to the wedding," he said, raising his voice. His candle was sputtering with a drop of water that had fallen on it. "We should be greatly upset if you did not."

"Nonsense. The countryside will soon tire of talking about it."

"You're damned insulting today. It's our wish that you should come. Mine and—"

"And Elizabeth's?"

"She especially asked that you should."

Ross checked a sentence on his tongue. "Very well. At what time?"

"Noon. George Warleggan is to be my groomsman."

"George Warleggan?"

"Yes. Had I known that you—"

"You see, the ground is rising a little. We're turning north now."

"We don't intend to have a big wedding," Francis said. "Just our families and a few friends. Cousin William-Alfred will officiate and Mr. Odgers will assist him. Ross, I wished to explain—"

"The air is improving here," Ross said grimly, pushing his way round an awkward corner of the confined tunnel and bringing down a shower of loose stones plop-plopping into the water.

They had climbed a few feet and were almost free of water. Ahead was a glimmer of light. Climbing still, they reached an air shaft, one of the numerous winzes driven down to make working conditions just supportable. Like the main shaft, this went deeper; it was full of water to within a few feet of them and was crossed by a narrow bridge of planks.

There was no ladder up this shaft.

They peered up at the small circle of daylight above.

"Where is this?" said Ross. "It must be the one beside the track to Reen-Wollas—"

"Or that at the edge of the sand hills. Look, Ross, I wished to explain. When I first met Elizabeth this spring past, there was no thought in my head of coming between her and you. It was like a stroke from the blue. Both she and I—"

Ross turned, his face high-strung and dangerous. "In the *devil's* name! Isn't it enough to—"

Such was his expression that Francis stepped back upon the wooden bridge crossing the shaft—the bridge broke to pieces like a biscuit and he was struggling in the water.

This happened so quickly that for a moment nothing could be done. Ross thought: Francis cannot swim.

In the semidarkness he came to the surface anyhow, an arm, fair hair, and the hard hat floating, his clothing a help before it became waterlogged. Ross fell on his stomach, leaned over the edge, nearly overbalanced, could not reach; a despairing face; the water was viscous. He pulled at a piece of the rotten bridge; it came away; he swung it down and a big iron nail caught on the shoulder of his cousin's coat; pulled and the coat tore; a hand grasped the end of the wood and Ross pulled again; before the wood crumpled they made contact.

Ross tensed his muscles on the slippery rock floor and hauled his cousin out of the shaft.

They sat there in silence for some moments, Francis gasping and spitting out the foul water.

"By God! What was your reason to flare up so?" he said in anger.

"By God, why don't you learn to swim!" Ross said.

There was another silence. The accident had released emotions within them; these for a time hung in the air like a dangerous gas, impossible to name but not to be ignored.

While they sat there, Francis took sidelong glances at his cousin. That first evening of Ross's return he had expected and understood Ross's disappointment and resentment. But in his casual, easygoing way he had had no idea of the extent of the emotion behind the finedrawn expression of his cousin's face. Now he knew.

He also sensed that the accident of his fall had not been the only danger in which he had stood... in which perhaps he still stood.

They had both lost their candles and had not brought spares. Francis glanced up at the disc of light high above them. Pity there was no ladder here. It would be an unpleasant journey back all the way they had come, groping in the dark...

After a minute he shook some water off his coat and began the trip back. Ross followed him with an expression which was now half grim, half ironical. For Francis the incident might have betrayed the extent of his cousin's resentment—but Ross felt it should also have shown him its limitations.

It had done that much for himself.

CHAPTER FOUR

1

IN THE WEEK BEFORE THE WEDDING ROSS LEFT HIS PROPERTY ONLY ONCE: TO
visit Sawle Church.

Joshua had expressed a wish to be buried in the same grave as his wife, so there
was little to see.

*Sacred to the memory of Grace Mary: beloved wife of Joshua Poldark, who departed this
life on the ninth day of May, 1770: aged 30 years.* Quid Quid Amor Jussit, Non Est
Contemnere Tutum.

And underneath Charles had had carved: *Also of Joshua Poldark, of Nampara, in the
County of Cornwall, Esqr., who died on the eleventh day of March, 1783, aged 59.*

The only other change was that the shrubs Joshua had planted had been
uprooted and the mound was thinly grown over with grass. Beside this on a
small headstone adjoining was: *Claude Anthony Poldark, died 9th January, 1771,
in the sixth year of his age.*

Four days later Ross returned to the church to bury the hopes he had carried
with him for more than two years.

All the time at the back of his mind had been the half conviction that somehow
the wedding would not be. It was as hard to believe as if someone had told him
he was going to die.

Sawle Church was half a mile from the village of Sawle at the head of the track
leading to the village. Today the main altar had been decorated with golden
chrysanthemums, and four musicians scraped out the hymns on fiddles and bass-
viols. There were twenty guests; Ross sat near the front in one of the tall pews
so convenient for sleeping, and stared across at the two figures kneeling at the
altar and listened to the drone of William-Alfred's voice forging the legal and
spiritual bond.

Soon, it seemed in no time at all for so vital a matter, they were out in the churchyard again where were gathered about four dozen villagers from Sawle, Trenwith, and Grambler. They stood at a respectful distance and gave out a thin little unrehearsed cheer when the bride and bridegroom appeared at the door.

It was a bright November day with areas of blue sky, intermittent sun, and grey-white monuments of cloud moving unhurriedly before the fresh wind. Elizabeth's veil of old lace blew in billows about her figure, making her seem unsubstantial and ethereal; she might have been one of the smaller clouds which had lost its way and been caught up in the human procession. Soon they were in their coach and were bumping off over the rough track, followed by the rest of the wedding party on horseback.

Elizabeth and her father and mother had come out from Kenwyn in the Chynoweth family coach, rattling and lurching along the narrow rutted lanes and throwing out behind a fog of grey dust which settled evenly over the staring people who gathered to watch it go by. For the appearance of such a vehicle in this barren countryside was an event of the first importance. Horseback and mule train were the unvarying means of travel. News of its coming moved faster than its large red iron-rimmed wheels could carry it, and tinners panning tin in nearby streams, cottagers and their wives, farm labourers, miners off duty, and the flotsam of four parishes turned out to see it pass. Dogs barked and mules brayed and naked children ran shouting after it through the dust.

As the drive was reached the coachman set the horses at a trot. Bartle on the back seat blew his horn, and they arrived before the front of Trenwith House in fine style with several of the following riders trotting and shouting alongside.

At the house a banquet had been prepared which put all other feasts in the shade. All were here who had been here on the night of Ross's return. Mrs. Chynoweth, beautiful as a well-bred female eagle; Dr. Choake and his silly, pretty wife; Charles, rising to the occasion in a large new wig, with a brown velvet coat finely laced about the cuffs, and a red waistcoat. Verity spent less than half her time at the table, being constantly up and down to see that things were going right, her fluffy dark hair becoming untidy as the afternoon advanced. Cousin William-Alfred, thin and pale and unapproachable, lent some solemnity and restraint to the proceedings. His wife Dorothy was not present, being ill of her old complaint, which was pregnancy. Aunt Agatha, taking her usual place at the foot of the table, wore an old-fashioned velvet gown with a whalebone hoop, and a cap of fine lace on her dusty wig.

Among the newcomers was Henshawe, captain of Grambler, a big young man with the lightest of blue eyes and small hands and feet, which allowed him to move easily for all his weight. Mrs. Henshawe was out of her depth here and paused now and then in her over-genteel eating to glance uneasily at the other guests; but her husband, though he had been down a mine since he was eight and could neither read nor write, was used to mixing with any class, and was soon picking his teeth with the two-pronged fork set for the sweetmeats.

Opposite them, trying not to notice this, was Mrs. Teague, the widow of a distant cousin with a small estate near St. Ann's; and dotted about the board in diminished thirds were her five marriageable daughters, Faith, Hope, Patience, Joan, and Ruth.

Next to her was a Captain Blarney, whom Ross had not met before, a quiet presentable man of about forty, master of one of the Falmouth-Lisbon packets. During the whole of the long meal, Ross saw the seaman speak only twice, and that was to Verity thanking her for something she brought. He drank nothing.

The other clergyman did not help Cousin William-Alfred with the dignities of the day. To the Revd. Mr. Odgers, a desiccated little man, was entrusted the cure of the village of Sawle with Grambler, and for this the rector, who lived in Penzance, paid him £40 a year. On this he kept a wife, a cow, and ten children. He took his seat at the feast in a suit going green with constant wear and in a faded horsehair wig, and he was constantly stretching out a hand, on which the dirt was ingrained and the nails broken, for another helping from some dish, while his narrow jaws worked to be rid of what was still before him. There was something rabbit-like in the quick furtive movements: nibble, nibble, before someone comes to frighten me away.

Making up the company were the Nicholas Warleggans, father, mother, and son.

They alone stood for the new-rich of the county. The elder Warleggan's father had been a country blacksmith who had begun tin-smelting in a small way; the smelter's son, Nicholas, had moved to Truro and built up a smelting works. From these roots all the tentacles of their fortune had sprung. Mr. Nicholas Warleggan was a man with a heavy upper lip, eyes like basalt, and big square hands still marked with their early labour. Twenty-five years ago he had married a Mary Lashbrook from Edgecumbe, and the first fruit of the union was present today in George Warleggan, a name which was to become famous in mining and banking circles and one which was already making itself felt where the father's was not.

George had a big face. All his features were on the same scale: the decisive nose drawn back a little at the nostrils as if prepared for opposition, the big intent brown eyes which he used more often than his neck when looking at what was not in front of him—a characteristic Opie had caught when painting his portrait earlier that year.

When the feast was at last over, the big table was pushed out of the way and the exhausted guests sat round in a circle to watch a cockfight.

Verity and Francis had protested that this form of entertainment was not suitable, but Charles had brushed them aside. One seldom had the chance of a tourney in one's own home; usually it meant riding into Truro or Redruth, a fagging business he was becoming less and less inclined for. Besides, Nicholas Warleggan had brought down Red Gauntlet, a bird with a reputation, and was willing to match him against all comers. Charles's own cockerels would become soft without fresh blood to meet them.

A servant of the Warleggans brought in Red Gauntlet and another bird, and a moment later Dr. Choake returned with a couple of his own fancies, followed by the boy Bartle with three of Charles's birds.

In the confusion Ross looked about for Elizabeth. He knew she hated cock-fighting; and sure enough she had slipped away to the end of the hall and was sitting on a settle beside the stairs drinking tea with Verity. Cousin William-Alfred, who disapproved of the sport on advanced Christian grounds, had withdrawn to a recess on the other side of the stairs where the Bible was kept on a three-legged mahogany table and family portraits frowned down over the scene. Ross heard him discussing with the Revd. Mr. Odgers the distressing condition of Sawle Church.

A faint flush coloured Elizabeth's skin as Ross came up to her.

"Well, Ross," said Verity, "and does she not look sweet in her wedding gown? And has it not all been a great success until now? These men with their cockfighting! Their food doesn't settle in their bellies unless they see blood flowing in some foolish pastime. Will you take tea?"

Ross thanked her and refused. "A wonderful feast. My only wish is to sleep after it."

"Well, I must go and find Mrs. Tabb: there is more to see to yet. Half our guests will be staying the night."

Verity left them and they listened a moment to the arguments and discussions going on about the space which had been cleared. With sport in prospect the company was quickly recovering from its food exhaustion. This was a vigorous age.

Ross said: "Are you among those who will stay?"

"Tonight we are to stay. Tomorrow we leave for Falmouth for two weeks."

He stared down at her as she gazed across the room. Her fair hair was short at the nape of the neck, with the ears bare and a single wisp of a curl in front of each. The rest was curled and piled on her head, with a small headdress in the shape of a single row of pearls. Her dress was high at the neck with tufted sleeves of fine lace.

He had sought this encounter and now didn't know what to say. That had often been the way when they first met. Her fragile loveliness had often left him tongue-tied until he came to know her as she really was.

"Ross," she said, "you must wonder why I wanted you to come today. But you hadn't been to see me and I felt I must speak to you." She stopped a moment to bite at her lower lip and he watched the colour come and go in it. "Today is my day. I do want to be happy and to feel that all those about me are the same. There's no time to explain everything; perhaps I couldn't explain it if there were. But I do want you to try to forgive me for any unhappiness I may have caused you."

"There's nothing to forgive," said Ross. "There was no formal undertaking."

She glanced at him a moment out of grey eyes which seemed to show a hint of indignation.

"You know that was not all—"

The first cockfight was over amidst shouting and applause, and the defeated bird, dripping blood and feathers, was rescued from the arena.

"Why, it was no fight at all," said Charles Poldark. "Aarf! Rarely have I seen five guineas earned so quick."

"No," said Dr Choake, whose bird had beaten one of the Warleggans'. "Paracelsus underrated his opponent. A fatal mistake."

"Eathily done!" said Polly Choake as she smoothed down the head of the victor while their manservant held it. "Conqueror looks none so vithious until hith temper be roused. People thay as how I am like that!"

"He has not come through unscathed, ma'am," said the servant. "You'll soil your gloves."

"Well, now I thall be able to afford me a new pair!" said Polly.

There was laughter at this, although her husband lowered his brows as at a breach of taste.

Charles said: "It was a poor show all the same. There's many a youngster could have done better. My Royal Duke could swallow either of 'em, and he little more than a stag!"

"Let us see this Royal Duke," said Mr. Warleggan politely. "Perhaps you would like to match him with Red Gauntlet."

"With who? With what?" asked Aunt Agatha, wiping a dribble from her chin. "Nay, that would be a shame, it would."

"At least we should see if his blood were really blue," said Mr. Warleggan.

"A battle royal?" said Charles. "I am not averse. What is the weight of your bird?"

"Four pounds exact."

"Then they fall in! Royal Duke is three pounds thirteen. Bring them in and let us see."

The two birds were brought forward and compared. Red Gauntlet was small for his weight, a vicious creature scarred and toughened with twenty fights. Royal Duke was a young bird which had fought only once or twice and that locally.

"And the stakes?" said George Warleggan.

"What you will." Charles glanced up at his guest.

"A hundred guineas?" said Mr. Warleggan.

There was a moment's silence.

"… And the whole range of columns supporting the roof," said Mr. Odgers, "are held together only by iron bars and clamps, which are constantly in need of reinforcement. The east and west walls are virtually tottering."

"Yes, yes, I'll back my fancy," shouted Charles. "Get on with the fight."

Preparations were begun with more care for detail than usual. Whatever might be the habits of Mr. Nicholas Warleggan, it was not the custom of the local squires of Mr. Poldark's financial status to wager so much.

"… You knew that was not all," Elizabeth repeated in an undertone. "Something was understood between us. But we were so young—"

"I don't see," said Ross, "in what way explanations will help. Today has made it—"

"Elizabeth," said Mrs. Chynoweth, coming on them suddenly. "You must remember this is your day. You must join in, not isolate yourself in this manner."

"Thank you, Mama. But you know I've no taste for this. I am sure I shall not be missed until it is over."

Mrs. Chynoweth straightened her back, and their eyes met. But she sensed the decision in her daughter's low voice and did not force an issue. She looked up at Ross and smiled without warmth.

"Ross, I know you are not uninterested in the sport. Perhaps you will instruct me in its finer points."

Ross smiled back. "I feel convinced, ma'am, that there are no subtleties of combat on which I can offer you any useful advice."

Mrs. Chynoweth looked at him sharply. Then she turned. "I'll send Francis to you, Elizabeth," she said as she left them.

There was silence before the opening of the fight.

"What is more," said Mr. Odgers, "the churchyard is worst of all. So full of graves is it that the ground can scarce be opened without turning up putrid bodies or skulls or skeletons. One is afraid to put in a spade."

"How dare you say that to my mother!" Elizabeth said.

"Is honesty always offensive?" Ross answered. "I'm sorry."

A sudden sharp murmur told that the fight had begun. From the start Red Gauntlet had the advantage. His little eyes gleaming, he flew in three or four times, finding his mark and drawing blood and knowing just when to withdraw before the other bird could use his own spurs. Royal Duke was game enough but in a different class.

This was a long fight, and everyone watching it became excited. Charles and Agatha led a chorus of encouragement and counter-encouragement. Royal Duke was down in a flutter of feathers with Red Gauntlet on top of him, but miraculously avoided the *coup de grace* and was up again and fighting back. At last they separated to spar for an opening, heads down and neck feathers out. Even Red Gauntlet was tiring and Royal Duke was in a sorry state. Gauntlet could do everything but finish him off.

"Withdraw!" yelled Aunt Agatha. "Charles, withdraw! We have a champion there. Do not let him be maimed in his first fight!"

Charles plucked at his bottom lip and was indecisive. Before he could make up his mind they were at it again. And suddenly, quite surprising everyone, Royal Duke took the initiative. He seemed to have drawn fresh reserves from his triumphant youth. Red Gauntlet, winded and taken unawares, was down.

George Warleggan grasped his father's arm, upsetting his snuffbox. "Stop the fight!" he said sharply. "The spurs are in Gauntlet's head."

He had been the first to see what they now all saw, that the Duke, by sheer staying power and some luck, had won the fight. If Warleggan did not at once intervene, Red Gauntlet would fight no more. He was wriggling round and round on the floor in a desperate and weakening effort to throw off the other bird.

Mr. Warleggan motioned back his manservant, bent and took up his snuffbox and put it away. "Let them go on," he said. "I don't encourage pensioners."

"We've got a champion!" crowed Aunt Agatha. "Ecod, we've got a champion, sure 'nough. Well, isn't the fight over? The bird's done for. Lor' bless us, he looks dead to me! Why wasn't they stopped?"

"I'll give you my draft for a hundred guineas," Warleggan said to Charles with an evenness which did not deceive anyone. "And if you wish to dispose of your bird, give me the first refusal. I believe something could be made of him."

"It was a lucky stroke," said Charles, his broad red face shining with sweat and pleasure. "A rare lucky stroke. I seldom saw a better fight or a more surprising finish. Your Gauntlet was a game bird."

"Game indeed," said Mr. Chynoweth. "A battle royal—um—as you said, Charles. Who is to fight next?"

"He that fights and runs away," said Aunt Agatha, trying to adjust her wig, "lives to fight another day." She chuckled. "Not against our Duke. He kills ere ever they can be separated. I must say you was all mortal slow. Or peevish. Was you peevish? Poor losers lose more'n they need."

Fortunately no one was attending to her, and two more cockerels were brought forward.

"You have no right," said Elizabeth, "no right or reason to insult my mother. What I have done I have done willingly and of my own mind. If you wish to criticize anyone, you must criticize me."

Ross glanced at the girl beside him, and the anger suddenly went out of him and left only pain that everything was over between them.

"I don't criticize anyone," he said. "What's done is done, and I don't want to spoil your happiness. I've my own life to live and... we shall be neighbours. We shall see something of each other—"

Francis withdrew himself from the crowd and dabbed a spot of blood from his silk stock.

"Someday," Elizabeth said in a low tone, "I hope you'll come to forgive me. We were so young. Later—"

With death in his heart Ross watched her husband approach.

"Not following this?" Francis said to his cousin. His handsome face was flushed with food and wine. "I don't blame you. An anti-climax after the other bout. It was an astonishing performance, that. Well, my dear, are you feeling neglected on your wedding day? It is shameful of me and shall be remedied. May I shrivel and waste if I leave you again today."

2

When Ross left Trenwith much later that evening, he mounted and rode for miles, blindly and blackly, while the moon climbed up the sky, until at last Darkie, not yet sound from her earlier injury, showed signs of lameness again. By then he was far beyond his own house in bare wind-swept country unfamiliar to him. He turned his mare about and allowed her to find her own way home.

This she lamentably failed to do, and the night was far gone before the broken chimney stack of Wheal Grace showed that he was on his own land.

He rode down into the valley and unsaddled Darkie and entered the house. He drank a glass of rum and went up to his bedroom and lay there on the bed fully clothed and booted. But his eyes were not closed when dawn began to lighten the squares of the windows. This was the darkest hour of all.

CHAPTER FIVE

1

For Ross the early part of the winter was endless. For days on end the driving mists filled the valley until the walls of Nampara House ran with damp and the stream was in yellow spate. After Christmas the frosts cleared the atmosphere, stiffening the long grass on the cliff edges, whitening the rocks and heaps of mining attle, hardening the sand and painting it salt-coloured until licked away by the unquiet sea.

Only Verity came often. She was his contact with the rest of the family, bringing him gossip and companionship. They walked miles together, sometimes in the rain along the cliffs when the sky was hung with low clouds and the sea drab and sullen as any jilted lover, sometimes on the sand at the sea's edge, when the waves came lumbering in, sending up mists of iridescence from their broken heads. He would stride on, sometimes listening to her, more seldom talking himself, while she walked swiftly beside him and her hair blew about her face and the wind stung colour into her cheeks.

One day in mid-March she came and stayed an unusual time, watching him hammering a support for one of the beams of the still-room.

She said: "How is your ankle, Ross?"

"I feel little of it." Not quite the truth, but near enough for other people. He limped scarcely at all, having forced himself to walk straight, but the pain was often there.

She had brought over some jars of her own preserves, and these she now began to take down from their shelves and rearrange.

"Father says if you are short of fodder for your stock, you can have some of ours. Also that we have seed of radish and French onion if you would like it."

Ross hesitated a moment. "Thanks," he said. "I put in peas and beans last week. There's room enough."

Verity stared at a label of her own writing. "Do you think you can dance, Ross?" she said.

"Dance? What do you mean?"

"Oh, not the reel or the hornpipe, but at a formal ball such as they are holding in Truro next Monday week, Easter Monday."

He paused in his hammering. "I might if I were so inclined. But as I am not the need doesn't arise."

She considered him a moment before speaking again. For all his hard work this winter he was thinner and paler. He was drinking too much and thinking too much. She remembered him when he had been a high-strung, light-hearted boy, full of talk and fun. He used to sing. This gaunt, brooding man was a stranger to her for all her efforts to know him. The war was to blame as well as Elizabeth.

"You're still young," she said. "There is plenty of life in Cornwall if you want it. Why don't you come?"

"So you are going?"

"If someone will take me."

Ross turned. "This is a new interest. And are not Francis and Elizabeth to be there?"

"They were, but have decided not."

Ross picked up his hammer. "Well, well."

"It is a Charity Ball," Verity said. "It is to be held at the Assembly Rooms. You might meet friends there whom you have not seen since your return. It would be a change from all this work and solitude."

"Certainly it would." The idea did not appeal. "Well, well, perhaps I'll think it over."

"It would not—it would not perhaps matter so much," said Verity, blushing, "if you did not want to dance a great deal—that is, if your ankle is painful."

Ross was careful not to notice her colour. "A long ride home in the dark for you, especially if it is wet."

"Oh, I have the offer of the night in Truro. Joan Pascoe, whom you know, will put me up. I will send in to ask them to accommodate you also. They would be delighted."

"You move too fast," he said. "I haven't said I would go. There's so much to do here."

"Yes, Ross," she said.

"Even now we're late with our sowing. Two of the fields have been under water. I cannot trust Jud to work alone."

"No, Ross," she said.

"In any case, I couldn't stay the night in Truro, for I have arranged to ride into Redruth to the fair on the Tuesday morning. I want more livestock."

"Yes, Ross."

He examined the wedge he had thrust under the beam. It was not secure yet. "What time shall I come round for you?" he asked.

That night he went line fishing on Hendrawna Beach with Mark and Paul Daniel and Zacky Martin and Jud Paynter and Nick Vigus. He had no zest for the old ways, but the drift of circumstances was leading him back to them.

The weather was cold and unsuitable, but the miners were too used to wet clothes and extremes of temperature to pay much heed to this, and Ross never took any notice of the weather. They caught no fish, but the night passed pleasantly enough for out of the driftwood on the beach they built a big fire in one of the caves and sat round it and told stories and drank rum while the dark cavern echoed with the noise they made.

Zacky Martin, father of Jinny and the other ten, was a quiet, keen little man with humorous eyes and a permanent grey stubble on his chin which was never a beard and never a clean shave. Because he could read and write, he was known as the scholar of the neighbourhood. Twenty odd years ago he had come to Sawle, a "stranger" from Redruth, and had overcome strong local prejudice to marry the smith's daughter.

While they were in the cave, he drew Ross aside and said Mrs. Zacky had gone on and on at him about some promise Mister Ross had made when he was over at their cottage soon after he came home. It was only about Reuben Clemmow and the way he was frightening young Jinny, making her life a misery, following her about, watching her, trying to get her away from her brothers and sisters to speak to her alone. Of course, he hadn't *done* anything yet: they'd deal with him themselves if he did; but they didn't want for that to happen, and Mrs. Zacky kept on saying if Mister Ross would speak to him perhaps it would bring him to see sense.

Ross stared across at Jud's bald head, which was just beginning to nod with the effects of the rum and the hot fire. He looked at Nick Vigus's pockmarked face glowing red and demonic through the flames, at Mark Daniel's long powerful back as he bent over the fishing tackle.

"I remember the offer well," he told Zacky. "I'll see him on Sunday—see if I can get some sense into him. If not I'll turn him out of his cottage.

They're an unhealthy family, the Clemmows; we should be better without the last of them."

2

Easter Monday came before Ross had faced up to his other promise. But on impulse he had undertaken to be Verity's escort at the ball, and out of affection for her he must go through with it.

The Assembly Rooms were full of people when Ross and Verity arrived. Many of the elite of Cornish society were present tonight. As Ross and Verity entered, the band was already tuning up for the first dance. The room was lit by scores of candles ranged along the walls. The murmur of voices met them, borne on a wave of warm air in which scents and perfumes were strongly mingled. They threaded their way across the room among talking groups and tapping heels and clicking snuffboxes and the rustle of silk gowns.

As was his custom when he went among the people of his own class, Ross had dressed with care; and Verity too, a little unexpectedly, had taken pains with herself. The bright colour of her crimson brocade frock lit up and softened the tan of her plain, pleasant face; she was far prettier than he had ever seen her. This was a different Verity from the one who in breeches and a smock ploughed about in the mud of Trenwith indifferent to rain and wind.

Mrs. Teague and her five daughters were here and were members of a party organized by Joan Pascoe, to which Ross and Verity were expected to attach themselves. While polite greetings were in progress, Ross turned his brooding gaze from one to the other of the five girls and wondered why none of them was married. Faith, the eldest, was fair and pretty, but the other four grew progressively darker and less attractive, as if the virtue and inspiration had gone out of Mrs. Teague as she produced them.

For once there were enough men, and Mrs. Teague, in a new frizzled wig and gold earrings, gazed over the scene with complacent eyes. There were half a dozen others to the party, and Ross was the senior among them. He felt it: they were so young with their artificial manners and parrot compliments. They called him Captain Poldark and treated him with a respect he did not look for—all, that is, except Whitworth, a swaggering beau who was doing nothing at Oxford with a view to entering the Church, and who was dressed in the extremity of fashion with a cutaway coat embroidered with silk thread flowers. He talked

in the loudest voice and clearly wished to take charge of the party, a privilege
which Ross allowed him.

Since he was here to please Verity, he decided to enter into the spirit of the
evening as much as possible, and he moved about from one girl to another,
offering the expected compliments and receiving the expected replies.

He found himself talking to Ruth Teague, the youngest and least attractive of
Mrs. Teague's quintet. She had been standing a little apart from her sisters and
for the moment had drifted out of range of her overpowering mother. It was her
first ball and she looked lonely and nervous. With an air of preoccupation Ross
raised his head and counted the number of young men the Teagues had brought.
There were, after all, only four.

"May I have the pleasure of the two second dances?" he said.

She went scarlet. "Thank you, sir. If Mama will permit me—"

"I shall look forward to it." He smiled and moved off to pay his respects to Lady
Whitworth, the beau's mother. A few moments later he glanced at Ruth and saw
she had now gone white. Was he so fearsome with his scarred face? Or was it the
reputation of his father which clung to his name like an odour of unsanctity?

He saw that another man had joined the party and was talking to Verity.
There was something familiar in that stocky, quietly dressed figure with the hair
done in an unpretentious pigtail. It was Captain Andrew Blarney, the Falmouth
packet captain, whom he had met at the wedding.

"Well, Captain," said Ross, "a surprise to see you here."

"Captain Poldark." Ross's hand was gripped, but the other man seemed
tongue-tied. Eventually he got out: "No dancing man, really."

They talked for some moment about ships, Captain Blarney mainly in mono-
syllables, looking at Verity. Then the band at last struck up and he excused
himself. Ross was to partner his cousin. They formed up to begin, the tilted
people in some order of precedence.

"Are you dancing the next with Captain Blarney?" he asked.

"Yes, Ross. Do you mind?"

"Not at all. I am promised to Miss Ruth Teague."

"What, the littlest of them all? How considerate of you."

"The duty of every Englishman," said Ross. Then as they were about to
separate he added in a gruff and very passable imitation: "No dancing man,
really." Verity met his eyes.

The formal dance went on. The soft yellow candlelight trembled over the
colours of the dresses, the gold and cream, the salmon and the mulberry. It made

the graceful and the beautiful more charming, the graceless and the ungainly tolerable; it smoothed over the tawdry and cast soft creamy-grey shadows becoming to all. The band scraped away, the figures pirouetted, moving and bowing and stepping, turning on heels, holding hands, pointing toes; the shadows intermingled and changed, forming and reforming intricate designs of light and shade, like some gracious depictment of the warp and woof of life, sun and shadow, birth and death, a slow interweaving of the eternal pattern.

The time came for his dance with Ruth Teague. He found her hand cold through its pink lace glove; she was still nervous and he wondered how he could put her at her ease. A poor plain little creature, but on examination, for which she gave him every opportunity by keeping her eyes down, she had some features to merit attention, a willful turn to her uplifted chin, a glow of vitality under her sallow skin, an almond shape to the eyes, which gave a hint of the original to her looks. Except for his cousin she was the first woman he had talked with who had not relied on a strong scent to drown the odours of the body. In finding a girl who smelt as clean as Verity he felt an impulse of friendship.

He summoned such small talk as he had and was successful at once in making her smile; in this newfound interest he forgot the aching of his ankle. They danced the two third together, and Mrs. Teague's eyebrows went up. She had expected Ruth to spend most of the evening beside her, as a dutiful youngest was under every obligation to do.

"What a genteel assembly," said Lady Whitworth, sitting beside Mrs. Teague. "I'm sure our dear children must be enjoying themselves. Who is the tall man distinguishing little Ruth? I missed his name."

"Captain Poldark. A nephew of Mr. Charles."

"What, a son of Mr. Joshua Poldark? And I never recognized him! Not at all like his father, is he? Not as handsome. Still... strikin' in his way—scar an' all. Is he taking an interest?"

"Well, that's how interest begins, isn't it?" said Mrs. Teague, smiling sweetly at her friend.

"Of course, my dear. But how embarrassin' for your two eldest if Ruth were to become attached before them. I always think it such a pity that the etiquette of comin' out is not more strictly followed in this county. Now in Oxfordshire no girls would be permitted by their parents to make themselves so free as Patience and Joan and Ruth are doin' until Faith and Hope were happily settled. I do think it makes for bitter feelin' within the family. Well, imagine that bein'

Mr. Joshua's son and I never recognized him. I wonder if they are alike in their ways. I remember Mr. Joshua well."

After this dance Ruth came to sit beside them. Her face, from being so pale, was now flushed. She fanned herself rapidly and her eyes were bright. Mrs. Teague was itching to question her, but so long as Lady Whitworth was irritatingly within hearing, nothing could be said. Mrs. Teague knew Joshua's reputation just as well as Lady Whitworth. Ross would be an excellent catch for little Ruth, but his father had had such a deplorable habit of snapping up the bait without getting caught on the hook.

"Miss Verity is quite forthcoming tonight," said Mrs. Teague to distract Lady Whitworth's attention. "I believe she is more vivacious than I have seen her."

"The young company, no doubt," said her friend drily. "I see Captain Blarney is here also."

"A cousin of the Roseland Blarneys, I understand."

"I have heard it said they prefer it to be known as a second cousinship."

"Oh, really?" Mrs. Teague pricked up her ears. "Why is that?"

"One hears these rumours." Lady Whitworth waved a gloved hand indifferently. "One does not, of course, repeat them when there are young ears to hear."

"What? Er—no, no, of course not."

Captain Blarney was bowing to his partner.

"Warm in here," he said. "Perhaps—some refreshment?"

Verity nodded, as tongue-tied as he. During the dancing they hadn't spoken at all. Now they went into the refreshment room and found a corner sheltered by ferns. In this seclusion she sipped French claret and watched people passing to and fro. He would drink only lemonade.

I must think of something to say, thought Verity; why have I no small talk like those girls over there; if I could help him to talk, he would like me more; he's shy like me, and I ought to make things easier, not harder. There's farming but he would not be attracted by my pigs and poultry. Mining I'm no more interested in than he. The sea I know nothing of except cutters and seiners and other small fry. The shipwreck last month… but that might not be a tactful thing to discuss. Why can't I just say, la, la, la, and giggle and be fanciful. I could say how well he dances, but that isn't true, for he dances like that big friendly bear I saw last Christmas.

"Cooler out here," said Captain Blarney.

"Yes," said Verity agreeably.

"A little overwarm for dancing in there. I don't believe that a breath or two of night air would do the room any harm."

"The weather, of course, is very mild. Quite unseasonable."

"How graceful you dance," said Captain Blarney, sweating. "I've never met anyone so, well—er—hm—"

"I greatly enjoy dancing," she said. "But I get little opportunity for it at Trenwith. Tonight is a special pleasure."

"And for me. And for me. I never remember enjoying anything—"

In the silence which followed this breakdown they listened to the laughter of the girls and men flirting in the next alcove. They were having a most agreeable time.

"What foolish things those young people are saying," Andrew Blarney got out abruptly.

"Oh, do you think so," she answered in relief.

Now I've offended her, he thought. It wasn't well framed. I meant no reflection on her. How pretty her shoulders are. I ought to take this opportunity of telling her everything; but what right have I to imagine she would be interested? Besides, I would tell it so clumsily that she'd be affronted at the first words. How clean her skin looks; she's like a westerly breeze at sunrise, rare and fresh, and good to get into your lungs and your heart.

"When do you next leave for Lisbon?" she asked.

"By the afternoon tide on Friday."

"I have been to Falmouth three times," she told him. "A fine harbour."

"The finest north of the equator. A farsighted government would convert it to its proper use as a great naval base and depot. Everything is in its favour. We shall need such a harbour yet."

"For what?" asked Verity, watching his face. "Aren't we at peace?"

"For a little while. A year or two, maybe; but there will be trouble with France again. Nothing is properly settled. And when war comes, sea power will decide it."

"Ruth," said Mrs. Teague in the other room. "I see Faith is sitting out this dance. Why do you not go and keep her company?"

"Very well, Mama." The girl rose obediently.

"What sort of rumours do you mean?" asked her mother when she was out of earshot.

Lady Whitworth raised her pencilled eyebrows.

"About whom?"

"Captain Blarney."

"About Captain Blarney? Dear me, I don't think it kind to lend too much credence to whispered stories, do you?"

"No, no, certainly not. I make a point of paying no attention to them myself."

"Mind you, I heard this on good authority; otherwise, I should not consider repeating it even to you." Lady Whitworth raised her fan, which was of chicken-skin parchment delicately painted with cherubs. Behind this screen she began to speak in an undertone into Mrs. Teague's pearl earring.

Mrs. Teague's black button eyes grew smaller and rounded as the tale proceeded; the creases in her eyelids moved down like little Venetian blinds which had come askew. "No!" she exclaimed.

"Is that so! Why, in that case he should not be allowed in the room. I shall consider it my duty to warn Verity."

"If you do so, my dear, pray leave it until another occasion. I have no wish to be drawn into the quarrel that might ensue. Besides, my dear, perhaps she already knows. You know what girls are these days: man mad. And, after all, she's twenty-five—the same as your eldest, my dear. She won't get many more chances."

On her way to join her sister, Ruth was intercepted by Ross. It was to ask her for the dance which was about to begin, a gavotte, that variation on the minuet which was now rivalling the minuet in favour.

He found this time that she smiled more easily, with less constraint. From being slightly scared by his attentions it had not taken her long to become flattered. A girl with four unmarried sisters does not come to her first ball with over-weening expectations. To find herself singled out by a man of some distinction was heady wine, and Ross should have been careful with his doses. But he, in a good-natured way, was only pleased to find pleasure in making someone's evening a success.

Rather to his own surprise he found he was enjoying the dance; there was a pleasure in mixing with people although he had tried to despise it. As they separated and came together again, he continued without break his whispered conversation with her, and she giggled abruptly, earning a glance of reproof from her second sister who was in the next square and dancing with two elderly men and a titled lady.

In the refreshment room Captain Blarney had produced a sketch.

"Now, you see, this is the foremast, mainmast, and mizzenmast. On the fore-mast is the mains'l, the—"

"Did you draw that?" Verity asked.

"Yes. It is a sketch of my father's ship. She was a ship o' the line. He died six years back. If—"

"It's uncommonly well drawn."

"Oh, that. One gets used to the pencil. You see, the foremast and the mainmast are square-rigged; that is to say they carry yards at—um—across the run of the ship. The mizzenmast is part square-rigged, but she carries a gaff and a spanker boom, and the sail is called the spanker. It was called a lateen in the olden days. Now this is the bowsprit. It is not shown in this sketch, but a sprits'l is set beneath it, so… Miss Verity, when can I see you again after tonight?"

Their heads were close together and she glanced up briefly into his intent brown eyes.

"That I couldn't say, Captain Blarney."

"It is all that I plan for."

"Oh," said Verity.

"… On the foremast, this is the mains'l. Then comes the lower tops'l and then the upper tops'l. This attachment to the bowsprit is called the jackstaff, and—and—"

"What is the jackstaff for?" Verity asked, short of breath.

"It is the—er— Dare I hope that—if I could hope that my interest was in the smallest way returned— If that were possible—"

"I think that is possible, Captain Blarney."

He touched her fingers for a moment. "Miss Verity, you give me a hope, a prospect which would inspire any man. I feel—I feel—But before I see your father, I must tell you something that only your encouragement would give me strength to venture—"

Five people entered the refreshment room, and Verity hastily straightened up, for she saw it was the Warleggans—with Francis and Elizabeth. Elizabeth saw her at once and smiled and waved and came across.

She was wearing a dress of peach-coloured muslin, with a white crepe turban close-fitting about her head.

"We'd no intention of coming, my dear," she said in amusement at Verity's surprise. "How pretty you're looking. How do you do, Captain Blarney."

"Your servant, ma'am."

"It was really George's fault," Elizabeth went on, excited and therefore radiantly beautiful. "We were supping with him and I believe he found our entertainment difficult."

"Cruel words from kind lips," said George Warleggan. "The fault is with your husband for wishing to dance this barbarous *ecossaise*."

Francis came across to them. His face was flushed with drink, and the effect also with him was a heightening of his good looks. "We've missed nothing that matters," he said. "All the fun's to come. I could not be sedate tonight if all England depended on it."

"Nor I," said Elizabeth. She smiled at Captain Blarney. "I hope our boisterous spirits don't jar on you, sir."

The sailor took a deep breath. "Not in the very least, ma'am. I have every reason to be happy myself."

In the ballroom Ruth Teague had returned and Lady Whitworth had gone.

"So Captain Poldark has left you at last, child!" said Mrs. Teague. "What explanation did he offer you for such conduct?"

"None, Mama," said Ruth, fanning herself brightly.

"Well, it is gratifying to be distinguished by such a genteel man, but there is reason in all things. You should know your manners if he does not. People are talking already."

"Are they? Oh, dear. I cannot refuse to dance with him; he is most polite and agreeable."

"No doubt, no doubt. But it is not becoming to make oneself too cheap. And you should think also of your sisters."

"He has asked me for the next dance after this."

"What? And what did you say?"

"I promised it for him."

"Uff!" Mrs. Teague shuddered fastidiously, but she was not as displeased as she sounded. "Well, a promise is a promise; you may dance it now. But you must not go into supper with him and leave Joan to her own devices."

"He has not asked me."

"You're very free with your answers, child. I think his attentions must have gone to your head. Perhaps I shall have a word with him after supper."

"No, no, Mama, you mustn't do that!"

"Well, we shall see," said Mrs. Teague, who really hadn't the slightest intention of discouraging an eligible man. Hers was a token protest to satisfy her sense of what was right and proper, of how she would behave if she had only one daughter and that one with a fortune of ten thousand pounds. With five on the books and no dowry for any of them, it deprived one of scope.

But they need not have concerned themselves. By the time the supper interval came, Ross had unaccountably disappeared. In his last dance with Ruth he had been stiff and preoccupied, and she wondered furiously whether in some manner her mother's criticisms had reached his ears.

As soon as the dance was over, he left the ballroom and walked out into the mild cloudy night. At the unexpected sight of Elizabeth his make-believe enjoyment had crumbled away. He wished more than anything to get out of her view. He forgot his obligations as Verity's escort and as a member of Miss Pascoe's party.

There were two or three carriages with footmen outside, and also a sedan chair. Lights from the bow windows of the houses in the square lit up the uneven cobbles and the trees of St Mary's churchyard. He turned in that direction. Elizabeth's beauty struck him afresh. The fact that another man should be in full enjoyment of her was like the torture of damnation. To continue to flirt with a plain little pleasant schoolgirl was out of the question.

As his hand closed about the cold railings under the trees, he fought to overcome his jealousy and pain, as one will to overcome a fainting fit. This time he must destroy it once and for all. Either he must do that or leave the county again. He had his own life to live, his own way to go; there were other women in the world, common clay perhaps, but charming enough with their pretty ways and soft bodies. Either break his infatuation for Elizabeth or remove himself to some part of the country where comparisons could not be made. A plain choice.

He walked on, waving away a beggar who followed him with a tale of poverty and want. He found himself before the Bear Inn. He pushed open the door and went down the three steps into the crowded taproom with its brass-bound barrels piled to the ceiling and its low wooden tables and benches. This night being Easter Monday, the room was very full, and the flickering smoky light of the candles in their iron sconces did not at first show him where a seat was to be found. He took one in a corner and ordered some brandy. The potman touched his forelock and took down a clean glass in honour of his unexpected patron. Ross became aware that at his coming a silence had fallen. His suit and linen were conspicuous in this company of ragged underfed drinkers.

"I'll have no more of such talk in 'ere," said the bartender uneasily, "so you'd best get down off of your perch, Jack Tripp."

"I'll stay where I am," said a tall thin man, better dressed than most of the others in a tattered suit sizes too big for him.

"Leave 'im stay," said a fat man in a chair below. "Even a crow's not denied its chimney pot."

There was a laugh, for the simile was apt enough.

Conversation broke out again when it became clear that the newcomer was too deeply set in his own thoughts to spare time for other people's. His only sign of life was to motion to the tapster from time to time to refill his glass. Jack Tripp was allowed to stay on his perch.

"It is all very well to say that, friend, but aren't we all men born of women? Does it alter our entry into the world or our exit out of it that we are a corn-factor or a beggar? Talk of it bein' God's devising that some should wallow in riches and others starve is so much clap-trappery. That is of man's devising, mark ee, the devising of the rich merchants and sich-like, to keep them where they be and other folk in chains. 'Tis fine and pretty to talk religion and bribe the clergy with food and wine—"

"Leave God alone," said a voice from the back.

"I've naught to say against God," croaked Jack Tripp. "But I don't hold with the God of the corn-factor's choosing. Didn't Christ preach justice for all? Where's justice in starving women and children? The clergy are stuffed wi' food while your womenfolk live on black bread and beech leaves, an' your children shrivel and die. And there's corn in Penryn, friends!"

There was a growl of assent.

A voice spoke in Ross's ear. "Buy a drink for a lady, will you, me lord? Unlucky to drink alone. The devil gets in brandy when you sup alone."

He stared into the bold dark eyes of a woman who had moved her position to sit beside him. She was tall, gaunt, about twenty-four or -five, dressed in a mannish blue riding suit which had once been smart but now was very shabby; it had perhaps been picked up at second or third hand. The stock was dirty and the lace front awry. She had high cheekbones, a wide mouth, bright teeth, wide bold, uncompromising eyes. Her black hair had been clumsily dyed copper.

Indifferently he motioned to the barman.

"Thanks, me lord," she said, stretching and yawning. "Here's to your health. You're looking wisht. Down in the mouth, y' know. Bit of company would do you no harm."

"Aye, there's corn in Penryn!" said Jack Tripp hoarsely. "And who be it for? Not for the likes of we. Nay, nay, sell the food abroad: that's the latest notion. They're not concerned wi' keeping us alive. Why is there no work in the mines? Because the tin and copper prices are so low. But why are they so low, friends? Because the merchants and the smelters fix the prices among theirselves to suit theirselves. Let the tinners rot! Why should the merchants care? Same wi' the millers! Same with all!"

Ross shifted on his elbow. These taproom agitators. His audience liked to be talked to in this manner; it gave mouth to grievances they had hardly begun to form.

The woman put her hand on his. He shook it off and finished his brandy.

"Lonely, me lord; that's what ails you. Let me read your palm." She put out her hand again and turned his up to examine it. "Ye-es. Ye-es. Bin disappointed in love, that's what it is. A fair woman has been false to you. But there's a dark woman here. Look." She pointed with a long forefinger. "See, she's close to you. Right close to you. She'll give you comfort, me lord. Not like these dainty maids who're afraid of a pair of breeches. I like the looks of you, if ye don't mind the expression. I'll wager you could give a woman satisfaction. But beware of some things. Beware o' being over partic'lar yourself, lest these dainty maids betray you into thinking love's a parlour game. Love's no parlour game, me lord, as you very well know."

Ross ordered another drink.

"Well, what of poor Betsey Pydar?" Jack Tripp said, shouting to drown the talk which had broken out. "What of that, I ask you, friends? What, *you* haven't heard of Widow Pydar? Hounded by the overseers and dying of starvation—"

The woman drained her glass at a draught but she did not release his hand.

"I can see a snug little cottage by the river. I like the look o' you, me lord. I feel an uncommon taking. I think you're the type of man who knows what's what. I've a talent for reading character, as you can see."

Ross stared at her, and she met his gaze boldly. Although they had only just set eyes on each other, it was as if a tremendous desire for him had flamed up in her. It wasn't all a matter of gold.

"And what did Parson Halse say when he was told?" asked Tripp. "He said that Betsey Pydar had brought this on herself by disobeying the laws of the country. That's your clergy for ee!— "

Ross got up, pulled his hand away, put down a coin for the potman, and threaded his way towards the door.

Outside the night was very dark and a light drizzle was falling. He stood a moment irresolute. As he turned away he heard the woman slip out of the inn.

She caught up with him quickly and walked tall and strong by his side. Then she took his hand again. His impulse was to wrench it away and have done with her importuning. But at the last moment his loneliness and dismay caught up with him like a slow-poisoning fog. What followed the rebuff? What was there for him to follow the rebuff? A return to the dance?

He turned and went with her.

CHAPTER SIX

1

Iᴛ ᴡᴀs ꜰᴏʀᴛᴜɴᴀᴛᴇ ᴛʜᴀᴛ Vᴇʀɪᴛʏ ʜᴀᴅ ᴀʀʀᴀɴɢᴇᴅ ᴛᴏ sᴘᴇɴᴅ ᴛʜᴇ ɴɪɢʜᴛ ᴡɪᴛʜ Joan Pascoe, for Ross saw no more of the ball. From the cottage of the woman Margaret he rode straight home, reaching Nampara as the first threads of daylight were unpicking the clustered clouds of the night.

This was Tuesday, the day of the Redruth Fair. He stripped off his clothes, went down to the beach and ran out into the surf. The cold boisterous water washed away some of the miasmas of the night; it was biting and tonic and impersonal. As he left the water, the cliffs at the far end of the beach were losing their darkness and the east sky had brightened to a brilliant cadmium yellow. He dried himself and dressed and woke Jud and they had breakfast with the first sun slanting through the windows.

They came to Redruth just before ten, slid down the steep greasy lane into the town, reached the chapel, crossed the river, and climbed the other hill to the fields where the fair was being held. The business of the day was already in progress with the buying and selling of livestock and farm and dairy produce.

It took Ross some time to find what he wanted, for he had no money to throw about, and by the time the various purchases had been made it was afternoon. In the second field every tradesman in the district had put up a stall. The better-class and larger tradesmen, with their saddlery and clothing and boots and shoes, clung to the upper part of the field; as the slope increased, one came to the gingerbread and sweetmeat stalls, the rope maker, the chair mender, the knife sharpener, the miscellaneous tents offering lanterns and brimstone matches, sealing-wax and silver buckles, bracelets of braided hair, secondhand wigs and snuffboxes, bed mats and chamber pots.

It would take Jud some hours to drive home the new oxen, so with time to spare Ross wandered round to see all there was to be seen. From the third field the substantial tradespeople were absent: this was the province of the professional rat catchers, the pedlars, the ha'penny peep-shows. One corner of this field belonged to the apothecaries and the herbalists. Men squatted on the ground and shouted before ill-spelt notices advertising their wares, which were the latest and most infallible cures for all the diseases of the flesh. Pectoral drops, Eau de Charm, nervous drops, spirit of benjamin, pomatum, fever powder, Jesuit drops. Here you could buy plantain and salad oil, angel water, hemlock for scrofulous tumours, and burdock burs for scurvy.

In the last field, which was the noisiest of all, were the side shows and the hurdy-gurdies, the Lilly-banger stall, where you cast dice for an Easter cake. In some sort of reaction from the bitterness and excesses of last night he found a relief in mingling with his fellow men, in accepting the simplicity of their pleasures. He paid his ha'penny and saw the fattest woman on earth, who, the man next to him was complaining, was not as fat as the one last year. For another ha'penny she offered to take you behind a screen and put your hand on a soft spot; but the man next to him said it was once-bitten-twice-shy, because all she did was put your hand on your own forehead.

He stood for fifteen minutes in a darkened booth watching a company of guise players performing a mime about St. George and the Dragon. He paid a ha'penny to see a man who in infancy had had his hands and feet eaten off by a pig and who sketched quite amazingly with a chalk in his mouth. He paid another ha'penny to see a mad woman in a cage tormented by her audience.

After he had seen the sights he sat down at a drinking booth and sipped a glass of rum and water. The words of Jack Tripp the agitator came to him as he watched the people pass by. For the most part they were weakly, stinking, rachitic, pockmarked, in rags—far less well found than the farm animals which were being bought and sold. Was it surprising that the upper classes looked on themselves as a race apart?

Yet the signs he had seen of a new way of life in America made him impatient of these distinctions. Jack Tripp was right. All men were born in the same way: no privilege existed which was not of man's own contriving.

He had chosen the last of the drinking booths at the extreme end of the ground. The noise and smell here was less overpowering; but just as he was ordering another drink, an uproar broke out behind the shop, and a number of people crowded to the corner to see what was on. Some of them began to laugh.

The uproar of squeals and barks went on. He rose to his feet and peered over the heads of the people standing near.

Behind the gin booth was a clearing where earlier some sheep had been quartered. Now it was empty except for a group of ragged boys watching a confused bundle of fur rolling over on the ground. This resolved itself into a cat and a dog, which the boys had tied tail to tail. The two animals were not much different in size, and after a fight, during which neither had the advantage, they now wanted to part company. First the dog pulled and the cat sprawled, spitting; then the cat with difficulty got to her feet and with slow convulsive movements, digging her claws into the earth, dragged the dog backwards.

The spectators roared with laughter. Ross smiled briefly and was about to sit down when a smaller boy broke away from two others who were holding him and ran towards the animals. He dodged one of the other boys who tried to stop him and reached the creatures, knelt down, and tried to loosen the knotted twine about their tails, ignoring the scratches of the cat. When it was seen what he was about, there was a murmur from the crowd who perceived that they were to be robbed of a free entertainment. But this murmur was drowned in a howl of fury from the other boys, who at once rushed in and fell upon the spoil-sport. He tried to put up a fight but soon went under.

Ross reached down for his drink but remained on his feet while he sipped it. A big man as tall as himself moved up and partly obscured the view.

"Sakes alive," said someone; "they'll maim the lad, a-kicking of him like that. 'Tis past a joke, the young varmints."

"And who's to say them nay?" queried a little merchant with a shade over one eye. "They're wild as cats. 'Tis a disgrace to the town the way they roam."

"Break your windows if you complain," said another. "And glad of the excuse. Aunt Mary Treglown, her's got a cottage over to Pool—"

"Ais, I knaw..."

Ross finished his drink and ordered another. Then he changed his mind and moved into the crowd.

"God preserve us!" said a housewife suddenly. "Is it a girl they're bating up? Or I'm mistook. An't any of ye going to stop 'em ?"

Ross took his riding crop from his boot and walked into the arena. Three of the urchins saw him coming; two fled, but the third stood his ground with bared teeth. Ross hit him across the face with the whip and the boy shrieked and fled. A stone flew through the air.

There were three other boys, two sitting on the figure while the third kicked it in the back. This last youth did not see the approach of the enemy. Ross hit him on the side of the head and knocked him out. One of the others he lifted by the seat of his breeches and dropped into a neighbouring pool of water. The third fled and left the figure of the spoil-sport lying on its face.

The clothing was certainly that of a boy; a loose shirt and coat, trousers too big and falling loosely below the knee. A round black cap lay in the dust; the tousled hair seemed overlong. A stone hit Ross's shoulder.

With the toe of his boot he pushed the figure on its back. Might be a girl. The child was conscious but too winded to speak; every intake of breath was half a groan.

A number of the townspeople had filtered into the clearing, but as the stones became more frequent they sheered off again.

"Have they hurt you, child?" Ross said.

With a convulsive wriggle she drew up her knees and pulled herself into a sitting position.

"Judas God!" she was at last able to get out. "… rot their dirty guts…"

The hail of stones was becoming more accurate and two more struck his back. He put his whip away and picked her up; she was no weight at all. As he carried her towards the gin shop, he saw that crofters had joined together and were going after the boys with sticks.

He set her down at the end of the trestle table he had recently left. Her head sank forward on the table. Now that the danger from missiles was over, people crowded round.

"What did they do to ee, my dear?"

"Scat un in the ribs, did they?"

"She'm fair davered, poor maid."

"I'd lace 'em…"

He ordered two glasses of rum. "Give the child air," he said impatiently. "Who is she and what is her name?"

"Never seed she afore," said one.

"She do come from Roskear, I bla'," said another.

"I know she," said a woman, peering. "She'm Tom Carne's daughter. They d' live over to Illuggan."

"Where is her father, then?"

"Down mine, I expect."

"Drink this." Ross put the glass against the girl's elbow and she picked it up and gulped at it. She was a thin scarecrow of a child of eleven or twelve. Her shirt was dirty and torn; the mop of dark hair hid her face.

"Are you with someone?" Ross asked. "Where is your mother?"

"She an't got one," said the woman, breathing stale gin over his shoulders. "Been in 'er grave these six year."

"Well, that cdn my fault," said the girl, finding her voice.

"Nor never said twas," said the woman. "And what you doing in your brother's clo'es? Young tomrigg! You'll get the strap for this."

"Go away, woman," said Ross in irritation at being so much the focus of attention. "Go away, all of you. Have you nothing better to gape at?" He turned to the girl. "Is there no one with you? What were you about?"

She sat up. "Where's Garrick? They was tormentin' him."

"Garrick?"

"My dog. Where's Garrick? Garrick! Garrick!"

"Ere 'e be." A crofter pushed his way through the others. "I got un for you. It was no easy job."

She got to her feet to receive a wriggling black bundle, and collapsed on the seat again with it in her lap. She bent over the puppy to see if it was hurt, getting her hands more bloody than they were. Suddenly she looked up with a wail, eyes blazing amid the dirt and hair.

"Judas God! The dirty nattlings! They've cut'n off his tail!"

"I done that," the crofter told her composedly. "Think I was going to get me 'ands tored for a mongrel cur? Besides, twas 'alf off already, and he'll be better placed without it."

"Finish this," Ross said to the girl. "Then if you can talk, tell me if you feel any bones broke in their handling." He gave the crofter sixpence, and the crowd, aware that the show was over, began to disperse, though for some time a ring of them remained at a respectful distance, interested in the gentleman.

The dog was an emaciated mongrel puppy of a muddy black colour, with a long thin neck and covered sparsely about the head and body with short black curls. Its parentage was unimaginable.

"Use this," said Ross, holding out his handkerchief. "Wipe your arms and see if the scratches go deep."

She looked up from fingering her body and stared at the linen square doubtfully.

"Twill foul it," she said.

"So I can see."

"It mayn't wash out."

"Do as you're bid and don't argue."

She used a corner of the kerchief on one bony elbow.

"How did you come here?" he asked.

"Walked."

"With your father?"

"Fathur's down mine."

"You came alone?"

"Wi' Garrick."

"You can't walk back like that. Have you friends here?"

"No." She stopped suddenly in her perfunctory wiping. "Judas, I feel some queer."

"Drink some more of this."

"No... 'tis that atop of nothin'..."

She got up and limped unsteadily to the corner of the gin shop. There, for the diversion and reward of the faithful spectators, she painfully lost the rum she had drunk. Then she fainted, so Ross lifted her back into the stall. When she recovered, he took her into the stall next door and gave her a square meal.

2

The shirt she was wearing had old tears in it as well as new; the breeches were of faded brown corduroy; her feet were bare and she had lost the round cap. Her face was pinched and white, and her eyes, a very dark brown, were much too big for it.

"What is your name?" he said.

"Demelza."

"Your Christian name, though?"

"Please?"

"Your first name."

"Demelza."

"A strange name."

"Mother were called that too."

"Demelza Carne. Is that it?"

She sighed and nodded, for she was well filled; and the dog under the table grunted with her.

"I come from Nampara. Beyond Sawle. Do you know where that is?"

"Past St. Ann's?"

"I am going home now, child. If you cannot walk I'll take you first to Illuggan and leave you there."

A shadow went across her eyes and she did not speak. He paid what he owed and sent word for his horse to be saddled.

Ten minutes later they were up and away. The girl sat silently astride in front of him. Garrick followed in desultory fashion, now and then dragging his seat in the dust or peering suspiciously round to see what had become of the thing he had sometimes chased and often wagged but now could not locate.

They cut across the moors by a mining track worn deep and hard and pitted by the passage of generations of mules. The countryside hereabout was entirely abandoned to the quest for minerals. All trees, except an occasional ragged pine, had been cut down for timber, every stream was discoloured, patches of cultivated land struggled among acres of mine refuse and mountains of stone. Engine sheds, wooden derricks, wheel stamps, windlasses, and horse gins were its adornment. Trenches and adits grew in the back gardens of the tiny cottages and huts; potatoes were hoed and goats grazed among the steam and the refuse. There was no town, scarcely even a hamlet, only a wide and sparse distribution of working people.

It was the first time he had been to Illuggan this way. With the improvement in the pumping engine and the new lodes of tin and copper available, Cornish mining had been going ahead until the slump of the last few years. People had migrated to these fortunate districts where the veins were richest, and the home population had increased rapidly. Now in the growing depression of the early eighties, many of the breadwinners were out of work and the doubt arose as to whether the population could be maintained. The danger was not immediate but the spectre was there.

The girl in front of him gave a wriggle.

"Could ee let me down 'ere?" she said.

"You're but halfway to Illuggan yet."

"I know. I doubt I shall be going 'ome yet awhile."

"Why not?"

There was no answer.

"Does your father not know you've been out?"

"Yes, but I was lended my brother's shirt and breeches. Fathur says I must go to fair whether or no, so he says I can borrow Luke's Sunday fligs."

"Well?"

"Well, I ain't got what I went for. And Luke's clothes is all slottery. So I reckon—"

"Why did you not go in your own clothes?"

"Fathur tored 'em last night when he give me a cooting."

They jogged on for some distance. She turned and peered back to be sure Garrick was following.

"Does your father often beat you?" Ross asked.

"Only when he's bin takin' too much."

"How often is that?"

"Oh… mebbe twice a week. Less when he 'an't got the money."

There was silence. It was now late afternoon and needed another two hours to dark. She began to fumble with the neck of her shirt and untied the string. "You can see," she said. "E used the strap last night. Pull me shirt back."

He did so, and it slipped off one shoulder. Her back was marked with weals. On some the skin had been broken, and these were partly healed, with dirt smeared on them and lice at the edges. Ross pulled the shirt up again.

"And tonight?"

"Oh, he'd give me a banger tonight. But I'll stay outdoors and not go 'ome till he's below again."

They rode on.

Ross was not oversensitive to the feelings of animals: it was not in his generation to be so, though he seldom hit one himself; but wanton cruelty to children offended him.

"How old are you?"

"Thirteen … sur."

It was the first time she had sirred him. He might have known that these undersized, half-starved waifs were always older than they looked.

"What work do you do?"

"Looking after the 'ouse and plantin' taties an' feeding the pig."

"How many brothers and sisters have you?"

"Six brothers."

"All younger than you?"

"Es-s." She turned her head and whistled piercingly to Garrick.

"Do you love your father?"

She looked at him in surprise. "Es-s—"

"Why?"

She wriggled. "Cos it says you must in the Bible."

"You like living at home?"

"I runned away when I was twelve."

"And what happened?"

"I was broft back."

Darkie swerved as a stoat scuttered across the path, and Ross took a firmer grip on the reins.

"If you stay out of your father's way for a time, no doubt he'll forget what you have done wrong."

She shook her head. "He'll save un up."

"Then what is the use of avoiding him?"

She smiled with an odd maturity. "Twill put un off."

They reached a break in the track. Ahead lay the way to Illuggan; the right fork would bring him to skirt St. Ann's whence he could join the usual lane to Sawle. He reined up the mare.

"I'll get down 'ere," she said.

He said: "I need a girl to work in my house. At Nampara, beyond St. Ann's. You would get your food and better clothing than you have now. As you are under age I would pay your wages to your father." He added: "I want someone strong, for the work is hard."

She was looking up at him with her eyes wide and a startled expression in them as if he had suggested something wicked. Then the wind blew her hair over them and she blinked.

"The house is at Nampara," he said. "But perhaps you do not wish to come."

She pushed her hair back but said nothing.

"Well then, get down," he continued with a sense of relief. "Or I will still take you into Illuggan if you choose."

"To live at your house?" she said. "Tonight? Yes, please."

The appeal, of course, was obvious; the immediate appeal of missing a thrashing.

"I want a kitchen maid," he said. "One who can work and scrub, and keep herself clean also. It would be by the year that I should hire you. You would be too far away to run home every week."

"I don't want to go home ever," she said.

"It will be necessary to see your father and get his consent. That may be hard to come by."

"I'm a good scrubber," she said. "I can scrub... sur."

Darkie was fidgeting at the continued check.

"We will go and see your father now. If he can be—"

"Not now. Take me with you. I can scrub. I'm a good scrubber."

"There is a law to these things. I must hire you from your father."

"Fathur don't come up from 'is core till an hour after cockshut. Then he'll go drink afore he do come 'ome."

Ross wondered if the girl were lying. Impulse had prompted him this far. He needed extra help as much in the house as in the fields, and he disliked the idea of handing this child back to a drunken miner. But neither did he wish to cool his heels in some bug-ridden hovel until dark with naked children crawling over him, then to be confronted by a gin-sodden bully who would refuse his suggestion. Did the child really want to come?

"About Garrick. I might not be able to keep Garrick."

There was silence. Watching her closely, he could plainly see the struggle which was going on behind the thin, anaemic features. She looked at the dog, then looked up at him and her mouth gave a downward twist.

"Him an' me's friends," she said.

"Well?"

She did not speak for a time. "Garrick an' me's done everything together. I couldn't leave 'im to starve."

"Well?"

"I couldn't, mister. I couldn't—"

In distress she began to slip off the mare.

He suddenly found that the thing he had set out to prove had proved something quite different. Human nature had outmaneuvered him. For if she would not desert a friend, neither could he.

3

They overtook Jud soon after passing the gibbet at Bargus, where four roads and four parishes met. The oxen were tired of the long trek and Jud was tired of driving them. He could not ride comfortably on blind Ramoth because four large baskets crammed with live chickens were slung across the saddle. Also he was deeply annoyed at having to leave the fair before he was drunk, a thing that had never happened to him since he was ten.

He looked round sourly at the approach of another horse and then pulled Ramoth off the track to let them pass. The oxen, being strung out in single file behind, followed suit quietly enough.

Ross explained the presence of the urchin in three sentences and left Jud to work it out for himself.

Jud raised his hairless eyebrows.

"He's all very well to play uppity-snap with a lame 'orse," he said in a grumbling voice. "But picking up brats is another matter. Picking up brats is all wrong. Picking up brats will get ee in trouble wi' the law."

"A fine one you are to talk of the law," Ross said.

Jud had not been looking where he was going, and Ramoth stumbled in a rut.

Jud said a wicked word. "Rot 'im, there 'e go again. 'Ow d'you expect for a man for to ride a blind 'orse. Ton my Sam, 'ow d'you expect for a 'orse for to see where he's going when he can't see nothin'. Tedn't in the nature o' things. Tedn't 'orse nature."

"I've always found him very sure," Ross said. "Use your own eyes, man. He's uncommonly sensitive to the least touch. Don't force him to hurry, that's the secret."

"Force 'im to 'urry! I should be forcin' meself over 'is 'ead into the nearest ditch if I forced 'im to go faster than a bullhorn leaving 'is slime twixt one stone and the next. Tedn't safe. One slip, one tumble, that's all; over you go, over 'is ears, fall on your nuddick, and *phit!* ye're dead."

Ross touched Darkie and they moved on.

"And a dirty bitch of a mongrel." Jud's scandalized voice followed them as he caught sight of their escort. "Lord Almighty, tes fit to duff you, we'll be adopting a blathering poorhouse next."

Garrick lifted a whiskery eye at him and trotted past. There had been talk concerning himself, he felt, at the fork roads, but the matter had been amicably settled.

On one point Ross was decided: There should be no qualifying of his position in the lice and bug battle. Six months ago the house, and particularly Prudie, had been alive with most of the things that crawl. He was not fussy but he had put his foot down over Prudie's condition. Finally the threat to hold her under the pump and give her a bath himself had had results, and today the house was almost free—and even Prudie herself except for the home-grown colonies in her lank black hair. To bring the child into the house in her present state would knock the props away from the position he had taken up. Therefore both she and the dog must be given a bath and fresh clothes found for her before she entered the house. For this duty Prudie herself would be useful.

They reached Nampara at sunset—a good half hour ahead of Jud, he reckoned—and Jim Carter came running out to take Darkie. The boy's health and physique had improved a lot during the winter. His dark Spanish eyes widened at the sight of the cargo his master brought. But in a manner refreshingly different from the Paynters, he said no word and prepared to lead the horse away. The girl stared at him with eyes already wide with interest, then turned again and gazed at the house, at the valley and the apple trees and the stream, at the sunset, which was a single vermilion scar above the dark of the sea.

"Where's Prudie?" said Ross. "Tell her I want her."

"She's not here, sur," said Jim Carter. "She left so soon as you left. She did say she was walking over to Marasanvose to see 'er cousin."

Ross swore under his breath. The Paynters had a unique gift for not being there when wanted.

"Leave Darkie," he said. "I'll attend to her. Jud is two miles away with some oxen I've bought. Go now and help him with them. If you hurry, you will meet him before he reaches the Mellingeyford."

The boy dropped the reins, glanced again at the girl, then went off at a rapid walk up the valley.

Ross stared a moment at the piece of flotsam he had brought home and hoped to salvage. She was standing there in her ragged shirt and three-quarter-length breeches, her matted hair over her face and the dirty half-starved puppy at her feet. She stood with one toe turned in and both hands loosely behind her back, staring across at the library. He hardened his heart. Tomorrow would not do.

"Come this way," he said.

She followed him, and the dog followed her, to the back of the house where between the still-room and the first barn the pump was set.

"Now," he said, "if you are to work for me, you must first be clean. D'you understand that?"

"Yes... sur."

"I cannot allow anyone dirty into the house. No one works for me if they are not clean and don't wash. So take off your clothing and stand under the pump. I will work the pump for you."

"Yes... sur." She obediently began to untie the string at the neck of her shirt. This done, she stopped and looked slowly up at him.

"And don't put those things on again," he said. "I'll find you something clean."

"P'r'aps," she said, "I could work the 'andle meself."

"And stand under at the same time?" he said brusquely. "Nonsense. And hurry. I have not all evening to waste over you." He went to the pump handle and gave it a preliminary jerk.

She looked at him earnestly for a moment, then began to wriggle out of her shirt. This done, a faint pink tinge was visible under the dirt on her face. Then she slipped out of her breeches and jumped beneath the pump.

He worked the handle with vigour. The first rinsing would not get rid of everything but would at least be a beginning. It would leave his position uncompromised. She had an emaciated little body, on which womanhood had only just begun to fashion its design. As well as the marks of her thrashings he could see blue bruises on her back and ribs where the boys had kicked her this afternoon. Fortunately, like her, they had been barefoot.

She had never had such a washing before. She gasped and choked as the water poured in spurts and volumes upon her head, coursed over her body, and ran away to the draining trough. Garrick yelped but refused to move, so took a good deal of the water at secondhand.

At length, fearing he would drown her, he stopped, and while the stream of water thinned to a trickle he went into the still-room and picked up the first cloth he could find.

"Dry yourself on this," he said. "I will fetch you something to put on."

As he re-entered the house he wondered what that something was to be. Prudie's things, even if they were clean enough, would smother the child like a tent. Jim Carter would have been the nearest choice for size if he had owned any other clothes but those he was wearing.

Ross went up to his own room and ransacked the drawers, cursing himself for never thinking more than one move ahead. One could not keep the child shivering there in the yard forever. Finally he picked out a Holland shirt of his own, a girdle, and a short morning gown of his father's.

When he went out he found her trying to cover herself with the cloth he had given her, while her hair still lay in wet black streaks on her face and shoulders. He did not give her the things at once but beckoned her to follow him into the kitchen, where there was a fire. Having just succeeded in shutting Garrick out of the house, he poked up the fire and told her to stand in front of it until she was dry and to put on the makeshift garments in what manner she chose. She blinked at him wetly, then looked away and nodded to show she understood.

He went out again to unsaddle Darkie.

CHAPTER SEVEN

1

DEMELZA CARNE SPENT THE NIGHT IN THE GREAT BOX BED WHERE JOSHUA Poldark had passed the last few months of his life. There was no other room where she could immediately go; later she could be put in the bedroom between the linen cupboard and the Paynters' room, but at present it was full of lumber.

To her, who had slept all her life on straw, with sacks for covering, in a tiny crowded cottage, this room and this bed were of unthought luxury and unimagined size. The bed itself was almost as big as the room she and four brothers slept in. When Prudie, grumbling and flopping, showed her where she had to spend the night, she guessed that three or four other servants would come in later to share the bed, and when no one came and it seemed she was to be left alone, a long time passed before she could bring herself to try it.

She was not a child who looked far ahead or reasoned deep; the ways of her life had given her no excuse to do either. With a cottage full of babies she had had no time at all to sit and think, scarcely any even to work and think; and what was the good of looking for tomorrow when today filled all your time and all your energy and sometimes all your fears? So that in this sudden turn in her fortunes, her instinct had been to accept it for what it was, and as long as it lasted, glad enough but as philosophically as she had taken the fight at the fair.

It was only this sudden luxury which scared her. The drenching under the pump had been unexpected, but its roughness and lack of concern for her feelings had run true to type; it fell in with her general experience. Had she then been given a couple of sacks and told to sleep in the stables she would have obeyed and felt there was nothing amiss. But this development was too much like the stories Old Meggy the Sumpman's mother used to tell her: It had some of the frightening, nightmare temper of those and some of the glitter of her mother's fairy tales in which everyone slept in satin sheets and ate off gold platters. Her imagination could gladly accept it in a story, but her knowledge of life could not accept it in reality. Her strange garments had been a beginning; they fitted nowhere and hung in ridiculous lavender-scented folds over her thin body; they were agreeable but suspect, as this bedroom was agreeable but suspect.

When at length she found the courage to try the bed, she did so with strange sensations; she was afraid that the big wooden doors of the bed would swing quietly to and shut her up forever; she was afraid that the man who had brought her here, for all his air of niceness and kind eyes, had some Evil Design, that as soon as she went off to sleep he would creep into the room with a knife or a whip—or merely creep into the room. From these fears her attention would be turned by the pattern of the tattered silk hangings on the bed, by the gold tassel of the bellpull, by the feel of the clean sheets under her fingers, by the beautiful curves of the bronze candlestick on the three-legged wicker table by the bed—from which candlestick guttered the single light standing between her and darkness, a light which by now should have been put out, and which would very soon go out of its own accord.

She stared into the dark chasm of the fireplace and began to fancy that something horrible might at any moment come down the chimney and plop into the hearth. She looked at the pair of old bellows, at the two strange painted ornaments on the mantelpiece (one looked like the Virgin Mary), and at the engraved cutlass over the door. In the dark corner beside the bed was a portrait, but she had not looked at it while the Fat Lady was in the room, and since the Fat Lady had left she had not dared to move out of the circle of the candlelight.

Time passed, and the candle was flaring up before it went out, sending smoky curls like wisps of an old woman's hair spiralling towards the beams. There were two doors, and that which led she-didn't-know-where held a special danger although it was tight shut every time she craned to look.

Something scratched at the window. She listened with her heart thumping. Then suddenly she caught something familiar in the noise, and she jumped from the bed and flew to the window. Minutes passed before she saw how to open it. Then when a six-inch gap had been slowly levered at the bottom, a wriggling black thing squirmed into the room, and she had her arms round Garrick's neck, half strangling him from love and anxiety that he should not bark.

Garrick's nearness changed the whole picture for her. With his long rough tongue he licked her cheeks and ears while she carried him towards the bed.

The flame of the candle gave a preliminary lurch and then straightened for a few seconds more. Hurriedly she pulled across the hearthrug and another rug from near the door, and with these made on the floor an improvised bed for herself and the puppy. Then as the light slowly died from the room and one object after another faded into the shadows, she lay down and curled herself up with the dog and felt his own excited struggles relax as she whispered endearments in his ear.

Darkness came and silence fell and Demelza and Garrick slept.

2

Ross slept heavily, which was not surprising, as he had had no sleep the night before, but a number of odd and vivid dreams came to disturb him. He woke early and lay in bed for a time looking out at the bright windy morning and thinking over the events of the past two days. The ball and the gaunt, wild Margaret: the aristocratic commonplace and the disreputable commonplace. But neither had been quite ordinary for him. Elizabeth had seen to that. Margaret had seen to that.

Then the fair and its outcome. It occurred to him this morning that his adoption of yesterday might have troublesome results. His knowledge of the law was vague and his attitude towards it faintly contemptuous, but he had an idea that one could not take a girl of thirteen away from her home without so much as a by-your-leave to her father.

He thought he would ride over and see his uncle. Charles had been a magistrate for over thirty years, so there was a chance he would have some views worth hearing. Ross also gave more than a thought to the violent court being paid to Verity by Captain Andrew Blarney. After the first, they had danced every dance together up to the time of his leaving the ballroom. Everyone would soon be talking, and he wondered why Blarney had not been to see Charles before now. The sun was high when he rode over to Trenwith. The air was exhilaratingly fresh and alive this morning, and all the colouring of the countryside was in washed, pastel shades. Even the desolate area round Grambler was not unsightly after the greater desolation he had seen yesterday.

As he came in sight of the house, he reflected again upon the inevitable failure of his father to build anything to rival the mellow Tudor comeliness of this old home. The building was not large, but gave an impression of space and of having been put up when money was free and labour cheap. It was built in a square about a compact courtyard, with the big hall and its gallery and stairs facing you as you entered, with the large parlour and library leading off on the right and the withdrawing room and small winter parlour on the left, the kitchens and buttery being behind and forming the fourth side of the square. The house was in good repair for its age, having been built by Jeffrey Trenwith in 1509.

No servant came out to take the mare, so he tethered her to a tree and knocked on the door with his riding whip. This was the official entrance, but the family more often used the smaller door at the side, and he was about to walk round to that when Mrs. Tabb appeared and bobbed respectfully.

"Morning, sur. Mister Francis you're wanting, is it?"

"No, my uncle."

"Well, sur, I'm sorry but they're both over to Grambler. Cap'n Henshawe come over this morning and they both walked back wi' him. Will ee come in, sur, while I ast how long they'll be?"

He entered the hall and Mrs. Tabb hurried off to find Verity. He stood a minute staring at the patterns made by the sun as it fell through the long narrow mullioned windows, then he walked towards the stairs where he had stood on the day of Elizabeth's wedding. No crowd of bedecked people today, no raucous cockfight, no chattering clergymen; he preferred it this way. The long table was empty except for its row of candlesticks. On the table in the alcove beside the stairs stood the big brass-bound family Bible, now seldom used except by Aunt Agatha in her pious moments. He wondered if Francis's marriage had yet been entered there, as all the others had for two hundred years.

He stared up at the row of portraits on the wall beside the stairs. There were others about the hall and many more in the gallery above. He would have had difficulty in picking out more than a dozen by name; most of the early ones were Trenwiths, and even some later portraits were unnamed and undated. A small faded painting in the alcove with the Bible, where it should not get too much light, was that of the founder of the male side of the family, one Robert d'Arqué, who had come to England in 1572. The oil paint had cracked and little was to be distinguished except the narrow ascetic face, the long nose, and the hunched shoulder. There was then discreet silence for three generations until one came to an attractive painting by Kneller of Anna-Maria Trenwith and another by the same artist of Charles Vivian Raffe Poldarque, whom she had married in 1696. Anna-Maria was the beauty of the collection, with large dark blue eyes and fine red-gold hair.

Well, Elizabeth would be a worthy addition, would grace the company if someone could be found to do justice to her. Opie might be too fond of the dark pigments.

He heard a door shut and a footstep. He turned, expecting Verity, and found Elizabeth.

"Good morning, Ross," she smiled. "Verity is in Sawle. She always goes on a Wednesday morning. Francis and his father are at the mine. Aunt Agatha is in bed with the gout."

"Oh yes," he said woodenly. "I had forgotten. No matter."

"I am in the parlour," she said, "if you would care to keep me company a few minutes."

He followed her slowly towards the parlour door; they entered and she sat down at the spinning wheel but did not resume what she had been doing.

She smiled again. "We see so little of you. Tell me how you enjoyed the ball."

He took a seat and looked at her. She was pale this morning, and her simple dress of striped dimity emphasized her youth. She was a little girl with all the appeal of a woman. Beautiful and fragile and composed, a married woman. A black desire rose in him to smash the composure. He subdued it.

"We were so pleased that you were there," she went on. "But even then you danced so little that we hardly saw you."

"I had other business."

"We had no intention of being there," she said, a little put out by the grimness of his tone, "it was quite on impulse that we went."

"What time will Francis and Charles be back?" he asked.

"Not yet, I'm afraid. Did you see how George Warleggan enjoyed the *écossaise*? He had sworn all along that nothing would persuade him to attempt it."

"I don't remember the pleasure."

"Did you wish to see Francis on something of importance?"

"Not Francis—my uncle. No. It can wait."

There was silence.

"Verity said you were going to Redruth Fair yesterday. Did you get all the stock you wanted?"

"Some of it. It was on a question of unexpected stock that I wished to see my uncle."

She looked down at the spinning wheel. "Ross," she said in a low voice.

"My coming here upsets you."

She did not move.

"I'll meet them on the way back," he said, rising.

She did not answer. Then she looked up and her eyes were heavy with tears. She picked up the woollen thread she had been spinning and the tears dropped on her hands.

He sat down again with a sensation as if he was falling off a cliff.

Talking to save himself, he said: "At the fair yesterday I picked up a girl, a child; she had been ill treated by her father. I needed someone to help Prudie in the house; she was afraid to go home; I brought her back to Nampara. I shall keep her as a kitchen maid. I don't know the law of the matter. Elizabeth, why are you crying?"

She said: "How old is the girl?"

"Thirteen. I—"

"I should send her back. It would be safer even if you had her father's permission. You know how hard people are judged."

"I shall not come here again," Ross said. "I upset you—to no purpose."

She said: "It's not your *coming*—"

"What am I to think, then?"

"It only hurts me to feel that you hate me."

He twisted his riding crop round and round. "You know I don't hate you. Good God, you should know that—"

She broke the thread.

"Since I met you," he said, "I've had no eyes and no thought for any other girl. When I was away, nothing mattered about my coming back but this. If there was one thing I was sure of, it wasn't what I'd been taught by anyone else to believe, not what I learned from other people was the truth but the truth that I felt in myself—about you."

"Don't say any more." She had gone very white. But for once her frailness did not stop him. It had to come out now.

"It isn't very pretty to have been made a fool of by one's own feelings," he said. "To take childish promises and build a—a castle out of them. And yet—even now sometimes I can't believe that all the things we said to each other were so trivial or so immature. Are you sure you felt so little for me as you pretend? D'you remember that day in your father's garden when you slipped away from them and met me in the summerhouse? That day you said—"

"You forget yourself," she whispered, forcing the words out.

"Oh no I don't. I remember you."

All the conflicting feeling inside her suddenly found an outlet. The mixed motives for asking him in; the liking, the affection, the feminine curiosity, the piqued pride; they suddenly merged into indignation to keep out something stronger. She was as much alarmed at her own feelings as indignant with him; but the situation had to be saved somehow.

She said: "I was wrong to ask you to stay. It was because I wanted your friendship, nothing more."

"I think you must have your feelings under a very good control. You turn them about and face them the way you want them to be. I wish I could do that. What's the secret?"

Trembling, she left the spinning wheel and went to the door.

"I'm married," she said. "It isn't fair to Francis to speak as you—as we are doing. I'd hoped that we could still be good neighbours—and good friends. We live so close—could help each other. But you can forget nothing and forgive nothing. Perhaps I'm expecting too much... I don't know. But, Ross, ours was a boy-and-girl attachment. I was very fond of you and still am. But you went away and I met Francis, and with Francis it was different. I *loved* him. I'd grown up. We were not children but grown people. Then came the word that you were dead... When you came back I was so happy; and so very sorry that I'd not been able to—to keep faith with you. If there'd been any way of making it up to you, I'd gladly have done it. I wished that we still should be close friends, and thought... Until today I thought that we could. But after this—"

"After this it's better that we shouldn't be."

He came up to the door and put his hand on it. Her eyes were dry enough now and exceptionally dark.

"For some time," she said, "this is goodbye."

"It's goodbye." He bent and kissed her hand. She shrank from his touch as if he was unclean. He thought he had become repulsive to her.

She went with him to the front door, where Darkie whinnied at the sight of him.

"Try to understand," Elizabeth said. "I love Francis and married him. If you could forget me, it would be better. There's no more I can say than that."

He mounted the mare and looked down at her.

"Yes," he agreed. "There's no more to say."

He saluted and rode away, leaving her standing in the dark of the doorway.

CHAPTER EIGHT

1

WELL, HE TOLD HIMSELF, THAT WAS OVER. THE SUBJECT WAS CLOSED. IF that queer perverted pleasure which came from striking with his barbed tongue at her composure—if that were satisfaction, then he had found some in the interview.

But all he felt was an ashen desolation, an emptiness, a contempt for himself. He had behaved badly. It was so easy to play the jilted lover, the bitter and sarcastic boor.

And even if he had upset her by his attack, yet her defence had more than levelled the score. Indeed, their positions being what they were, she could in a single sentence strike more surely at him than he at her with all the ingenuity his hurt could devise.

He was past Grambler and nearly home before he realized he had not seen either Charles or Verity, and the two questions he had gone to Trenwith to ask remained unanswered.

He rode down the valley, too full of a deadly inertia of spirit to find satisfaction in the sight of his land, which was at last beginning to show signs of the attention it was receiving. On the skyline near Wheal Grace he could see Jud and the boy Carter busy with the six yoked oxen. At present they were not used to working as a team, but in a week or so a child would be able to drive them.

At the door of Nampara he climbed wearily down from his horse and stared at Prudie, who was waiting for him.

"Well, what is it?" he said.

"Thur's three men to see ee. They stank into the 'ouse without so much as a by-your-leave. They're in the parlour."

Uninterested, Ross nodded and entered the living-room. Three workingmen were standing there, big and square-shouldered and stolid. From their clothes he could tell they were miners.

"Mister Poldark?" the eldest spoke. There was no seemly deference in his tone. He was about thirty-five, a powerfully built, deep-chested man with bloodshot eyes and a heavy beard.

"What can I do for you?" Ross asked impatiently. He was in no mood to receive a delegation.

"Name of Carne," said the man. "Tom Carne. These my two brothers."

"Well?" said Ross. And then after he had spoken, the name stirred in his memory. So the matter was to resolve itself without Charles's advice.

"I hear tell you've gotten my dattur."

"Who told you that?"

"The Widow Richards said you took 'er 'ome."

"I don't know the woman."

Carne shifted restlessly and blinked his eyes. He had no intention of being sidetracked.

"Where's my dattur?" he said grimly.

"They've searched the 'ouse," came from Prudie at the door.

"Hold your noise, woman," said Carne.

"By what right do you come here and talk to my servant like that?" Ross asked with malignant politeness.

"Right, by God! You've slocked my dattur. You 'ticed her away. Where is she?"

"I have no idea."

Carne thrust out his bottom lip. "Then you'd best find out."

"Aye!" said one of the brothers.

"So that you may take her home and beat her?"

"I do what I choose wi' me own," said Carne.

"Her back is already inflamed."

"What right ha' you to be seein' her back! I'll have the law on you!"

"The law says a girl may choose her own home when she is fourteen."

"She's not fourteen."

"Can you prove it?"

Carne tightened his belt. "Look 'ere, man; tedn't fur me to prove nothing. She's my dattur, and she'll not go to be plaything to a rake-hell dandy, not now, nor when she's forty, see?"

"Even that," said Ross, "might be better than caring for your pigsty."

Carne glanced at his brothers.

"He ain't going to give 'er up."

"We can make un," said the second brother, a man of about thirty with a pockmarked face.

"I'll go fetch Jud," said Prudie from the door, and went out flapping in her slippers.

"Well, mister," said Carne. "What's it to be?"

"So that's why you brought your family," said Ross. "Without the spunk to do a job yourself."

"I could 'a brought two 'undred men, mister." Carne thrust his face forward. "We don't 'old wi' cradle thiefs down Illuggan way. Scat un up, boys."

Immediately the other two turned; one kicked over a chair, the other upended the table on which were some cups and plates, Carne picked up a candlestick and dashed it on the floor.

Ross walked across the room and took down from the wall one of a pair of French duelling pistols. This he began to prime.

"I'll shoot the next man who touches furniture in this room," he said.

There was a moment's pause. The three men stopped, plainly thwarted.

"Where's my dattur?" shouted Carne.

Ross sat on the arm of a chair. "Get off my land before I have you committed for trespass."

"We'd best go, Tom," said the youngest brother. "We can come back wi' the others."

"Tes my quarrel." Carne plucked at his beard and stared obliquely at his opponent. "Will ye buy the girl?"

"What d'you want for her?"

Carne considered. "Fifty guineas."

"Fifty guineas, by God!" shouted Ross. "I should want all seven of your brats for that."

"Then what'll you give me for 'er?"

"A guinea a year so long as she stays with me."

Carne spat on the floor.

Ross stared at the spittle. "A thrashing, then, if that's what you want."

Carne sneered. "Tes easy to promise from behind a gun."

"It is easy to threaten when it's three to one."

"Nay, they'll not interfere if I tell 'em no."

"I prefer to wait until my men arrive."

"Aye, I thought you would. Come us on, boys."

"Stay," said Ross. "It would give me pleasure to wring your neck. Take off your coat, you bastard."

Carne peered at him narrowly, as if to decide whether he was in earnest. "Put down your gun, then."

Ross laid it on the drawers. Carne showed his gums in a grin of satisfaction. He turned on his brothers with a growl.

"Keep out o' this, see? He's my affair. I'll finish him."

Ross took off his coat and waistcoat, pulled off his neckerchief, and waited. This, he realized, was just what he wanted this morning; he wanted it more than anything in life.

The man came at him, and at once by his moves it was plain that he was an expert wrestler. He sidled up, snatched Ross's right hand, and tried to trip him. Ross hit him in the chest and stepped aside. Keep your temper; size him up first.

"I don't love you," Elizabeth had said; well, that was straight; discarded like a rusty ornament; thrown aside; women; now badgered in your own parlour by a damned insolent red-eyed bully; keep your temper. He was coming again and taking the same grip, this time swiftly with his head under Ross's arm: the other arm was round Ross's leg and he was lifting. Famous throw. Fling your whole weight back; just in time; side-slip and push his head up with a snap. Good, that was good; break his damned neck. The hold slipped, tightened again; they both fell to the floor with a clatter. Carne tried to get his knee into Ross' stomach. Knuckles on his face; twice; free now; roll over and on your feet.

The second brother, breathing heavily, pulled the overturned table out of the way. Fight him afterwards. And the third. Carne on his feet like a cat grasped at the collar of Ross' shirt.

The stuff held; they stumbled back against a tall cupboard which rocked dangerously. Good Irish cloth was bad now. Mooning about an assembly ball like a lovesick calf; going off bleating at the sight of his mistress. Seeking the squalid… Stuff would not tear. Hand up and take the man's wrist. Left elbow violently down on Carne's forearm. The grip broke, a grunt of pain. Ross took a hold on the man's side: the other arm gripped his own right to increase the strength of it. Butted his head low. Carne tried to jab with his own right elbow, but they were too close together. In time the miner kicked with his boots, but all the same he was swung off the ground and flung three feet against the panelled wall of the room. Seeking the squalid he had found the squalid: drink and whores. God, what a solution! This was better. Carne was on his feet again and rushed. Two full punches did not stop him; he tackled Ross about the waist.

"Now ye've got un!" shouted the second brother.

Man's greatest strength was in his arms. He did not try to throw now, but ever tightened his hug and bent Ross back. He had injured a number of men this way. Ross grinned with pain, but his back was strong; after a moment he bent no further at the waist but at the knees, hands on Carne's chin, toes just off the ground—as if kneeling on Carne's thighs. Solid straining. Black spots danced across the walls; Carne lost his balance and they again crashed to the floor. But the grip did not relax. Letting blood of this drunken bully; thrashing his own child till her back bled; spots and blood; he'd get his lesson; break the swine; break him. Ross convulsively jerked his knees up; thrust sideways; was free. On his feet first: as Carne got up he swung on him with the full weight of his body to the side of the jaw. Carne went staggering back and collapsed into the fireplace amid a clatter of irons and kindling logs. A little slower getting up this time.

Ross spat redly on the floor. "Come, man, you're not beat yet."

"Beat!" said Carne. "By a simpering young sucking bottle wi' a fancy mark on his face. Beat, did ye say?"

2

"All right," growled Jud. "I can't walk no fasterer. An' what's to do when we git there? Tes only three agin three, then. An' one of us is a slit of a boy, as thin as a stalk o' wheat an' delicut as a lily."

"Here, leave off," said Jim. "I'll take my chance."

"Ye don't think to count me, an?" said Prudie, rubbing her big red nose. "Thur's no man born o' woman I can't deal with if I've the mind. Puffed up pirouettes, that's what men are. Hit 'em acrost the 'ead wi' a soup ladle, an' what happens? They crawl away as if you'd 'urt 'em."

"I'll run on," said Jim Carter. He was carrying a leather whip, and he broke into a trot to take him down the hill.

"Whur's the brat?" Jud asked his wife.

"Dunno. They searched the 'ouse afore Cap'n Ross come home. A wonder to me ye didn't see 'em and come down. And I wonder ye didn't 'ear me just now when I was shouting. 'Oarse, I am."

"Can't be every place at once," said Jud, changing shoulders with his long pitchfork. "Tedn't to be expected of mortal man. If there was forty-six Jud

Paynters poddlin' about the farm, then mebbe one of 'em would be in the right place to suit you. But as there's only one, Lord be thanked—"

"Amen," said Prudie.

"All right, all right. Then ye can't expect 'im to be within earshot every time you start cryin' out."

"No, but I don't expect 'im to be deaf on purpose, when I'm only one field away. The knees of your britches was all I seen, but I knew twas you by the patches on 'em and by the factory chimney puffin' smoke hard by."

They saw Jim Carter emerge from among the apple trees and run across the garden to the house. They saw him reach it and enter.

Prudie lost one of her flapping slippers and had to stop to retrieve it. It was Jud's turn to grumble. They reached the plantation of apple trees, but before they were through it they met Jim Carter returning.

"'Tis all right. They're… fighting fair. 'Tis a proper job to watch—"

"What?" snapped Jud. "Wrastling? 'Ere, 'ave we missed it?"

He dropped his pitchfork, broke into a run, and reached the house ahead of the other two. The parlour was in ruin, but the best of the struggle was over. Ross was trying to get Tom Carne out through the door, and Carne, though too spent to do further harm, was yet fighting fanatically to save the ignominy of being thrown out. He was clinging partly to Ross and partly to the jamb with a wicked, mulish will not to admit himself beaten.

Ross caught sight of his servant and showed his teeth. "Open the window, Jud—"

Jud moved to obey, but the youngest brother instantly stepped in his path.

"No, ye don't. Fair's fair. Leave 'em be."

With the respite Carne abruptly showed more fight again and took a wild grip of Ross's throat. Ross loosed his own hold and hit the man twice more. The miner's hands relaxed and Ross swung him round, grasped him by the scruff of the neck and below the seat of the breeches. Then he half ran, half carried him through the door, across the hall, and out through the farther door, knocking Prudie aside as she panted upon the scene. The brothers waited uneasily, and Jud grinned at them knowingly.

There was a splash, and after a few moments Ross came back gasping and wiping the blood from the cut on his cheek.

"He will cool there. Now then." He glared at the other two. "Which of you next?"

Neither of them moved.

"Jud."

"Yes, sur."

"Show these gentlemen off my property. Then come back and help Prudie to clear up this mess."

"Yes, sur."

The second brother relaxed his tense attitude slowly and began to twist his cap. He seemed to be trying to say something.

"Well, he got out at last. Brother's in the right, mister, and you be in the wrong. That's for sartin. But for all that, twas a handsome fight. Best fight ever I saw outside of a ring."

"Damme," said the youngest, spitting. "Or inside of one. Many's the time 'e's laced me. I never thought to see 'im beat. Thank ee, mister."

They went out.

Ross's body was beginning to ache with the crushing and straining it had had. His knuckles were badly cut and he had sprained two fingers. Yet his general feeling was one of vigorous, exhausted satisfaction, as if the fight had drained ugly humours out of him. He had been blooded, as a physician blooded a man with fever.

"Aw, my dear!" said Prudie, coming in. "Aw! I'll get ee rags and some turpletine."

"None of your doctoring," he said. "Doctor the furniture. Can you repair this chair? And here's some plates been broke. Where is the child, Prudie? You may tell her to come out now."

"Gracious knows where she's to. She seed her fadder a-coming and scuddled to me all of a brash. I have a mind she's somewhere in the house for all their searchings."

She went to the door. "Tes all clear now, mite! Yer fadder's gone. We've drove un off. Come out, wherever you be!"

Silence.

The cut on his cheek had almost stopped bleeding. He put on his waistcoat and coat again over his torn and sweaty shirt, stuffed the neckerchief in a pocket. He would take a drink, and then when Jud came back to confirm that they were gone he would go down and bathe in the sea. The salt would see that no harm came of the scratches and strains.

He went to the big cupboard which had rocked so perilously during the fight and poured himself a stiff glass of brandy. He drank it off at a draught, and as his head went back, his eyes met those of Demelza Carne, very dark and distended, staring at him from the top shelf of the cupboard.

He let out a roar of laughter that brought Prudie hurrying back into the room.

CHAPTER NINE

THAT NIGHT ABOUT NINE O'CLOCK JIM CARTER CAME BACK FROM VISITING Jinny Martin. There had been some friendship between them before he came to work here, but it had ripened quickly during the winter.

He would normally have gone straight to his stable loft to sleep until dawn, but he came to the house and insisted on seeing Ross. Jud, already in the know, followed him unbidden into the parlour.

"It's the Illuggan miners," the boy said without preliminary. "Zacky Martin's heard tell from Will Nanfan that they're a-coming tonight to pay you back for stealing Tom Carne's girl."

Ross put down his glass but kept a finger in his book.

"Well, if they come, we can deal with them."

"I aren't so sartin 'bout that," said Jud. "When they're in ones an' twos ye can deal wi' 'em as we dealt wi' 'em today, but when they're in 'undreds, they're like a great roarin' dragon. Get across of 'em and they'll tear ee to shreds as easy as scratch."

Ross considered. Shorn of its rhetoric, there was some truth in what Jud said. Law and order stood aside when a mob of miners ran amok. But it was unlikely that they would walk all this way on so small a matter. Unless they had been drinking. It was Easter week.

"How many guns have we in the house?"

"Three, I reckon."

"One should be enough. See that they're cleaned and ready. There's nothing more to do beyond that."

They left him, and he heard them whispering their dissatisfaction outside the door. Well, what else was there to do? He had not seen that his casual adoption of a child for a kitchen wench would produce such results, but it was done now and all hell should crackle before he retracted. Two years abroad had led him to forget the parochial prejudices of his own people. To the tinners and small holders of the county someone from two or three miles away was a foreigner. To take a child from her home to a house ten miles away, a *girl* and under age, however gladly she might come, was enough to excite every form of passion and prejudice. He had given way to a humane impulse and was called an abductor. Well, let the dogs yap.

He pulled the bell for Prudie. She shuffled in ponderously.

"Go to bed, Prudie, and see that the girl goes also. And tell Jud that I want him."

"He's just went out, just this minute. Went off wi' Jim Carter, the pair of 'em, he did."

"Never mind, then." He would soon be back, having probably gone no farther than to light the boy to his loft. Ross got up and went for his own gun. It was a French flintlock breechloader, one his father had bought in Cherbourg ten years ago, and it showed a greater reliability and accuracy than any other gun he had used.

He broke the barrel and squinted up it, saw that the flint and hammer were working, put powder carefully in the flashpan, loaded the charge, and then set the gun on the window seat. There was no more to do, so he sat down to read again and refilled his glass.

Time went on and he grew impatient for Jud's return. There was little wind tonight and the house was very silent. Now and then a rat moved behind the wainscoting; occasionally Tabitha Bethia, the mangy cat, mewed and stretched before the fire, or a billet of wood shifted and dropped away to ashes.

At ten-thirty he went to the door and peered up the valley. The night was cloudy and out here the stream whispered and stirred; an owl flitted from a tree on furtive wings.

He left the door open and went round the house to the stables. The sea was very dark. A long black swell was riding quietly in. Now and then a wave would topple over and break in the silence with a crack like thunder, its white lip vivid in the dark.

His ankle was very painful after the horseplay of this afternoon, his whole body was stiff, his back aching as if he had cracked a rib. He entered the stables and went up to the loft. Jim Carter was not there.

He came down, patted Darkie, heard Garrick scuffle in the box they had made for him, returned the way he had come. Devil take Jud and his notions. He surely had sense enough not to leave the property after the boy's warning. Surely he had not ratted.

Ross went into the downstairs bedroom. The box bed was empty tonight, for Demelza had been moved to her new quarters. He mounted the stairs and quietly opened the door of her bedroom. It was pitch dark, but he could hear a sharp excited breath. She at least was here, but she was not asleep. In some manner she had come to know of the danger. He did not speak but went out again.

From the room next door came a sound like a very old man cutting timber with a rusty saw, so he had no need to locate Prudie. Downstairs again, and an attempt to settle with his book. He did not drink any more. If Jud returned, they would take it in two-hour watches through the night; if he did not, then the vigil must be kept singlehanded.

At eleven-thirty he finished the chapter, shut the book, and went to the door of the house again. The lilac tree moved its branches with an errant breeze and then was still. Tabitha Bethia followed him out and rubbed her head in companionate fashion against his boots. The stream was muttering its unending litany. From the clump of elms came the rough thin churring of a nightjar. In the direction of Grambler the moon was rising.

But Grambler lay southwest. And the faint glow in the sky was not pale enough to reflect either a rising or a setting moon. Fire.

He started from the house and then checked himself. The defection of Jud and Carter meant that he alone was left to guard his property and the safety of the two women. If in truth the Illuggan miners were on the warpath, it would be anything but wise to leave the house unprotected. Assuming the fire to have some connection with these events, he would surely meet the miners if he went to look and they were on their way here. But some might slip around him and gain the house. Better to stay than risk its being set afire.

He chewed his bottom lip and cursed Jud for a useless scoundrel. He'd teach him to rat at the first alarm. This desertion somehow loomed larger than all the neglect before he came home.

He limped up as far as the Long Field behind the house and from there fancied he could make out the flicker of the fire. He returned and thought of waking Prudie and telling her she must care for herself. But the house was as silent as ever and dark, except for the yellow candlelight showing behind the curtains of the parlour; it seemed a pity to add needlessly to anyone's alarm. He wondered what the child's feelings were, sitting up there in the dark.

Indecision was one of the things he most hated. After another five minutes he cursed himself and snatched up his gun, and set off hastily up the valley.

Rain was wafting in his face as he reached the copse of fir trees beyond Wheal Maiden. At the other side he stopped and stared across to Grambler. Three fires could be seen. So far as he could make out they were not large, and he was thankful for that. Then he picked out two figures climbing the rising ground towards him, one carrying a lantern.

He waited. It was Jim Carter and Jud.

They were talking together, Carter excited and breathless. Behind them, emerging out of the shadows, were four other men: Zacky Martin, Nick Vìgus, Mark and Paul Daniel, all from the cottages at Mellin. As they came abreast of him he stepped out.

"Why," said Jud, showing his gums in surprise, "if tedn't Cap'n Ross. Fancy you being yurabouts. I says to meself not five minutes gone: now, I says, I reckon Cap'n Ross'll be just going off to sleep nice and piecemeal; he'll be just stretching his feet down in the bed. I thought I wished I was abed too, 'stead of trampling through the misty-wet, a mile from the nearest mug of toddy—"

"Where have you been?"

"Why, only down to Grambler. We thought we'd go visit a kiddley an' pass the evening sociable—"

The other men came up and paused, seeing Ross. Nick Vigus seemed disposed to linger, his sly face catching the light from the lantern and creasing into a grin. But Zacky Martin tugged at Vigus' sleeve.

"Come on, Nick. You'll not be up for your core in the morning. Good night, sur."

"Good night," said Ross, and watched them tramp past. He could see more lanterns about the fires now and figures moving. "Well, Jud?"

"Them fires? Well, now, if ye want to hear all about un, twas like this—"

"Twas like this, sur," said Jim Carter, unable to hold his impatience. "What with Will Nanfan saying he'd heard tell the Illuggan miners was coming to break up your house—on account of you taking Tom Carne's maid, we thought twould be a good thing if we could stop 'em. Will says there's about a hundred of 'em carrying sticks and things. Well, now then, Grambler men owes Illuggan men a thing or two since last Michaelmas Fair, so I runs along to Grambler and rouses 'em and says to 'em—"

"Oo's telling this old yarn?" Jud said with dignity.

But in the excitement Jim had lost his usual shyness.

"—and says to 'em, 'What d'you think? Illuggan men are coming over 'ere bent on a spree.' Didn't need to say more'n that, see? Alf Grambler men was in the kiddleys, having a glass, and was fair dagging for a fight. While this, Jud runs down to Sawle and tells 'em same story. It didn't work so well there, but he comes back wi' twenty or thirty—"

"Thirty-six," said Jud. "But seven o' the skulks turned into Widow Tregothnan's kiddley, and still there for all I'd know, drowning their guts. Twas Bob Mitchell's fault. If he—"

"They was just there in time to help build three bonfires—"

"Three bonfires," said Jud, "and then—"

"Let the boy tell his story," said Ross.

"Well, now then, we builded three bonfires," said Carter, "and they was just going pretty when we heard the Illuggan men coming, four or five scores of 'em, headed by Remfrey Flamank, as drunk as a bee. When they come up, Mike Andrewartha mounts on the wall and belves out to 'em, 'What d'you want, Illuggan men? What business 'ave you hereabouts, Illuggan men?' And Remfrey Flamank pulls open his shirt to show all the hair on his chest and says, 'What bloody consarn be that of yourn?' Then Paul Daniel says, 'Tis our consarn, every man jack of us, for we don't want Illuggan men poking their nubbies about in our district.' And a great growl goes up, like you was teasing a bear."

Jim Carter stopped a moment to get his breath. "Then a little man with a wart on his cheek the size of a plum shouts out, 'Our quarrel's not wi' you, friends. We've come to take back the Illuggan maid your fancy gentleman stole and teach 'im a lesson he won't forget, see? Our quarrel's not wi' you.' Then Jud 'ere belves out, 'Oo says there's aught amiss wi' hiring a maid, like anyone else. And he took her in fair fight, ye bastards. Which is more'n any of you could do back again. There never was an Illuggan man what—'"

"All right, all right," interrupted Jud in sudden irritation. "I knows what I says, don't I! Think I can't tell what I said meself—" In his annoyance he turned his head and showed that one eye was going black.

"He says, 'There never was an Illuggan man what wasn't the dirty cross-eyed son of an unmarried bitch wi' no chest and spavin shanks out of a knacker's yard.' I thought twas as good as the preacher. And then someone hits him a clunk in the eye."

Ross said: "Then I suppose everyone started fighting."

"Nigh on two hundred of us. Lors, twas a proper job. Did ee see that great fellow wi' one eye, Jud? Mark Daniel was lacing into him, when Sam Roscollar came up. An' Remfrey Flamank—"

"Quiet, boy," said Jud.

Jim at last subsided. They reached home in a silence which was only once broken by his gurgling chuckle and the words, "Remfrey Flamank, as drunk as a bee!"

"Impudence," said Ross at the door. "To go off and involve yourselves in a brawl and leave me at home to look after the women. What d'you think I am?"

There was silence.

"Understand, quarrels of my own making I'll settle in my own way."

"Yes, sur."

"Well, go on to bed, it's done now. But don't think I shall not remember it."

Whether this was a threat of punishment or a promise of reward Jud and his partner could not be sure, for the night was too dark to see the speaker's face. There was a catch in his voice which might have been caused by a barely controlled anger.

Or it might have been laughter, but they did not think of that.

CHAPTER TEN

1

A T THE EXTREME EASTERN END OF THE POLDARK LAND, ABOUT HALF A MILE from the house of Nampara, the property joined that of Mr. Horace Treneglos, whose house lay a couple of miles inland behind the Hendrawna sand hills and was called Mingoose. At the point where the two estates met on the cliff edge was a third mine.

Wheal Leisure had been worked in Joshua's day for surface tin but not at all for copper. Ross had been over it during the winter and the desire to restart at least one of the workings on his own land had, after consideration of Wheal Grace, come to centre upon this other mine.

The advantages were that drainage could consist of adits running out to the cliff face, and that in some of the last samples taken from the mine and hoarded by Joshua there were definite signs of copper.

But it needed more capital than he could find; so on the Thursday morning of Easter week he rode over to Mingoose. Mr. Treneglos was an elderly widower with three sons, the youngest in the navy and the others devoted fox hunters. He was himself a scholar and unlikely to care for mining adventures; but since the mine was partly on his land, it was the smallest courtesy to approach him first.

"Seems to me you've got so little to go on; almost like digging virgin ground. Why not start Wheal Grace where there's shafts already sunk?" shouted Mr. Treneglos. He was a tall, heavily built man whom deafness had made clumsy. He was sitting now on the edge of an armchair, his fat knees bent, his tight knee breeches stretched to a shinier tightness, his buttons under a strain, one hand stroking his knee and the other behind his ear.

Ross gave his reasons for preferring Wheal Leisure.

"Well, my dear," shouted Mr. Treneglos, "it is all very convincing, I believe you. I have no objection to your making a few holes in my land. We did ought to be good neighbours." He raised his voice. "Financially, now, I'm a bit costive this month; those boys of mine and their 'unters. Next month perhaps I could loan you fifty guineas. We did ought to be good neighbours. How would that do?"

Ross thanked him and said that if the mine were started he would run it on the cost-book system, whereby each of a number of speculators took up one or more shares and paid towards the outlay.

"Yes, excellent notion." Mr. Treneglos thrust forward an ear. "Well, come round and see me again, eh? Always glad to help, my boy. We did ought to be good neighbours, and I'm not averse to a little flutter. Perhaps we shall find another Grambler." He rumbled with laughter and picked up his book. "Perhaps we shall find another Grambler. Ever read the classics, my boy? Cure for many ills of the modern world. I often try to get your father interested. How is he, by the way?"

Ross explained.

"Why damn me, yes. A poor job. It was your uncle I was thinking of. It was his uncle I was thinking of," he added in an undertone.

Ross rode home feeling that half a promise from Mr. Treneglos was as much as he could expect at this stage; it remained for him to get some professional advice. The man to approach for this was Captain Henshawe of Grambler.

Jim Carter was working in one of his fields with the three young Martin children. As Ross passed, Carter ran over to him.

"I thought I'd tell ee a bit of news, sir," he said quietly. "Reuben Clemmow's runned away."

So much had happened since their meeting last Sunday that Ross had forgotten the last of the Clemmows. The interview had not been a pleasant one. The man had been shifty but defiant. Ross had reasoned with him, trying to get at him through a blank wall of suspicion and resentment. But even while doing it he had been conscious of failure, and of the enmity towards himself—something that couldn't be met or turned by good advice or a friendly talk. It was too deeply rooted for that.

"Where has he gone?"

"Dunno, sur. What you said to him 'bout turning of him out must have frightened him."

"You mean he isn't at the mine?"

"Not since Tuesday. Nobody's seed him since Tuesday."

"Oh well," said Ross, "it will save trouble."

Carter looked up at him. His high-boned young face was very pallid this morning. "Jinny d' think he's still hanging around, sur. She says he hasn't gone far."

"Someone would surely have seen him."

"Yes, sur, that's what I d' say. But she don't believe we. She says, sur, if you'll excuse it, sur, to look out for yourself."

Ross's face creased into a smile.

"Don't worry your head about me, Jim. And don't worry about Jinny, neither. Are you in love with the girl?"

Carter met his gaze and swallowed.

"Well," said Ross, "you should be happy now you've lost your rival. Though I doubt if he seriously competed."

"Not in that way," said Jim. "Tes only that we was afraid—"

"I know what you were afraid of. If you see or hear anything, let me know. If not, don't see bogles in every corner."

He rode on. Very well for me to talk, he thought. Perhaps the lout has run off to his brother in Truro. Or perhaps he has not. No telling with that type. It would be better for the Martins if he was under lock and key.

2

Although he went to Truro several times, Ross saw nothing more of Margaret. Nor had he the desire to. If his adventure with her on the night of the ball had not cured him of his love for Elizabeth, it had proved to him that to seek lust for its own sake was no solution.

The child Demelza settled into her new home like a stray kitten into a comfortable parlour. Knowing the great strength of family ties among the miners, he had been prepared after a week to find her curled in a corner weeping for her father and his thrashings. Had she shown any signs of homesickness he would have packed her off at once; but she did not, and Prudie gave her a good character.

The fact that within three hours of her coming Demelza had found her way into the good graces of the monstrous Prudie was another surprise. Perhaps she appealed to some half-atrophied mother instinct, as a starving duckling might to a great auk.

So after a month's trial he sent Jim Carter—Jud would not go—to see Tom Carne with two guineas for the hire of the girl's services for a year. Jim said that Carne had threatened to break every bone in his body; but he didn't refuse the gold, and this suggested that he was going to acquiesce in the loss of his daughter.

After their one large-scale invasion, the miners of Illuggan made no move. There was always a chance of trouble when the next feast day came, but until then the distance between the places would save accidental clashes. Ross suspected for a time that they might try to take the child away by force, and he told her that she was not to go far from the house. One evening, riding home from St. Ann's, a hail of stones was flung at him from behind a hedge, but that was the last sign of public disfavour. People had their own concerns to think of.

Turning over the lumber in the library, Prudie came upon a piece of stout printed dimity, and this, washed and cut up, made two sacklike frocks for the girl. Then an old bedspread with a deep lace edge was cut up into two pairs of combinations. Demelza had never seen anything like them before, and when she was wearing them, she always tried to pull them down so that the lace showed below the hem of her skirt.

Much against her will, Prudie found herself enlisted in a campaign in which she had no personal belief: the war on lice. It was necessary to point out to Demelza at frequent intervals that her new master wouldn't tolerate dirty bodies or dirty hair.

"But how do he know?" the girl asked one day when the rain was trickling down the bottle-green glass of the kitchen window. "How do he know? My hair's dark and there an't that change whether you d' wash it or no."

Prudie frowned as she basted the meat which was roasting on a spit over the fire. "Yes. But it d' make a powerful difference to the number of cra'lers."

"Cra'lers?" echoed Demelza, and scratched her head. "Why, everyone's got cra'lers."

"He don't like 'em."

"Why," said Demelza seriously, "*you've* got cra'lers. You've got cra'lers worser than what I have."

"He don't like 'em," Prudie said stubbornly.

Demelza digested this for a moment.

"Well, how do you get rid of 'em?"

"Wash, wash, wash," said Prudie.

"Like a blathering duck," said Jud, who had just entered the kitchen.

Demelza turned her head and gazed at him with her interested dark eyes. Then she looked again at Prudie.

"'Ow is it you an't got rid of 'em, then?" she asked, anxious to learn.

"An't washed enough," said Jud sarcastically. "Tedn't right fur human beings to 'ave skins. They must scrub theirselves raw as a buttock of beef to please some folk. But then again it depend 'pon how cra'lers do attach their selves. Cra'lers is funny, kicklish creatures. Cra'lers like some folk better'n other folk. Cra'lers 'ave a natural infinity with some folk, just like they was brother and sister. Other folk, God makes 'em clean by nature. Look at me. You won't find no cra'lers on *my* head."

Demelza considered him.

"No," she said, "but you an't gotten any hair."

Jud threw down the turfs he had brought in. "If you learned her to hold 'er tongue," he said pettishly to his wife, "twould be a sight betterer than learning 'er that. If you learned 'er manners, how to speak respectable to folk and answer respectable an' *be* respectable to her elders an' betters, twould be a sight betterer than that. Then ye could pat yourself on the 'ead and say, 'Thur, I'm doing a tidy job, learning her to be respectable.' But what are ee doing? Tedn't 'ard to answer. Tedn't 'ard to see. You're learning her to be sassy."

That evening Jim Carter was sitting in the Martins' cottage talking to Jinny. With the family of Martins he had become fondly familiar during the winter of his work at Nampara. As his attachment for Jinny grew, he saw less and less of his own family. He was sorry for this, for his mother would miss him, but he could not be in two places at the same time, and he felt more at home, more able to expand and talk and enjoy himself in the easygoing cottage of these people who knew him less intimately.

His father, an expert tributer, had earned good money until he was twenty-six, and then the phthisis with which he had been threatened for years became the master, and in six months Mrs. Carter was a widow with five young children to bring up, the eldest, Jim, being eight.

Fred Carter had gone to the lengths of paying sixpence a week for him to attend school at Aunt Alice Trevemper's, and there had been talk of the child staying there another year. But necessity blew away talk as wind blows smoke and Jim became a jigger at Grambler. This was "grass" or surface work, for the Cornish miners did not treat their children in the heartless fashion of the up-country people. But jigging was not ideal, since it meant sieving copper ore in water and standing in a doubled-up position for ten hours a day. His mother was worried because he brought up blood when he got home. But many other boys did the same. The one and threepence a week made a difference.

At eleven he went below, beginning by working with another man and wheeling the material away in barrows; but he had inherited his father's talent and by the time he was sixteen he was a tributer on his own pitch and earning enough to keep the household. He was very proud of this, but after a couple of years he found himself losing time through ill health and saddled with a thick loose cough like his father's. At twenty, with a deeply laid grievance against fate, he allowed his mother to bully him into leaving the mine, into throwing away all his earning power, into handing over his pitch to his younger brother and applying for work as a *farm labourer*. Even with the fair wages paid by Captain Poldark, he would earn less in a quarter than he usually made in a month; but it was not only the loss of money, not even the loss of position which upset him. He had mining in his blood; he liked the work and wanted the work.

He had given up something that he wanted very much. Yet already he was stronger, steadier. And the future had lost most of its fear.

In the Martins' cottage he sat in a corner and whispered to Jinny, while Zacky Martin smoked his clay pipe on one side of the fireplace, reading a newspaper, and on the other side Mrs. Zacky nursed on one arm Betsy Maria Martin, aged three, who was recovering from a perilous attack of measles, while on the other arm their youngest, a baby of two months, grizzled fitfully. The room was faintly lighted by a thin earthenware lamp or "chill," with two wicks in little lips at the sides of the well. The well contained pilchard oil and the smell was fishy. Jinny and Jim were seated on a homemade wooden form and were glad of the comfortable obscurity of the shadows. Jinny would not go out after dark yet, even with Jim for escort—the only sore point in their friendship—but she swore she hadn't a minute's peace when every bush might hide a crouching figure. Better here, even with all her family to play gooseberry.

In the dim light only portions of the room showed up, surfaces and sides, curves and ends and profiles. The table had just been cleared of the evening meal of tea and barley bread and pease pudding; a wet circle showed where the ancient pewter teapot had leaked. At the other end was a scattering of crumbs left by the two youngest girls. Of Zacky could be seen only the thick brush of his red-grey hair, the jutting angle of his pipe, the curl of the closely printed *Sherborne Mercury,* grasped in a hairy hand as if it was in danger of flying away. Mrs. Zacky's steel-rimmed spectacles glinted and each side of her flat face with its pursed whistling lips was illuminated in turn like different phases of the moon as she gazed first at one fretful child and then the other. The only thing to be seen of the infant Inez Mary was a grey shawl and a small chubby fist clasping and unclasping air as if asserting her frail stake in existence. A shock of red hair and a freckled nose slumbered uneasily on Mrs. Zacky's other shoulder.

On the floor Matthew Mark Martin's long bare legs glimmered like two silver trout; the rest of him was hidden in the massive pool of shadow cast by his mother. On the wall beside Jinny and Jim another great shadow moved, that of the tawny cat, which had climbed on the shelf beside the chill and blinked down on the family.

This was the best week of all, when Father Zacky was on the night core, for he allowed his children to stay up until nearly nine o'clock. Use had accustomed Jim to this routine, and he saw the moment approaching when he must leave. At once he thought of a dozen things he still had to say to Jinny, and was hurrying to say them, when there came a knock on the door and the top half swung open to show the gaunt, powerful figure of Mark Daniel.

Zacky lowered his paper, unscrewed his eyes, and glanced at the cracked hourglass to reassure himself that he had not overstayed his leisure.

"Early tonight, boy. Come in and make yourself 'tome, if you've the mind. I've not put so much as foot to boot yet."

"Nor me neither," said Daniel. "Twas a word or two I wanted with ee, boy, just neighbourly, as you might say."

Zacky knocked out his pipe. "That's free. Come in and make yourself 'tome."

"Twas a word in private," said Mark. "Asking Mrs. Zacky's pardon. A word in your ear 'bout a little private business. I thought mebbe as you'd step outside."

Zacky stared and Mrs. Zacky whistled gently to her fretful charges. Zacky put down his paper, smoothed his hair, and went out with Mark Daniel.

Jim gratefully took advantage of the respite to add to his whisperings: words of importance about where they should meet tomorrow, if she had finished mine work and housework before dark and he his farming… She bent her head to listen. Jim noticed that in whatever shadow they sat some light attached itself to the smooth pale skin of her forehead, to the curve of her cheeks. Light, there was always light for her eyes.

"Tes time you childer was all asleep," said Mrs. Zacky, unpursing her lips. "Else you'll be head-in-the-bed when you did ought to be up. Off now, Matthew Mark. And you, Gabby. And Thomas. Jinny, m' dear, it is hard to lose your young man s'early in the day, but you know how tis in the morning."

"Yes, Mother," said Jinny, smiling.

Zacky returned. Everyone gazed at him curiously, but he affected to be unaware of their scrutiny. He went back to his chair and began folding the newspaper.

"I don't know," said Mrs. Zacky, "that I holds wi' secret chatter between grown men. Whispering together just like they was babies. What was you whispering about, Zachariah?"

"About how many spots there was on the moon," said Zacky. "Mark says ninety-eight and I says an hundred and two, so we agrees to leave it till we see the preacher."

"I'll have none of your blaspheming in here," said Mrs. Zacky. But she said it without conviction. She had far too solid a faith in her husband's wisdom, built up through twenty years, to do more than make a token protest at his bad behaviour. Besides, she would get it out of him in the morning.

Greatly daring among the shadows, Jim kissed Jinny's wrist and stood up. "I think it is about time I was going, Mr. and Mrs. Zacky," he said, using what had come to be a formula of farewell. "And thank ee once again for a comfortable welcome. Good night, Jinny; good night, Mr. and Mrs. Zacky; good night, all."

He got to the door but Zacky stopped him there. "Wait, boy. I d' feel like a stroll, and there's swacks of time. I'll take a step or two with you."

A protest from Mrs. Zacky followed him into the drizzling darkness. Then Zacky shut the doors and the night closed in on them, dank and soft with the fine misty rain falling like spider's webs on their faces and hands.

They set off, stumbling at first in the dark but soon accustomed to it, walking with the surefootedness of countrymen on familiar ground.

Jim was puzzled at his company and a little nervous, for there had been something grim in Zacky's tone. As a person of "learning," Zacky had always been of some importance in his eyes: whenever Zacky took up the tattered *Sherborne Mercury,* the magnificence of the gesture struck Jim afresh; and now too he was Jinny's father. Jim wondered if he had done something wrong.

They reached the brow of the hill by the Wheal Grace workings. From there the lights of Nampara House could be seen, two opal blurs in the dark.

Zacky said: "What I d' want to tell you is this. Reuben Clemmow's been seen at Marasanvose."

Marasanvose was a mile inland from Mellin Cottages. Jim Carter had a nasty feeling of tightness come upon his skin as if it were being screwed up.

"Who seen him?"

"Little Charlie Baragwanath. He didn't know who twas, but from the describing there's little room to doubt."

"Did he speak to un?"

"Reuben spoke to Little Charlie. It was on the lane twixt Marasanvose and Wheal Pretty. Charlie said he'd got a long beard, and a couple of sacks over his shoulders."

They began to walk slowly down the hill towards Nampara.

"Just when Jinny was getting comfortable," Jim said angrily. "This'll upset her anew if she'd get to know."

"That's why I didn't tell the womenfolk. Mebbe something can be done wi'out they knowing."

For all his disquiet, Jim felt a new impulse of gratitude and friendship towards Zacky for taking him into his confidence in this way, for treating him as an equal, not as a person of no account. It tacitly recognized his attachment for Jinny.

"What are ee going to do, Mr. Martin?"

"See Cap'n Ross. He did ought to know."

"Shall I come in with ee?"

"No, boy. Reckon I'll do it my own way."

"I'll wait outside for you," Jim said.

"No, boy; go to bed. You'll not be up in the morning. I'll tell ee what he advise tomorrow."

"I'd rather wait," said Jim. "That's if it is all the same with you. I've not the mind for sleep just now."

They reached the house and separated at the door. Zacky slipped quietly round to the kitchen. Prudie and Demelza were in bed, but Jud was up and yawning his head off, and Zacky was taken in to see Ross.

Ross was at his usual occupation, reading and drinking himself to bed. He was not too sleepy to listen to Zacky's story. When it was done, he got up and strolled to the fire, stood with his back to it staring at the little man.

"Did Charlie Baragwanath have any conversation with him?"

"Not what you'd rightly call conversation. It was just passing the time o' day, as you might say, till Reuben seized his pasty and ran off with un. Stealing a pasty from a boy often!"

"Hungry men feel different about these things."

"Charlie says he went off running into the woods this side of Mingoose."

"Well, something must be done. We can get up a manhunt and drive him out of his burrow. The moral difficulty is that so far he has done no wrong. We cannot imprison a fellow because he is a harmless idiot. But neither do we want to wait until he proves himself the reverse."

"He must be living in a cave, or mebbe an old mine," said Zacky. "And living off of somebody's game."

"Yes, there's that. I might persuade my uncle to stretch a point and make out an order for his arrest."

"If you thought we was doing right," said Zacky, "I think twould satisfy folk better if we caught un ourselves."

Ross shook his head. "Leave that as a last resort. I'll see my uncle in the morning and get an order. That will be the best. In the meantime, see Jinny does not go out alone."

"Yes, sur. Thank you, sur." Zacky moved to go.

"There's one thing that might lead towards a solution so far as Jinny is concerned," Ross said. "I've been thinking of it. My boy who works here, Jim Carter, seems very taken with her. Do you know if she also likes him?"

Zacky's weather-beaten face glinted with humour.

"They're both bit wi' the same bug, I bla'."

"Yes, well I don't know your view of the boy, but he seems a steady lad. Jinny's seventeen and the boy's twenty. If they were married it might be for their good, and there is the likelihood that it would cure Reuben of his ambitions."

Zacky rubbed the stubble on his chin; his thumb made a sharp rasping sound. "I like the boy; there's no nonsense about him. But tis part a question of wages and a cottage. There's small room for raising of another family in ours. And for labouring he gets little more than enough to pay the rent of a roof, wi'out vittles for two. I had the mind to build a lean-to to our cottage, but there's bare room for it."

Ross turned and kicked at the fire with the toe of his boot.

"One cannot afford to pay mining wages to a farm boy. But there are two empty cottages at Mellin, in the other row. They bring in nothing as they are, and Jim could live in one for the repairing. I should ask no rent from him so long as he worked for me."

Zacky blinked. "No rent? That'd make a difference. Have you mentioned it to the boy?"

"No. It's not my business to order his life. But talk it over with him sometime if you're so disposed."

"I will tonight. He's waiting outside... No, I'll wait till tomorrow. He'd be over to our place, reg'lar as clockwork." Zacky stopped. "It is very handsome of you. Wouldn't you like to see 'em both together, then you could tell 'em yourself."

"No, no, I'll have no hand in it. It was a passing suggestion. But make what arrangements on it you please."

When the little man was gone Ross refilled his pipe and lit it and turned back to his book. Tabitha Bethia jumped on his knee and was not pushed off. Instead he pulled her ear while he read. But after turning a page or two he found he had taken nothing in. He finished his drink but did not pour himself another.

He felt righteous and unashamed. He decided to go to bed sober.

3

The wet weather had put him out of contact with Trenwith House during the last few weeks. He had not seen Verity since the ball, and he sensed that she was avoiding him so that he should not twit her on her friendship with Captain Blarney.

The morning following Zacky's call he rode over in pouring rain to see his uncle, and was surprised to find the Revd. Mr. Johns there. Cousin William-Alfred, his scrawny neck sticking well out above his high collar, was in sole possession of the winter parlour when Mrs. Tabb showed him in.

"Your uncle is upstairs," he said, offering a cold but firm grasp. "He should be down soon. I hope you're well, Ross?"

"Well, thank you."

"Hm," said William-Alfred judicially. "Yes. I think so. You *look* better than when I last saw you. Less heavy under the eyes, if I may say so."

Ross chose to pass this. He liked William-Alfred for all his bloodless piety, because the man was so sincere in his beliefs and in his way of life. He was worth three of the politically minded Dr. Halse.

He enquired after his cousin's wife, and expressed polite gratification that Dorothy's health was improving. In December, God had given them another daughter, the blessing of another lamb. Ross then asked after the health of the occupants of Trenwith House, wondering if the answer would explain William-Alfred's presence. But no. All were well, and there was nothing here to bring William-Alfred all the way from Stithians. Francis and Elizabeth were spending a week with the Warleggans at their country home at Cardew. Aunt Agatha was in the kitchen making some herb tea. Verity—Verity was upstairs.

"You have ridden far on so unpleasant a morning," Ross said.

"I came last evening, Cousin."

"Well, that was no better."

"I hope to leave today if the rain clears."

"Next time you're here venture another three miles and visit Nampara. I can offer you a bed, if not quite the accommodation you have here."

William-Alfred looked pleased. It was seldom that he received open gestures of friendship. "Thank you. I will certainly do that."

Charles Poldark entered, blowing like a sperm whale with the effort of coming downstairs. He was still putting on weight and his feet were swollen with gout.

"Ho, Ross; so *you're* here, boy. What's to do: is your house a-floating out to sea?"

"There's some danger if the rain keeps on. Am I interrupting you in important business?"

The other two exchanged glances.

"Have you not told him?" Charles asked.

"I could not do that without your permission."

"Well, go on, go on. Aarf! It is a family affair and he is one of the family, even though an odd one."

William-Alfred turned his pale-grey eyes to Ross.

"I came out yesterday not so much to pay a social call as to see Uncle Charles on a matter of outstanding import to our family. I hesitated some time before intruding upon ground which was—"

"It is about Verity and this Captain Blarney fellow," Charles said briefly. "Damme, I couldn't ha' believed it. Not that the girl should—"

"You know, do you not," said William-Alfred, "that your cousin has become friendly with a seafaring man, one Andrew Blamey?"

"I know that I've met him."

"So have we all," said Charles explosively. "He was here at Francis's wedding!"

"I knew nothing of him then," said William-Alfred. "That was the first time I had seen him. But last week I learned his history. Knowing that he was becoming that there had been a considerable talk linking his name and Cousin Verity's, I came over at the earliest opportunity. Naturally, I was at pains first to verify the information which reached me."

"Well, what is it?" said Ross.

"The man has been married before. He is a widower with two young children. Perhaps you know that. He is also, however, a notorious drunkard. Some years ago in a drunken frenzy he kicked his wife when she was with child and she died. He was then in the Navy, the commander of a frigate. He lost his rank and lay in a common prison for two years. When released he lived on the charity of his relatives for a number of years until he obtained his present commission. There is, I understand, an agitation afoot to boycott the packet he commands until the company discharges him."

William-Alfred finished his unemotional recital and licked his lips. There had been no animosity in his tones, a circumstance which made the indictment worse. Charles spat through the open window.

Ross said: "Does Verity know?"

"Yes, damme!" said Charles. "Would you believe it of the girl? She's known for more than two weeks. She says it don't make any difference!"

Ross went to the window, bit his thumb. While he had been concerned with his own day-to-day affairs, this had been happening.

"But it must make a difference," he said, half to himself.

"She says," William-Alfred observed judicially, "that he will touch no drink now at all."

"Yes, well—" Ross paused. "Oh yes, but—"

Charles exploded again. "God's my life, we all drink! Not to drink is unnatural in a man. Aarf! But we do not become murderous in our cups. To kick a woman in that condition is beyond forgiveness. I don't know how he got off so light. He should have been hanged from his own yardarm. Drunk or sober makes little difference."

"Yes," said Ross slowly. "I'm inclined to agree."

"I do not know," said William-Alfred slowly, "if marriage was his intention; but if it was, can we let a gentle girl like Verity marry such a man?"

"By God, no!" said Charles, empurpled. "Not while I am alive!"

"What's her attitude?" Ross asked. "Does she insist on wanting to marry him?"

"She says he has been reformed! For how long? Once a drunkard always a drunkard. The position is impossible! She's in her room and will stay there until she sees reason."

"I've been very friendly with her this winter. It might help if I saw her and we talked things over."

Charles shook his head. "Not now, my boy. Later perhaps. She's as pigheaded as her mother. More so, in truth, and that's saying volumes. But the association's got to be broke. I'm mortal sorry for the girl. She's not had many admirers. But I'll not have any wife-kicking skunk bedding with my flesh and blood. That's all there is to it."

So for the second time that spring Ross rode home from Trenwith having done nothing that he had set out to do.

He felt restless and uneasy at the thought of Verity's misery. Very well for Charles to say "that's all there is to it"; but he had come to know Verity better than her own father and brother did. Her affections were slow to take and hard to break. He was not even sure that this one would be broken by Charles's veto. It might be that she would defy everyone and marry Blarney, and that only then would the affection break.

That was the worst prospect of all.

CHAPTER ELEVEN

"EVERYTHING ARRANGED NOW, JIM?"

It was a week later and they had met in the stable. Jim Carter's gratitude was dumb. Two or three times before he had struggled with his tongue, but it wouldn't move. Now at last he got out:

"'Tis what I d' want more than anything. I'd not thought to hope for it, hardly begun to. An' I've to thank you for it."

"Oh, nonsense," said Ross. "Don't owe your happiness to anyone. Tell Zacky tonight that the warrant for Clemmow's arrest has been issued. As soon as he is located, we can put him away for a space to cool his head."

"It is the cottage I have to thank ee for," Jim persisted, now that he was at last launched. "That d' make all the difference. You see, if we had no hope for that—"

"Which have you decided on?" Ross asked to cut short his thanks. "Reuben's or the one next door?"

"The one next door, the one next to Joe and Betsy Triggs. We reckoned, sur, if twas all the same to you, that we'd not go into Reuben's cottage. It don't seem too comfortable, if you follow me. And the other's clean 'nough after five year. Smallpox have gone long since."

Ross nodded. "And when are you to be married?" Jim flushed. "Banns will be called for the first time next Sunday. I can't hardly… We're startin' repairing the roof tonight if the weather clears. There's little enough to do. Jinny would dearly like to come and thank you herself."

"Oh, there's no need of that," Ross said in alarm. "I'll call and see you when you are nicely settled."

"And we'd like," Jim struggled on, "if we d' get on, to pay you a rent… just to show—"

"Not while you're working for me. But it's a good thought."

"Jinny d' hope to stay on at the mine, at least to begin. With my two brothers doing well for theirselves, Mother hasn't the same need of my help… So, I believe twill work—"

A sneeze attracted Ross's attention and he saw Demelza crossing the yard with a pile of logs held in her pinafore. It was raining and she was without a hat. Behind her Garrick, grown tall and ungainly in mid-puppyhood, black and tailless and sparsely curled, gambolled like a French poodle. Ross wanted to laugh.

"Demelza," he said.

She stopped instantly and dropped one of the logs. She could not see where the voice came from. He stepped out of the darkness of the stable.

"You're not allowing Garrick in the house?"

"No, sur. He come no further than the door. He come that far just to keep me company. He's awful sore at not coming no further."

He picked up the log and put it back on the bundle in her arms.

"Perhaps," she said, "he could come in just so far as the kitchen when he's rid of cra'lers too."

"Crawlers?"

"Yes, sur. The things that crawl in your hair."

"Oh," said Ross. "I misdoubt if he ever will be."

"I do scrub him every day, sur."

Ross eyed the dog, which was sitting on its haunches and scratching its floppy ear with one stiff hind leg. He looked again at Demelza, who looked at him. "I'm pleased that Prudie is directing you so well. I believe his colour is a thought lighter. Does he like being scrubbed?"

"Judas God, no! He d' wriggle like a pilchard."

"Hm," Ross said drily. "Well, bring him to me when you think he's clean and I'll tell you then."

"Yes, sur."

Prudie appeared at the door. "Oh, there you are, you black worm!" she said to the girl, and then she saw Ross. A faint sheepish smile creased her shiny red face. "Miss Verity's here, sur. I was just going to tell 'er to go seek ee."

"Miss Verity?"

"Just come this inster. I was rushin' out for to tell ee. Hastenin' I was and no one can say different."

He found Verity in the parlour. She had taken off her grey cloak with its fur-lined hood and was wiping the rain from her face. The bottom of her skirt was black with rain and splashed with mud.

"Well, my dear," he said. "This is a surprise. Have you walked in this weather?"

Her face had become sallow under its tan, and there were heavy shadows below her eyes.

"I had to see you, Ross. You understand better than the others. I had to see you about Andrew."

"Sit down," he said. "I'll get you some ale and a slice of almond cake."

"No, I mustn't stay long. I—slipped out. You… came over on Thursday last, did you not? When William-Alfred was there."

Ross nodded and waited for her to go on. She was out of breath, either from haste or from the press of her feelings. He wanted to say something that would help her, but couldn't find the right words. Life had clutched at his kind little Verity.

"They—told you?"

"Yes, my dear."

"*What* did they tell you?"

As close as he could remember, he gave William-Alfred's account. When he finished, she went to the window and began pulling at the wet fur of her muff.

"He didn't kick her," she said. "That is a lie. He knocked her down and—and she died. The rest—is the truth."

He stared at the trickles of water running down the windowpane. "I'm more sorry than I can say."

"Yes, but… They want me to give him up, to promise never to see him again."

"Don't you think that would be for the best?"

"Ross," she said, "I love him."

He didn't speak.

"I'm not a child," she said. "When he told me—he told me the day after the ball—I felt so sick, so ill, so sorry—for him. I couldn't sleep, couldn't eat. It was so terrible hearing it direct from him, because I had no hope that it wasn't true. Father doesn't understand me because he thinks that I am not revolted. Of course I was revolted. So much so that for two days I was in bed of a fever. But that—that doesn't make me not love him. How can it? One falls in love for good or ill. You know that."

"Yes," he said. "I know that."

"Knowing him, knowing Andrew, it was almost impossible to credit. It was terrible. But one cannot turn one's back on the truth. One cannot wish it away, or pray it away, or even live it away. He did do such a thing. I told myself again and again the thing he had done. And the repetition, instead of killing my love, killed my horror. It killed my fear. I said to myself: He has done this and he has paid for it. Isn't that enough? Is a man to be condemned forever? Why do I go to church and repeat the Lord's Prayer if I don't hold to it, if there is no forgiveness? Is our own behaviour higher than the Founder of Christianity, that we should set a higher standard for others?"

She had been speaking quickly and fiercely. These were the arguments her love had forged in the quietness of her bedroom.

"He never touches drink now," she ended pathetically.

"Do you think he will keep to that?"

"I am sure of it."

"What do you intend to do?"

"He wishes me to marry him. Father forbids it. I can only defy him."

"There are ways of coercion," Ross said.

"I am of age. They can't stop me."

He went across and threw another log on the fire. "Has Blarney seen Charles? If they could talk it over—"

"Father won't consider seeing him. It is… so unfair. Father drinks. Francis gambles. They're not saints. Yet when a man does what Andrew has done they condemn him unheard."

"It's the way of the world, my dear. A gentleman may get drunk so long as he carries his drink decent, or slips beneath the table with it. But when a man has been sent to prison for what Blarney did, then the world is not at all prepared to forgive and forget, despite the religion it subscribes to. Certainly other men are not prepared to entrust their daughters to his care with the possibility of their being treated in like manner." He paused, struggling to find words. "I am inclined to agree with that attitude."

She looked at him painfully a moment, then shrugged.

"So you side with them, Ross."

"In principle, yes. What do you wish me to do?"

She picked up her wet cloak, stood with it between her fingers, looking at it. "I can't ask anything if you feel like that."

"Oh yes, you can." He walked over and took the cloak from her and stood beside her at the window. He touched her arm. "For me, Verity, the winter is over. That and much more. Without you I don't know what the end would have been. Not this. If your winter is to come, am I to refuse to help you because I take another view in principle? I don't bring myself yet to like the idea of your marrying Blarney; but that's because I care so

greatly for your welfare. It doesn't mean I'll not help you in any manner
I can."

For a moment she did not answer. Suddenly he despised himself for what he
had just said. Qualified help was weak and timid. Either you come out dead
against the attachment or else help without reservation, without giving the
impression of reluctance and disapproval.

Very difficult. Because of their special friendship the first was impossible. The
second was against his better judgment—for he had no personal love or belief to
sustain him, except his belief in Verity.

But it was not good enough. The choice was difficult, but he must see
more clearly than he had done. What would Verity have done if positions
were reversed?

He released her arm. "Forget what I said. There's no question of my disapproval. None at all. I'll do whatever you wish."

She sighed. "You see, I have to come to you, for there is no one else. Elizabeth
is very understanding, but she cannot openly side with me against Francis. And
I don't really think she wishes to. Besides I thought—Thank you."

"Where is Andrew now?"

"At sea. He'll not be back for two weeks at least. When he comes… I thought
if I could write him telling him to meet me here—"

"At Nampara?"

She looked at him. "Yes."

"Very well," he said instantly. "Let me know the day before and I will
make arrangements."

Her lips trembled and she looked as if she was going to cry.

"Ross dear, I am indeed sorry to implicate you in this. There is enough—But
I could not think—"

"Nonsense. It's not the first time we shall have been conspirators. But look,
you must put a stop to this worrying. Or he will not wish to see you when he
comes. The less you fret, the braver will things turn out. Go home and go about
your normal life as if nothing was to do. Make a show that you have nothing
to worry over and it will be easier to carry. God knows, I have no licence to
preach, but it's good advice nevertheless."

"I'm sure of it." She sighed again and put a hand to the side of her tired face.
"If I can come here and *talk* with you, that will help more than you know. To
be contained within my own thoughts all the day, and surrounded by hostile
ones. Merely to talk to someone with understanding is like—"

"Come when you like. And as often. I am always here. You shall tell me all there is to know. I'll get you something warm to drink while Jud saddles Darkie. Then I'll ride you back."

CHAPTER TWELVE

1

J IM CARTER AND JINNY MARTIN WERE MARRIED AT 1 P.M. ON THE LAST MONDAY in June. The ceremony was taken by the Revd Mr. Clarence Odgers, whose fingernails were still black from planting his onions. As he had kept the party waiting a few minutes while he donned his vestments, he thought it only right to keep them no longer than strictly necessary over the actual ceremony.

He therefore began:

"Dearly beloved, we are gathered together here in the sight of God, anin the face this congregashun nay—num—num—this man and this woman holy matrimony; which is an—num—state—num—signifying unto us a mythical union—num—nite—murch—num—nar duly considering the causes for which matrimony is ordained. First it was ordained for the procreation of children to be brought up in the num—nurcher—num. Secondly it was ordained for a remedy against sin nar—num fornication nar—nar undefiled members of Christ's body. Thirdly it was ordained for the mutual society, help, comfort, num—num—perity—versity—nar—num—man—shew—num—or else hereafter forever hold his peace.

"I require and charge you both—num—num—num—"

Jinny's red-brown hair was brushed and combed until it glistened beneath the homemade white muslin bonnet set well back on her small head.

She was far the more composed of the two. Jim was nervous and halted several times in his responses. He was self-conscious in his own splendour, for Jinny had bought him a bright blue kerchief from a pedlar, and he had bought himself a secondhand coat almost as good as new, of a warm plum colour with bright buttons. This would perhaps have to last him as a best coat for the next twenty years.

"… and live according to thy laws; through Jesus Christ our Lord, Amen. Those whom God hath joined let no man put asunder. For as much as N. and N.—er—forasmuch as James Henry and Jennifer May have consented together in holy wedlock and've nessed—name—no—given—nar—nar—reeve—ring—hands—I pronounce that they be man and wife together. In the name Far, Son, Holy Ghost, Amen." Mr. Odgers would soon be back with his onions.

A meal was provided in the Martins' cottage for all who could attend. Ross had been invited, but had refused on a plea of urgent business in Truro, feeling that the gathering would be likely to enjoy itself more freely in his absence.

As there were eleven of the Martins without the bride and six of the Carters not counting the groom, the accommodation for outsiders was limited. Old Man Greet doddered and creaked in a corner by the fireplace, and Joe and Betsy Triggs kept him company. Mark and Paul Daniel were there, and Mrs. Paul, and Mary Daniel. Will Nanfan and Mrs. Will were there as uncle and aunt of the bride; Jud Paynter had taken the afternoon off to come—Prudie was laid up with a bunion—and somehow Nick Vigus and his wife had managed to squeeze in—as they always managed to squeeze in when anything was going free.

The room was so full that all the children had to sit on the floor, and the juveniles, those from nine to sixteen, were arranged two by two up the wooden ladder to the bedroom—"just like the animiles in the ark," as Jud benevolently told them. The wooden bench that Jim and Jinny had used during most of the dark quiet evenings of the winter had been raised to the status of a bridal chair, and on this the married couple were perched like love birds where, for once, everyone could see them.

The feast was a mixture of food designed to tempt the appetite and upset the digestion, and port and homebrewed mead were in lavish supply to wash it all down and make the company more boisterous.

When the feast was over and Zacky had made a speech and Jim had said thank you for all your good wishes and Jinny had blushed and refused to say anything at all, when even with the door open the room had become insufferably hot and sticky and nearly everyone was suffering from cramp, when the babies were becoming fractious and the children quarrelsome and the grownups sleepy from heavy food and lack of air, then the women and children went to sit outside, leaving the men room to stretch their legs and light their pipes or take their snuff, and freedom to drink their port and gin and yarn contentedly about how the tamping got wet on the 120 level, or the chances of a good pilchard season.

The preparations of the men to finish up the celebrations after their own fashion were much frowned on by Mrs. Martin and Mrs. Paul Daniel; but Zacky, although he agreed that he had found the Lord at a revival meeting at St Ann's a couple of years ago, still refused to lose his toddy as a consequence, and the others took their cue from him.

The port was cheap stuff for which Zacky had paid 3s 6d a gallon, but the gin had quality. On a quiet evening in September, eight of them had taken a Sawle cutter round to Roscoff, and among the cargo they brought back were two large tubs of fine gin. One tub they had divided among themselves at once, but the other they had decided to keep for a feast. So Jud Paynter, who was one of the eight, had hidden the tub by lowering it into the broken rainwater barrel beside the conservatory at Nampara, where it would be safe from the prying eyes of any suspicious revenue man who might come around. There it had remained all through the winter. Jud Paynter and Nick Vigus had brought it along for this occasion.

While the women, having for the most part been barred from the new home, were now shown over it, with broods of children dragging at their heels, the men prepared to drink themselves into a comfortable stupor.

"They do say," came the thin sleek voice of Nick Vigus over the top of his mug, "that all the mines'll be closed down afore long. They do say as a man called Raby 'as bought all the big slag 'eaps in the county, and there's a process as he can treat the attle with as will give all the copper England d' want for a hundred year."

"Tedn't feasible," said Will Nanfan, hunching his big shoulders.

Zacky took a swig of gin from his mug. "It won't need that for to put us in poor shape if things go on as they be going now. United Mines of St. Day showed a loss of nigh on eight thousand pounds last year, and gracious knows what Grambler will show when tis next accounted. But this edn fitty talk for a wedding feast. We've got our pitches and our homes, and money d' come in. Mebbe it edn so much as we should like, but there be swacks of folk ready to change—"

"Mortal strange gin, this, Zacky," said Paul Daniel, wiping his moustache. "Never have I tasted gin like un. Or mebbe once… Mebbe once—"

"Well now," said Zacky, licking his lips, "if I 'adn been so concentrated on what I was saying I might have thought the very same. Now you call it to mind, it d' taste more like— more like—"

"More like turpentine," said Mark Daniel.

"Mortal fiery," said Old Man Greet. "Mortal fiery. But in my day twas expected that a nip of gin should bite ee. Twas expected. When I was on Lake Superior in '69, when I was thur 'specting for copper, there was a store that sold stuff as'd take the skin off your 'and—"

Joe Triggs, the doyen of the party, was given a mug of it. Everyone watched him take a draught and watched the expression on his deeply corrugated old face with its sprouting side whiskers. He pursed his lips and opened them with a loud smack, then drank again. He lowered the empty mug.

"Tedn't near so good as what ee got from Roscoff back last Septemby," was his growling verdict.

"But that's what tis," two or three exclaimed.

There was a moment's silence.

"A different tub," said Jud. "Tastes all right to me, but tedn't so mature. That's what's amiss with un. Did ought to have been kept awhile longerer. Like Uncle Nebby's old cow." He began to mumble a little tune to himself:

There was an old couple and they was poor, Tweedle, tweedle, go twee—

It seemed that the same terrible suspicion had leapt unasked into everyone's mind. They all stared silently at Jud while he went on humming and trying to look unconcerned.

Eventually the little song gave out.

Zacky looked down at his glass. "It is powerful strange," he said quietly, "that two tubs of gin should have such opposite flavours."

"Powerful strange," said Paul Daniel.

"Damnation strange," said Mark Daniel.

"Mebbe we was swindled," said Jud, showing his two big teeth in an unconvincing smile. "Them Frenchies is as cuzzle as a nest o' rats. Can't trust 'em no furtherer than ye can spit. Wouldn't turn me back on one no how. Cross one and turn your back, and he outs with his knife, and *phit!* ye're dead."

Zacky shook his head. "Who's ever been cheated by Jean Lutté?"

"He always do do the straight thing by we," said Will Nanfan.

Zacky rubbed his chin, and seemed to regret he had shaved that morning. "He told me they was two proper tubs of gin, and both same brand, mark ee. That's what's powerful strange. Both same brand. Seems to me as someone's been tampering wi' this one. I wonder who could be?"

"I've a damnation thundering good notion," said Mark Daniel, who had already drunk three pints of port and had just been ready to get down to the serious work of the evening.

"No need to get in a pore about un," said Jud, sweating. "Tes naught to do wi' me. There an't no proof o' nothing. Nobody can't say where the fault do lay. Anybody could 'ave tankered with un—that's if so be as somebody 'as, which if they 'as I doubt. But I suspicion tis the Frenchie. Never trust a Frenchie, say I. That Frenchie at Roscoff, he d' look all right, he d' talk all right; but do he act all right? He d' look ee in the eye like a Christian; but what do that surmount to? Only that he's two-faced like the rest but more so."

"When I was a tacker," said Old Man Greet perseveringly, "they had some proper gin down to Sawle Village where Aunt Tamsin Nanpusker lived. She that died in '58, fell down a shaft she did when she was well gone in liquor. An' not surprising when—"

"'S. I well remember old Aunt Tamsin," said Nick Vìgus, incautiously. "She as rode down Stippy-Stappy Lane one day on the back of her old sow, wi' all the little uns wagging away be'ind. Regular procession, twas. Some drink old Aunt Tamsin had to put away—"

"Damme!" roared Mark Daniel. "Ef I don't see it all now! That's where I tasted un before. It is Nick's doing. It is all Nick's doing! We're suspicioning the wrong man. You call to mind that poison brew Nick Vigus did hatch in his own back kitchen out o' devil knows what to sell to the poor fools wi' money to burn last Michaelmas Fair! Gin, he called it, ye recollect. Well, it was near enough the taste o' this to be brother an' twin to un."

"Aye," said Will Nanfan. "Aye, that's truth. God's truth, for I drank some meself and wished I never touched un. It give a twist to yer innards, a twist like a reefer knot. Nick Vigus has cheated we!"

Vigus' sly pockmarked face went red and white by turns as the accusing stares focused themselves on him. Mark Daniel took another sup to be sure, and then went to the window and sprayed it about the vegetable bed.

"Pah, the very same, or I'm a heathen. Nick Vìgus, ye're a damnation crawling cheat and it is time ye was learned a lesson." He began to roll up his sleeves, showing his great hairy forearms.

Nick backed away, but Paul Daniel blocked his escape to the door. There was some horseplay, then Mark Daniel took a firm grip and turned Vigus upside down and stood him on his head.

"Twas none o' my doing," Nick shouted. "Jud Paynter wur the one! Jud Paynter come to me last week and said to me, 'e said—"

"Don't ee believe a word of un!" Jud said loudly. "I'm a honest man as ye all d' know, not given to tankering wi' the word o' truth. But Nick's a greasy liar as ye all d'know, and would sell his mother to save the skin off his nose. And as—as ye all d' know—"

"Shake un up, Mark," Zacky said. "We shall be getting at the truth by and by."

"Jud come to me last week and says to me, 'e says, 'Can ee make us some o' your gin, boy? Cos that there tub I was keeping, all the gin 'as runned away into the ground—' Turn me right face up, Mark, or I shall sh-mother—"

Mark gripped his victim more firmly round the middle, and with a great heave stamped his kicking feet upon one of the beams of the cottage ceiling.

"Come, my dear," he said gently. "Speak up, for else ye may die unshrived—"

"'E says all the gin 'as runned away into the ground on account of the rats had gnawled away a 'ole in the tub—ah, ah ... And on account of he didn't want to disappoint ee, would I make—would I make—"

"Catch 'im, Paul!" Will Nanfan shouted, as Jud Paynter, like an obsequious bulldog, tried to leave unnoticed.

They caught him in the doorway, and a great deal of heaving and muttering went on before the elder Daniel and Will Nanfan came back with him.

"Tedn't true!" shouted Jud, toothless with indignation. "You're barking up the wrong door. What for do ee want to take that man's word 'fore mine. Tedn't fair. Tedn't just. Tedn't *British*. I dare swear if the truth be known that he stole 'alf the tub fur his self. Why blame a man ye know wouldn't rob—"

"If I had the 'alf, you 'ad the rest," came from the upended Vigus.

"Let me get atun!" swore Jud, suddenly struggling. "I'll tear his britches off. Let me face un and have un out. Ye pack of cowards: two to one! Let me get at un. I'll face ee one by one, ye cowards. Take yer 'ands off me and I'll poam ee: I'll poam ee—"

"Wait awhile and I'll poam ye myself," said Mark Daniel. "Man to man as ye'd like, see. Now out o' the way, boys—"

He carried Nick Vigus still inverted to the door. Unfortunately at this moment some of the women, hearing the uproar, had left the other cottage and reached this door led by Mrs. Vigus. On seeing her husband presented to her at an unusual angle, she let out a piercing scream and rushed forward to the rescue, but Mark fended her off and carried Nick across to the cottage of Joe and Betsy

Triggs. At the back of this was a slimy green pool which contained among other things most of their sewage. Since Reuben Clemmow had disappeared this had held pride of place for smells in the neighbourhood.

At the brink of the water Mark sharply upended the half-choked man, grasped him again by the seat of his breeches, and flung him on his face into the middle of the pool.

Mark breathed deeply and spat on his hands.

"Now for the next of un," he said.

And thither also Jud Paynter went in his turn.

2

As Ross rode home from Truro that evening in the gathering windy dusk, he thought of the two young people who were starting life together. If the mine were started, he would offer Jim a surface job, some sort of clerical work perhaps, which would give him a better chance.

His outing today had been to do with Wheal Leisure. After buying things for the house, flour and sugar, mustard and candles, huckaback linen for towels, a new pair of riding boots for himself and a brush and comb, he had called on Mr. Nathanial Pearce, the notary.

Mr. Pearce, as effusive, as purple, and as gouty as ever, sitting in an armchair poking the fire with a long iron curtain rod, listened with interest. Mr. Pearce said, well now, and how pleasant, and I declare a most takable suggestion. Mr. Pearce scratched at a louse under his wig while his eyes grew speculative. Was Captain Henshawe investing some of his own money? Dear, dear, now Captain Henshawe's reputation was high in the Truro district. Well now, dear sir, speaking as an indigent notary, he personally had only a little free capital, but there were, as Captain Poldark suggested, a certain number of his clients who were always on the lookout for a good speculative investment. He would be willing to give the matter his further consideration and see what could be done.

Events were moving slowly, but movement there was, and the momentum would increase. In a couple of months they might be sinking the first shaft.

As he led the mare into the stable and unbuckled the saddle, he wondered whether to offer Charles and Francis a share.

He had come home at a good pace to reach the house before dark, and Darkie was steaming and sweaty. She was unsettled too and did not want to keep still while he wiped her down.

For that matter, the other horses showed the same uneasiness; Ramoth kept tossing his old head and whinnying. He wondered if there was a snake in the stable or a fox in the loft above. The pale square of the stable door still let in some light, but he could see nothing in the shadows. He patted Ramoth's soft old nose and returned to his task. This done he gave Darkie her feed and turned to leave.

Near the door were the steps to the loft where Carter had slept. As he glanced up there, something grazed past his head and struck him a numbing blow on the shoulder. He fell to his knees and there was a thud on the straw of the floor. Then he got quickly to his feet again, staggered to the door, was through it and leaning with his back to it, holding his shoulder.

For a few seconds the pain made him feel sick, but it began to pass. He felt his shoulder and could find no broken bone. The thing which had struck him still lay on the floor inside the stable. But he had seen what it was, and that was why he had moved so quickly into the open.

It was the rock drill, the iron jumper he had last seen in the hands of Reuben Clemmow.

3

They were all in the kitchen when he went in. With a piece of coarse thread and a large bent needle, Demelza was trying to mend a tear in her skirt; Jud was sitting back in a chair with a look of patient suffering on that part of his face which was not hidden by a large bandage; Prudie was drinking tea.

"Why, Cap'n Ross," said Jud in a weak and trembling voice, "we didn't hear ee come. Shall I go and wipe down the 'oss?"

"I have done that. Why are you back from the wedding so soon? What is wrong with your face? Prudie, keep my supper for ten minutes. I have something to see to."

"The wedding is over," said Jud. "Twas a poor affair, a more poorer affair never I saw. Naught but Martins and Carters, the whole dashed danged blathering boiling of 'em, and a few o' the riffraff of the mines. I thought better o' Zacky than to invite such a poor lot of folk. Out o' my element I was—"

"Is aught amiss, sur?" Demelza asked.

Ross stared at her. "Amiss? No, what should there be?"

"An' on the way back," Jud said, "hard by Wheal Grace I turned me heel 'pon a stone an' fell—"

But Ross had walked through into the house.

"You'd best keep yer tongue still when he's in one o' them moods," Jud said severely to Demelza, "'or twon't be only your father you'll be gettin' a cuff from. Interrupting of your elders shows you been bad brought up—"

Demelza gazed at him wide-eyed but did not reply.

Ross could not see his gun in the parlour but found it in his bedroom. There he carefully loaded and primed it and pulled back the hammer to half cock. He had bolted the door of the stable so there should be no escape this time. He felt as if he had cornered a mad dog.

In the gathering darkness he lit a storm lantern, and this time left the house by the front door, making a circuit of the building to reach the stable. Better not leave the man too long or he might do some hurt to the horses.

Quietly he drew the bolt of the door and waited for a gust of wind to die before lifting the latch. Then he pushed the door wide, entered, put the lantern down just out of the draught, and stepped away into the shadows of the stalls.

Darkie whinnied at his sudden entry; wind blew in, disturbing the straw and leaves; a bat fluttered away from the light; there was silence. The iron bar had gone.

"Reuben," Ross said. "Come out. I want to talk to you.'

No reply. He hadn't expected one. You could hear the fluttering of the bat's wings as it circled in the darkness. He went on into the stable.

As he reached the second horse, he thought he heard a move behind him and turned swiftly, his gun up. But nothing stirred. He wished now he had brought the lantern farther, for its feeble light did not reach the deeper shadows.

Squire moved suddenly, stamping his hoofs on the floor. All the horses knew there was mischief about. Ross waited five minutes, tense by the stall, knowing that now it was a test of patience, of whose nerve would stand the longest. He was sure of his own, but as time passed he found that sureness urging him to go on. The man might have gone back to the loft with his weapon. He might be cowering there, prepared to see the night through.

Ross heard Jud come out of the house and tramp across the cobbles. He thought at first he might be coming here, but heard him enter the earth closet next door. Presently he went back to the house and the door was shut. Still no movement in the stable.

Ross turned to go back for the lantern, and as he did so there was a hum of air behind him and a crash as the jumper was swung and hit the partition where he had been standing. Wood splintered and he turned and fired straight into the figure which came up in the darkness. Something hit him across the head and the figure was making for the door. As the man was outlined he pulled the trigger again. But this time the touch powder did not ignite; before he could pull back the cock Reuben Clemmow was gone.

He ran to the door and stared out. A figure moved beside the apple trees and he discharged the second barrel at it. Then he wiped a trickle of blood from his forehead and turned towards the house, from which Jud and Prudie and Demelza were just issuing in alarm.

He was angry and frustrated at the man's escape, even though there was every likelihood of his being found in the morning.

It would be very difficult for him not to leave a trail.

CHAPTER THIRTEEN

1

H E WAS OUT AT DAWN FOLLOWING THE BLOODSTAINS WHICH CLEMMOW had left behind; but just before they reached Mellin, they turned north towards the sand hills and he lost track of them. In the days that followed nothing more was heard of the man, and the most reasonable conclusion was that he had lain down somewhere in that waste of sand and died of weakness and exposure. It was well to be finally rid of him, and nobody asked any questions. The fact that he had ever reappeared became a secret kept by the four members of the Nampara household and Zacky, whom Ross told.

During all the months of that summer the house of Nampara was seldom without flowers. This was Demelza's doing. She was always up at dawn and, now that the dread of being kidnapped and taken home for a thrashing had left her, she wandered at will in the fields and lanes, the lolloping Garrick trailing at her heels, to return with a big bunch of wildflowers, which found their way into the parlour.

Prudie had tried to break her of the habit, since it was not the duty of a kitchenmaid to brighten up the house with her gleanings; but Demelza went on bringing in the flowers, and her obstinacy and Prudie's inertia won the day. Sometimes it was a bunch of meadowsweet and ragged robin, sometimes an armful of foxgloves or a posy of sea pinks.

If Ross ever noticed these, he made no comment.

The child was like a young animal which had spent fourteen years in blinkers, narrowing her gaze to the smallest domestic circle and the most primitive purposes; the first nine years linked closely to her mother in a succession of illnesses and ill treatment and poverty and childbirths, the last five facing all except the last alone. It was not surprising now that she expanded in body and in mind. She grew an inch in four months, and her interest in flowers was a symbol of her widening outlook.

She had taken to combing her hair and tying it back, where it sometimes stayed, so that her features had come out into the open. She was not an ill-looking girl and had a good clear skin and a quick mobility of expression; her eyes were intelligent and very frank. In another couple of years some young miner like Jim Carter would be courting her.

She was a very quick learner and something of a mimic, so that she began to add words to her vocabulary and to know how to pronounce them. She also began to lose some. Ross had consulted Prudie—always a flattering way of approach—and Prudie, who could outswear a trooper when she chose, found herself committed to the reduction of Demelza's curse words.

Sometimes, faced by Demelza's probing questions, Prudie felt as if she were in a trap. Prudie knew what was right and proper, and Demelza did not. And it might be possible to teach some girls to behave themselves without taking care of your own behaviour, but Demelza was not one of them. She was much too quick in her conclusions; her thoughts raced ahead and met one on the rebound.

So the process became not merely the willing education of Demelza but the unwilling regeneration of Prudie. It was not possible, she found, even to get drunk decently these days.

Ross looked on with amusement. Even Jud was not immune, but he bore the situation less graciously than his wife. He seemed to consider it an added grievance that she had not hit him with a broom handle for more than two months.

It was not a question of their being reformed by contact with the pure and lovely spirit of a child, for the child had as much original sin as they had.

If Demelza grew and developed, Garrick was a beanstalk. When he came he had been more of a puppy than anyone thought, and with proper food he enlarged so rapidly that one began to suspect the sheep dog in his ancestry. The sparse black curls of his coat remained, and his lack of tail made him curiously clumsy and unbalanced. He took a great fancy to Jud who couldn't bear the sight of him, and the ungainly dog followed the bald old rascal everywhere. In July Garrick was pronounced free of parasites and admitted to the kitchen. He celebrated his entry by bounding across to Jud at the table and upsetting a jug of cider in his lap. Jud got up in a flood of cider and self-pity and aimed the jug at the dog, which scuttled out again, while Demelza fled into the dairy and covered her head with her hands in a paroxysm of laughter.

One day, to Ross's surprise, he received a visit from Mrs. Teague and her youngest daughter, Ruth.

They had ridden over to Mingoose, Mrs. Teague explained, and thought it sociable to call in at Nampara on the way home. Mrs. Teague had not visited Nampara for nearly ten years and was so interested, she said, to see how Ross was managing for himself. Farming was such an engaging hobby, Mr. Teague had always said.

"More than a hobby with me, ma'am," Ross said. He had been mending the fence which bounded part of his land, and was dirty and dishevelled, his hands scarred and soiled and rusty. When he greeted them in the parlour the contrast with Mrs. Teague's over-bright riding costume could not be ignored. Ruth too was got up to kill today.

Looking at her while they drank the cordial he ordered for them, he saw what it was that had taken him at the ball: the latent prettiness of the slightly rouged mouth, the unusual oblique set of her grey-green eyes, the lift of her willful little chin. With some last despairing effort Mrs. Teague had put a vitality into her youngest daughter that the others lacked.

They talked prettily about this and that. They had really been to call at the invitation of Mr. John Treneglos, the eldest son of Mr. Horace Treneglos of Mingoose. John was master of the Garnbarrow Hunt and had expressed supreme admiration for the way Ruth rode. He had invited them over so often that at last they felt impelled to gratify his request. What a noble house Mingoose was, was it not? The Gothic style and so very spacious, said Mrs. Teague, looking round. Mr. Treneglos was a most charming old gentleman; one could not help but notice how frail he had become.

How disappointing that Captain Poldark did not ride to hounds! Would it not do him a great matter of benefit, the mixing with other people of his own station and the thrill of the chase? Ruth always rode; it was her abiding passion; not of course that she was not highly accomplished in the gentler arts; one had to taste her syllabubs to know their richness; she had always believed, Mrs. Teague said, in bringing up her children to be accomplished about the house; this piece of lace which she wore as a fichu had been made entirely by Ruth and Joan, though Joan had not the industry of her younger sister.

During all this Ruth looked uncomfortable, pouting her mouth and glancing obliquely about the room and tapping her riding whip against one of her small well-shod feet. But when her mother was otherwise occupied, she found the opportunity to send him some knowledgeable and inviting looks. Ross thought of the few hours of daylight left and realized he would not complete the repair of the fence today.

Did he see much of the rest of the family? Mrs. Teague asked. There had not been a single Poldark at the Lemon ball. Of course, one could not expect Elizabeth to go about so much as usual, now that she was expecting a confinement. Ruth blushed, and a sharp stab of pain went through Ross.

Was it true, Mrs. Teague wondered, that Verity was still meeting that man, that Captain Blarney, somewhere in spite of her father's veto? One heard the rumour. No, well, of course, Ross wouldn't know, with being so much out of touch with the world.

At five-thirty they rose to go. They thanked him but would not stay to supper. It had been agreeable seeing him. Would he come over to visit them if they wrote fixing a day? Very well, one day at the beginning of next month. He had made Nampara most comfortable again. One felt, perhaps, that the touch of a woman's hand was needed to set it off, to give it graciousness and gentility. Did he not ever feel that way?

They moved to the front door, Mrs. Teague chatting amiably, Ruth sulky and sweet by turns, trying to catch his eye and re-establish the flirtatious companionship of the ball. Their man-servant brought their horses forward. Ruth mounted first, lightly and easily. She had the grace of youth and of the born horsewoman; she sat in the saddle as if made for it. Mrs. Teague then mounted, satisfied with his approving glances, and he walked with them as far as the boundary of his land.

On the way Demelza passed them. She was carrying a basket of pilchards from Sawle, where the first catch of the season had just been landed. She was in the better of her two frocks of pink printed dimity and the sun shone on her tousled hair. A child, a girl, thin and angular with a long-legged stride; and then she raised her unexpected eyes.

She blinked once, curtsied awkwardly, passed on.

Mrs. Teague took out a fine lace handkerchief and flicked a little dust from her habit. "I heard you had—um—adopted a child, Captain Poldark. That is she?"

"I have adopted no one," Ross said. "I needed a kitchen wench. The child is old enough to know her own mind. She came. That is all there is about it."

"A nice little thing," said Mrs. Teague. "Yes, she looks as if she would know her own mind."

2

The affairs of Verity and Captain Blarney came to a head at the end of August. It was unfortunate that this should occur on the day Ross had accepted Mrs. Teague's invitation to return her call.

Verity had met Andrew Blarney four times at Nampara during the summer, once each time he was ashore.

Ross could not bring himself to dislike the seaman, for all his history. A quiet man with no small talk, a man with self-possessed eyes offset by an unusual modesty of bearing; the word one would instinctively choose to describe him was "sober." Yet sober was the last thing he had once been, if one merely accepted his own confession. Sometimes it was possible to sense a conflict. He had the reputation, Ross knew, for being a driver aboard his ship; and in the deliberate self-control, the self-containment of all his movements, one caught the echo of past struggles and guessed the measure of the victory won. His deference and tenderness towards Verity were obviously sincere.

If there was anyone he could dislike, it was himself and the role he was playing. He was abetting the meeting of two people whom common sense would emphasize were better apart. If things went wrong, he would be more to blame than anyone else. One could not expect clearsightedness from two people deeply in love.

Nor was he at all comfortable about the progress of events. He was not present at their interviews, but he knew Blarney was trying to persuade Verity to run away with him, and that so far Verity had not brought herself to the point of agreement, still hoping that there might be a reconciliation between Andrew and her father. She had, however, agreed to go with him to Falmouth sometime soon and meet his children, and Ross had a suspicion that if she went she would not return. One could not go so far in a few minutes and be back without anyone being the wiser. This would be the thin end of defiance. Once there he would persuade her to marry him rather than come back and face the storm.

The week before, Mrs. Teague had sent a letter by one of her grooms inviting him to "a small afternoon party" they were holding next Friday, at four. Heaping abuse on himself, he wrote out an acceptance while the man waited. The next

day Verity came over to ask if she might meet Andrew Blarney at Nampara on
Friday afternoon at three.

There was no need for Ross to be in while they met, except a convention
which, knowing Verity, he didn't subscribe to; so he raised no objection, and
only delayed long enough to welcome them.

Having seen them into the parlour and left word they were not to be disturbed,
he got his horse and rode up the valley, casting regretful eyes about at all the
work he might have been doing instead of riding away to play at foppery with a
half-dozen silly young men and women. At the head of the valley, just beyond
Wheal Maiden, he met Charles and Francis.

For a moment he was put out.

"A pleasure to welcome you on my land, Uncle," he said. "Were you thinking
to pay me a visit? Another five minutes and you would have found me away."

"That was our intention," said Francis shortly.

Charles jerked his horse's head up. They were both looking flushed and angry.

"There's a rumour afoot that Verity is meeting that Blarney fellow at your
house, Ross. We are riding over to discover the truth of it."

"I'm afraid I can't offer you my hospitality this afternoon," Ross said. "I have
an engagement at four—at some distance."

"Verity's at your house now," said Francis. "We intend going down to see if
Blarney is there, whether you like it or not."

"Aarf!" said Charles. "There's no need to be unpleasant, Francis. Perhaps we
are mistaken. Give us your word of honour, boy, and we'll ride back without
the need of a quarrel."

"Well, but what is she doing there?" Francis asked truculently.

Ross said: "Since my word of honour would not remove Captain Blarney, I
can't give it."

He watched Charles's expression change. "God damn you, Ross, have you no
sense of decency, no loyalty to your family, leaving her down there with that
son of a whore?"

"I told you it was so!" Francis exclaimed and without waiting for further talk
turned his horse at a trot down the valley towards Nampara.

"I think you misjudge the man," Ross said slowly.

Charles snorted. "I think I have misjudged you." He followed his son.

Ross watched them nearing the house with an unpleasant premonition of ill.
Their words and looks left no doubt of the attitude they would take.

He pulled at Darkie's head and followed in their wake.

3

When he reached the house Francis was already in the parlour. He could hear the raised voices as Charles slid laboriously from his horse.

When they got inside, Captain Blarney was standing beside the fireplace, one hand on Verity's sleeve, as if to stop her from coming between him and Francis. He was in his captain's laced coat of fine blue cloth with a white wing collar and black cravat. He wore his most self-contained look, as if all unruly passion were locked away, bolted and unreachable, guarded by all the controls of his own choosing and testing. He looked sturdy and middle-aged against the flushed handsome arrogance of Francis's youth. Ross noticed that Charles was carrying his riding whip.

"… no way to speak to your sister," Blarney was saying. "Any hard words you've a mind to speak can come to me."

"Dirty skunk!" Charles said. "Sneaking behind our backs. My only daughter."

"Sneaking," said Blarney, "because you would not meet to talk over the matter. Do you think—"

"Talk it over!" said Charles. "There's nothing to talk over wi' wife murderers. We don't like 'em in this district. They leave a nasty stink in the nostrils. Verity, get your horse and go home."

She said quietly: "I have a right to choose my own life."

"Go, dear," said Blarney. "It's no place for you now."

She shook off his hand. "I stay."

"Then stay and be damned!" said Francis. "There's only one way of treating your sort, Blarney. Words and honour don't count. Perhaps a thrashing will." He began to take off his coat.

"Not on my land," said Ross. "Begin any brawl here and I'll throw you off it myself."

There was a moment's nonplussed silence.

"God's name!" exploded Charles. "You have the impudence to take his side!"

"I take no one's side, but you won't change the issue with horseplay."

"One skunk and another," said Francis. "You're small matter better than he is."

"You heard what your sister said," Captain Blarney interposed quietly. "She has the right to choose her own life. I have no wish to quarrel, but she is coming away with me."

"I'll see you in hell first," Francis said. "There'll be no cleaning of your boots on our family."

Captain Blarney suddenly went very white. "You insolent puppy!"

"Puppy, is it now!" Francis leaned forward and smacked Captain Blarney with an open hand across his cheek.

The red mark showed, and then Blarney hit Francis in the face and Francis went to the floor.

There was a brief pause. Verity had backed away from them both, her face small and sick.

Francis sat up and with the back of his hand wiped a streak of blood from his nose. He got to his feet.

"When will it be convenient for you to meet me, Captain Blarney?"

Having found outlet, the seaman's anger had ebbed. But somehow his composure was not the same. If only for a moment, the controls had been broken.

"I leave for Lisbon by tomorrow's tide."

Francis's expression was contemptuous. "That, of course, is what I would have expected."

"Well, there is still today."

Charles stepped forward. "Nay, there's no call for these damned Frenchy methods, Francis. Let's thrash the beggar and then go."

"There'll be none of that, neither," said Ross.

Francis licked his lips. "I demand satisfaction. You can't deny that. The fellow once laid claims to be a gentleman. Let him come outside and meet me—if he's got the guts."

"Andrew," Verity said. "Don't agree to anything—"

The sailor glanced at the girl distantly, as if her brother's hostility had already separated them.

"Fight it out with fists," said Charles stertorously. "The skunk's not worth the risk of a pistol ball, Francis."

"Nothing else will discourage him," said Francis. "I'll trouble you for weapons, Ross. If you refuse them I'll send over to Trenwith for my own."

"Send over, then," snapped Ross. "I'll be no party to your blood-letting."

"They're on the wall behind you, man," said Blarney, between his teeth.

Francis turned and took down the silver duelling pistols with which Ross had threatened Demelza's father. "Will they still fire?" he said coldly, addressing Ross.

Ross did not speak.

"Come outside, Blarney," Francis said.

"Look, boy," said Charles. "This is stuff and nonsense. It's my quarrel and—"

"Nothing of the sort. He knocked me down—"

"Come away and have no truck with the varmint. Verity will come with us, won't you, Verity?"

"Yes, Father."

Francis looked at Ross. "Call your man and get him to see these pistols are properly primed."

"Get him yourself."

"There are no seconds," said Charles. "There's no suitable arrangements."

"Formality! One needs no formality when stalking a crow."

They went outside. It was easy to see that Francis was determined to have his satisfaction. Blarney, white about the nostrils, stood apart, as if the business didn't concern him. Verity made a last appeal to her brother, but he snapped at her that some solution to her infatuation must be found and he had chosen this one.

Jud was outside so there was no need to call him. He was visibly interested and impressed by the responsibility thrust on him. He had only seen such a thing once before and that thirty years ago. Francis told him to act as referee and to count out fifteen paces for them; Jud glanced at Ross, who shrugged.

"Yes, sur, fifteen did ye say."

They were in the open space of grass before the house. Verity had refused to go indoors. She held to the back of the garden seat.

The men stood back to back, Francis an inch or more the taller, his fair hair glinting in the sun.

"Ready, sur?"

"Aye."

Ross made a movement forward but checked himself. The headstrong fool must have his way.

"Then go. One, two, three, fower, five, six—"

As Jud counted the two men paced away from each other, and a swallow dipped and swerved between them.

At the word fifteen they turned. Francis fired first and hit Blarney in the hand. Blarney dropped his pistol. He bent and picked it up with his left hand and fired back. Francis put up a hand to his neck and fell to the ground.

4

Ross's thought as he went forward was, I should have stopped them. What will this mean to Elizabeth if Francis...?

He turned Francis over upon his back and ripped away the ruffles of his shirt. The ball had gone into the base of the neck by the shoulder but had not come out again. Ross lifted him and carried him into the house.

"My God!" said Charles, following helplessly with the others. "The boy's dead... My boy—"

"Nonsense," Ross said. "Jud, take Mr. Francis's horse and ride for Dr. Choake. Say there has been a shooting accident. Not the truth, mind."

"Is the hurt serious?" Captain Blarney said, with a handkerchief about his hand. "I—"

"Get out of here!" said Charles, empurpled. "How dare you come into the house again!"

"Don't crowd about him," Ross urged, having laid Francis on the sofa. "Prudie, get me some clean rags and a bowl of hot water."

"Let me help," said Verity. "Let me help. I can do something. I can—"

"No, no. Leave him be."

There was silence for some moments until Prudie returned in haste with the bowl. Ross had kept the wound from bleeding excessively until now by pressing on it with his own coloured kerchief. Now he lifted this and pressed a damp cloth in its place. Francis winced and groaned.

"He'll be all right," said Ross. "Only give him room to breathe."

Captain Blarney picked up his hat and left the room.

Outside he sat a moment on the seat beside the front door and put his head in his hands.

"God's blood, that gave me a fright," said Charles, wiping his face and neck and under his wig. "I thought the boy was gone. A mercy the fellow didn't shoot with his right hand."

"Perhaps then he would have missed more cleanly," Ross said.

Francis turned and muttered and opened his eyes. It took some moments for full consciousness to return. The rancour had left his eyes.

"Has the fellow gone?"

"Yes," said Ross.

Francis grinned wryly. "I winged him. It was your pesty duelling arms, Ross. Their sighting must be awry. Ach! Well, this will save the leeches for a week or two."

Outside in the garden Verity had rejoined Andrew Blarney.

He had withdrawn completely within himself. In the space of fifteen minutes their relationship had been irrevocably changed.

"I must go," he said, and they both at once noticed the pronoun. "It's better before he comes round."

"Oh, my dear, if you could have—shot wide—or not at all—"

He shook his head, oppressed with the complex struggles of his own nature and with the futility of trying to explain.

She said: "This—I know it was his seeking all this quarrel. But he is my brother. It makes it so *impossible* for me—"

He struggled to find the hope to argue. "In time it will cool, Verity. Our feelings can't change."

She did not answer but sat with lowered head.

He stared at her hard for some seconds. "Perhaps Francis was right. There has been only trouble. Perhaps I shouldn't ever have thought of you—have looked at you."

She said: "No, Francis wasn't right. But after this… there can never be any reconciling."

After a minute he got up.

"Your hand," she said. "Let me tie it."

"It's only a scratch. A pity his aim wasn't better."

"Can you ride? Your fingers—"

"Yes, I can ride."

She watched him walk round the house. He held his shoulders like an old man. He came back mounted.

"Goodbye, my love. If there's nothing else, give me leave to keep the memory."

She watched him cross the stream and ride slowly up the valley until the image in her eyes was suddenly misted and smeared.

CHAPTER FOURTEEN

T HE WHOLE PARTY WAS BACK AT TRENWITH. FRANCIS, TEMPORARILY PATCHED, had ridden his horse home, and now Choake was with him, making a showy job of the dressing. Charles, belching wind and the remnants of his anger, had stumped off to his own room to take a vomit and rest until supper.

Elizabeth had almost fainted at the sight of her husband. But recovering herself, she had flown up and downstairs to hasten Mrs. Tabb and Bartle in supplying Dr. Choake's needs and in tending to the wounded man's comfort. As would be the case all through her life, she had a store of nervous energy, unavailable at ordinary times but able to serve her in sudden need. It was a fundamental reserve which a stronger person might never know.

And Verity had gone to her room…

She felt herself detached from this household of which she had been a part for twenty-five years. She was among strangers. More than that, they were hostile strangers. They had drawn away from her, and she from them, for lack of understanding. In an afternoon she had shrunk inside herself; there would grow up a core of friendlessness and isolation.

She pushed the bolt across the door and sat abruptly in the first chair. Her romance was over; even though she rebelled against the fact, she knew that it was so. She felt faint and sick, and desperately tired of being alive. If death could come quietly and peacefully, she would accept it, would sink into it as one sank into a bed wanting only sleep and self-forgetfulness.

Her eyes moved round the room. Every article in it was familiar with the extreme unseeing intimacy of everyday association.

Through the long sash window and the narrow window in the alcove she had looked with the changing eyes of childhood and youth. She had looked out on the herb garden and the yew hedge and the three bent sycamores in all the seasons of the year and in all the moods of her own growth. She had seen frost draw its foliate patterns on the panes, raindrops run down them like tears on old cheeks, the first spring sun shine dustily through them on the turkey rug and the stained oak boards.

The old French clock on the carved pine chimneypiece, with its painted and gilt figures, like a courtesan from the days of Louis XIV, had been in the room all Verity's life. Its thin metallic bell had been announcing the hours for more than fifty years. When it was made, Charles was a thin strip of a boy, not a breathless empurpled old man breaking up his daughter's romance. They had been together, child and clock, girl and clock, woman and clock, through illness and nightmare and fairy stories and daydreams, through all the monotony and the splendour of life.

Her eyes went on, to the glass-topped display table with the carved legs, to the two pink satin bedroom chairs, the cane rocking-chair, the stumpy brass candlesticks with the candles rising in steps, the pincushion, the embroidered workbasket, the two-handled washing urn. Even the decorations of the room, the long damask curtains, the flock wallpaper with its faded crimson flowers on an ivory ground, the white plaster roses of the cornice and ceiling, had become peculiarly and completely her own.

She knew that here in the privacy of her own room, where no man except her brother and her father ever came, she could give way, could lie on the bed and weep, could abandon herself to sorrow. But she sat on the chair and didn't move at all.

There were no tears in her. The wound went too deep, or she was not so constituted to give way to it. Hers would be the perpetual ache of loss and loneliness, slowly dulled with time until it became a part of her character, a faint sourness tinged with withered pride.

Andrew would be back in Falmouth by now, back in the lodgings she had heard of but never seen. Through his quiet talk she had seen the bleakness of his life ashore, the two rooms in the lodging house by the quay, the drab woman who looked after him.

She had thought to change all that. They had planned to rent a cottage over-looking the bay, a place with a few trees and a small garden running down to the shingle beach. Though he had scarcely ever spoken of his first marriage, she had understood enough to be certain that much of the fault of the failure lay with her—however inexcusable on his side the end might have been. She had felt that she could make up for that first failure. With her busy hands and managing ability and with their mutual love she would have made for him a home such as he had not had before.

Instead this room, which had seen her grow to maturity, would see her dry up and fade. The gilt mirror in the corner would bear its dispassionate testimony.

All these ornaments and furnishings would be her companions through the years to come. And she realized that she would come to hate them, if she didn't already hate them, as one hates the witnesses of one's humiliation and futility.

She made a halfhearted attempt to shake herself out of this mood. Her father and her brother had acted in good faith, true to their upbringing and principles. If as a result she remained at their beck and call until she was old, it was not fair to blame them for the whole. They thought they had saved her from herself. Her life in Trenwith would be more peaceful, more sheltered than as the wife of a social outcast. She was among relatives and friends. The long summer days were full of interest about the farm: the sowing, the haymaking, the harvesting; butter and cheeses to superintend, syrups and conserves to make. The winter ones were full too. Needlework in the evening, making curtains and samplers and stockings, spinning wool and flax with Aunt Agatha, brewing simples; playing at quadrille when there were guests, or helping Mr. Odgers to train the choir at Sawle Church, dosing the servants with possets when they were ill.

This winter too there would be a newcomer in the house. If she had gone, Elizabeth would have been doubly lost; Francis would have found the well-run routine of the house suddenly out of joint, Charles would have no one to arrange his cushions or see that his silver tankard was polished before each meal. For these and a hundred other small needs the household depended on her, and if they did not repay her with overt thanks, they showed her a tacit affection and friendship she couldn't disregard.

And if she had not found these duties irksome in the past, was it not just the first flush of disappointment which said they must be so in the future?

So she might argue, but Andrew said no. Andrew sitting now with his head in his hands in the dismal lodgings in Falmouth, Andrew next week in the Bay of Biscay, Andrew tramping the streets of Lisbon by night, or next month back in his lodgings, Andrew eating and drinking and sleeping and waking and *bang,* said no. He had taken a place in her heart, or taken a *part* of her heart, and nothing would be the same again.

Last year she had drifted on a tide of custom and habit. She might have so drifted, without protest, into a contented and unambitious middle age. But this year, from now on, she must swim against the stream, not finding stimulus in the struggle but only bitterness and regret and frustration.

She sat there in the room by herself until darkness came and the shadows of the room closed about her like comforting arms.

CHAPTER FIFTEEN

1

WHEAL LEISURE WAS NOT STARTED THAT SUMMER.

After some hesitancy Ross invited Francis to join them. Francis refused rather brusquely; but something more imponderable than this held up the project. The price of copper in the open market fell to £80 a ton. To begin a new seeking venture at such a time would be asking for failure.

Francis mended rapidly from his neck wound, but Ross's part in Verity's love affair still rankled with him and his father. Rumour had it that Poldark and his young wife had been spending money at an extravagant rate, and now that Elizabeth did not go out much Francis went everywhere with George Warleggan.

Ross saw little of Verity, for during the rest of the summer she scarcely left Trenwith. He wrote to Mrs. Teague apologizing for his default, "owing to unforeseen and unavoidable circumstances." There was very little else he could say. He did not receive a reply. Later he learned that the "small party" was Ruth's birthday party, at which he was to have been the guest of honour. It was by then too late to implement his apology and the damage was done.

After the postponement of the Wheal Leisure venture Jim Carter left his employment. He was not the sort of young man to be a farm labourer all his life, and Grambler reclaimed him.

He came to Ross one evening in August after they had spent all day cutting a field of barley, and explained that Jinny would not be able to work at Grambler after Christmas—at least not for the time—and they could not afford to be without her earnings. So, as he had never felt better in his life, he had taken a tribute on the forty-fathom level.

"I'm proper sorry to be leaving, sir," he said. "But it's a good pitch. I know that. Wi' luck I shall make thirty or thirty-five shillings a month, and that's what we've got to think on. If we could stay on at the cottage, we'd like to pay rent for it."

"So you shall," said Ross, "when I think you can afford it. Don't be so generous with your money till you see if it goes round."

"No, sir," said Jim inarticulately. "Twasn't exactly that—"

"I know, boy; I'm not blind. Nor, by the way, am I deaf. I heard it whispered that you had been out poaching the other night with Nick Vigus."

Jim went crimson. He stammered and seemed about to deny it, then abruptly said, "Yes."

"It's a dangerous pastime," Ross said. "Whose land did you go on?"

"Treneglos."

Ross suppressed a smile. His warning was, in fact, deadly serious, and he had no wish to weaken it.

"Keep away from Nick Vigus, Jim. He'll lead you into trouble before you know it."

"Yes, sir."

"What does Jinny say?"

"The same as you, sir. I… promised her not to go again."

"Then keep your promise."

"Twas for 'er that I went. I thought something tasty—"

"How is she?"

"Proper, sir, thank you. We're that happy, just the two of us, that I wish, in a manner o' speaking, that there weren't going to be another. Still, Jinny's happy about that too. It isn't she that's afraid."

2

Subtle changes were continuing to take place in the relationship between Demelza Carne and the rest of the Nampara household. Her mind having outstripped the Paynters, she turned elsewhere for information, and this brought her more into contact with Ross, who found some pleasure in helping her. He wanted to laugh at her remarks much more often than he allowed himself.

At the end of August, during the week the corn was being ricked, Prudie slipped and hurt her leg and had to lie up.

For four days Demelza flew about the house, and although Ross was not in to see what she did, the midday meal was always brought out on time and the larger evening meal was always ready when they came wearily home. Demelza

did not cling to her newfound authority when Prudie got up, but their relationship was never again that of housekeeper and scullery maid. The only comment
on the change came from Jud, who told his wife that she was getting as soft as
an old mare.

Ross did not speak to Demelza about her efforts on those four days, but when
he was next in Truro, he bought her one of the scarlet cloaks which were so
fashionable in the mining villages of West Cornwall. When she saw it, she was
speechless—an unusual symptom—and bore it off to her bedroom to try it on.
Later he caught her looking at him in a peculiar manner; it was as if she felt it
only right and proper for her to be aware of his likes and wants—that was what
she was here for; but for him to know hers was not quite in the bargain.

In place of Jim, Ross took an elderly man called Jack Cobbledick. He was a
saturnine man, slow of thought and speech, with a ginger-grey drooping moustache, through which he strained all his food, and a long heavy-legged gait, as if
he was always mentally striding through tall grass. Demelza nearly got into trouble
several times when walking across the yard lifting her own long legs in imitation.

In September, when the pilchard season was at its height, Ross rode into
Sawle now and then to see the fish brought in or to buy a half hogshead for
salting down when the quality was good. In this he found Demelza, with her
experience of catering for a large and poor family, a better judge than himself,
so she sometimes rode behind him on his horse or walked on half an hour in
advance. Sometimes Jud would drive over with a couple of oxen yoked to a
rickety cart and buy up a load of the broken and damaged fish for half a guinea
to dig into the land as manure.

From the church of Sawle you went down Stippy-Stappy Lane, and at the
bottom was a narrow humped bridge and a green square surrounded by sheds
and cottages which was the nucleus of the village of Sawle. From here it was a
few yards to the high bar of shingle and the shallow inlet of the bay.

Just clear of the bar were two gaunt fish-packing houses, and about these the
summer industry of the village centred. Here the fish were picked over and
packed into cellars for a month or so until the oil and blood had drained off them
and they could be preserved and exported in hogsheads to the Mediterranean.

3

Elizabeth's child was born at the end of October. It was a difficult and protracted
birth, but she stood the strain well and would have rallied more quickly had

not Dr. Choake decided to bleed her the day afterwards. As a result of that she spent twenty-four hours going off into dead faints which alarmed everyone and from which it needed any number of burnt feathers held under the nose to revive her.

Charles was delighted at the event, and the news that it was a boy roused him from his after-dinner stupor.

"Splendid!" he said to Francis. "Well done, my boy. I'm proud of you. So we have a grandson, eh? Damme, that's just what I wanted."

"You have Elizabeth to thank, not I," said Francis pallidly.

"Eh? Well, I expect you did your part?" Charles quivered with subterranean laughter. "Never mind, boy; I'm proud of you both. Didn't think she had it in her. What are you going to name the brat?"

"We have not yet decided," Francis said sulkily.

Charles prised his great bulk out of the chair and waddled into the hall to stare around. "Well, we've a fine variety of names in the family without going farther afield. Let's see, there's Robert, and Claude... and Vivian... and Henry. And two or three Charleses. What's wrong with Charles, eh, boy?"

"It must be for Elizabeth to decide."

"Yes, yes, she'll do that, I expect. Anyhow, I hope she doesn't choose Jonathan. Infernal silly name. Where's Verity?"

"Upstairs now, helping."

"Well, tell me when the brat's open to receive its grandfather. A boy, eh? Well done, both of you."

Elizabeth's weakness delayed the christening until early December, and then it took place on a quieter scale than Charles would have liked. There were only eighteen present including the immediate family.

Dorothy Johns, Cousin William-Alfred's wife, had been caught between her pregnancies and was with him. She was a dried-up prim little woman of forty with a reserved, sub-acid smile and inhibitions ahead of her outspoken age. She never used the word "bowels" even in private conversation, and there were subjects which she did not mention at all, a matter for astonishment among most of her women friends. Her last two confinements had told heavily on her, and Ross thought that she looked drawn and wrinkled. Would Elizabeth some day come to look like this? Her first child seemed even to have improved her looks.

She lay on the couch where Francis had carried her. A great log fire was blazing and the flames leapt up the chimney like chained hounds. The big room was warm and people's glances were lit by the reflection of the fire; outside the grey cold day curled in a thin fog over the windows. There were flowers in the room, and Elizabeth lay among them like a lily while everyone moved around her. Her fine clear skin was waxen about the arms and throat, but in her cheeks there was more colour than usual. She had the hot-house bloom of the lily.

They named the child Geoffrey Charles. A bundle of blue silk and lace, with a small round fluffy head, deep blue eyes, and Aunt Agatha's gums. During the christening he made no protest and afterwards he went back to his mother, uncomplaining. A model baby, they all agreed.

Over the meal which followed, Charles and Mr. Chynoweth discussed cockfighting, and Mrs. Choake talked to anyone who would listen of the latest rumours about the Prince of Wales.

Mrs. Chynoweth talked to George Warleggan and monopolized his attention, much to Patience Teague's annoyance. Aunt Agatha munched crumbs and strove hard to hear what Mrs. Chynoweth was saying. Verity sat silent and stared at the table. Dr. Choake pulled his eyebrows down, and from under them told Ross some of the charges which ought to be preferred against Hastings, the governor general of Bengal. Ruth Teague, embarrassingly near Ross, tried to carry on a conversation with her mother as if he were not there.

Ross was faintly amused at Ruth's attitude, but a little puzzled at a constraint towards himself in one or two of the other ladies—Dorothy Johns and Mrs. Chynoweth and Mrs. Choake. He had done nothing to offend them. Elizabeth went out of her way to be kind.

And then in the middle of the luncheon Charles climbed laboriously to his feet to propose a toast to his grandson, spoke for some minutes breathing like a bulldog, then banged his chest, exclaimed impatiently, "This wind, this wind," and slid sideways to the floor.

With clumsy-handed care they upended the mountain of flesh, levering him first upon a chair, then bearing him step by step upstairs to his bedroom: Ross and Francis and George Warleggan and Dr. Choake.

Once on the massive four-poster bed with its heavy stuff-brown hangings, he seemed to breathe more easily, but he did not move or speak. Verity, roused from her lethargy, hurried about doing the doctor's bidding. Choake bled him and listened to his heart and straightened up and scratched the bald patch at the back of his own head, as if that might help.

"M' yes," he said. "I think we will do now. A heart stroke. We must be left perfectly quiet and warm. Have the windows kept shut and the curtains of the bed drawn so that there is no risk of a chill. He is so very big, hm; one must hope for the best."

When Ross returned to the subdued company downstairs, he found them settling to wait. It would be impolite to leave until there was some more definite word from the doctor. Elizabeth was much upset, they said, and had asked to be excused.

Aunt Agatha was gently rocking the cradle and plucking at the white hairs on her chin. "A bad omen," she said. "On little Charles's christening day for big Charles to go down like that. Just like an elmin tree strick by lightning. I hope nothing will come of it."

Ross went into the large parlour. There was no one there and he moved to the window. The gloomy day had grown heavier and darker, and there was a freckle of rain on the glass.

Change and decay. Was Charles, then, to go so soon the way of Joshua? He had been failing for some time, getting purpler and looser and more unwieldy. Old Agatha and her omens. How would it affect Verity? Little enough except for her bereavement. Francis would become master of this house and all the land. He would have a free rein to go the pace with Warleggan if he chose. Perhaps responsibility would sober him.

He moved out of the parlour into the next room, the library, which was small and dark and smelt of mildew and dust. Charles had been no more of a reader than his brother; their father, Claude Henry, had done most of the collecting.

Ross glanced over the shelves. He heard someone come into the parlour talking, but took no particular notice, for he had found a new edition of Dr. Burns's *Justice of the Peace*. He had turned to the chapter on lunacy when Mrs. Teague's voice, coming through the open door, took his attention.

"Well, dear child, what else can one expect? Like father like son, I always say."

"My dear ma'am"—it was Polly Choake—"the tales one hears about old Jothua! Most comical. I only do wish as I had been in these parts then."

"A gentleman," said Mrs. Teague, "knows where to draw the line. Towards a lady of his own class his intentions should be most strictly honourable. His attitude to a woman of a lower class is different. After all, men are men. It is very disagreeable, I know; but if a thing is gone about in the right way and the wench is provided for, there is no reason for anyone to come to harm. Joshua would never face up to the distinction. That was why I disapproved of him; that was why all the county disapproved of him and he was always fighting with fathers and husbands. He was too *loose* with his affections."

Polly giggled. "Pwomithcuouth, as you might thay!"

Mrs. Teague warmed to her subject. "The tales I could tell you of the hearts he broke! Scandal followed scandal.

"But even Joshua kept his own house free from sluts and queans. Even he did not kidnap a starveling beggar wench before she had reached the age of consent and seduce her on his own hearth. And to keep her openly for what she is: that is the worst part! It would be different if he kept her in her place. It's not good for the vulgars to know that one of their sluts is living in a position of equality with a man of Ross's standing. It puts ideas into their heads. To tell the truth when I was last over to see him—just a passing call, you understand, and that many months ago—I saw the creature. A hussy. Already beginning to put on airs. You can tell the type anywhere."

"Hardly a day patheth," Polly Choake said, "but what he comes widing into Thawle, with she behind on the same horthe, all fligged up in a scarlet cloak."

"It isn't good enough at all. It isn't good for the family. I wonder they don't tell him it must stop."

"Maybe they don't fancy to." Polly giggled. "They do thay as how he ith a quick-tempered man. Mythelf, I shouldn't like to do it, for he might stwike one a blow."

"Charles has been too easygoing," came a fresh voice. So Mrs. Chynoweth was there. She sounded annoyed. "When Charles is gone Francis will take a different line. If Ross refuses to listen, he must accept the consequences." There was the sound of a door opening and shutting.

Polly Choake giggled again. "No doubt she would dearly like to be mistreth of Trenwith 'stead of Elizabeth. P'waps then she would weform Francis too. My husband, Dr. Choake, tells me as how he lost a hundred guineas on the turn of a card last night."

"Gambling is a gentleman's pastime, Polly," said Mrs. Teague. "Possibly—"

Polly's giggle became louder. "Don't tell me bedding ith not!"

"Hush, child; you must learn to moderate your voice. It isn't—"

"That ith what the doctor always thays—"

"And very rightly. Especially is it unseemly to raise one's voice in laughter in a house of sickness. Tell me, child, what are the other rumours you have heard about him?"

CHAPTER SIXTEEN

1

CHARLES WAS INCONSIDERATE ENOUGH NOT TO GAIN HIS SENSES IN TIME TO satisfy the christening guests. Ross's parting picture of the unusually quiet house was of Aunt Agatha still rocking the baby and a thin bead of saliva trickling down one of the wrinkles of her chin as she muttered, "Tis an omen, for sure. I wonder what will come of it."

It was not, however, of Charles's illness or Geoffrey Charles's future that Ross thought on the way home.

At Nampara they had been preparing for the winter by lopping some of the branches of the elm trees for kindling wood. One tree only was condemned, whose roots, in the soft ground by the stream, were uncertain after the autumn gales. Jud Paynter and Jack Cobbledick had a rope tied to one of the higher branches and were using a two-handled saw on the trunk. When they had worked for a few minutes, they would walk away and tug at the rope to see if the trunk would snap off. The rest of the household had come out in the afternoon twilight to watch. Demelza was dancing about trying to help, and Prudie, her muscular arms crossed like the knotted roots of the tree, was standing by the bridge giving unwelcome advice.

She turned and bent her heavy brows at Ross.

"I'll take the mare. And 'ow went the christening, an? Did ee get a nice drop of bed-ale? And the brat, dear of 'm; like Mr. Francis, is 'e?"

"Like enough. What is the matter with Demelza?"

"One of 'er moods. I says to Jud, that girl, I says, will come to mischief in one o' them moods. She's bin like that ever since 'er fadder left."

"Her father? What was his business here?"

"No more'n a 'alf hour after you'd left, he come. By 'is self this time, and in his Sunday britches. 'Want to see my dattur,' 'e says, quiet like an old bear; and she come tripping over 'erself out of the house to meet him."

"Well?"

"Ye want for to draw at the old tree from the other side," Prudie advised in a voice like a pipe organ. "He won't come down just by playin' maypole with un."

Jud's reply was happily carried away down-wind. Ross walked slowly towards the men, and Demelza came running to meet him, running with an occasional hop as she did when excited.

So absence had made the heart grow fonder and there was a reconciliation between father and daughter at last. No doubt she would want to return home, and the silly malicious gossip would lose its point.

"He won't come down," she said, turning as she reached him and pushing back her mop of hair to gaze at the tree. "He's stronger than we suspicioned."

Silly malicious gossip. Wicked empty dirty gossip. He could have wrung Polly Choake's useless little neck. He might not have got Elizabeth but he had not yet sunk so low as to seduce his own kitchenmaid. Demelza of all wenches, whose dirty, skinny little body he had deluged with cold water when she came not so many months ago it seemed. She had grown since then. He supposed that the gossips of the countryside could not conceive of the son of Joshua living a celibate life. Some women had minds like addle-gutters; if there was no stench they had to create one.

Demelza shifted and glanced at him uneasily, as if aware of his scrutiny. She reminded him of a restive foal, with her long legs and wayward eye. When she was in one of her moods, as Prudie called them, there was no foreseeing what she would do next.

"Your father has been here," he said.

Her face lighted up. "Yes-s-s! I've made en up with him. I'm some happy 'bout that!" Her look changed as she tried to read his expression. "Did I do wrong?"

"Of course not. When does he wish you to return?"

"If 'e'd wanted that, I couldn't have made en up, could I?" She laughed with pleasure, an infectious bubbling laugh. "He don't want for me to go back, for he's wed again. He was marre'd again last Monday! So now he's ready to be friendly an' I don't have to feel every night, what's Brother Luke doing and do Brother Jack miss me. The Widow Chegwidden will look after him betterer than ever I could. Widow Chegwidden is Methody, and she'll look after they all right."

"Oh," said Ross. So he was not to be rid of his charge after all.

"I believe she think to reform Fathur. She believe she can make him tee-tottle. That's where she'll be mistook, I reckon."

The two men, having sawed for a few minutes, solemnly walked away to the end of the rope and began to pull. Ross joined them and added his weight. A perverse spirit within him was glad that he was not to have the easy way of meeting the scurrilous gossip. Let them talk till their tongues dropped out.

But surely Elizabeth wouldn't believe such a story.

He gave an extra hard tug on the rope, and it snapped where it had been knotted to a branch of the tree. He sat down with the other two men. Garrick, who had been out on a private rabbit hunt and missing the fun, came rushing down the valley and gambolled about the three men, licking Jud's face as Jud got to his knees.

"Dang the blathering whelp!" said Jud, spitting.

"It's poor stuff you rely on," said Ross. "Where did you find it?"

"In the library—"

"Twas soggy at one end," said Demelza. "The rest is sound."

She picked up the rope and began to climb the tree like a playful cat.

"Come back!" Ross said.

"She put en up thur first time," said Jud, aiming a kick at Garrick.

"She had no business to. But now—" Ross went nearer. "Demelza! Come down!"

She heard him this time and stopped to peer through the branches, "What's to do? I'm all but there."

"Then tie it at once and come down."

"I'll loop en over at the next branch." She put her foot up and climbed a few feet higher.

"Come down!"

There was an ominous crack.

"Look for yourself!" shouted Jud.

Demelza paused and looked down, more than ever like a cat now which had found its foothold insecure. She gave a squeak as the tree began to go. Ross jumped out of the way.

The tree fell with a drawn-out noise exactly like the tipping of a load of slates. One second it was all noise, and the next there was complete silence.

He ran forward but could not get very near because of the far-flung branches. Right in the middle Demelza suddenly appeared, climbing with pawing movements among the branches. Prudie came flapping across from the stables, shouting, "My ivers! My ivers!"

Jack Cobbledick reached the girl first from his side, but they had to cut away some of the smaller branches before they could get her clothing free. She crawled out laughing. Her hands were scraped and her knees bleeding, the calf of one leg was interlaced with scratches but otherwise she had come to no harm.

Ross glowered at her. "You'll do as I tell you in future. I want no broken limbs here."

Her laughter faded before his glance. "No." She licked the blood off one palm, then glanced down at her frock. "Dear life, I've breeked my dress." She screwed her neck round at an impossible angle to see the back.

"Take the child and give her something for those cuts," Ross said to Prudie. "She's beyond me now."

2

In Trenwith House the evening moved towards its close.

When those guests had gone who were not staying the night, a flatness and lethargy fell on the house. The absence of wind and the glowing ashes of the great log fire made the hall unusually cosy, and five high-backed well-padded chairs supported a semicircle of relatives drinking port.

Upstairs in his great curtained bed Charles Poldark, at the end of his active life, took short and anxious gasps at the vitiated air which was all medical science allowed him. In another room farther along the west passage Geoffrey Charles, at the beginning of his active life, was taking in the nourishment his mother could offer him, with which medical science had not found a means to tamper.

During the last month Elizabeth had known all kinds of new sensations. The birth of her child had been the supreme experience of her life, and looking down now at the crown of Geoffrey Charles's fluffy pale head so close to her own white skin, she was filled with a frightening sense of pride and power and fulfillment. In the instant of his birth her existence was changed; she had accepted, had seized upon a life-long commission of motherhood, a proud and all-absorbing task beside which ordinary duties became void.

After a long period of great weakness, she had suddenly begun to pick up, and during the last week had felt as well as ever in her life. But she was dreamy, indolent, happy to lie a little longer and think about her son and gaze at him and let him sleep in the crook of her arm. It would have distressed her very much to feel that by staying in bed she was putting more responsibility on Verity, but she could not yet summon up the resolve to break the spell of invalidism and move about as before. She could not bear the separation from her son.

This evening she lay in bed and listened to the sound of movement about the old house. During her illness, with her very quick ears she had come to identify every noise; each door made a different sound when opened: the treble and bass creak of unoiled hinges, the click and scrape of different latches, the loose board here and the uncarpeted patch there, so that she could follow the movements of everyone in the west part of the house.

Mrs. Tabb brought her supper, a slice of capon's breast, a coddled egg, and a glass of warm milk, and about nine Verity came in and sat for ten minutes. Verity had got over her disappointment very well, Elizabeth thought. A little quieter, a little more preoccupied with the life of the household. She had wonderful strength of mind and self-reliance. Elizabeth was grateful for her courage. She thought, quite wrongly, that she had very little herself, and admired it in Verity.

Father had opened his eyes once or twice, Verity said, and had been persuaded to swallow a mouthful of brandy. He did not seem to recognize anyone, but he was sleeping more easily and she had hopes. She was going to sit up in case he wanted anything. She would be able to doze in his armchair.

At ten Mrs. Chynoweth came upstairs and insisted on saying good night to her daughter. She talked in so determined a voice about poor Charles that she woke her grandson; then she stayed on talking while he was fed, a thing Elizabeth hated. But at last she was gone and the child asleep, and Elizabeth stretched her limbs in the bed and listened happily to Francis moving about in the room next to hers. Soon he would come in to say good night and then there would be a great stretch of darkness and peace until the early morning.

He came in, stepping with exaggerated care and pausing a moment to peer at the sleeping child, then he sat on the edge of the bed and took Elizabeth's hand.

"My poor wife, neglected as usual," he said. "Your father has been talking for hours without a break on his grievances against Fox and Sheridan, while you have been up here alone missing all the delights of conversation."

In his banter there was a certain amount of true feeling—he had been a little annoyed that she had come to bed so early—but at the sight of her his grudge vanished and his love returned.

For some minutes they talked in low tones, then he leaned forward to kiss her. She offered him her lips unthinkingly, and it was only when his arms went about her that she realized that tonight the friendly little salute would not do.

After a minute he sat back, smiled at her in rather a puzzled way.

"Is something wrong?"

She made a gesture towards the cot. "You'll surely wake him, Francis."

"Oh, he's new fed. He sleeps heavy then. You've told me so yourself."

She said: "How is your father? Is he any better? Somehow one does not feel—"

He shrugged, feeling himself put in the wrong. He was not happy at his father's collapse; he was not indifferent to the outcome; but that was something quite separate. The two conditions existed at the same time. Today he had carried her downstairs, lifting the weight of her, sorry that she was not heavier but happy to feel the substance under her frailty. From that moment the scent of her seemed to cling in his nostrils. Pretending to busy himself with the guests, he had really had eyes for no one else.

She said: "I'm not well tonight. Your father's illness upset me very much."

He struggled with his feelings, trying to be reasonable. Like all proud men, he hated to be rebuffed in this way. It made him feel like a lascivious schoolboy.

"Sometime," he said, "will you feel well again?"

"That's not fair, Francis. It isn't my choosing that I'm not very strong."

"Nor mine." Recollection of his restraint during these months bubbled up in him. That and other things. "I notice you didn't frown or look faint at Ross this afternoon."

Indignation flickered in her eyes. From the very beginning the things Ross had said to her had found excuse and justification in her mind. She had seen nothing of him and was sorry for him; during the months while her baby was coming she had thought a good deal of Ross, of his loneliness, of his pale eyes and wild scarred face. Like all human beings she could not refrain from idly comparing what she had with what she might have had.

"Please leave him out of this," she said.

"How can I?" he rejoined, "when you will not."

"What d'you mean? Ross is nothing to me."

"Perhaps you're beginning to regret it."

"I think you must be drunk, Francis, to speak to me like this."

"A splendid fuss you made of him this afternoon. 'Ross, sit here beside me.' 'Ross, is my baby not pretty?' 'Ross, take a piece of that cake.' Dear, dear, what a to-do."

She said, almost too angry to speak: "You're being utterly childish."

Francis got up. "Ross, I am sure, would not be childish."

She said, deliberately trying to hurt him back: "No, I'm sure he would not."

They stared at each other.

"Well, that's pretty straight, isn't it?" he said, and left her.

He flung into his own room, slamming the door without regard to the sick man or the sleeping child. Then he undressed anyhow, leaving his clothes on the floor, and got into bed.

He lay with his hands behind his head and eyes open for an hour or more before he went to sleep. He was consumed with disappointment and jealousy. All the love and desire in him had turned to bitterness and aridity and desolation.

There was no one to tell him that he was wrong in being jealous of Ross. There was no one to tell him that another and more powerful rival had recently arisen.

There was no one to warn him about Geoffrey Charles.

CHAPTER SEVENTEEN

1

Iɴ ᴛʜᴇ ɢʀᴏᴡᴛʜ ᴏꜰ Dᴇᴍᴇʟᴢᴀ'ꜱ ɪɴᴛᴇʟʟɪɢᴇɴᴄᴇ ᴏɴᴇ ʀᴏᴏᴍ ᴀᴛ Nᴀᴍᴘᴀʀᴀ ᴘʟᴀʏᴇᴅ
a distinctive part. That room was the library.

It had taken her a long time to overcome her distrust of the gaunt and dusty
lumber room, a distrust which derived from the one night she had spent in, or
beside, the great box bed. She had found afterwards that the second door in that
bedroom led through into the library, and some of the fear of that first hour
stuck to the room beyond the second door.

But fear and fascination are yokefellows, oxen out of step but pulling in the
same direction, and once inside the room she was never tired of returning
to it. Since his return Ross had shunned the place because every article in it
brought back memories of his childhood and of his mother and father and
their voices and thoughts and forgotten hopes. For Demelza there were no
memories, only discoveries.

Half the articles she had never seen before. For some of them even her inge-
nious brain could not invent a use, and so long as she could not read, the piled
yellow papers and the little signs and labels scrawled and tied on certain articles
were no help.

There was the figurehead of the *Mary Buckingham,* which had come ashore,
Jud told her, in 1760, three days after Ross was born. She liked tracing the
carving of this with her finger. There was the engraved sea chest from the little
fore-and-aft schooner which had broken its back on Damsel Point, drifted upon
Hendrawna Beach and darkened the sands and sand hills with coal dust for weeks
afterwards. There were samples of tin and copper ore, many of them lacking
labels and all useless anyhow. There were spare strips of canvas for patching sails,
and four ironbound chests at whose contents she could only guess. There was

a grandfather's clock with some of its inside missing—she spent hours over this with the weights and wheels, trying to discover how it could have worked.

There was a coat of mail armour, terribly rusty and antique, two rag dolls and a homemade rocking horse, six or seven useless muskets, a spinet which had once belonged to Grace, two French snuffboxes and a music box, a roll of moth-eaten tapestry from some other ship, a miner's pick and shovel, a storm lantern, a half keg of blasting powder, a sketch map pinned on the wall of the extent of Grambler workings in 1765.

Of all the discoveries, the most exciting to her were the spinet and the music box. One day, after an hour's tinkering, she persuaded the music box to work, and it played two thin trembling minuets. In excitement and triumph she danced all round the instrument on one leg, and Garrick, thinking this a new game, jumped round too and bit a piece out of her skirt. Then when the music was over she hurriedly went and hid in a corner lest someone should have heard it and come and find them there. A greater discovery was the spinet, but this had the drawback that she could not make it play a tune. Once or twice when she was sure there was no one about she ventured to try, and the sounds fascinated her even when they were discordant. She found herself perversely taken with such sounds and wanting to hear them again and again. One day she discovered that the farther her fingers moved to the right the thinner became the sound, and this seemed to give the puzzle away. She felt it would be much simpler to conjure tunes out of this than to make sense of the horrible spidery trails that people called writing.

2

Charles Poldark made an obstinate recovery from his heart attack, but was confined to the house for the rest of the winter. He still put on weight. Soon it was all he could do to struggle downstairs in the afternoon and sit panting and eruptive and purple before the parlour fire. There he would remain scarcely speaking for hours, while Aunt Agatha worked the spinning wheel or read the Bible to herself in an audible undertone. Sometimes in the evenings he would talk to Francis, asking him questions about the mine, or he would tap a mild accompaniment on the arm of his chair when Elizabeth played an air on the harp. He seldom spoke to Verity except to complain that something was not to his liking, and usually dozed off and snored in his chair before he would allow himself to be supported up to bed.

Jinny Carter's child was born in March. Like Elizabeth's child, it was a boy; and he was christened, by permission, Benjamin Ross.

A fortnight after the christening Ross had an unexpected visitor; Eli Clemmow had walked in the rain all the way from Truro. Ross had not seen him for ten years, but he instantly recognized his loping walk.

Unlike his elder brother, Eli was built on a narrow economical scale, with a suggestion of the Mongol in his features. When he spoke he slopped and slurred with his teeth as if his lips were waves washing over half-tide rocks.

To begin with he was ingratiating, asking about his brother's disappearance, enquiring if no trace at all had been found. Then he was complacent, mentioning with satisfaction the good position he had got. Personal servant to a lawyer; a pound a month and all found; snug little room, light work, drop of toddy every Saturday night. Later, when he brought up the question of his brother's belongings, and Ross said candidly that he was welcome to what he found in the cottage but doubted if there was anything worth the effort of carrying away, Eli's eyes betrayed the malice which had all the time been hiding away behind his obsequious manner.

"No doubt," he said, sucking with his lips, "all the neighbours will have took anything of value."

"We don't encourage thieves," Ross observed. "If you want to make remarks of that kind, make them to the people you accuse."

"Well," said Eli, blinking, "I shouldn't be saying more'n I've the right if I said Brother 'ad been drove out of his home by lying tongues."

"Your brother left his home because he couldn't learn to control his appetites."

"And did 'e do anything?"

"Anything?"

"Anything wrong."

"We were able to prevent that."

"Yes, but he was drove out of his 'ome fur doing nothing at all, and mebbe starved to death. Even the law don't say ye can punish a man before 'e do do a wrong."

"He was not driven from his home, man."

Eli fingered his cap. "Of course 'tis common knowledge that ye've always had a down on we. You and father. Your father had Reuben put in the stocks for next to nought. 'Tis 'ard not to remember that."

"You're fortunate," Ross said, "not to receive something else to remember. I give you five minutes to be off my land."

Eli swallowed something and sucked again. "Why, sur, ye just said I could go down fur to take anything of Brother's away that's worth the carrying. Ye've just said so. That be common justice."

"I don't interfere with the lives of my tenants unless they interfere with mine. Go to the cottage and take what you choose. Then go back to Truro and stay there, for you're not welcome in this district."

Eli Clemmow's eyes gleamed and he seemed about to say more, but he changed his mind and left the house without a word.

So it came about that Jinny Carter, nursing her baby by the upstairs window, saw the man come over the hill in the rain with his slow dipping stride and go into the next cottage. He was inside for about half an hour, and then she saw him leave with one or two articles under his arm.

What she did not see was the thoughtful expression on his sly Mongolian face. To one of Eli's peculiar perceptions it was clear that the cottage had been inhabited by someone less than a week ago.

3

That night the wind got up with violence and blew unabated through the following day. The next night about nine news came that a ship was in the bay and drifting ashore between Nampara and Sawle.

Demelza had spent most of the afternoon as she was coming to spend many afternoons when heavy rain stopped all but the most urgent outdoor work. Had Prudie been of an industrious turn of mind she would have taught the girl something more than the neat but primitive sewing she now understood; and there was weaving and spinning to learn, the drying and dipping of rushes for making rushlights. But these things were beyond Prudie's idea of housecraft. When work was inescapable she did it, but any excuse was good enough to sit down and take off her slippers and brew a dish of tea. So soon after dinner Demelza had sneaked off to the library.

And this afternoon by the purest chance she made the greatest discovery of all. Just as a premature dusk was falling she found that one of the big chests was not really locked but only held by a trick clasp. She lifted the lid and found the box full of clothing. There were dresses and scarves, three-cornered hats and fur-lined gloves, a periwig and red and blue stockings, a pair of lady's green lace slippers with blue heels. There was a muslin neck scarf and an *ostrich feather*. There was a bottle with liquid that smelt of gin, the only intoxicant she knew, and another half full of scent.

Although she had already stayed longer than usual, she could not bring herself to leave, and went over and over the velvet and the lace and the silk, stroking it and shaking out the crumbs of dry lavender. She couldn't put down the slippers with the lace and the blue heels; they were too dainty to be real. The ostrich feather she sniffed and pressed against her cheek. Then she tried it round her neck and put on a fur hat and pirouetted up and down on her toes, pretending to be a great lady, with Garrick crawling at her heels.

With darkness closing in on her she lived in a dream, until she woke and found she could no longer see and was alone in the sombre room with the draught blowing cold and rain seeping through the shutters.

Frightened, she rushed to the box, pushed in everything she could find and shut the lid, and slipped through the big bedroom and thence to the kitchen.

Prudie had had to light the candles, and delivered an ill-tempered lecture, which Demelza, not yet anxious to go to bed, adroitly steered round until it became a continuation of the story of Prudie's life. Hence the girl had only just gone upstairs and was not asleep when Jim Carter and Nick Vigus called in to say there was a ship in distress. When Ross, disturbed from his book, made ready to go with them he found Demelza, a kerchief about her hair and two old sacks on her shoulders, waiting to ask that she might go too.

"You're better in bed," Ross said. "But as you please if you want the wetting."

They set out, Jud carrying a strong rope in case there should be a chance of giving help.

The night was so black as to be sightless. Out of the shelter of the house the wind struck a blow that was not temporary but enduring. They tried to overcome it, taking steps forward that should have been an advance. One of the storm lanterns went out, the other swayed and flickered, thrusting out a hoop of light which danced along with them clownlike and showed their heavy boots squelching across the dripping grass. Once or twice the force of the wind was so great that they were all brought to a stop, and Demelza, struggling voicelessly beside them, had to clutch Jim Carter's arm to hold her ground.

As they neared the cliff top the rain came again, drenching them in a few seconds, splashing, into their mouths and eyes. They had to turn their backs and crouch behind a hedge until it was over.

There were people at the edge of the cliff. Lanterns winked here and there like glowworms. Below them, about a hundred feet down, more lights gleamed. They went down a narrow path until they came to a group of people on a broad ledge all staring out to sea.

Before they could learn much a figure appeared from the lower path, coming out of the darkness like a demon out of a pit. It was Pally Rogers from Sawle, naked and dripping with his hairy body and great spade beard.

"It's no manner of good," he shouted. "They struck not fifteen minutes since—" The wind bore his voice away. "If they was farther in, we could get them a rope." He began to pull on his breeches.

"Have you tried to get out to them?" Ross shouted.

"Three of us 'ave tried to swim. The Lord was agin the venture. She'll not last long now. Caught beam on she be, wi' water spouting over 'er. By daylight she'll be driftwood."

"Any of the crew come ashore?"

"Two. But the Lord God had taken their souls. Five more there'll be afore sun-up."

Nick Vigus sidled between them, and a gleam from the lantern showed up his shining pink face with its toothless pockmarked innocence. "What cargo do she carry?"

Pally Rogers screwed the water out of his beard. "Taper and wool from Padstow they do say."

Ross left them and with Jud went farther down the cliff. Not until they were near the bottom did he find that Demelza had followed.

Here they were sheltered from the wind, but every few seconds a wave would hit a ridge of rock and deluge them in spray. The tide was coming in. Below them, on the last few square feet of sand, was a cluster of lanterns where men still sat waiting for any slackening of the sea to risk their lives and swim to the wreck. From here it was possible to make out a dark lump which might have been a rock but which they knew was not. There were no lights on it and no sign that anyone still lived.

Ross slipped on the greasy path, and Jim Carter grasped his arm.

Ross thanked him. "There's nothing to be done here," he muttered.

"What d'you say, sir?"

"There's nothing to be done here."

"No, sir, I think I'll be getting back. Jinny may be getting narvous."

"There's another un coming in," screamed an old woman near by. "See 'im there, bobbin' 'bout like a cork. Head first, then tail. There'll be a pretty find for the morning tide! There'll be driftwood for ee!"

A flurry of spray fell on them like a swarm of insects.

"Take this girl back with you," Ross said.

Demelza opened her mouth to protest, but wind and spray came together and took her breath.

Ross watched them climbing until they were out of sight, then went down to join the little group of lanterns on the sand.

CHAPTER EIGHTEEN

1

J INNY CARTER STIRRED IN HER BED. SHE HAD BEEN DREAMING, HALF DREAMING that she was baking starry-gazey pie, and all the fishes had suddenly blinked their eyes and changed into babies and begun to cry. She was wide awake now but the cry was still in her ears. She sat up and listened for her own baby in its wooden box that Jim had made, but there was no sound at all. It must have been her imagination working on the beat of the rain against the tight-closed shutters, on the howl of the gale as it whirled past the cottages and roared inland.

Why had Jim left his comfortable bed and gone out into the wild night just in the hope of picking up some bit of wreckage? She had asked him not to go, but he had taken no notice. That was the way: always she asked him not to go, and always he made an excuse and went. Two or three nights every week he would be absent—to return in the small hours with a pheasant or a plump partridge under his arm.

He had changed a good deal these last few months. It had really begun in January. One week he had been away from the mine and laid up, cough, cough, cough. The next he had gone out two nights with Nick Vigus and returned with food for her that the loss of his earnings would have made impossible. It was no good to tell him she would rather do without the food any number of times over than that he should be caught breaking the law. He didn't see it that way and was hurt and disappointed if she didn't seem delighted.

She slid out of bed with a shiver and went to the shutters. She made no effort to open them, or the rain would have burst full into the room; but through a crack where the rain was trickling she could tell that the night was as dark as ever.

She fancied there was a noise in the room below. All the woodwork in the cottage creaked and stirred under the strain. She would be glad when Jim was back.

Almost she would have been glad if Benjy had cried, for then there would have been the excuse to take him into her own bed for comfort and to feel the clutch of his tiny predatory hands. But the child slept.

She slipped back into bed and pulled the blanket up to her nose. Jim's bad habits were really all Nick Vigus's fault. He was the bad influence, with his evil baby face. He put things to Jim that Jim would never have thought of, ideas about property and the right to take food for one's belly that was not one's own. Of course Nick used such arguments only as an excuse for any of his sly doings that took him outside the law. But Jim accepted them seriously, that was the trouble. He would never have thought of robbing to feed himself, but he was beginning to feel himself in the right in stealing to feed his family.

A heavy squall buffeted against the shutter; it was as if an enormous man was leaning against the house and trying to push it over. She dozed for a minute, dreaming of a happy life when the food was plentiful for all and children grew up laughing, without the need to work as soon as they could walk. Then she started into wakefulness, aware that there was a light somewhere. She saw three or four nicks coming through the floor and felt a warm pleasure that Jim was home. She thought of going down to see what news he brought to be back so early, but the warmth of her bed and the draughtiness of the room robbed her of the will. She dozed again and then was wakened by the noise of something falling in the room below.

Jim had perhaps brought back some prize and was stacking it in a corner. That was why he had returned so soon. Strange there was no one with him, no voices of Nick or her father. Perhaps they had stayed on. But the best chance of salvage would come with the morning light. She hoped they had all been careful. It was less than two years since Bob Tregea had been drowned trying to get a line out to a ship—and left a widow and young children.

Jim did not call up to her. Of course he would think her asleep. She opened her mouth to call down, and as she did so suddenly wondered with an unpleasant prickly sensation round her heart if the man below really was Jim.

Some heavy movement had induced the doubt. Jim was so light on his feet. Now she sat up in bed and listened.

If it was Jim, then he was searching for something, clumsily, drunkenly. But Jim had touched no more than a mug of light ale since he was married. She waited, and an idea which had blown from somewhere into her mind suddenly germinated and grew.

There was only one man, it seemed to her, who would come in like this while Jim was away, who would move about so clumsily, who might at any moment come creeping up the ladder—and he had disappeared months ago, was thought dead. Nothing had been seen of him for so long that the cloud in her mind had gone.

She crouched there and listened to the gale and to the movements of the visitor. She didn't move an inch for fear of making a noise. It was as if her stomach and her lungs were slowly becoming frozen. She waited. Perhaps if there was no sound he would go away. Perhaps he would not come up, to find her here alone. Perhaps very soon Jim would really be back.

Or perhaps he was still down there by the rocks watching the efforts made to save men he had never seen before, while at home his wife lay like a stone in bed and a half-starved lustful madman lumbered about the room below.

And the child began to cry.

The fumbling below stopped. Jinny tried to get out of bed, but she had lost every bone in her body; she couldn't move and she couldn't swallow. The child stopped, began again more confidently: a thin wail competing against the buffeting of the wind.

She was out of bed at last, had picked him up, almost dropping him from her fumbling hasty hands.

The light below quivered and winked. There was a creak on the ladder.

She no longer had words to pray, nor resources to turn and hide. She stood at the side of the bed, her back against the wall, the child stirring feebly in her tightened arms, while the trap door slowly lifted.

She knew then, as soon as she saw the hand grasping the knotted wood of the floor, that her instinct had not been mistaken, that now she had to face something she had never known before.

2

By the light of the candle he carried it was possible to see the changes that months of living in lonely caves had brought. The flesh had shrunk from face and arms. He was in rags and barefoot, his beard and hair straggling and wet as if he had come from some underwater cave. Yet it was the same Reuben Clemmow she had always known, with the pale self-centred eyes and the uncertain mouth and the white creases in the sun-reddened face.

She fought down a wave of illness and stared at him.

"Where's my fry pan?" he said. "Stole my fry pan."

The child in her arms wriggled and gasped for breath and began to cry again.

Reuben climbed up the steps, and the trap door slammed back into place. For the first time he saw the bundle that she clutched. Recognition of her was slow in dawning. When it came, all the rest came with it, remembrance of the injury done him, of why he was forced to shun people and frequent his cottage only at night, of the ten-month-old wound still festering in his side, of his lust for her, of his hatred for the man that had got her this squealing infant, Ross Poldark.

"Lily," he muttered. "White lily... sin—"

He had been so long apart from people that he had lost the faculty of making them understand. Speech was for him alone.

He straightened himself awkwardly, for the muscles had contracted about the wound.

Jinny was praying again.

He took a step forward. "Pure Lily—" he said, and then something in the girl's attitude sent his brain clicking over upon an old forgotten rhythm of his childhood. "Why standest thou so far off an' hidest thy face in the needful time o' trouble. The ungodly for 'is own lust doth persecute; let 'im be taken in the crafty wiliness that they 'ave imagined. For the ungodly'th made a boast of his heart's desire, an' speaketh good of the covetous." He took out his knife, an old trapper's knife, with the blade worn down to about four inches from years of sharpening and use. In the months of isolation desire for her had become confused with revenge. In lust there is always conquest and destruction.

The candle began to tremble and he put it on the floor, where the draught blew the light in gusts about the room and sweated tallow on the boards. "He sittest lurkin' in the thievish corners o' the streets, and privily in 'is lurkin' dens doth 'e murder the innocent."

Jinny lost her head and began to scream. Her voice went up and up.

As he took another step forward, she forced her legs to move; she was halfway across the bed when Reuben caught her and stabbed at the child; she partly parried the blow, but the knife came away red.

The girl's scream changed its note, became more animal in sound. Reuben stared at the knife with passionate interest, then recovered himself as she reached the trap door. She turned as he came rushing up. He stabbed at her this time and felt the knife go into her. Then inside him all that had been tense and hard and burning suddenly ran away through his veins: he dropped the knife and watched her fall.

An extra gust of wind blew the candle out.

He shouted and groped for the trap door. His foot slipped on something greasy and his hand touched a woman's hair. He recoiled and screamed, banged on the boarding of the room: but he was shut in here forever with the horror he had created.

He pulled himself upwards by the bed, blundered across the room, and found the shutters of the window. He fought, shouting, with these but could not find the bolt. Then he thrust forward his whole weight and the fastenings gave way before him. With a sense of breaking from a prison, he fell forward out of the window, out of the prison, out of life, upon the cobbles below.

BOOK TWO

APRIL–MAY 1787

CHAPTER ONE

R OUND THE DINING TABLE OF THE PARLOUR OF NAMPARA HOUSE ONE WINDY afternoon in 1787 six gentlemen were seated.

They had dined and wined well, off part of a large cod, a chine of mutton, a chicken pie, some pigeons, and a fillet of veal with roasted sweetbreads; apricot tart, a dish of cream, and almonds and raisins. Mr. Horace Treneglos of Mingoose, Mr. Renfrew from St. Ann's, Dr. Choake from Sawle, Captain Henshawe from Grambler, Mr. Nathaniel Pearce the notary from Truro, and their host, Captain Poldark.

They had met to approve the preliminary work which had been undertaken at Wheal Leisure, and to decide whether good gold should be risked by them all with the aim of raising copper. It was an important occasion which had lured Mr. Treneglos from his Greek, Dr. Choake from the hunting field, and Mr. Pearce from his gouty fireside.

"Well," said Mr. Treneglos, who from his position and seniority occupied the head of the table, "well, I'm not going to go against expert advice. We've been hummin' and ha'ing for more'n two years; and if Captain Henshawe says we should begin, well, damme, it's his money being risked as well as mine, and he's the one as did ought to know!"

There was a murmur of assent and some qualifying grunts. Mr. Treneglos put a hand behind his ear to gather up the crumbs of comment.

Dr. Choake coughed. "Naturally we all defer to Captain Henshawe in his experience of working mines. But the success of this venture does not depend on the working of the lode; otherwise, we should have begun a twelvemonth since. It is conditions in the trade which must determine our course. Now only last week we had occasion to attend upon a patient in Redruth who was suffering with an imposthume. In fact he was not our patient but Dr. Pryce called us in for further advice. The poor fellow was far gone when I arrived at his considerable house, which had a fine drive and a marble staircase and other evidences of good taste and the means to gratify it; but between us we were able to alleviate the condition.

"This gentleman was a shareholder in Dolly Koath Mine, and he let fall the information that it had been decided to close all the lower levels."

There was silence.

Mr. Pearce, purple and smiling, said: "Well now, in fact I heard much the same thing; I heard it only last week." He stopped a moment to scratch under his wig, and Dr. Choake said:

"If the largest copper mine in the world is reducing its work, what chance has our small venture?"

"That doesn't follow if our overheads are smaller," said Ross, who was at the other end of the table, his bony distinguished face a shade flushed with what he had eaten and drunk. By growing longer side pieces he had partly hidden his scar, but one end of it still showed as a paler brown line across his cheek.

"The price of copper may fall still lower," said Dr. Choake.

"What's that you say? What's that?" asked Mr. Treneglos. "I couldn't hear him," he explained to himself. "I wish he'd speak up."

Choake spoke up.

"Or it may equally well rise," was the reply.

"I look at it this way, gentlemen," said Ross. He drew at his long pipe. "The moment is, on the face of it, a bad one for the starting of ventures large or small. But there are points in our favour which must be borne in mind. Supply and demand rule the prices of ore. Now two large mines have closed this year, and any number of small ones. Dol Koath may soon follow Wheal Reath and Wheal Fortune. This will halve the output of the Cornish industry, so supply to the markets will be less and the price of copper should rise."

"Hear, hear," said Captain Henshawe.

"I agree wi' Captain Poldark," said Mr. Renfrew, speaking for the first time. Mr. Renfrew was a mine chandler from St. Ann's, and therefore had a double interest in this venture; but so far he had been overawed by the presence of so many gentlemen at the meeting.

The blue-eyed Henshawe had no such diffidence. "Our costs wouldn't be one half what Wheal Reath's was, ton for ton."

"What I should like to know," said Mr. Pearce deprecatingly, "speaking of course for the parties I represent, Mrs. Jacqueline Trenwith and Mr. Aukett, as well as for myself, is what figure we should have to obtain for our crude ore in order to show a profit at all. What do you say to that?"

Captain Henshawe picked his teeth. "It is so much a lottery what the blocks do fetch. We all know that the copper companies are out to get the stuff dirt cheap."

Ross said: "If we get nine pounds a ton, we shall come to no harm."

"Well," said Mr. Treneglos, "let's see your plan on paper. Where's the map of the old workings? We can follow better then."

Henshawe rose and brought over a big roll of parchment, but Ross stopped him.

"We'll have the table clear for this." He rang a hand bell, and Prudie came in followed by Demelza.

This was Demelza's first appearance, and she was the object of a number of curious glances. Everyone, except Mr. Treneglos, who lived in his own private world, knew something of her history and of the rumours which surrounded her presence here. The talk was old talk now, but scandal died hard when its cause was not removed.

They saw a girl of just seventeen, tall, with dark untidy hair and big dark eyes which had a disconcerting glint in them when they happened to meet your own. The glint suggested unusual vitality and a latent mettlesomeness; otherwise, there was nothing special to remark.

Mr. Renfrew peered at her with puckered astigmatic eyes, and Mr. Pearce, while keeping his gouty feet ostentatiously out of danger, ventured to raise his quizzing glass when he thought Ross was not looking. Then Mr. Treneglos eased off the top button of his breeches, and they bent to peer over the map which Captain Henshawe was unrolling on the table.

"Now," said Ross. "Here we have the old workings of Wheal Leisure and the direction of the tin-bearing lode." He went on to explain the situation, the angle of the shafts to be sunk, and the adits which would be driven in from the face of Leisure Cliff to unwater the mine.

"What's this here?" Mr. Treneglos put a stubby, snuff-stained finger on a corner of the map.

"That's the limit of the workings of Trevorgie Mine so far as it is known," said Ross. "All accurate maps have been lost. These workings were old when my great-grandfather came to Trenwith."

"Um," said Mr. Treneglos. "They knew what they was about in those days. Yes," he agreed *sotto voce,* "they knew what they was about."

"What do you mean, sir?" enquired Mr. Renfrew.

"What do I what? Well, damme, if the old men was working tin here and here they was working the back of Leisure lode before it was discovered on my land. That's what I mean."

"I think he's right," said Henshawe, with a sudden quickening of interest.

"In what way does that assist us?" asked Mr. Pearce, scratching himself.

"It only means," Ross said, "that the old men would not have driven all this way under such conditions for nothing. It was their custom to avoid all but the shallowest underground work. They had to. If they went this far, they must have found some good return as they went along."

"Think you it is all one great lode, eh?" said Mr. Treneglos. "Could it run so far, Henshawe? Has any been known to run so far?"

"We don't know and shan't know, sir. Looks to me as if they was following tin and struck copper. That's how it seems to me. It is very feasible."

"I've a very great respect for the ancients," said Mr. Treneglos, opening his snuffbox. "Look at Xenophanes. Look at Plotinus. Look at Democritus. They were wiser than we. It is no disgrace to follow where they led. What will it cost us, dear boy?"

Ross exchanged a glance with Henshawe.

"I am willing at the outset to be manager and head purser without payment; and Captain Henshawe will supervise the beginnings at a nominal salary. Mr. Renfrew will supply us with most of the gear and tackle at the lowest margin of profit to himself. And I have arranged for Pascoe's Bank to honour our drafts up to three hundred guineas for the buying of winches and other heavy equipment. Fifty guineas each would cover the expense of the first three months."

There was a moment's silence, and Ross watched their faces with a slight cynical lift of his eyebrow. He had cut down the opening figure to the lowest possible, knowing that a big demand would result in another stalemate.

"Eight fives," said Mr. Treneglos. "And three from Pascoe's, that's seven in all. Seven hundred on an outlay of fifty each seems very reasonable to me, what? Expected a hundred at least," he added to himself. "Quite expected a hundred."

"That's only a first outlay," said Choake. "That's only the first three months."

"All the same it is very reasonable, gentlemen," said Mr. Renfrew. "These are expensive days. You could hardly expect to become interested in a gainful venture for less."

"Quite true," said Mr. Treneglos. "Well, then, I'm for starting right away. Decide by a show of hands, what?"

"This loan from Pascoe's Bank," said Dr. Choake heavily. "That means we should put all our business through them? But what's wrong with Warleggan's? Might we not get better terms from them? George Warleggan is a personal friend of ours."

Mr. Pearce said: "A matter I was about to raise myself, sir. Now if—"

"George Warleggan is a friend of mine too," Ross said. "But I don't think friendship should come into a matter of business."

"Not if it be detrimental to the business, no," said the doctor. "But Warleggan's is the biggest bank in the county. And the most up-to-date. Pascoe's has old-fashioned ideas. Pascoe's has not advanced in forty years. I knew Harris Pascoe when he was a boy. He's a stick-in-the-mire and always has been."

Mr. Pearce said: "My clients, I b'lieve, quite understood it would be Warleggan's Bank."

Ross filled his pipe.

Mr. Treneglos unfastened another button of his breeches. "Nay, one bank's the same as another to me. So long as it's sound, eh? That's the point, eh? You had a reason for going to Pascoe's, Ross, I suppose, what?"

"There is no grudge between the Warleggans and me, father or son. But as a banking partnership they own too many mines already. I do not wish them to come to own Wheal Leisure."

Choake bent his heavy eyebrows. "I should not care to let the Warleggans hear you say that."

"Nonsense. I say nothing that everyone does not know. Between them and their puppet companies they own a dozen mines outright and have large interests in a dozen others, including Grambler and Wheal Plenty. If they chose to close Grambler tomorrow they would do so, as they have closed Wheal Reath. There is nothing underhand in that. But if Wheal Leisure is opened, then I prefer to keep such decisions in the hands of the venturers. Big concerns are dangerous friends for the small man."

"I quite agree, gentlemen," Mr. Renfrew concurred nervously. "There was bad feeling in St. Ann's about the closing of Wheal Reath. We know it was not an economical mine to maintain, but that does not help the shareholders who have lost their money, nor the two hundred miners who have lost their work. But it helps Wheal Plenty to offer only starvation wages, and it gives young Mr. Warleggan a chance of showing a tidy profit!"

The issue had touched some sore point in Mr. Renfrew's memory. A wrangle broke out, with everybody talking at once.

Mr. Treneglos banged on the table with his glass. "Put it to the vote," he shouted. "It is the only sensible way. But first the mine. Let's have the faint-hearts declare themselves afore we go any further."

The vote was taken and all were for opening.

"Good! Splendid!" said Mr. Treneglos. "We're getting on at last. Now this question of the bank, eh? Those in favour of Pascoe's—"

Renfrew, Henshawe, Treneglos, and Ross were for Pascoe's; Choake and Pearce for Warleggan's. As Pearce carried with him the votes of his nominees, the voting was even.

"Damme," mumbled Mr. Treneglos. "I knew that lawyer fellow would baulk us again." Mr. Pearce could not miss hearing this and tried hard to be offended.

But secretly he was looking for a share in Mr. Treneglos's estate business; and finding Mr. Treneglos firm on his course, he spent the next ten minutes tacking round to the old man's point of view.

Left alone, Choake gave in, and the absent Warleggans were defeated. Ross knew their adventure was so small as to be hardly worth the attention of a large banking firm, but that they had received it he was in no doubt George would be annoyed.

Now that the chief hurdles had been taken, the rest of the business went through quickly enough. Captain Henshawe stretched his big legs, got up and, with a nod from Ross, passed the decanter round the table.

"I don't doubt you'll pardon the liberty, gentlemen. We've sat round this table as equals, and we're equal partners in the venture. Nay, though I'm the poorest, my share stands biggest in the general pool for my reputation's there as well as my fifty guineas. So here's a toast. Wheal Leisure."

The others rose and clinked their glasses.

"Wheal Leisure!"

"Wheal Leisure."

"Wheal Leisure!"

They drained their glasses.

In the kitchen Jud, who had been whittling a piece of wood and humming his favourite tune, raised his head and spat expertly across the table into the fire.

"Something's moving at last. Dang me if it don't sound like they're going to open the blatherin' mine after all."

"Dirty ole black worm," said Prudie. "You nearly spit in the stew pot that time."

CHAPTER TWO

1

WHEN HIS NEW PARTNERS HAD GONE, ROSS LEFT THE HOUSE AND STROLLED across his land towards the site of his mine. He did not go down to the beach and across the sand hills, but made a semicircular detour which kept to the high ground. Wheal Leisure was on the first promontory midway along Hendrawna Beach, where the sand hills gave place to rock.

There was as yet little to see. Two shallow tunnels slanting down and a number of trenches, all made by the old men; a new tunnel with a ladder, and a few turfs cut to show where the new work was to be. Rabbits dodged and dipped their tails as he moved about; a curlew cried; a strong wind murmured through the coarse grass. Little to see, but by the end of the summer the view would be changed.

During the years of planning and frustration, this idea had grown on him until it took first interest in his mind. The venture would have been started eighteen months ago if it had not been for Mr. Pearce, who felt a natural care for the safety of his nominees' money, and the hesitances and pessimism of Choake, whom Ross was now sorry to have brought in. All the others were gamblers, ready and eager to take a chance. Despite all the fine arguments today, there was really no improvement in prospects over a year ago; but old Mr. Treneglos had happened to be in boisterous spirits and had carried the others with him. So the gamblers had at last had their way. The future would decide the rest.

He stared across to where the chimneys of Mellin Cottages were just visible in the valley.

He would be able to help Jim Carter now, help him without suspicion of charity, which the boy would never accept. As assistant purser at the mine, he could be brought in to relieve Ross of some of the supervision, and later, when he had learned to read and write, there was no reason why he shouldn't be paid forty or more shillings a month. It would help both Jim and Jinny to forget the tragedy of two years ago.

Ross began to pace out again the position where the first shaft would be sunk. The irony of that tragedy at Mellin Cottages was that physically, actually, it could have been so much worse. In the end only one life had been lost, that of Reuben Clemmow himself. The baby Benjamin Ross had suffered a cut on the head and cheek, which would never be more than a minor disfigurement, and Jinny had escaped with a stab which closely missed her heart. She had been in bed for weeks, with internal bleeding, which her mother, eventually forgetting her Methody scruples, swore she cured with a lock of her grandmother's hair. But that was long ago, and Jinny was well and had had a baby girl, Mary, since then.

It could have been so much worse. But just as baby Benjamin would always show the marks of the attack on his face, so it seemed Jinny was to carry them on her spirit. She had become listless, silent, unpredictable of mood. Even Jim was often not sure what she was thinking. When Jim was at the mine, her mother would trot over and stay for an hour, amiably prattling about the happenings of the day. Then she would kiss her daughter and trot the few steps back to her own kitchen with an uneasy feeling that Jinny had not been listening at all.

Jim too had lost his buoyancy because of the sense of guilt that he could not be rid of. He would never forget the moment when he came back to find Reuben Clemmow dying on his doorstep, and the entry into his own bedroom with his child crying in the darkness and a weight that had to be pushed off the trap door. He could not escape from the fact that had he not gone out the tragedy would not have happened. He gave up his association with Nick Vigus, and no more pheasants made their appearance in his kitchen.

In fact these were no longer needed, for the whole neighbourhood took their case to heart. A public subscription was raised and all manner of presents were sent them, so that while Jinny was laid up and for some time afterwards they enjoyed a bounty they had never known before. But it was a bounty Jim privately disliked, and he was relieved when it tapered off. His pitch at Grambler was yielding good results and they had no need of charity. What they had need of was something which would wipe out the memory of that night.

Ross finished his pacing and stared down at the sandy earth. The eternal enigma of the prospector faced him: whether this acre of ground held under its surface riches or frustration. Time and work and patience…

He grunted and looked up at the sky, which promised rain. Well, if the worst came to the worst, they would be giving a few miners the chance of feeding their families. Conditions, everyone agreed, could hardly be worse throughout the county, or indeed throughout the country as a whole.

2

Conditions could hardly be worse, they thought, with the 3 percents at fifty-six

The whole nation felt down in the mouth after the unequal struggle against France and Holland and Spain, the perverse unbrotherly war with America, and the threat of further enemies in the north. It was a spiritual as well as a material slough. Twenty-five years ago she had been leader of the world, and the fall had been all the greater. Peace had come at last, but the country was too weary to throw off the effects of war.

A tenacious prime minister, at twenty-seven, was holding his uneasy position in the face of all the coalitions to upset him; but the coalitions had hopes. Money had to be found, even for peace and reform; taxes had gone up 20 percent in five years and the new ones were dangerously unpopular. Land tax, house tax, servants' tax, window tax. Horses and hats, bricks and tiles, linen and calicoes. Another impost on candles hit directly at the poor. Last winter the fishermen of Fowey had saved their families from starvation by feeding them on limpets.

It would take fifty years, some people said, before things righted themselves.

Even in America, Ross had been told, disillusion was no less. The United States had so far been united only in a dislike for overlordship, and with that gone and all the afterwar problems in train, they seemed on the point of breaking up into local self-governing republics quarrelling endlessly among themselves like the cities of medieval Italy. Frederick of Prussia, tapping away with gouty fingers on his piano in the Sans Souci Palace at Potsdam, had been heard to say that the country was so unwieldy that now they had got rid of George the Third the only solution was to set up a king of their own. The remark even found its way into the fastnesses of Cornish society.

Other things too the Cornish knew, or sensed, with their constant illicit traffic between the French ports and their own. England might be down in the mouth, but things were even worse in Europe. Strange whiffs of a volcanic unrest came to them from time to time from across the Channel. Dislike for an old enemy as much as idealism for a new friend had tempted France to pour out her gold and men to help American freedom. Now she found herself with an extra war debt of fourteen hundred million livres and a knowledge of the theory and practice of revolution bred in the minds and blood of her thinkers and soldiers. The crust of the European despotisms was being weakened at its weakest spot.

In two years Ross had seen little of his own family and class. What he had overheard in the library on the day of Geoffrey Charles's christening had filled him with contempt for them, and though he would not have admitted to being influenced one way or the other by Polly Choake's gossip, an awareness of their clacking tongues made him dislike the idea of going among them. Monthly, out of common courtesy, he went to enquire after the invalid Charles, who refused either to die or get better, but when he found company there, his conversation didn't touch on the popular subjects. He was not as concerned as they about the return of Maria Fitzherbert from the Continent or the scandal of the Queen of France's necklace. There were families in the district without enough bread and potatoes to keep them alive, and he wanted these families to be given gifts in kind, so that the epidemics of December and January should not have such easy prey.

His listeners felt uncomfortable when he was speaking, and resentful when he had finished. Many of them were hard hit themselves by the slump in mining and the increased taxation. Many were helping those hard cases with which they came in contact, and if that barely touched the fringe of the distress they did not see that Ross was doing any more. What they were not prepared to accept was that they had any sort of liability for the hardships of the day, or that laws could be framed to offer some less soul-destroying form of relief than the poorhouse and the parish cart. Even Francis could not see it. Ross felt like another Jack Tripp preaching reform from an empty tub.

He topped the crest of the hill on the way home and saw Demelza coming to meet him. Garrick was trotting at her heels like a small Shetland pony.

She hopped from time to time as she came up.

"Jud d' tell me," she said, "that the mine is to open at last!"

"Just as soon as we can hire the men and buy the tackle."

"Hooray! Garrick, go down. I'm real pleased 'bout that. We was all disappointed last year when we thought twas all set, sur. Garrick, be quiet. Will it be as big as Grambler?"

"Not yet." He was amused at her excitement. "Quite a little mine to begin."

"I'm sure twill soon be a big un wi' great chimney stacks and things."

They walked down the hill together. Normally he took her very much for granted, but the interest of the others today made him steal a sidelong glance at her now. A well-grown and developing girl, barely recognizable as the scrawny half-starved urchin he had swilled under the pump.

More changes had come about during the last year. Demelza was now a sort of general housekeeper. Prudie was far too indolent to wish to manage anything if there was a way out of it. Her leg had given trouble two or three times more, and when she came downstairs again, it was easier to potter about the kitchen brewing tea for herself and doing a little light work than contriving the meals and cooking them, which Demelza so much seemed to enjoy. The burden was off her shoulders; Demelza never dictated, and was quite willing to continue doing her own work as well, so what was there to object to in that?

Apart from one violent quarrel, life in the kitchen was more peaceful than when Jud and Prudie shared it alone; a rough camaraderie had grown up between the three, and the Paynters did not seem to resent Ross's friendship with the girl. There were plenty of times when he was lonely and glad of companionship. Verity no longer had the heart to come over, and Demelza took her place.

Sometimes she even sat with him in the evening. It had begun with her going to ask him for orders about the farm, by her staying to talk; and then somehow she was sitting in the parlour with him two or three evenings a week.

She was, of course, the most amenable of companions, being content to talk if he wanted to talk, or to persevere with her reading if he wanted to read, or willing to slip out at once if her presence was unwelcome. He still drank heavily.

She was not quite a perfect housekeeper. Though she came near enough to it for normal needs, there were times when her temperament played a part. The "moods" of which Prudie had spoken still took her. Then she could outswear Jud, and once had nearly outfought him. Her sense of personal danger was at all times nonexistent; but at such times even her industry was misdirected.

One dark rainy morning of last October she had chosen to clean out part of the cattle shed, and began pushing the oxen around when they got in the way. Presently one resented this and she came out boiling with indignation and wounded in a manner that made sitting down impossible for a week. Another time she chose to move all the kitchen furniture while Jud and Prudie were out. But one cupboard was too much even for her energy, and she pulled it over on herself. Prudie came back to find her pinned underneath, while Garrick barked his appreciation at the door.

The affair of the quarrel with Jud had a more serious side and was now discreetly forgotten by all. Demelza had tasted the bottle of spirits in the old iron box in the library, and, liking the taste, had finished the bottle. Then she went prancing in to Jud, who by mischance had also been having a private sup. She so tormented him that he fell upon her with some indistinct notion of slaying her. But she fought back like a wildcat, and when Prudie came in, she found them struggling on the floor. Prudie had jumped instantly to the wrong conclusion and had attacked Jud with the hearth shovel. Ross's arrival was only just in time to prevent most of his staff from being laid up with serious injuries.

A frozen equanimity had fallen on the kitchen for weeks after that. For the first time Demelza had felt the acid sting of Ross's tongue and had curled up and wanted to die.

But that was twelve months ago. It was a grisly spectre buried in the past.

Without further speech they passed through the apple trees and walked towards the house, through the garden on which Demelza had put in so many extra hours last summer. All the weeds had been cleared, leaving much bare earth and a few straggling remnants of the plants Ross's mother had grown.

There were three lavender bushes, tall and ungainly from the press of weeds; there was a bush of rosemary, freed from its tangle and promising flower. She had also unearthed a damask rose with its bright splashed flowers of pink and white, and a moss rose and two monthly roses; and in her quest about the countryside she had begun to bring home seeds and roots from the hedgerows. These were no easy things to rear: They had all the waywardness of wild things, ready to luxuriate in desolate places of their own choosing but apt to pine and die when confined within the luxury of a garden. But last year she had had fine spurs of viper's bugloss, a patch of sea pinks, and a row of crimson foxgloves.

They stopped now, Demelza explaining what she proposed to do here and here, suggesting that she might take cuttings from the lavender bush and try to root them to make a hedge. Ross looked about him with a tolerant eye. He was not greatly interested in flowers, but he admired the neatness and the colour; and herbs which could be cooked or infused were useful.

Recently he had given her a little money for her own use, and with this she had bought a bright kerchief to wrap around her head, a pen to learn to write, two copy books, a pair of shoes with paste buckles, a big cloam mug to hold flowers, a sunbonnet for Prudie and a snuffbox for Jud. Twice he had let her mount Ramoth and ride with him into Truro, once when he had promised to visit the cockpit and watch Royal Duke fight for a fifty-guinea purse. This entertainment, to his surprise and amusement, quite disgusted her.

"Why," she said, "tis no better than Fathur do do." She had expected something more refined of a cockfight patronized by the nobility and gentry.

On the way home she had been unusually silent. "Don't you think animals d' feel hurt like we?" she got out eventually.

Ross considered his answer. He had been led once or twice before into pitfalls by making unthinking replies to her questions.

"I don't know," he said briefly.

"Then why do veers squeal like they do when you put rings through their noses?"

"Cockerels aren't pigs. God made it their nature to fight."

She did not speak for a time. "Yes, but God didn' give 'em steel spurs to fight with."

"You should have been a lawyer, Demelza," he commented, and at that she had been silent again.

He thought of these things while they talked in the garden. He wondered if she knew what Nat Pearce and the others had been thinking when they stared at her in the parlour a couple of hours ago, and whether she agreed with him that no idea could be more ridiculous. When he wanted that sort of pleasure he would call for Margaret in Truro, or one of her kind.

It seemed to him sometimes that if pleasure lay in the unsubtle sport that a harlot afforded, then he had not quite the normal appetites of a normal man. Well, there was an odd satisfaction in asceticism, a cumulative self-knowledge and self-reliance.

He thought very little about it these days. He had other interests and other concerns.

CHAPTER THREE

1

Before she left him Demelza said she had seen Jinny Carter early that day, and Jim was sick with a pleurisy. But Jim with his uncertain health was often laid up for a few days, and Ross did not take account of it. All the next fortnight he was busy with matters concerning the opening of the mine, and he put off seeing Jim until he could offer him certain cut-and-dried duties. He did not want this to seem a made-up job.

The library at Nampara was to serve as a mining office, and the domestic life of the house was disrupted while part of this was cleared and repaired. News that a mine was to open instead of close spread quickly, and they were besieged with miners from up to eighteen miles distant, anxious to take the work at any price. Ross and Henshawe tried to strike bargains fair to both sides. They engaged forty men, including a "grass" captain and an underground captain, who would be responsible to Henshawe.

At the end of the fortnight Ross met Zacky Martin and enquired about Jim. Jim was up, Zacky said, though not yet back at the mine, being troubled with his cough.

Ross thought over the arrangements so far as they had gone. Next Monday eight men would begin the adit from the face of the cliff, and another twenty would be at work on the first shaft. It was time for the assistant purser to be brought in.

"Tell him to come round and see me tomorrow morning, will you?" Ross said.

"Yes," said Zacky. "I'll see Jinny tonight. I'll tell her to tell him. She won't forget."

2

Jim Carter was not asleep and heard the faint tapping on the door almost as soon as it began.

Very cautiously, so as not to wake Jinny or the babies, he slid out of bed and began to gather up his clothes. Once he trod on a loose floor board, and he stood still for some seconds suppressing a cough, until the girl's regular breathing reassured him. Then he pulled on his breeches and shirt and picked up his boots and coat.

The hinge of the trap door usually groaned when it was moved, but he had put grease on it earlier in the day and it opened now with no noise. He was halfway through when a voice said:

"Jim."

He bit his lip in annoyance but did not reply; she might yet be only speaking in her sleep. There was silence. Then she went on:

"Jim. You're going out with Nick Vigus again. Why didn't you tell me?"

"I knew you'd only make a fuss."

"Well, you needn't go."

"Yes, I do. I promised Nick yesterday."

"Tell 'im you've changed your mind."

"I haven't."

"Cap'n Poldark wants you in the morning, Jim. Have you forgotten that?"

"I shall be back long afore morning."

"Maybe he'll want ee to take a pitch at the new mine."

Jim said: "I couldn't take it, Jinny. 'Tis a speculation, no more and no less. I couldn't give up a good pitch for that."

"A good pitch is no good if you've to wade to your chin in water going forth and back to it. No manner of wonder you cough."

"Well, when I go out to get a bit of extry, all you do is complain!"

"We can manage, Jim. Easy. I don't want more. Not that way. It fair sticks in my throat when I think how you've come by it."

"I aren't all that Methody."

"No more am I. 'Tis knowing the danger you've been in to get it."

"There's no danger, Jinny," he said in a softer tone. "Naught to fret about. Honest. I'll be all right."

A faint tapping was heard on the door again.

He said: "'Tis only while I'm not earning. You know that. I shan't be up of nights when I'm back on my pitch. Goodbye now."

"Jim," she said urgently, "I wisht you wouldn't go tonight. Not tonight."

"Hush, you'll wake the babies. Think on them, and the other one coming. We got to keep you well fed, Jinny dear."

"I'd rather starve—"

The three words floated down into the dark kitchen as he descended, but he heard no more. He unbolted the door and Nick Vigus slipped inside like a piece of rubber.

"You been some long time. Got the nets?"

"All ready now. Brrr... 'tis cold."

Jim put on his coat and boots and they went out, Nick whispering to his dog. Their walk was to be a fairly long one, about five miles each way, and for some time they tramped in silence.

It was a perfect night, starlit and clear but cold, with a north-westerly breeze thrusting in from the sea. Jim shivered and coughed as he walked.

Their way lay southeast, skirting the hamlet of Marasanvose, climbing to the main coaching road and then dropping into the fertile valley beyond. They were entering Bodrugan land, profitable country but dangerous, and they began to move with the utmost caution. Nick Vigus led the way and the thin lurcher made a second shadow at his heels. Jim was a few paces behind carrying a stick about ten feet long and a homemade net.

They avoided a carriage drive and entered a small wood. In the shadow Nick stopped.

"They blasted stars are as sharp as a quarter moon. I misdoubt if we'll have as fair a bag."

"Well, we can't go back wi'out a try. It 'pears to me—"

"Sst... Quiet."

They crouched in the undergrowth and listened. Then they went on. The wood thinned out, and a hundred yards ahead the trees broke into a big clearing half a mile square. Fringing one side was a stream and about the stream a thicket of bushes and young trees. It was here that the pheasants roosted. Those in the lower branches were easy game for a quick man with a net. The danger was that at the other end of the clearing stood Werry House, the home of the Bodrugans.

Nick stopped again.

"What did ee hear?" Jim asked.

"Somethin'," whispered Vigus. The starlight glistened on his bald pink head and made little shadows of the pits in his face. He had the look of a perverted cherub. "They keepers. On the prowl tonight."

They waited for some minutes in silence. Jim suppressed a cough and put his hand on the dog's head. It moved a moment and was still.

"Lurcher's all right," said Nick. "Reckon twas a false alarm."

They began to move again through the undergrowth. As they neared the edges of the clearing it became a question not so much of disturbing the keepers, who perhaps had not been there at all, but of not flushing the pheasants until it was too late for them to fly. The brightness of the night would make this difficult.

They whispered together and chose to separate, each man taking one net and closing in on the covey from an opposite direction. Vigus, who was the more practised, was to make the longer detour.

Jim had a gift for stealthy movement, and he went on very slowly until he could see the dark shapes of the birds, podlike among the branches and in the low forks of the tree just ahead. He unwound the net from his arm, but decided to give Nick another two minutes lest he should spring the trap half set.

As he stood there he could hear the wind soughing in the branches above him. In the distance Werry House was a dark alien bulk among the softer contours of the night. One light still burned. The time was after one, and he wondered about the people who lived there and why they were keeping such late hours.

He wondered what Captain Poldark would have to say to him. He owed a lot there, but that made him feel he couldn't accept any more favours. That was, always supposing he could keep his health. It would be no benefit to Jinny to do as his father had done and die at twenty-six. Jinny made a to-do about him having to wade through water to his working pitch every day, but she didn't realize that they were all wet and dry most of the time. If a man couldn't put up with that, he wasn't fitted to be a miner. At present he was free of the blasting powder, and that was something to be thankful for.

An animal stirred in the thicket near him. He turned his head and tried to see but could not. The tree beyond was gnarled and misshapen. A young oak, one would guess from the dead leaves on its branches. They hung there rustling in the breeze all the winter through. A peculiar swollen shape.

And then the shape changed slightly.

Jim screwed up his eyes and stared. A man was standing against the tree.

So their visit of Saturday had not gone unmarked. Perhaps every night since then there had been gamekeepers waiting patiently for the next visit. Perhaps he had already been seen. No. But if he moved forward, he was as good as caught. What of Nick coming round from the north?

Jim's mind was frozen by the need to make an instant choice. He began to move slowly away.

He had not taken two steps when there was the sound of a broken twig behind him. He twisted in time to avoid a grasp on his shoulder and plunged towards the pheasants, dropping his net as he ran. In the same second there was a scuffle at the other side and the discharge of a musket; suddenly the wood came to life—with the cry of cock pheasants and the beating of their startled wings as they rose, with the stirring of other game disturbed, with men's voices shouting directions for his capture.

He came to open ground and ran flatly, skirting the edge of the stream and keeping as much as possible in the deep shadow. He could hear running footsteps behind and knew that he was not outdistancing them; his heart pounded and his breath grew tight.

At a break in the trees he swerved and ran amongst them. He was not now far from the house, and he could see that this was a formal path he followed. In here it was darker, and the undergrowth between the trees was so dense that it would be hard to force a way through it without giving them time to catch up.

He came upon a small clearing; in the middle was a circular marble pavilion and a sundial. The path did not go beyond this point. He ran towards the pavilion, then changed his mind and made for the edge of the clearing where a big elm tree leaned out and away. He scrambled up the trunk, scratching his hands and breaking his nails on the bark. He had just reached the second branch when two gamekeepers pounded into the clearing. He lay still, drawing thinly at the air.

The two men hesitated and peered about the clearing, one with head bent forward listening.

" ... not gone fur... Hiding out..." floated across to the tree.

They walked furtively into the clearing. One went up the steps and tried the door of the pavilion. It was locked. The other stepped back and stared up at the circular domed roof. Then they divided and made a slow circuit of the open space.

As one of the men approached his tree Jim suddenly felt that peculiar stirring in his lung which he knew meant an attack of coughing. The sweat came out afresh on his forehead.

The gamekeeper slowly went past. Jim saw that he carried a gun. Just beyond the leaning elm the man stopped at a tree which looked more scalable than the rest and began to peer up through its branches.

Jim gasped at the air and choked and got a breath and held it. The second man had made his tour and was coming to rejoin his companion.

"Seen aught of 'im?"

"No. Bastard must've escaped."

"Did they catch the other un?"

"No. Thought we'd got this un though."

"Ais."

Jim's lungs were expanding and contracting of their own accord. The itch welled up irresistibly in his throat and he choked.

"What's that?" said one of the men.

"Dunno. Over yur."

They came sharply towards the elm but mistook the direction by twenty feet, frowning into the tangled undergrowth.

"Stay thur," said one. "I'll see what I can find." He forced his way through the bushes and disappeared. The other stood against the bole of a tree with his gun at the cock.

Jim grasped at the branch above him in a frantic effort to hold his cough. He was soaked now with sweat, and even capture seemed little more fearful than this convulsive strain. His head was bursting. He would give the rest of his life to be able to cough.

There was a trampling and a cracking and the second gamekeeper came out, cursing his disappointment.

"He's gone, I reckon. Let's see what Johnson's done."

"How 'bout getting the dogs?"

"They've nought to go on. Maybe we'll catch 'em proper next week."

The two men moved off. But they had not gone ten paces when they were stopped by a violent explosion of coughing just above and behind them.

For a moment it alarmed them, echoing and hollow about the trees. Then one recovered himself and ran back towards the elm.

"Come down!" he shouted. "Come down out of there at once, or I'll shoot the life out of you."

CHAPTER FOUR

1

ROSS DID NOT HEAR OF THE ARREST UNTIL TEN O'CLOCK, WHEN ONE OF THE Martin children brought the news to him at the mine. He at once went home, saddled Darkie and rode over to Werry House.

The Bodrugans were one of the decaying families of Cornwall. The main stem, having scored a none-too-scrupulous trail across local history for nearly two hundred years, had given out in the middle of the century. The Werry Bodrugans were following suit. Sir Hugh, the present baronet, was fifty and a bachelor, under-sized, vigorous and stout. He claimed to have more hair on his body than any man living, a boast he was ready to put to the proof for a fifty-guinea bet any evening with the port. He lived with his stepmother, the Dowager Lady Bodrugan, a hard-riding, hard-swearing woman of twenty-nine, who kept dogs all over the house and smelt of them.

Ross knew them both by sight, but he could have wished that Jim had found other preserves to poach on.

He wished it still more when he came to the house and saw that the Carnbarrow Hunt was meeting there. Conscious of the stares and whispers of the people in their red coats and shining boots, he got down and threaded a way among horses and yapping dogs and went up the steps of the house.

At the top a servant barred his way.

"What do you want?" he demanded, looking at Ross's rough working clothes.

Ross stared back at him. "Sir Hugh Bodrugan, and none of your damned impudence."

The manservant made the best of it. "Beg pardon, sir. Sir Hugh's in the library. What name shall I say?"

Ross was shown into a room full of people drinking port and canary sack. Conditions could hardly be more difficult for what he had to ask. He knew many of the people. Young Whitworth was here and George Warleggan and Dr. Choake, and Patience Teague and Joan Pascoe. And Ruth Teague with John Treneglos, eldest son of old Mr. Horace Treneglos. He looked over the heads of most of them and saw Sir Hugh's squat form by the fireplace, legs astraddle and glass raised. He saw the manservant approach and whisper in Sir Hugh's ear and heard Bodrugan's impatient, "Who? What? What?" This much he was able to hear because there had been a temporary dropping off in conversation. Someday he might come to accept this as a natural event when he entered a room.

He nodded and half smiled to some of the guests as he walked through them towards Sir Hugh. There was a sudden outburst of barks and he saw that Constance Lady Bodrugan was on her knees on the hearthrug tying up a dog's paw, while six black spaniels licked and lurched about her.

"Blast me, I thought it was Francis," said Sir Hugh. "Your servant, sir. The hunt starts in ten minutes."

"Five is all I need," Ross said pleasantly. "But those I should like in private."

"There's nowhere private in the house this morning unless it's the Jericho. Speak up, for there's too much noise for anyone to eavesdrop on your private affairs."

"The man who left this bloody glass about," said his stepmother. "I'd horse-whip him, by God."

Ross took the wine offered him and explained his mission to the baronet. A poacher had been taken on Bodrugan land last night. A boy known personally to himself. Sir Hugh, being a magistrate, would no doubt have something to do with the hearing of the case. It was the boy's first offence and there was strong reason to believe that he had been led away by an older and more hardened rogue. Ross would consider himself under an obligation to make good any loss if the boy could be dismissed with a severe warning. Moreover, he would be personally responsible...

At this stage Sir Hugh burst into a roar of laughter. Ross stopped.

"Blast me, but you come too late, sir. Too late by half. I had him up before me at eight o'clock this morning. He's on his way to Truro now. I've committed him for trial at the next quarter sessions."

Ross sipped his wine.

"You were in haste, Sir Hugh."

"Well, I didn't want to be delayed dealing with the fellow when it was the day of the meet. I knew by nine o'clock the house would be in a pandemonium."

"The poacher," said Lady Bodrugan, struck with the idea as she released the dog. "I suspicion it was he who dropped the glass. I'd have him flogged at the cart wheel, by God! The laws are too easy on the varmints."

"Well, he'll not be troubling my pheasants for a week or two," said Sir Hugh, laughing heartily. "Not for a week or two. You must agree, Captain Poldark, it's a standing disgrace the amount of good game that's lost in a year."

"I'm sorry to have intruded on your hunting time."

"Sorry your mission ain't a happier one. I've a nag to lend you if you've a mind to join the hunt."

Ross thanked him but refused. After a moment he made his excuses and left. There was no more he could do here. As he moved away from them he heard Lady Bodrugan say:

"You don't mean you'd have let me varmint go free, Hughie?"

He couldn't hear her stepson's reply, but there was a ripple of laughter among those who did.

The attitude of the Bodrugans to his idea of letting a poacher off with a warning was, he knew, the attitude all society would adopt, though they might dress it in politer phrases. Even Cornish society, which looked with such tolerance on the smuggler. The smuggler was a clever fellow who knew how to cheat the government of its revenues and bring them brandy at half price. The poacher not only trespassed literally upon someone's land, he trespassed metaphorically upon all the inalienable rights of personal property. He was an outlaw and a felon. Hanging was barely good enough.

Ross came up against the same attitude a few days later when he spoke to Dr. Choake. Jim was not likely to be brought up for trial before the last week in May. He knew that Choake, in his capacity of mine surgeon, had treated Jim as recently as February and he asked him his opinion of the boy.

Choake said, well, what could you expect with phthisis in the family? By auscultation he had detected a certain morbid condition in one lung, but how far it had developed it was not possible to say. Of course the complaint had various forms; mortification of the lung might set in early or late; he might even live to be forty, which was a fair age for a miner. One couldn't tell.

Ross suggested that the information would be of use at the quarter sessions. Evidence of serious ill health, together with a plea from himself, might possibly get the charge dismissed. If Choake would give evidence at the trial…

Choake knit his brows in a perplexed stare. Did he mean…

Ross did mean. Choake shook his head incredulously.

"My dear sir, we'd do much for a friend, but don't ask us to testify on behalf of a young vagrant who's been caught poaching. We couldn't do it. 'Twould come unnatural to us, like mothering a Frenchie."

Ross pressed, but Choake would not budge.

"To tell the truth, I haven't a deal of sympathy for your aims," he said at length. "No good will come of being sentimental about such folk. But I'll set you out a note of what I've said about the boy. Signed with my own hand and sealed like a writ. That will be just as good as going there and standing in the box like a felon. We couldn't do that."

Ross grudgingly accepted.

The following day Wheal Leisure had its first official visit from Mr. Treneglos. He stumped over from Mingoose with a volume of Livy under his arm and a dusty three-cornered hat stuck on top of his wig. There was mining blood in the Treneglos family.

He saw what there was to be seen. Three shafts were being sunk, but it was hard going. They had struck ironstone almost at once. This in places meant working with steel borers and then blowing with gunpowder. The layer ran east to west and seemed to be of some size, so the next few weeks were likely to be tedious for all.

Mr. Treneglos said, well, that would mean more expense, but the circumstance was not discouraging. Rich lodes of copper were often found in ironstone. "Nature's safe," he said. "She keeps her treasures under lock and key."

They went to the edge of the cliff and stared over the edge to the flimsy wooden platform halfway down, from which eight men in twelve-hour cores of four had begun driving an adit into the cliff. They had long since gone from view; all that could be seen from the cliff top was a boy of twelve who appeared from time to time with a barrow whose contents, the refuse of the four tunnelling beetles, he emptied onto the sand below. They too, Ross said, had met ironstone and were trying to find a way round it.

Mr. Treneglos grunted and said he hoped those two old women Choake and Pearce wouldn't start whinnying about the expense at the next meeting. How long had they reckoned on it taking them to bring home that adit to the mine, eh?

"Three months," Ross said.

"It will take all of six," said Mr. Treneglos to himself. "It will take all of six," he assured Ross. "By the by, have you heard the news?"

"What news?"

"My son John and Ruth Teague. They've made it up together. They are going to be wed, y' know."

Ross didn't know. Mrs. Teague would be in transports.

"She's done well for herself," the old man said, as if for once he spoke Ross's thoughts instead of his own. "She's done well for herself getting John, even though he is a small matter boisterous in his cups. I could have wished for some maid with money to her name, for we're none too easy set for our position. Still, she takes a fence well and she's suitable enough other ways. I heard of a fellow the other day who was carrying on with his kitchen wench. I can't remember who twas. Serious, I mean, not for a lark. It all depends how you treat a thing like that. I well remember John put one of our serving girls in the straw before ever he was seventeen."

"I hope they'll be happy."

"Eh? Oh yes. Well, I shall be glad to see him settled. I shan't last forever, and there hasn't been a bachelor master of Mingoose for eighty years."

"You're a magistrate," Ross said. "What is the sentence for poaching?"

"Eh? Eh?" Mr. Treneglos clutched at his old hat just in time to save it from the wind. "For poaching? It all depends, dear boy. All depends. If a man is caught with a whippet and snare in his keeping, then if tis a first conviction he may be given three or six months. If he's been convicted before or has been caught in the act, as the saying is, then no doubt he'll be sent for transportation. You have to be strong on the rogues, else we'd have no game at all. How's your uncle, boy?"

"I haven't seen him this month."

"I doubt if *he* will go magistrating again. I s'pose he takes it easy? Perhaps he pays too much heed to the physical profession. I mistrust 'em myself. Rhubarb's my cure. As for the doctors: *timeo Danaos et dona ferentes;* that's my motto. That's my motto," he added to himself. "Should be Charles's."

2

The trial took place on the thirtieth of May.

It had been a cold and unsettled spring with strong winds and days of chilly rain, but in the middle of the month the weather began to clear and the last week was quiet and suddenly very warm. Spring and midsummer were telescoped into one week. In six days of blazing sunshine the entire countryside grew and set into its richest green. The delayed spring blossoms came out overnight, bloomed as in a hothouse, and were gone.

The day of the trial was very warm, and Ross rode into Truro early with the songs of the birds all the way. The courtroom would have been gloomy and decrepit at the best of times. Today the tunnels of sunlight streaming in through the dirty windows fell on the gnarled old benches and showed up the big cobwebs in the corners of the room and hanging from the rafters. It picked out the emaciated clerk of the court bending over his papers with a pendulous drop glinting from his nose, and fell in patches on the ill-kempt spectators crowded together whispering and coughing at the back.

There were five magistrates, and Ross was pleased to find that he had some acquaintance with two of them. One, the chairman, was Mr. Nicholas Warleggan, George's father. The other was the Revd. Dr. Edmund Halse, whom Ross had last met in the coach. A third he knew by sight: a fat elderly man called Hick, one of the gentry of the town, who was drinking himself to death. During most of the morning Dr. Halse kept his fine cambric handkerchief before his sharp thin nose. No doubt it was well soaked with extract of bergamot and rosemary, a not unwise precaution with so much fever about.

Two or three cases were got through quickly enough in the heavy airless atmosphere, and then James Carter was brought into the box. In the well of the court Jinny Carter, who had walked the nine miles with her father, tried to smile as her husband glanced towards her. During the period of his remand his skin had lost its tan and thick smudges below his dark eyes showed up.

As the case began the usher glanced up at the big clock on the wall, and Ross could see him deciding there would be just time for this case before the midday break.

The magistrates were of the same opinion. Sir Hugh Bodrugan's gamekeeper had a tendency to wander in his evidence, and twice Mr. Warleggan sharply instructed him to keep to the point. This gave the witness stagefright, and he mumbled through to the end in a hurry. The other gamekeeper bore out the story, and that completed the evidence. Mr. Warleggan looked up.

"Is there any defence in this case?"

Jim Carter did not speak.

The clerk got up, pushing away a dew drop with his hand. "There's no defence, Your Worship. There's been no previous conviction. I have a letter 'ere from Sir Hugh Bodrugan complaining of how much game 'e's lost this year and saying as how this is the first poacher they has been able to catch since January."

The magistrates put their heads together. Ross cursed Sir Hugh.

Mr. Warleggan looked at Carter. "Have you anything to say before sentence of this court is passed?"

Jim moistened his lips. "No, sir."

"Very well, then—"

Ross got up. "If I might ask the indulgence of the court—"

There was a stir and a mutter, and everyone turned to see who was disturbing the magisterial dust.

Mr. Warleggan peered through the shafts of sunlight and Ross nodded slightly by way of recognition.

"You have some evidence you wish to give in this man's defence?"

"I wish to give evidence of his good character," Ross said. "He has been my servant."

Warleggan turned and held a whispered conference with Dr. Halse. They had both recognized him now. Ross continued to stand up, while people shifted their positions and peered over each other's shoulders to get a view of him. Among those just to his left he saw a face he recognized, one it was impossible to mistake: the moist, prominent mouth and slant eyes of Eli Clemmow. He had perhaps come to gloat over Carter's downfall.

"Will you take the witness stand, sir," Warleggan said in his deep careful voice. "Then you may say what you have to say."

Ross left his seat and walked across the court to the witness box. He took the oath and made a pretence of kissing the greasy old Bible. Then he put his hands over the edge of the box and looked at the five magistrates. Hick was blowing as if asleep; Dr. Halse was dabbing lightly with his handkerchief, no trace of recognition in his eyes; Mr. Warleggan was looking through some papers.

"No doubt, gentlemen, on the evidence you have heard, you will see no reason to look for anything exceptional in this case. In your long experience there must be many cases, especially at a time of distress such as this, when there are circumstances—of hunger, of poverty, of sickness which extenuate the offence in some degree. But naturally the laws must be administered, and I should be the last to ask of you that the ordinary poacher, who is a trouble and expense to all of us, should be allowed to go unpunished. I have, however, a close knowledge of the circumstances of this case which I should like to put before you." Ross gave them a summary of Jim's vicissitudes, with particular stress on his ill health and the brutal assault made upon his wife and child by Reuben Clemmow. "Living as he does in poverty, I have reason to believe that the prisoner fell into bad company and was persuaded away from certain promises he had made direct to me. I personally am sure of this boy's honesty. It is not he who should be in court but the man who led him astray."

He paused and felt that he had the interest of his listeners. He was about to go on when someone sniggered loudly in the well of the court. Several of the magistrates looked across, and Dr. Halse frowned severely. Ross had no doubt who it was.

"The man who led him astray," he repeated, trying to regain the wandering attention of his listeners. "I repeat that Carter has been led astray by a man much older than himself who has so far escaped punishment. It's he who should bear the blame. As for the prisoner's present health, you have only to look at him to see what it is today. In confirmation of that I have here a statement from Dr. Thomas Choake of Sawle, the distinguished mine surgeon, that he has examined James Carter and finds him to be suffering from a chronic and putrid inflammation of the lung which is likely to prove fatal. Now I am prepared to re-engage him in my employment and to stand surety for his good behaviour in the future. I ask for the consideration of these facts by the court, and that they should be taken into careful account before any sentence be passed."

He handed to the clerk the piece of notepaper on which, in watery ink, Choake had scrawled his diagnosis. The clerk stood hesitantly with it in his hand until Mr. Warleggan impatiently beckoned him to pass it to the bench. The note was read and there was a brief consultation.

"Is it your contention that the prisoner is not in a fit state of health to be sent to prison?" Warleggan asked.

"He is very gravely ill."

"When was this examination made?" Dr Halse asked coldly.

"About three months ago."

"Then he was in this state when he went poaching?"

Ross hesitated, aware now of the unfriendly nature of the question. "He has been ill for some time."

Dr. Halse sniffed at his handkerchief. "Well, speaking for myself, I feel that if a man is—hm—well enough to go stealing pheasants, he is—hm—well enough to take the consequences."

"Aye, true 'nough," came a voice.

Mr. Warleggan tapped on the desk. "Any further disturbance—" He turned. "You know, Mr. Poldark, I'm of a mind to agree with my friend, Dr Halse. It is no doubt a misfortune for the prisoner that he suffers these disabilities, but the law gives us no opportunity to draw fine distinctions. The degree of a man's need should not determine the degree of his honesty. Else all beggars would be thieves. And if a man is well enough to err, he is surely also well enough to be punished."

"Yet," Ross said, "bearing in mind the fact that he has already suffered nearly four weeks' imprisonment—and bearing in mind his good character and his great poverty, I cannot help but feel that in this case justice would be best served by clemency."

Warleggan thrust out his long upper lip. "You may feel that, Mr. Poldark, but the decision rests with the bench. There has been a marked increase in lawlessness during the last two years. This, too, is a form of lawbreaking both difficult and expensive to detect, and those who are apprehended must be prepared to bear their full share of the blame. Nor can we apportion the guilt; we can only take cognizance of the facts." He paused. "In view, however, of the medical testimony and of your own testimony as to Carter's former good character, we are willing to take a more lenient view of the offence than we should otherwise have done. The prisoner is sentenced to two years' imprisonment."

There was a murmur in the court, and someone muttered a word of disgust.

Ross said: "I trust I may never have the misfortune to have the leniency of the court extended to me."

Dr. Halse lowered his handkerchief. "Have a care, Mr. Poldark. Such remarks are not entirely outside our jurisdiction."

Ross said, "Only mercy enjoys that privilege."

Mr. Warleggan waved a hand. "Next case."

"One moment," said Dr. Halse. He leaned forward, putting his fingertips together and pursing his thin lips. He disliked this arrogant young squireen afresh every time they met: at school, in the coach, in court. He was particularly gratified at having been able to put that sharp little question about dates which had turned the other magistrates to his own way of thinking. But even so the young upstart was trying to have the last word. It would not do. "One moment, sir. We don't come here and administer justice according to the statute book without a considerable sense of our privileges and responsibilities. As a member of the Church, sir, I feel that responsibility with especial weight. God has given to those of his ministers who are magistrates the task of tempering justice with clemency. That task I discharge to the best of my poor ability, and I think it has been so discharged now. Your insinuations to the contrary are offensive to me. I do not think you have the least idea what you are talking about."

"These savage laws," Ross said, controlling his temper with the greatest difficulty, "these savage laws which you interpret without charity send a man to prison for feeding his children when they are hungry, for finding food where he can when it's denied him to earn it. The book from which you take your teaching, Dr. Halse, says that man shall not live by bread alone. These days you're asking men to live without even bread."

A murmur of approval at the back of the court grew in volume.

Mr. Warleggan rapped angrily with his hammer.

"The case is closed, Mr. Poldark. You will kindly step down."

"Otherwise," said Dr. Halse, "we will have you committed for contempt of court."

Ross bowed slightly. "I can only assure you, sir, that such a committal would be a reading of my inmost thoughts."

He left the box and pushed his way out of court amid much noise and the shouts of the usher for silence. In the narrow street outside he took a breath of the warm summer air. The deep gutter here was choked with refuse and the smell was unsavoury, but it seemed agreeable after the smell of the court. He took out a kerchief and mopped his forehead. His hand was not quite steady from the anger he was trying to control. He felt sick with disgust and disappointment.

A long mule train was coming down the street with the heavy panniers of tin slung on each side of the animals and with a number of travel-stained miners plodding slowly along by their side. They had walked miles since dawn from some outlying district with this tin for the coinage hall, and would ride home on the backs of the weary mules.

He waited until they were past and then was about to cross the narrow street. A hand touched his arm.

It was Jinny, with her father, Zacky Martin, in the rear. There were pink flushes in her cheeks, showing up against the pale freckled skin.

"I want to thank ee, sur, for what you said. Twas more'n good of you to try so 'ard for Jim. And what you said—"

"It did no good," Ross said. "Take her home, Zacky. She'll be best with you."

"Yes, sur."

He left them abruptly and strode off up Coinagehall Street. To be thanked for his failure was the last straw. His disgust was partly levelled at himself for having lost his temper. Be as independent as you liked when it was your own freedom you were bartering; but at least have a greater restraint when it was someone else's. His whole attitude, he told himself, had been wrong. A good beginning, and then it had gone awry. He was the last person to make a success of such a job. He should have been obsequious, flattering to the bench. He should have upheld and praised their authority, as he had begun by doing, and at the same time have brought it home to them that a lenient sentence might be passed out of the benevolence of their hearts.

Deep down he wondered if even the golden voice of Sheridan would have charmed them from their prey. An even better approach, he thought now, would have been to see the magistrates before the court opened and have pointed out to them how inconvenient it would be for him to be deprived of his manservant. That was the way to get a man off, not by the testimony of doctors or sentimental appeals for clemency.

He was in Prince's Street by this time, and he turned down into the Fighting Cock's Inn. There he ordered a bottle of brandy and set about drinking it.

CHAPTER FIVE

1

IN THE HOT SUNSHINE OF THE EARLY SUMMER AFTERNOON, DEMELZA AND PRUDIE were thinning out the young turnips which had been sown in the lower half of the Long Field.

Prudie was not slow in her complaints, but if Demelza heard, she did not pay any attention. She thrust and dragged rhythmically with her hoe, breaking the young weeds at the same time as she cleared spaces for the growth of the plants. Now and then she paused, hands on hips, to stare out over Hendrawna Beach. The sea was very quiet under the hot sun. Faint airs moved across from time to time, brushing dark gentle shadows over it as over the down of a bird's wing. Where the water was shallow, its surface was an ever-shifting pattern of mauve and bottle-green wrinkles.

Sometimes she hummed a tune, for she loved warmth of any kind, especially the warmth of the sun. Much to Prudie's disapproval, she had taken off her blue bonnet and worked now in one of her blue print frocks with sleeves rolled up and bare legs and hard wooden-soled shoes.

With a groan and a pressing of hands, as if this were a movement not often to be made, Prudie straightened her back and stood upright. With one dirty finger she lifted her bonnet and tucked away a strand of black hair.

"I'll be that stiff in the morning. There's no more I can do today. My hips! I'll 'ave no easement all the night." She plucked at the heel of one slipper, which was tucked under and was letting in a trickle of soil. "You'd best finish too. There's calves to be meated and I can't do all—Now who be this?"

Demelza turned and frowned into the sun.

"Why, it's—What can *he* be wanting?"

She dropped her hoe and ran across the field towards the house. "Father!" she called.

Tom Carne saw her and stopped. She ran up to him. Since his last visit when he had announced his coming marriage her feelings for him had changed. The memory of his ill treatment was faded, and now that there was no point at issue between them she was willing to let bygones be bygones and to offer him affection.

He stood there with his round hat on the back of his head, feet planted stolidly apart, and allowed Demelza to kiss the prickles of his black beard. She noticed at once that his eyes were less bloodshot and that he was dressed in respectable clothes: a jacket of coarse grey cloth, a grey waistcoat, with thick trousers turned up some inches at the bottoms, showing brown worsted stockings and heavy shoes with bright brass clasps. She had forgotten that the Widow Chegwidden had a long purse.

"Well, dattur," he said, "so you be still 'ere."

She nodded. "And happy too. Hope you're the same."

He pursed his lips. "That's as may be. Is there any place we can talk, maid?"

"There's no one can hear us here," she answered. "'Cept the crows and they're not interested."

At this he frowned and stared across at the house, lying close and warm in the sun.

"I don't know as 'tis any place for a dattur o' mine," he said harshly. "I don't know 'tall. I bin much troubled about ee."

She laughed. "What's to do wi' a dattur of yourn?" She was lapsing into the broader speech she had begun to lose. "And how's Luke and Samuel and William and John and Bobbie and Drake?"

"Brave enough. 'Tis not o' they I'm thinking." Tom Carne shifted his position and took up an even firmer one. The gentle breeze just stirred his whiskers. "Now look ee here, Demelza, I've walked all this way to see ee, an' I've come to ask ee to come home. I've come to see Cap'n Poldark to explain why."

As he spoke she had a feeling as if something were freezing inside her. The newfound daughterly affection would be among the first things to go if all this had to be thrashed out again. Surely it wouldn't have to be. But this was a new and more reasonable father than she had known before. He was not blustering or shouting or even ordinarily drunk. She shifted to leeward of him to see if she could catch any smell of spirits. He would be more dangerous if one could not so easily put him in the wrong.

"Cap'n Poldark's in to Truro. But I've told ee afore. I want to stay here. And what about... how is she... the Wid... your—"

"Well-a-fine. 'Tis she in part do feel you be betterer wi' we than 'ere in this house exposed to all the temptations o' the world, the flesh, and the devil. You're but sixteen yet—"

"Seventeen."

"No matter. You're too young to be wi'out guidance." Carne thrust out his bottom lip. "Do ee ever go to church or meetin' house?"

"Not so often."

"Mebbe if you coined back to us you'd be saved. Baptized in the Holy Ghost."

Demelza's eyes widened. "What's to do? What's the change in ee, Father?"

Tom Carne met his daughter's eyes defiantly.

"When you left me, I was in the darkness and the shadow o' death. I was the servant o' the devil and was iniquitous and a drunkard. Last year I was convinced o' sin under Mr. Dimmick. Now I am a noo man altogether."

"Oh," said Demelza. So the Widow Chegwidden had been successful after all. She had underrated the Widow Chegwidden. But perhaps indeed it was more than the widow. It would need Something Awful to have changed the man she knew.

"The Lord," said Tom Carne, "hath brought me out of a horrible pit of mire an' clay, and set my feet 'pon a rock and hath put a new song in my mouth. There's no more drinkings and living in sin, Dattur. We d' live a good life an' we'd be willing to welcome ee back. Tis your natural place in the world."

Demelza stared a moment at her father's flushed face, then looked down bleakly at her shoes.

Tom Carne waited. "Well, maid?"

"It's mortal kind of you, Fathur. I'm that glad there's been a change. But I been here so long now that this is my home. It would seem like leaving home to come back wi' you. I learned all 'bout farming here and everything. I'm part of the house. They'd not be able to get along without me. *They* need me, not you. One day I'll walk over and see ee... you an' the boys and all. But you don't need me. You got she to look after you. There's nought I can do 'cept eat your food."

"Oh yes there is." Carne stared over the horizon. "The Lord has blessed our union. Nellie is six months forward an' will be delivered in August month. 'Tis your proper place and your bounden duty to come 'ome and look after us."

Demelza began to feel that she was caught in a trap which was only just beginning to show its teeth.

There was silence. A curlew had come down in the field and was taking its little run forward, crested head down, and uttering its sad "pee-wit" sound. She looked across at Prudie, who had gathered up her tools and was ambling untidily towards the house. She stared at the field of turnips, half thinned out, the other half to do. Her eyes went across the sand and the sand hills to the cliff where two huts were being built and men moved like ants on the summer skyline. Wheal Leisure.

She couldn't leave this. Not for anything. She had come to look upon it all, quick and dead, all things alike, as owned by it and owning. She was fiercely attached to it. And of course to Ross. If this were anything for him she was being asked to do it would be different, but instead she was expected to desert him. Not until she came here had she lived at all. Though she did not consciously reason so, all the early part of her life was like a dark prenatal nightmare, thought and imagined and feared rather than suffered.

"Where's Cap'n Poldark?" Tom Carne said, his voice having hardened again at her silence. "I come to see him. I got to explain and then 'e'll understand. There'll be no call for wrastling this time."

That was true. Ross would not stop her going. He might even expect it of her.

"He's from home," she said bluntly. "'E'll not be back till dark."

Carne moved round to meet her gaze, as in the old days he had sidled round to grip an opponent.

"You can't do nothing 'bout un. You got to come."

She looked at him. She saw for the first time how coarse and common he really was. His cheeks sagged and his nose was crossed with tiny red veins. But then all the gentlemen were not like the one she served.

"You can't expect me to say 'yes,' just like that and come away, after all these years. I got to see Cap'n Ross. He engaged me by the year. I'll see what he says and leave you know." That was it. Get him off the farm before Ross came back, get him away and allow herself time to think.

Tom Carne was eyeing his daughter in return, keenly, with a tinge of suspicion. Only now did he take in the full change in her, the way she had advanced, matured, grown to a woman's shape. He was not a man to mince matters.

"Is there any sin twixt you and Poldark?" he demanded in a low sharp voice, in the old voice of old Tom Carne.

"Sin?" said Demelza.

"Aye. Don't look so innocent."

Her mouth tightened. The instinct of an outgrown fear saved him from a reply he would not quite have expected from a daughter's lips—even though they were words she had learned from him.

"There's nought twixt us except what should be between master and servant. But you did ought to know I'm hired by the year. I can't walk out without so much as a by-your-leave."

"There's talk about you," he said. "Talk that comes so far as Illuggan. Whether us all lies or no, tedn't right for a young girl to be mixed up in such talk."

"It's nothing to do wi' me what folks say."

"That's as may be. But I don't want for a dattur o' mine to be mingled up in such talk. When will he be home?"

"Not till nightfall, I say. He's gone to Truro."

"Well, 'tis a long way for me to walk 'ere again. Tell un what I've telled you and then come you over to Illuggan. If you're not back by the end of the week, I'll come over again. If 'tis Cap'n Poldark putting obstacles, I'll talk un over with 'im."

Tom Carne hitched up his trousers and fingered the buckle of his belt. Demelza turned and walked slowly towards the house, and he followed.

"After all," he said on a more palliative note, "I'm not asking more'n any dattur would do."

"No," she said. (Buckle end of a strap when it suited him; sores on her back, ribs you could count, dirt and crawlers; not more than any daughter would do!)

As they reached the house Jud Paynter came out with a bucket of water. He raised his bald eyebrows at the sight of the other man.

Tom Carne said: "Where's your master?"

Jud stopped and set down his bucket and eyed Carne and spat. "Over to Truro."

"What time will 'e be home?"

Demelza held her breath. Jud shook his head. "Tonight mebbe. Or tomorrow."

Carne grunted and walked on. At the front of the house he sat on the seat and took off his boot. Complaining of his corns, he began to press the boot into a more comfortable shape. Demelza could have screamed at him. Jud had told the truth as far as he knew it. But Ross had told her he expected to be back for supper at six. It was now after five.

Tom Carne began to tell her about her brothers. The five eldest were all at work in mines—or had been until two were put off when Wheal Virgin closed. The youngest, Drake, was starting as forge boy at a wheelwright's next week. John and Bobbie were both saved and had joined the society, and even Drake nearly always went to the meetings, although he was too young to be admitted. Only Samuel was erring. His conviction had worn away and the Lord had not seen fit to send him mercy. It was to be hoped that when she, Demelza, came back among them, she would soon lay hold of the blessing.

At another time she would have found quiet fun in his new talk, which for all its glibness fitted him as ill as a Sunday suit. She took in the news of her brothers, of whom she was as fond as they had allowed her to be. But above all was the need to see him gone. She could have kicked him to move his great slow body, fallen on him with her nails and drawn red scratches across his coarse complacent face. Even when he left she didn't know what was to be done. But at least she would have time to think. She would have time. But if he stayed here talking all day until Ross came home, then Ross would hear of it tonight and that would be the end. Ross would invite her father to sleep here and bundle them off in the morning.

She stood quivering and watched him while he bent to pull on his boot, angrily offered to buckle it, jerked upright and stood again silently watching him while he picked up his stick and made ready to go.

She walked with him, two paces ahead of him to the bridge, and then he stopped again.

"You've nought much to say," he observed, eyeing her again. "Tedn't like ee to be so silent. Have you still enmity and uncharitableness in your heart?"

"No, Father," she said quickly. "No, Father. No."

He swallowed and sniffed again. Perhaps he too felt a strangeness in talking this flowery language to the child he had been wont to order and bully around. In the old days a grunt and a curse had been enough.

He said slowly and with an effort: "I forgive ee fully and altogether for leavin' me when you did, and I ask forgiveness, God's forgiveness, fur any wrong I did ee with the strap in my drink. There'll be no more o' that, dattur. We'll welcome you among us like the lost sheep back to the fold. Nellie too. Nellie'll be a mother to ee—what you've lacked this pretty many year. She's been a mother to my flock, and now God's giving her her own."

He turned and stumped off across the bridge. Standing on one leg and then the other, she watched him go up slowly into the young green of the valley and prayed urgently and angrily—was it to the same God?—that he should not meet Ross on the way.

2

"They calves want feeding," said Prudie. "An' my poor feet is tryin' me something bitter. Sometimes I'd like to saw off me toes one by one. Saw 'em off I would, wi' that old garden saw."

"Here," said Demelza.

"What's that?"

"The carving knife. Chop 'em off and then you'll be settled. Where's the meal porridge?"

"Well to jest," said Prudie, wiping her nose on her hand. "Iggerance always jests. You wouldn't jest when the knife were gratin' on the bone. And I'd do it if twere not for considering what Jud would do without un. In bed he says my feet are as good as a warmin' pan; nay, bettcrcr, for they don't cool down as the night goes on."

If she went, Demelza thought, there was no need to go so soon. August, he had said. Tomorrow was the last day of May. She need not stay more than a month; then she could come back here to her old duties.

She shook her head. Things would not turn out like that. Once home she stayed home. And whether the ruling force was the leather strap or religious zeal she had a feeling that her job would be the same. She tried to remember what the Widow Chegwidden had looked like behind the counter of her little shop. Dark and small and fat, with fluffy hair under a lace cap. Like one of those little black hens with red combs that would never lay their eggs in the box, but always hid them away and then before you knew where you were they were sitting on a dozen and had gone broody. She had made Tom Carne a good wife; would she make a good stepmother? Plenty worse, maybe.

Demelza didn't want a stepmother, nor a father, nor even a spawn of brothers back. She was not afraid of work, but there she would be working in a home where no kindness had ever been shown her. Here, for all her ties, she was free; and she worked with people she had grown to like and for a man she adored. Her way of seeing things had changed; there were happinesses in her life she had not understood until they were on her. Her soul had blossomed under them. The abilities to reason and think and talk were new to her—or they had grown in a way that amounted to newness, from the gropings of a little animal concerned only for its food and safety and a few first needs. All that would be stopped. All these new lights would go out; snuffers would be put on the candles and she would see no more.

Not heeding Prudie, she slopped the meal porridge into a bucket and went out with it for the six calves. They greeted her noisily, pushing at her legs with their soft damp noses. She stood there and watched them eat.

Her father, by asking if there was any sin between herself and Ross, meant of course exactly the same as those women at Grambler and Sawle who sometimes would turn and stare after her with greedy curious eyes. They were all thinking that Ross...

Red-faced, she gave a little half-scornful titter in the shadows. People were always thinking things; it was a pity they couldn't think up something more likely. Did they think that if she... that if Ross... would she then be living and breathing as an ordinary servant? No. She would be so filled with pride that everyone would know the truth without having to whisper and peer and pry.

Ross Poldark lying with the child he had befriended and swilled under the pump and scolded and taught and joked with over the pilchards in Sawle! He was a man, and maybe he wanted his pleasures like any other man, and maybe he took them on his visits to town. But she would be the last person he would turn to, she whom he knew so well, who had no strangeness, no pretty dresses, no paint and powder, no shy secrets to hide from him. Fools people were with their double-damned, soft-silly imaginings.

The six calves were fussing round her, rubbing their heads against her body, sucking at her arms and frock with their wet mealy mouths. She pushed them away and they came back again. They were like thoughts, other people's and her own, pressing upon her, worrying her all at one time, sly and impossible and suggestive, importunate and friendly and hopeful.

What a fool her father was! With the sudden adultness of a growing wisdom she saw that for the first time. If there was *anything* between herself and Ross, like he suggested, would she even for an instant have listened to him asking her to go back? She would have said: "Back? I'm not coming back! This is where I belong!"

Perhaps it was. Perhaps Ross would refuse to let her go. But there was no proper feeling for her on his part, not beyond a kindly interest. He would as soon become used to her not being in the parlour as he had to her being there. That was not enough, not near enough...

One of the calves trampled on the bucket and sent it rolling to the back of the stall. She went after it, picked it up, and in the darkness of the shed, in the corner right away from the light, she came up against the most terrible thought of her life. It startled her so much that she dropped the bucket again. The bucket clattered and rolled and was still. For several moments she stood there holding to the partition, her mind cold and frightened.

Madness. He would think her drunk and turn her out of the house, as he had threatened her after that fight with Jud.

But then she must go; by any reckoning she must go... There would be no loss. But she would have to take his contempt with her. A big price to pay. Even if she succeeded, she might still earn his contempt. But *she would not go*. She picked up the bucket again and gripped it with whitening knuckles.

The calves came again, pushing at her frock and hands. Her mood wilted. It was not the right or the wrong that troubled her. It was the fear of his contempt. The idea was bad. Put it away. Lose it. Bury it.

She pushed the calves impatiently aside, let herself out and walked across the cobbles to the kitchen. Prudie was still there rubbing her flat bunioned feet on a dirty towel.

The kitchen smelt of feet. She was still grumbling, might never have noticed that Demelza had been away.

"One o' these days I shall go off like a snip o' the finger. *Then* folk'll be sorry for driving of me. Then folk'll be sorry. But what good will that do me, an? What good do it do to shed bitter tears over a cold corpse? 'Tis a little more kindness I want now while the breathin's still in me." She glanced up. "Now don't tell me you've caught a fever. Don't tell me that."

"There's nothing wrong wi' me."

"There must be. You're sweating awful."

"It's *hot*," said Demelza.

"An' what're ee doing bringing that bucket sloppering in 'ere?"

"Oh," she said. "I forgot. I'll leave it outside."

CHAPTER SIX

1

HE WAS NOT BACK. SHE COULD NOT MAKE UP HER MIND WHETHER TO WISH for his coming. The clock showed eight. Very soon both Jud and Prudie would be in bed and asleep. It would be right for her to stay up and see to his supper. But if he did not come soon, he would be staying in Truro overnight. Zacky and Jinny were back. Jack Cobbledick had seen them and the news was about. Everyone was sorry for Jim, and feeling ran high against Nick Vigus. Everyone was sorry for Jinny and the two children. No man was the same when he came out of prison.

Demelza looked at the frock and bit her lip and looked at it again. Then she hastily threw bed linen over it as she heard Prudie flip-flopping laboriously up the stairs.

"I'm going to bed, dear," said Prudie, a bottle of gin in her hand. "Ef I don't I shall come over faint. Many's the time when I was a girl I used to swoon off without a breath o' warning. If me mother knowed what I 'ave to bear now she'd stand up in 'er grave. She'd walk. Many's the time I've expected of her to walk. You can see for his supper, an?"

"I'll see for it."

"Not that he's like to be home tonight. I said so much to Jud, but the ole mule says, no, 'e'll wait five and twenty minutes more, so wait 'e will."

"Good night," said Demelza.

"*Good* night? It will be a shock if I get so much as a wink."

Demelza watched her through to her room, then turned back the linen to stare again at the frock. After some moments she covered it and went downstairs.

In the kitchen there was a savoury smell of pie. Jud was sitting before the fire whittling a piece of hard driftwood into a new poker for raking out the burnt furze from the clay oven. As he whittled he quietly muttered his song:

There was an old couple and they was poor, Tweedle, tweedle go twee—

"It's been a handsome day, Jud," she said.

He looked at her suspiciously.

"Too 'ot. All wrong for the time o' year. There'll be rain soon. Swallows is flying low."

"You shouldn't sit so near the oven."

"What did Fathur say?"

"He wanted for me to go stay with them for a few weeks."

Jud grunted. "An' 'oo's to do your work?"

"I said I couldn't go."

"Should think as not. Start o' the summer too." He lifted his knife. "That a horse? Reckon it's Mr. Ross, just when I'd given un up."

Demelza's heart gave a lurch. Jud set down the stick and went out to take Darkie to the stables. After a few seconds Demelza walked after him through the hall.

Ross had just dismounted and was untying from behind the saddle the parcels and goods he had bought. His clothes were thick with dust. He looked very tired, and his face was flushed. He glanced up as she came to the door and smiled briefly but without interest. The sun had just set over the western ridge of the valley and the skyline was lit with a vivid orange glow. All round the house the birds were singing.

"… extra feed," he was saying. "The meal they gave her was skinny. Wugh, there's no air tonight." He took off his hat.

"Will you be wanting me again?" Jud asked.

"No. Go to bed when you wish." He walked slowly to the door and Demelza drew aside to let him pass. "You also. Serve my supper and then you can go."

Yes, he had had a drink; she could tell that. But she could not tell how much.

He went into the parlour where the table was set for his meal. She heard him struggling to pull off his boots and silently entered with his slippers and helped him to be rid of the boots. He looked up and nodded his thanks.

"Not an old man yet, you know."

She went out to take the pie from the oven. When she returned, he was pouring himself a drink. She set the pie on the table, cut him a piece, put it on his plate, cut him some bread, waited without speaking while he sat down and began the meal. All the windows were open. The furnace glow over the hill had faded. High in the sky a ruffle of cloud was saffron and pink. Colours in the house and in the valley were flaunting themselves.

"Shall I light the candles?"

He looked up as if he had forgotten her.

"No, there's time enough. I'll do them later."

"I'll be back and light 'em," she said. "I'm not goin' to bed yet."

She slipped out of the room, went through the low square hall into the kitchen. So the way was open that she might return. She didn't now know what to do. She wanted to pray for something that she knew the Widow Chegwidden's God disapproved of. She knelt and stroked Tabitha Bethia and went to the window and stared across at the stables. She chopped up some odds and ends for Garrick and by that means lured him into an outhouse and locked him up. She returned and raked out the fire. She picked up Jud's wooden poker and slipped a shaving off it with his knife. Her knees were weak and her hands ice cold. She took a bucket to the pump and drew fresh water. One of the calves was crying. A group of seagulls were winging their way slowly out to sea.

This time Jud followed her back into the kitchen, whistling between his two big teeth. Darkie was fed and watered. He put away the knife and the stick.

"You'll not be astir in the morning."

She knew very well who was not likely to be astir in the morning, but for once did not answer him. He went out and she heard him climbing the stairs. She followed. In her room she stared again at the dress. She would have given anything for a glass of brandy, but that was barred. If he smelt anything on her breath, that would end it. There was nothing for it but a cold, hard face, or else to run like a badger to her hole. The bed looked fine. She had only to shed the decision with her clothes and drop into it. But tomorrow would come. Tomorrow offered nothing to hope for.

She took out her broken bit of comb and went to the square of mirror she had found in the library, and began to tug at her hair.

2

The frock was one she had found at the bottom of the second tin trunk, and from the outset it had enticed her as the apple did Eve. It was made of pale blue satin, the bodice cut low and square. Below the tight waist the gown billowed out at the back like a blue cabbage. She thought it an evening gown, but really it was one Grace Poldark had bought for a formal afternoon. It was the right length for Demelza, and other alterations she had contrived on wet afternoons. There was a thrill in trying it on, even though no one would ever see her wear it...

She peered at herself in the half light and tried to see. Her hair she had combed up and parted at the side and drawn away from the ears to pile it on top of her head. At any other time she would have been pleased with her looks and preened herself, walking up and down peacock fashion to hear the *rough rough* of the silk. But now she stared and wondered and stared. She had no powder, as a real lady would have; no rouge, no scent. She bit at her lips to redden them. And this bodice. Ross's mother might have been made different, or perhaps she had worn a muslin fichu. She knew that if the Widow Chegwidden saw her she would open her tight little mouth and scream the word "Babylon!"

She stiffened. She had set to go. There was no more to do, no drawing back.

The flint and steel were clumsy in her hands, and she was hard put to it to light the candle. At last a flame flickered, and the rich blueness of the gown showed up more vividly. She rustled as she moved to the door, then slowly, candlestick in hand, went down the stairs.

At the door of the parlour she paused, swallowed something foreign in her throat, licked her lips, went in.

He had finished his meal and was seated in the half darkness in front of the empty fire grate. His hands were in his pockets and his head was down. He moved slightly at her entry but did not look up.

"I've brought the light," she said, speaking in a voice unlike her own, but he didn't notice.

Slowly she walked round, conscious of the noise her skirt was making, lit the two candle sconces. With each candle she lit the room grew a shade lighter, the squares of the windows a shade darker. All the sky over the hill was an ice blue, bright and clear and empty as a frozen pool.

He stirred again and sat more upright in his chair. His voice came as a shock to her ears. "You heard that Jim Carter has gone to prison for two years?"

She lit the last candle. "Yes."

"I doubt if he'll survive it."

"You did all you could."

"I wonder." He spoke as if he were talking to himself rather than to her.

She began to draw the curtains over the open windows.

"What else could you've done?"

"I'm not a good pleader," he said; "being too infernal conscious of my own dignity. The dignified fool, Demelza, gets nowhere beside the suave flattering rogue. Gentle obsequious compliments were the order of the day, and instead I tried to teach them their business. A lesson in tactics, but Jim Carter may pay the bill with his life."

She pulled the last curtain. A moth came fluttering in, wings beating the green figured damask.

"No one else'd 've done what you did," she said. "No other squire. It was none of your fault that he went poaching and was caught."

Ross grunted. "To be frank, I don't think my interference greatly altered the situation. But that is no matter for—" He stopped. He stared. This was the moment now.

"I haven't brought the other candles," she got out. "We was short and you said you'd get some today."

"Have you been drinking again?"

She said desperately: "I've never touched nothing since you told me. Honest. I swear to God."

"Where did you get that dress?"

"From the library—" Her ready lies were forgotten.

"So now you wear my mother's clothes!"

She stammered: "You never told me that. You told me that I mustn't drink, an' I've never touched nothing since. You never told me not to touch the clo'es!"

"I tell you now. Go and take those things off."

It couldn't have been worse. But in the depths of horror and despair one comes to a new steadiness. There is no farther to fall. She moved a foot or two into the yellow gleam of the candlelight.

"Well, don't you like it?"

He stared at her again. "I've told you what I think."

She came to the end of the table, and the moth fluttered past the candles and across the blue of her dress and pattered its reckless wings against the cupboard by the wall.

"Can I not... sit and talk for a while?"

Astounding the change. The hair combed up gave her face an altered, a more oval shape. Her youthful features were cleancut and wholesome, her look was adult. He felt like someone who had adopted a tiger cub without knowing what it would grow into. The imp of a sturdy disrespect for his own position tempted him to laugh.

But the incident wasn't funny. If it had been, he would have laughed with a clear mind. He didn't know why it wasn't funny.

He said in a withdrawn voice: "You came here as a maid and have been a good one. For that you've been allowed certain liberties. But the liberty of dressing yourself in those things is not one of them."

The chair on which he had been sitting at the table was still half out, and she subsided on the edge of it. She smiled nervously, but with more brilliance than she thought.

"Please, Ross, can't I stay? No one'll ever know. Please—" Words bubbled to her lips, overflowed in a whisper. "I aren't doing no 'arm. 'Tis no more'n I've done many and many an evening before. I didn't mean no 'arm putting on these clothes. They was rotting away in the old tin box. It d' seem a shame to leave all they pretty things there rotting away. I only meant it to please you. I thought you'd maybe like it. If I stay 'ere now till tis time to go—"

He said: "Get off to bed at once and we'll say no more of it."

"I'm seventeen," she said mutinously. "I been seventeen for weeks. Are ee always going to treat me like a child? I'll *not* be treated like a child! I'm a woman now. Can I not please myself when I d' go to bed?"

"You can't please yourself how you behave."

"I thought you liked me."

"So I do. But not to let you rule the house."

"I don't want to rule the house, Ross. I only want to sit here and talk to you. I've only old clo'es to work in. This is so—to have somethin' like this on—"

"Do as I say, or you'll go home to your father in the morning."

From the first desperately shy beginning she had succeeded in working up a feeling of grievance against him; for the moment she really believed that the issue was whether she should be given certain privileges.

"Well then," she said, "turn me out! Turn me out tonight. I don't care. Hit me if you want to. Like Father used to. I'll get drunk an' shout the house down, an' then you'll have good reason!"

She turned and picked up his glass from the table. She poured out some brandy and took a gulp of it. Then she waited to see what effect it would have on him.

He quickly leaned forward and picked up the wooden poker and rapped her sharply across the knuckles with it, so that the glass broke and spilled its contents down the disputed frock.

For a moment she looked more surprised than hurt, then she put her knuckles into her mouth. The mature and defiant seventeen became a desolate and unfairly rebuked child. She stared down at the frock where the brandy was soaking through the skirt. Tears came into her eyes, beading upon her thick dark lashes till she blinked them away, beading again and trembling at the rim without falling. Her attempt at coquetry had been a painful failure, but nature was coming to her help.

"I shouldn't have done that," he said.

He didn't know why he had spoken or why he should apologize for a just and necessary rebuke. Quicksands had moved under his feet.

"The frock," she said. "You shouldn't 've spoiled the frock. It was that pretty. I'll go tomorrow. I'll go as soon as the light comes."

She got up from the chair, tried to say something more, then suddenly was kneeling by his chair, her head on his knees, sobbing.

He looked down at her, at the head with its tumble of dark hair beginning to come awry, at the gleam of her neck. He touched her hair with its light and dark shadows.

"You little—" he said. "Stay on if you want to."

She tried to dry her eyes but they kept filling up again. For the first time then he put his hands on her, lifted her up. Yesterday the contact would have meant nothing. Without direct intention she came to be sitting on his knee.

"Here." He took out his handkerchief and wiped her eyes. Then he kissed her on the cheek and patted her arm, trying to feel the act as a paternal one. His authority was gone.

That didn't matter.

"I like that," she said.

"Maybe. Now go you off and forget this ever happened."

She sighed and swallowed. "My legs are wet." She pulled up the front of the pink petticoat and began to wipe her knee.

He said angrily: "You know what people say of you, Demelza?"

She shook her head. "What?"

"If you act like this, what they say of you will become true."

She looked at him, candidly this time, without coquetry and without fear.

"I live only for you, Ross."

A breeze lifted the curtain at one of the open windows. The birds outside were quiet at last and it was dark. He kissed her again, this time on the mouth. She smiled unsteadily through the remnants of her tears, and the candlelight lent a cream-gold charm to her skin.

Then by some mischance she put up a hand to push back her hair and the gesture reminded him of his mother.

He got up, lifting her to her feet so sharply that she almost fell, went to the window, stood with his back to her.

It was not the gesture but the frock. Perhaps the smell of it: something that brought up to him the taste, the flavours of yesterday. His mother had lived and breathed in that frock, in this room, in that chair. Her spirit moved and quickened between them.

Ghosts and phantoms of another life.

"What's to do?" she asked.

He turned. She was standing at the table, holding to it, the broken glass at her feet. He tried to remember her as a thin little urchin trailing across the fields with Garrick behind her. But that was no use at all. The urchin was gone forever. It was not beauty she had grown overnight but the appeal of youth, which was beauty in its own right.

"Demelza," he said, and even her name was strange. "I didn't take you from your father—for—to—"

"What do it matter what you took me for?"

"You don't understand," he said. "Get out. Get out."

He felt the need to soften what he had said, the need to explain. But the slightest movement on his part would throw restraint away.

He stared at her and she did not speak. Perhaps she was silently admitting defeat, but he didn't know, he couldn't read her. Her eyes were the eyes of a stranger who had usurped familiar ground. They stared at him with a challenge grown hostile and hurt.

He said: "I am going to bed now. You also go to bed and try to understand."

He picked up one of the candles, blew out the others in that sconce. He glanced at her briefly, forced a half smile.

"Good night, my dear."

Still she did not speak or move. When the door closed behind him, then at last in the silent room with only the frustrated moth for company she turned and picked up a candle for herself and one by one began to blow out the others he had left.

3

In his bedroom he was beset by a wave of cynicism of quite surprising violence. What sort of a monk and anchorite was he becoming? Shades of his own father seemed to rise and whisper, "Young prude!"

Heaven! he said to himself. What moral code had he drawn for himself that he had to obey these nice distinctions? You could fritter away a whole youth tracing the petty differences between one moral obligation and another. Slender refined Elizabeth, gaunt lascivious Margaret, Demelza with her flowering maidenhood. A passionate child rolling in the dust with her ugly dog; a girl driving oxen; a woman… Did anything else matter? He owed no one anything; certainly not Elizabeth. She was nothing any longer to him. This was no blind seeking after sensation in order to drown a hurt, as it had been on the night of the ball. God, he had never been so drunk on so little brandy before. That old stiff silk dress, part of an older love…

He sat on the bed uncertainly and tried to think. He tried to think over the incidents of the day. The beginning was frustration and the end was frustration. "Frankly, Mr. Poldark, I am inclined to agree with my friend, Dr. Halse. It is no doubt very unfortunate that the prisoner is suffering from this disability—" Who but a dolt would have expected the magistrates to do anything but agree with each other. "Must back each other up, *esprit de carps,* good of the community, good of the class." That was what he had ignored. One did not stand up in a witness box and argue against one's own class in public, let alone harangue them in front of a crowd of court idlers. It wasn't done. Well, he had his own standards of behaviour, though no one gave him credit for them. It was nothing out-of-the-way for the younger gentry of the neighbourhood to tumble their kitchenmaids. They didn't kidnap them when they were under age, that was all. Well, she was of age now, age enough to know her own mind and sense enough to read his before he knew it himself. What was the matter with him? No sense of humour to leaven life? Must every act be dead serious, a weight upon his head and hands? Loving was a recreation; all the poets sang of its lightness, its levity; only the dull clod raised barriers of creed or conscience.

There was no air tonight. The temperature didn't often keep up after dusk.

At least he had in some way earned the increased gratitude of Jinny. These years would seem even longer for her than for Jim. Would he see them through? "Quite the sentimental fool. Quite the renegade. Mixing with the Indians and fighting against the whites. Traitor to one's own station in life…" "Then come kiss me, sweet and twenty…" "Beauty is but a flower which wrinkles will devour…"

"Upsetting himself about some farm labourer with a bad cough. Rather unbalanced, one supposes. After all, one has to accept the rough with the smooth. Last year when my prize mare took the blood poisoning…"

"Every wise man's son doth know."

He got up and went to the north window to see if it was open. The sophistries of the poets. Tonight he could see nothing straight. Were sweet singers the best counsellors? Yes, the window was wide open. He pulled back the curtain and stared out. In twenty-seven years he had worked out some sort of a philosophy of behaviour; did one throw it over at the first test? There was a tap on the door.

"Come in," he said.

He turned. It was Demelza, carrying a candle. She did not speak. The door swung to behind her. She hadn't changed and her eyes were like lamps.

"What is it?" he said.

"This frock."

"Well?"

"The bodice unfastens down the back."

"Well?"

"I can't reach the hooks."

He frowned at her a moment.

She came slowly up to him, turned, set the candle clumsily upon a table. "I'm sorry."

He began to undo the dress. She felt his breath on her neck.

There was still one scar of those he had seen on the way home from Redruth Fair.

His hands touched the cool skin of her back. Abruptly they slipped inside her frock and closed about her waist. She leaned her head back against his shoulder and he kissed her until the room went dark before her eyes.

But now at this last moment when all was won she had to confess her deceit. She couldn't die unshriven.

"I lied," she whispered, crying again. "I lied about the hooks. Oh, Ross, don't take me if you h–hate me. I lied... I lied—"

He said nothing, for now nothing counted, not lies nor poets nor principles nor any reservations of mind or heart.

He released her and lit another candle.

CHAPTER SEVEN

S HE WOKE AT DAWN. SHE YAWNED, AT FIRST NOT AWARE OF THE CHANGE. THEN she saw that the rafters overhead ran a different way…

The pipe and the silver snuffbox on the mantelshelf, the oval mildewed mirror above it. His bedroom. She turned and stared at the man's head with its copper-dark hair on the pillow.

She lay quite still with closed eyes while her mind went over all that had happened in this room, and only her breathing coming quick and painful showed she was not asleep.

The birds were waking. Another warm still day. Under the eaves the finches made liquid sounds like water dripping in a pool.

She slid quietly to the edge of the bed and slipped out, afraid of waking him. At the window she stared across the outhouses to the sea. Tide was nearly full. Mist lay in a grey scarf along the line of the cliffs. The incoming waves scrawled dark furrows in the silver-grey sea.

Her frock—that frock—lay in a heap on the floor. She snatched it up and wrapped it round her, as if by so doing she hid from herself. On tiptoe across to her own bedroom. She dressed while the square of the window slowly lightened.

No stirrings in the house. She was always the first abroad, had often been to the end of the valley for flowers before Jud and Prudie grumblingly saw the light. Today she must be out of the house first.

Barefoot down the short shallow stairs and across the hall. She opened the front door. Behind the house might be the old grey sea; but in the valley was all the warmth and fragrance which the land had stored up during the short summer night. She stepped out and the warm air met her. She filled her lungs with it. In odd parts of the sky clouds lay thin and streaky, motionless and abandoned as by the sweeping of a careless broom.

The damp grass was not cold to her bare feet. She walked across the garden to the stream, sat on the wooden footbridge with her back to the rail and dipped her toes in the trickle of water. The hawthorn trees growing along its banks were in bloom, but the blossom had lost its whiteness, was turning pink and falling, so that the stream was full of drifting tiny petals like the remnants of a wedding.

In her loins and in her back there was pain; but the frightening recollections of the night were fading before the remembrance of its triumphs. She had no twinges of conscience as to the way she had gained that end, for to live and fulfill the purpose of life seemed to absolve all. Yesterday it couldn't happen. Today it had happened. Nothing could touch that; nothing.

In a few minutes the sun would be up, lighting the ridge of the valley behind which a few short hours ago it had set. She drew up her legs, sat a moment on the bridge, then knelt, scooped up the water in her hands and bathed her face and neck. Then she stood up and in a sudden excess of feeling hopped and skipped across to the apple tree. A thrush and a blackbird were competing from neighbouring branches. Under the trees some leaves touched her hair, sprinkling her ear and neck with dew. She knelt and began to pick a few of the bluebells which made a hazy carpet under the trees. But she had taken no more than a dozen when she gave it up and sat against a lichened tree, her head back, the thin juicy stems of the bluebells clutched to her breast.

She sat so still, her neck curved in lassitude, her skirts drawn up, her bare legs in sensuous contact with the grass and the leaves, that a chaffinch hopped down and began its "pink-pink" cry beside her hand. Her throat ached to join in, but she knew she would only croak.

A big fly came down also and settled on a leaf close to her face; he had two round brown knobs on his head and at this range looked enormous, a prehistoric animal which had roamed the jungles of a forgotten world. First he stood on four front legs and rubbed the two back ones with sinuous ease up and down his wings; then he stood on the four back and rubbed the two front ones like an obsequious shopkeeper. "Buzz, buzz!" said Demelza. He went with a sudden hum but was back again in the same position almost at once, this time rubbing his head as if over a wash tub.

A spider's web was outlined in fine beads of moisture above her head. The blackbird which was singing stopped his song, balanced a moment with a tail like a lady's fan, flew away. Two last petals of pink-brown apple blossom, disturbed by the movement, floated indolently to earth. The finch began to peck at one of them.

She put out her hand and made an encouraging sound, but he wouldn't be deceived and fluttered sidelong to a safer distance. In the fields a cow lowed.

There was still that about the early hour which set it apart from men. At the back of all the chatter of the birds was the quietness of a world not yet awake.

A rook flew low overhead, his shabby plumage gilded, his wings making a creaky sound as they beat the air. The sun rose and flooded into the valley, casting dewy silent shadows and shafts of long pale light among the trees.

CHAPTER EIGHT

Ross woke late. It was seven before he was stirring. When he got up he had a nasty taste in his mouth. It had been poor stuff at the Fighting Cock's Inn.

Demelza… Stiff old silk of the dress… The hooks. What had got into her? He had been drunk, but was it with liquor? The expense of spirit in a waste of shame is lust in action… past reason hated—how did it go? He had not thought of *that* sonnet last night. The poets had played him false. A strange affair.

At least there had been an expense of spirit…

And the whispering shrews of three villages had only anticipated the truth. Not that that mattered. What mattered was Demelza and himself. What would he find her this morning: the friendly drudge of daylight or the silk-mouthed stranger he had imagined through the summer night?

She had had her way and at the last had seemed to fear it.

The acme of futility was to regret a pleasure that was past, and he had no intention of doing so. The thing was done. It would change the very pith of their personal ways; it would intrude on their growing friendship, distorting every act and image and introducing false values.

His rejection of her in the parlour had been the only sane course. Prudish if you liked, but how far were prudery and restraint confused in the mind of the cynic?

His reasoning was all questions and no answers this morning.

Whichever way one looked at it, a recollection of last night held something distasteful: not Demelza's fault, not his, but arising out of the history of their association. Was this nonsense? What would his father have said? "High-flown claptrap to explain a thick head."

He struggled into his clothes. For a time he allowed his mind to slur over the outcome. He went down and swilled himself under the pump, glancing from time to time at the distant cliff line where Wheal Leisure could be seen.

He dressed again and had breakfast, waited on by a backbent muttering Prudie. She was like a fisherman angling for sympathy. She got no bites this morning. When he had finished he sent for Jud.

"Where is Demelza?"

"Dunno. She belong to be somewhere about. I seed en pass through the 'ouse an hour gone."

"Are the Martin children here?"

"In the turmut field."

"Well, Prudie and Demelza can join them when she is ready. I shall not be going to the mine this morning. I'll help you and Jack with the hay. Time it was begun."

Jud grunted and ambled out. After sitting a few minutes, Ross went out to the library and did half an hour's work on the business of the mine. Then he took a scythe from the farmshed and set about giving it a keener edge on the grindstone. Work as a solvent for the megrims of the night. The expense of spirit in a waste of shame... Last night before the final episode he had reflected that the day had begun in frustration and ended in frustration. This morning all the old restraints were rising to persuade him that the judgment still held good. Life seemed to be teaching him that the satisfaction of most appetites carried in them the seeds of frustration, that it was the common delusion of all men to imagine otherwise.

The first principles of that lesson had ten-year-old roots. But then, he was not a sensualist so perhaps he couldn't judge. His father had been a sensualist and a cynic; his father took love at its face value and took it as it came. The difference was surely not so much that *he* was frigid by nature (far from it) but that he expected too much.

The sense of separateness from others, of loneliness, had not often been so strong as this morning. He wondered if in fact there was any true content in life, if all men were as troubled as he with a sense of disillusion. It had not always been so. His childhood had been happy enough in the unthinking way that childhoods are. He had enjoyed in a measure the roughness and dangers of active service. It was since he returned home that the evil eye of discontent had been on him, making empty air of his attempts to find a philosophy of his own, turning to ashes whatever he grasped.

He put the scythe on his shoulder and tramped over to the hayfield, which lay on the northeast side of the valley beyond the apple trees and stretching up to Wheal Grace. A large field unenclosed by walls or hedges, and the hay in it was a good crop, better than last year, yellowed and dried by the last week of sun. He took off his coat and hung it over a stone at the corner of the field. He was bare-headed and could feel the warmth of the climbing sun on his hair and open neck. Natural enough that in the old days men were sun worshippers; especially in England, where the sun was elusive and fitful and always welcome, in a land of mists and cloud and drifting rain.

He began to cut, bent a little forward and using the body as a pivot, swinging in a wide semicircle. The grass toppled reluctantly, long sheafs of it bending over and sinking slowly to the earth. With the grass went patches of purple scabious and moon daisies, chervil and yellow buttercups, flowering illicitly and suffering the common fate.

Jack Cobbledick appeared, climbing the field with his high-stepping stride, and then Jud, and they worked together all through the morning while the sun rose high and beat down on them. Every now and then one or another would stop to sharpen his scythe upon a stone. They spoke little, all preferring to keep their own thoughts tight and tidy and untouched. Two larks remained with them most of the morning, fluttering dots in the high sky, singing and diving and singing.

At noon they stopped and sat in a group amongst the slain grass and took long drinks of buttermilk and ate rabbit pasties and barley cakes, Jack Cobbledick meantime remarking in a voice as slow and drawling as his walk that this here weather made you that dry you wanted to drink down more than you could rightly hold; and he'd heard tell the marrying next month at Mingoose was to be the biggest party for years: all the tip-top folk, and he'd seed old Joe Triggs last forenoon and he'd said it was a mortal shame for Jim Carter to lie in prison while Nick Vigus went scot-free, and there was many folk of the same mind; and it was said as Carter was being sent to Bodmin Gaol, which they did say was one of the best in the West Country and fever was not so prevalious there as Launceston or the Plymouth hulks. Was that true, did Cap'n Poldark know? Ross said, yes, that was true.

Jack Cobbledick said it was common belief that if Cap'n Poldark hadn't stood up in court and preached to the magistrates, Carter would have been sent for seven years' transportation, and folks said as the justices was fair mad about it.

Jud said he knew a man who was sent to Bodmin Gaol for next to nothing, and the first day he was there he got the fever and the second day he was dead.

Cobbledick said folk were saying that if more of the gentry was like Someone They All Knew there wouldn't be all this distress and closing down of mines and crying out for bread.

Jud said the fever was that bad at Launceston in '83 that the gaoler and his wife was strick down with it the same night and was both cold before the light of day.

Cobbledick said the Greets and the Nanfans were for getting up a crowd of men to drive Nick Vigus out of the district but that Zacky Martin had said they mustn't do nothing of the shape; two wrongs didn't make a right, nor never would.

Jud said it was his firm belief that Jim Carter's third child would be born posthumorously.

Presently they were up and off again. Ross soon forged ahead of his companions, driven on by private necessities of his own. As the sun declined, he stopped again for a few minutes and saw that they had nearly done. His forearms and back were aching with the exercise, but he had worked some dissatisfaction out of himself. The regularity of the sweeping scythe, the pivoting movement of the body, the steady advance round the edge of the field, eating into the grass and gradually approaching the centre, had helped to lay the uncomfortable ghosts of his discontent. There was a faint north breeze stirring, and the heat of the sun had become a mellow warmth. He took deep breaths and mopped his brow and stared at the other men behind him. Then he glanced at the dwarfed figure of one of the Martin children coming towards him from the house.

It was Maggie Martin, aged six, a cheerful child with the family red hair.

"If ee plaise, sur-r," she piped in her singsong voice, "thur be a leddy to see ee."

He put a forefinger under the child's chin. "What manner of lady, my dear?"

"Mistress Poldark, sur. Over from Trenwith."

It was months since Verity had been to see him. This might be the beginning of a resumption of their old friendship. He had never needed it more.

"Thank you, Mag. I'll come at once."

He fetched his coat, and with this and the scythe slung over his shoulder went down the hill to the house. She had come by horse this time, it seemed.

He put the scythe at the door and, swinging his coat, entered the parlour. A young woman was seated in a chair. His heart gave a lurch.

Elizabeth was in a long dark brown riding habit with fine Ghent lace at the cuffs and throat. She wore a three-cornered felt hat trimmed with lace which set off the oval of her face and crowned the bright sheen of her hair.

She extended a hand with a smile that hurt him with a memory of things past. She was a lady and very beautiful.

"Why, Ross, I thought we hadn't seen you for a month, and since I was passing this way—"

"Don't make excuses for your coming," he said. "Only for not having come before."

She flushed and her eyes showed a hint of pleasure. Her frailty and charm had not been altered by her motherhood. At every meeting he was surprised afresh.

"It's a hot day to be riding," he said. "Let me get you something to drink."

"No, thank you, I'm quite cool." And she looked it. "First tell me how you are, what you have been doing. We see so little of you."

Conscious of his damp shirt and ruffled hair, he told what he had been doing. She was a little ill at ease. He saw her glance once or twice round the room as if she sensed some alien presence, or as if she was surprised at the comfortable though shabby nature of the furnishings. Her eyes went to a bowl of wood anemones and hart's tongue ferns on the window seat.

"Verity told me," she said, "that you were not able to get your farm boy a lighter sentence. I am sorry."

Ross nodded. "A pity, yes. George Warleggan's father was chairman of the bench. We parted in mutual dislike."

She glanced at him from under her lashes. "George will be sorry. Perhaps if you had approached him it might have been arranged. Though it is true, isn't it, that the boy was caught red-handed?"

"How is Uncle?" Ross changed the subject, feeling that his views on the Carter episode might offend her.

"He grows no better, Ross. Tom Choake bleeds him regular, but it brings him only a temporary relief. We had all hoped that this fine weather would put him on his feet again."

"And Geoffrey Charles?"

"Doing splendid, thank you. We feared last month that he had taken the measles after escaping all the epidemic, but it was no more than a teething rash." Her tone was controlled but something remained in it to give him a twinge of surprise. He had not heard that snuffed possessive inflexion before.

They chatted for some minutes with a sort of anxious agreeableness. Elizabeth asked about the progress of the mine, and Ross went into technical details which he doubted if she understood and was sure she could not be as interested in as she seemed. She spoke of the forthcoming wedding taking it for granted that he had been invited, and he had not the heart to correct her. Francis wanted her to go to London this autumn, but she thought Geoffrey Charles young for the journey. Francis did not seem to understand that Geoffrey Charles could not be left behind. Francis thought, etc... Francis felt...

Her small composed face clouded at this stage, and she said, pulling at her gloves:

"I wish you could see more of Francis, Ross."

Ross politely agreed that it was a pity he had not more time to spend in visiting his cousin.

"No, I do not mean quite in the sense of an ordinary visit, Ross. I do wish somehow you could have worked together. Your influence on him—"

"My influence?" he said in surprise.

"It would have steadied him. I think it would help to steady him." She glanced up painfully, then looked away. "You will think it strange my speaking in this way. But you see, I have been worried. We are both so friendly with George Warleggan, have stayed in Truro with him and at Cardew. George is very kind. But he is so wealthy, and to him gambling is just a pleasant recreation. Not so to us now, not so to Francis. When one plays for higher stakes than one can afford... It seems to have a hold of Francis. It is the breath of life to him. He wins a little and then loses so much. Charles is too ill to stop him and he has control of everything. We really cannot go on as we are doing. Grambler is losing money, as you know."

"Do not forget," Ross said, "that I lost money myself before I went away. My influence might not have been so good as you think."

"I should not have spoken of it. I hadn't intended to. I have no right to burden you with my troubles."

"I take it as a true compliment."

"But when you mentioned Francis... And our old friendship... You were always one to understand."

He saw that she was genuinely distressed, and turned towards the window to give her time to recover. He wanted to justify her faith in him; he would have given a lot to have been able to put some suggestion to ease the distress from her face. His resentment of her marriage had quite gone. She had come to him.

"I wondered if I should tell Charles," she said. "I'm so afraid it would make him more ill—and that would not help us at all."

Ross shook his head. "Not that. Let me see Francis first. God knows, I am not likely to succeed where—where others have failed. What I cannot begin to understand—"

"What?"

But she sensed something of what he left unsaid. "He is reasonable in so many things, but I cannot influence him in that. He seems to take my advice as an interference."

"So he will certainly take mine the same. But I will try."

She looked at him. "You have a strong will, Ross. I knew it once. What a man dislikes to hear from his—his wife he may accept from a cousin. You have a way of making your point. I think you could influence Francis very much if you chose."

"Then I will choose."

She rose. "Forgive me, I hadn't intended to say so much. I can't tell you how I appreciate the way you've welcomed me."

Ross smiled. "Perhaps you'll promise to come more often."

"Gladly. I should have liked to come before but felt I had not the right to come."

"Don't feel that again."

There was a footstep in the hall and Demelza came in carrying a great sheaf of fresh-picked bluebells.

She stopped dead when she saw she was intruding. She was in a plain blue linen dress, homemade, with open neck and a bit of embroidery to ornament the belt. She looked wild and unkempt, for all afternoon, shamefully neglecting Prudie and the turnips, she had been out lying in the grass of another hayfield on the high ground to the west of the house, staring down at Ross and the men working on the hill opposite. She had lain there sniffing at the earth and peering through the grass like a young dog, and finally had turned over and gone to sleep in the sweet warmth of the declining sun. Her hair was ruffled and there was grass and burrs on her frock.

She returned Ross's gaze and glanced with wide eyes at Elizabeth. Then she muttered an apology and turned to withdraw.

"This is Demelza of whom you've heard me speak," Ross said. "This is Mistress Elizabeth Poldark." Two women, he thought. Made of the same substance? Earthenware and porcelain.

Elizabeth thought: Oh, God, so there *is* something between them. "Ross has often mentioned you to me, my dear," she said.

Demelza thought: She's one day too late, just one day. How beautiful she is; how I hate her. Then she glanced at Ross again, and for the first time like the stab of a treacherous knife it occurred to her that Ross's desire for her last night was a flicker of empty passion. All day she had been too preoccupied with her own feelings to spare time for his. Now she could see so much in his eyes.

"Thank you, ma'am," she said with horror and hatred in her fingertips. "Can I get you anything, sur?"

Ross looked at Elizabeth. "Reconsider your decision and take tea. It would be made in a few minutes."

"I must go. Thank you all the same. What pretty bluebells you've picked."

"Would you like them?" said Demelza. "You can have 'em if you'd like."

"That is kind of you!" Elizabeth's grey eyes flickered round the room just once more. This is her doing, she thought; those curtains. I thought Prudie wouldn't have the idea to hang them so; and the velvet draping on the settle, Ross would never have thought of that. "I came by horse, though, and unhappily could not carry them. Keep them yourself, my dear, but thank you for the kind thought."

"I'll tie en up for you and loop them over the saddle," Demelza said.

"I'm afraid they would droop. See, they're drooping already. Bluebells are like that." Elizabeth picked up her gloves and crop. I can't come here again, she thought. After all this time, and now it's too late. Too late for me to come here. "You must call and see Uncle, Ross. He often asks for you. Hardly a day goes by."

"I'll be over next week," he said.

They went to the door and Ross helped her to mount her horse, which she did with that peculiar grace of her own. Demelza had not followed them, but watched while seeming not to watch from the window.

She's slenderer than me, she thought, even though she's had a child. Skin like ivory; never done a day's work. She's a lady and Ross is a gentleman, and I am a slut. But not last night, not last night. (The memory of it swelled up in her.) I can't be a slut: I'm Ross's woman. I hope she gets fat. I do hope and dearly pray she gets fat and catches the pox and her nose drips and her teeth fall out.

"Did you mean what you said about Francis?" Elizabeth said to Ross.

"Of course. I'll do anything I can—little as it's likely to be."

"Come to see Charles. For dinner, that would suit. Any day. Goodbye."

"Goodbye," he said.

It was their first complete reconciliation since his return; and they were both aware, while not knowing that the other was aware, that the reconciliation had come just too late to count for what it might.

He watched her ride slowly up the valley. Once he saw the glint of her hair as it caught the light from the slanting sun. In this shadowed valley the birds were breaking out into their evening song.

He was tired, so tired, and wanted to rest. But his peace of mind, hardly bought during the day, was dissipated with her visit.

He turned on his heel and tramped into the house, through to the kitchen. Prudie was preparing the evening meal. He grunted at some complaint she made and went to the stables.

For some minutes he busied himself with the small tasks of the farm; these done he came back to the house and to the living-room.

Demelza was still there, standing by the window. She held the bluebells in her arms. He did not seem to notice her, but went slowly across to his favourite chair, took off his coat, and sat for some time staring with a little frown at the opposite wall. Presently he leaned back.

"I'm tired," he said.

She turned from the window, and moving quietly, as if he were asleep, she came towards his chair. On the rug at his feet she sat down. She began idly, but half contentedly, to arrange and re-arrange the bluebells in heaps upon the floor.

BOOK THREE

JUNE–DECEMBER 1787

CHAPTER ONE

1

ROSS AND DEMELZA WERE MARRIED ON THE TWENTY-FOURTH OF JUNE, 1787. The Revd Mr. Odgers performed the ceremony, which took place very quietly in the presence only of the necessary number of witnesses. The register shows that the bride gave her age as eighteen, which was an anticipation of fact by three-quarters of a year. Ross was twenty-seven.

His decision to marry her was taken within two days of their first sleeping together. It was not that he loved her but that such a course was the obvious way out. If one overlooked her beginnings she was a not unsuitable match for an impoverished farmer squire. She had already proved her worth about the house and farm, none better, and she had grown into his life in a way he had hardly realized.

With his ancient name, he could of course have gone into society and paid violent court to some daughter of the new rich and have settled down to a life of comfortable boredom on the marriage dowry. But he couldn't see such an adventure seriously. He realized with a sense of half-bitter amusement that this marriage would finally damn him in the eyes of his own class. For while the man who slept with his kitchenmaid only aroused sly gossip, the man who married her made himself personally unacceptable in their sight.

He did not go to dinner at Trenwith as he had promised. He met Francis by design at Grambler the week before the wedding and told him the news. Francis seemed relieved rather than shocked; perhaps he had always lived with an underlying fear that his cousin would one day cast off the skin of civilization and come and take Elizabeth by force. Ross was a little gratified at this unhostile reception of the news and forgot almost until they were separating his promise to Elizabeth. He did, however, then fulfill it, and they parted in a less friendly manner than they might have done.

Out of his old friendship for Verity, Ross would much have liked her to be at the wedding, but he learned from Francis that the doctor had ordered her a fortnight in bed. So Ross held back his letter of invitation and instead sent her a longer one explaining the circumstances and inviting her to come and stay with them when she was better. Verity knew Demelza by sight, but had not seen her for the better part of two years, and Ross thought she would be unable to imagine what germ of senile decay had got into his brain.

If this were so, she did not say as much in her letter of reply.

Dearest Ross,

Thank you for writing me so fully and explaining about your marriage. I am the last one to be able to criticize your attachment. But I should like to be the first to wish you the happiness I pray will be yours. When I am well and Papa is better, I will come and see you both.

Love,

Verity

The visit to Sawle Church changed more than the name of the one-time kitchenmaid. Jud and Prudie were inclined to take it badly at first, resenting, so far as they dared show it, the fact that the child who had come here as a waif and stray, infinitely beneath themselves, should now be able to call herself their mistress. They might have sulked for a long time if it had been anybody but Demelza. But in the end she talked them or hypnotized them into the view that she was in part their protegee and so her advancement reflected a certain glory on them. And after all, as Prudie remarked privately to Jud, it was better than having to take orders from some fudgy-faced baggage with drop curls.

Demelza did not see her father again that year. A few days after the banns were called she persuaded Ross to send Jud to Illuggan with a verbal message that they were to be married in a fortnight. Carne was down the mine when Jud arrived, so he was able only to deliver the message to a fat little woman in black. Thereafter silence fell. Demelza was nervous that her father might turn up and create a scene at the wedding, but all passed quietly. Tom Carne had accepted his defeat.

On the tenth of July a man called Jope Ishbel, one of the oldest and foxiest miners in the district, struck a lode of red copper at Wheal Leisure. A great amount of water came with the discovery, and all work was held up while pumping gear was brought. The adit from the cliff face was making fair progress, but some time must pass before it could unwater the workings. All this water was looked on as a good sign by those who professed to know.

When news of the find was brought to Ross, he opened an anker of brandy and had big jugs of it carried up to the mine. There was great excitement, and from the mine they could see people climbing the ground behind Mellin Cottages a mile away and staring across to see what the noise was about.

The find could not have been more opportune, for the second meeting of the venturers was due in a week's time, and Ross knew that he must ask for a further fifty pounds from each of them. Jope Ishbel's strike armed him with tangible results, for even from the poor quality of the ore that Ishbel had brought to the surface they could expect to get several pounds a ton more than from ordinary copper ore. The margin of profit was widened. If the lode was a reasonably big one, it meant the certainty of a fair return.

He did not fail to point this out when the meeting took place in Mr. Pearce's overheated offices in Truro, and the general effect was such that further drafts were voted without demur.

This was the first time Ross had seen Mr. Treneglos since the great day at Mingoose when his son married Ruth Teague, and the old man went out of his way to be agreeable and complimentary. Over dinner they sat together, and Ross was afraid that an apology was impending for the breach of manners between old neighbours in his not having been invited to the wedding. He knew the fault did not lie with Treneglos and steered conversation away from the subject.

Mr. Renfrew caused an awkward moment by getting above himself in his cups and following up a toast to the happy pair by proposing that they should not forget the bridegroom in their midst.

There was a constrained silence, and then Mr. Pearce said:

"Indeed, yes. We must certainly not forget that." And Dr Choake said: "That would be most remiss." And Mr. Treneglos, who fortunately had caught the trend of the conversation, immediately got to his feet and said: "My privilege, gentlemen. My pleasure and privilege. Our good friend, damme, recently embarked upon matrimony himself. I give you the toast: Captain Poldark and his young bride. May they be very happy."

Everyone rose and drank.

"Twould have looked bad if nobody'd mentioned it," said Mr. Treneglos, not quite to himself as they sat down.

Ross seemed the least embarrassed of them all.

2

She had already grown into his life. That was what he thought. What he meant was that she had grown into the life of the house, seeing to his needs eagerly but without fuss, a good servant and an agreeable companion.

Under the new arrangement this didn't much alter. Legally an equal, she remained in fact his inferior. She did what he said, no less eagerly, no less unquestioningly, and with a radiant good will to illuminate it all. If Ross had not wished to marry her, she would not have fretted for something else; but his decision to make the union legal and permanent, his honouring her with his name, was a sort of golden crown to set upon her happiness. Those few bad moments when Elizabeth called were almost forgotten and altogether discarded.

And now she was growing into his life in a different way. There was no going back for him, even if he had wished it, which he found he did not. There was now no mistaking that he found her desirable: Events had proved it to be no delusion of a single summer night. But he was not yet at all sure how far it was she personally who was desirable to him, how far it was the natural needs of a man that she as a woman met.

She did not seem to be troubled with any heart searchings of her own. If she had grown and developed quickly before, now her personality flowered overnight.

When a person is as happy as she was that summer, it is hard for others to be unaffected, and after a time the atmosphere she created began to have its effect on all in the house.

The additional freedoms of marriage came to her slowly. Her first attempt in this direction was a mild suggestion to Ross that some day it would be a good thing to have the mine office moved from the library, as the men walked across her flower beds in their big boots. No one was more surprised than she when a week later she saw a file of men carrying the mine papers up to one of the wooden sheds on the cliff.

Even then weeks passed before she could bring herself to steal into the library without the old sense of guilt. And it needed all the hardihood in the world to sit there trying to conjure tunes out of the derelict spinet when anyone was within hearing.

But her vitality was so abundant that gradually it overcame the barriers which custom and subservience had set up. She began to strum more openly and to sing low-voiced chants of her own devising. One day she rode in with Ross and brought back a few broad-sheets of verse which she learned by heart and then hummed to her own tunes at the spinet, trying to fit in sounds where they sounded right.

As if to collaborate with Demelza's happiness, the summer was the warmest for years, with long weeks of bright quiet weather and rare full days of rain. After the epidemics of the winter, the fine clean weather was welcome to all, and the level at which many families spent the summer seemed like plenty compared with what had gone before.

Work on Wheal Leisure was going slowly but well. With the adit making progress towards the workings, every attempt was made to avoid the heavy cost of a pumping engine. Horse whims were devised one beside another and the water thus raised was ingeniously dammed in a hollow and released down a teat to turn a water wheel, which itself worked a pump to raise more water. Copper was being mined now. Soon there would be enough to send a consignment into Truro for one of the ticketings.

3

She had already grown into his life, he thought.

Often now he wished he could separate the two Demelzas who had become a part of him. There was a matter-of-fact, daytime Demelza with whom he worked and from whom for a year or more he had derived certain definite pleasures of companionship. This one he had grown to like and to trust—to be liked and trusted by her. Half servant, half sister, comradely and obedient, the direct and calculable descendant of last year and the year before. Demelza learning to read, Demelza fetching wood for the fire, Demelza shopping with him and digging the garden and never still about her tasks.

But the second was still a stranger. Although he was husband and master of them both, this one was incalculable with the enigma of her pretty candlelit face and fresh young body—all for his carnal satisfaction and increasing pleasure. In the first days he had held this one in a certain contempt. But events had moved beyond that. Contempt had gone—but the stranger was still left.

Two not-quite-distinct persons, the stranger and the friend. It was unsettling in the day, in moments of routine and casual encounter, to get some sudden reminder of the young woman who could somehow call herself into being at will, whom he took and owned, yet never truly possessed. Still more odd was it in the night to see sometimes peering from the drugged dark eyes of this stranger the friendly untidy girl who had helped him with the horses or cut out his supper. At such times he was perturbed and not quite happy, as if he found himself trampling on something that was good in its own right.

He wished he could separate these two. He felt he would be happier if he could separate them entirely. But as the weeks passed it seemed that the reverse of what he wanted was taking place. The two entities were becoming less distinct.

It was not until the first week of August that a fusion of the two occurred.

CHAPTER TWO

PILCHARDS HAD COME LATE TO THE COAST THAT YEAR. THE DELAY HAD CAUSED anxiety, for not only did the livelihood of many people depend on the arrival of the fish but virtually in these times their existence. In the Scillies and the extreme south, the trade was already in full swing, and there were always wiseacres and pessimists who were ready to predict that the shoals would miss the northern shores of the county this year and go across to Ireland instead.

A sigh of relief greeted the news that a catch had been made at St. Ives, but the first shoal was not sighted off Sawle until the afternoon of the sixth of August.

A huer, watching from the cliff, as he had been watching for weeks, spotted the familiar dark red tinge far out to sea, and the cry he let out through his old tin trumpet inspirited the village. The seining boats instantly put out, seven men to each of the leading boats, four to the follower.

Towards evening it was known that both teams had made catches much above the average, and the news spread with great speed. Men working on the harvest at once downed tools and hurried to the village, followed by every free person from Grambler and many of the miners as they came off core.

Jud had been into Grambler that afternoon and came back with the news to Demelza, who told Ross over their evening meal.

"I'm that glad," she said. "All Sawle've been wearing faces down to their chins. Twill be a rare relief; and I hear it is a handsome catch."

Ross's eyes followed her as she rose from the table and went to trim the wicks of the candles before they were lighted. He had been at the mine all day and had enjoyed his supper in the shadowy parlour with the evening stealing into and about the room. There was no real difference between now and that evening two months ago when he had come home defeated and it had all begun. Jim Carter was still in prison. There was no real change in the futility of his own life and efforts.

"Demelza," he said.

"Um?"

"It is low tide at eleven," he said. "And the moon's up. What if we rowed round to Sawle and watched them putting down the tuck net."

"Ross, that would be lovely!"

"Shall we take Jud to help row us?" This to tease.

"No, no, let us go, just the two of us! Let us go alone. You and I, Ross." She was almost dancing before his chair. "I will row. I am as strong as Jud any day. We'll go an' watch, just the two of us alone."

He laughed. "You'd think it was a ball I'd invited you to. D'you think I can't row you that far myself?"

"When shall we start?"

"In an hour."

"Good, good, good. I'll make ready something to eat an' brandy in a flask, lest it be cold sitting, an'—an' a rug for me, and a basket for some fish." She fairly ran from the room.

They set off for Nampara Cove shortly after nine. It was a warm still evening with the three-quarter moon already high. In Nampara Cove they dragged their small boat from the cave where it was kept, across the pale firm sand to the sea's edge. Demelza got in and Ross pushed the boat through the fringe of whispering surf and jumped in as it floated.

The sea was very calm tonight and the light craft was quite steady as he pulled towards the open sea. Demelza sat in the stern and watched Ross and looked about her and dipped a hand over the gunnel to feel the water trickling between her fingers. She was wearing a scarlet kerchief about her hair and a warm skin coat which had belonged to Ross as a boy and now just fitted her.

They skirted the high bleak cliffs between Nampara Cove and Sawle Bay, and the jutting rocks stood in sharp silhouette against the moonlit sky. The water sucked and slithered about the base of the cliffs. They passed two inlets which were inaccessible except by boat at any tide, being surrounded by steep cliffs. All this was as familiar to Ross as the shape of his own hand, but Demelza had never seen it. She had only once been out in a boat before. They passed the Queen Rock, where a number of good ships had come to grief, and then rounded a promontory into Sawle Bay and came on the first fishers.

They had let down the seine—net a fine strong mesh of great length, with corks on the upper side and lead on the lower—some distance past the promontory and about half a mile from the shore. With this great net the seiners had enclosed about two acres of water and, they hoped, many fish. There was always the possibility, of course, that they had been wrongly directed by the man on the cliffs who alone could see the movement of the shoal, or that some flaw on the sea bed should have prevented the net from falling cleanly and so allowed the fish to slip away. But short of such accidents there was every hope of a good catch. And although in calm weather it might be possible to keep the net in position by means of grapnels for ten days or a fortnight, no one had the least intention of relying on good weather a minute longer than they had to.

And tonight there was a moon.

As low tide approached the boat known as the follower and carrying the tuck net was rowed cautiously into the enclosed area marked by the bobbing corks supporting the great stop seine. The boat was rowed round within the area while the tuck net was lowered and secured at various points. This done, they began to haul in the tuck net again.

It was at this crucial stage that Ross and Demelza came closely on the scene. They were not the only spectators. Every boat that would float and every human being that could sit in one had come out from Sawle to watch. And those who had no craft or were too infirm stood on the shelving beach and shouted advice or encouragement. There were lights and lanterns in the cottages of Sawle and all along the shingle bar and moving up and down on the blue-white waters of the cove. The moon lit up the scene with an unreal twilight.

Sea gulls flapped and screamed low overhead. No one took much notice of the new arrivals. One or two called friendly greetings. The arrival of Ross on the scene did not embarrass them as the arrival of others of the gentry might have done.

He rowed his boat close to where the master seiner was standing in his craft giving brief orders to the men who were within the circle hauling in the net. As it became clear that the net was heavy a short silence fell. In a moment or two it would be known whether the catch was a fine or a poor one, whether they had trapped a good part of the shoal or some part with fish too small for salting and export, whether by some mischance they might have caught a shoal of sprats instead, as had happened a couple of years ago. On the result of the next few minutes the prosperity of half the village hung.

The only sound now was the bobble and swish of water against fifty keels and the deep "Yoy… ho! Hoy… ho!" chorus of the men straining to haul in the net.

Up and up came the net. The master seiner had forgotten his words of advice and stood there biting his fingers and watching the waters within the tuck net for the first sign of life.

It was not long in coming. First one of the spectators said something, then another exclaimed. Then a murmur spread round the boats and increased to what was more a shout of relief than a cheer.

The water was beginning to bubble, as if in a giant saucepan; it boiled and frothed and eddied, and then suddenly broke and disappeared and became fish. It was the miracle of Galilee enacted over again in the light of a Cornish moon. There was no water any more: only fish, as big as herrings, jumbled together in their thousands, jumping, wriggling, glinting, fighting and twisting to escape.

The net heaved and lurched, the big boats heeled over as the men strained to hold the catch. People talking and shouting, the splash of oars, the excited shouts of the fishers; the earlier noise was nothing to this.

The tuck net was now fast and the fishermen were already dipping baskets into the net and tipping them full of fish into the bottom of the boat. It seemed as if everyone was mindful of the haste necessary to take full advantage of good fortune. It was as if a storm waited just over the summit of the nearest cliff. Two big flat-bottomed boats like barges were ferried alongside, and men hanging over the side began to work with fury to fill them. Other small boats quickly surrounded the net to take in the catch.

Sometimes the moonlight seemed to convert the fish into heaps of coins, and to Ross it looked like sixty or eighty darkfaced sub-human pygmies scooping at an inexhaustible bag of silver.

Soon men were up to their ankles in pilchards, soon up to their knees. Boats broke away and were rowed gingerly towards the shore, their gunnels no more than two inches above the lapping water. On shore the activity was no less; lanterns were everywhere while the fish were shovelled into wheelbarrows and hurried towards the salting cellars for picking over and inspection. Still the work round the net went on amongst the springing gleaming fish.

At the other side of the bay, another but lesser catch was being hauled in. Ross and Demelza ate their cakes and took a sip of brandy from the same flask and talked in lowered voices of what they saw.

"Home now?" Ross said presently.

"A small bit longer," Demelza suggested. "The night is so warm. It is grand to be 'ere."

He dipped his oars gently and straightened the bows of the boat towards the gentle lift and fall of the sea. They had drifted away from the crowds of boats, and it rather pleased him to get this detached view.

He found, quite to his surprise, that he was happy. Not merely happy in Demelza's happiness but in himself. He couldn't think why. The condition just existed within him.

They waited and watched until the tuck net was almost cleared and the fishermen were going to lower it again. Then they waited to see if the second haul would be as big as the first. Whenever they were about to leave some fresh interest held them. Time passed unnoticed while the moon on its downward path came near the coast line and picked out a silver stitching on the water.

At last Ross slowly exerted his strength on the oars and the boat began to move. As they passed near the others Pally Rogers recognized them and called, "Good night!" Some of the others paused, sweating from their labours and also shouted.

"Good catch, eh, Pally?" Ross said.

"'Andsome. More'n a quarter of a million fish, I reckon, afore we're done."

"I'm very glad. It will make a difference next winter."

"Night, sur."

"Good night."

"Night, sur."

"Night…"

They rowed away, and as they went the sounds of all the voices and human activity slowly faded, into a smaller space, into a little confined murmur in the great night. They rowed out towards the open sea and the sharp cliffs and the black dripping rocks.

"Everyone is happy tonight," Ross said, half to himself.

Demelza's face gleamed in the stern. "They like you," she said in an undertone. "Everyone d' like you."

He grunted. "Little silly."

"No, 'tis the truth. I know because I'm one of 'em. You and your father was different from the others. But mostly you. You're—you're—" She stumbled. "You're half a gent and half one of them. And then you trying to help Jim Carter and giving food to people—"

"And marrying you."

They passed into the shadow of the cliffs. "No, not that," she said soberly. "Maybe they don't like that. But they like you all the same."

"You're too sleepy to talk sense," he said. "Cover your head and doze off till we're home."

She did not obey, but sat watching the dark line where the shadow of the land ended and the glinting water began. She would have preferred to be out there. The shadow had lengthened greatly since they came out, and she would have rather made a wide circuit to keep within the friendly light of the moon. She stared into the deep darkness of one of the deserted coves they were passing. To these places no man ever came. They were desolate and cold. She could picture unholy things living there, spirits of the dead, things come out of the sea. She shivered and turned away.

Ross said: "Take another nip of brandy."

"No." She shook her head. "No. Not cold, Ross."

In a few minutes they were turning into Nampara Cove. The boat slipped through the ripples at the edge and grounded in the sand. He got out and as she made to follow caught her about the waist and carried her to dry land. He kissed her before he put her down.

When the boat was drawn up into its cave and the oars hidden where a casual vagrant could not find them, he rejoined her where she was waiting just above high-watermark. For a while neither of them made a move and they watched the moon set. As it neared the water, it began to grow misshapen and discoloured like an overripe blood orange squeezed between sea and sky. The silver sword across the sea became tarnished and shrank until it was gone and only the old moon remained, bloated and dark, sinking into the mists.

Then without words they turned, walked across the sand and shingle, crossed the stream at the stepping-stones, and walked together hand in hand the half mile to the house.

She was quite silent. He had never done what he had done tonight. He had never kissed her before except in passion. This was something different. She knew him to be closer to her tonight than he had ever been before. For the very first time they were on a level. It was not Ross Poldark, gentleman farmer, of Nampara, and his maid, whom he had married because it was better than being alone. They were a man and a woman, with no inequality between them. She was older than her years and he younger; and they walked home hand in hand through the slanting shadows of the new darkness.

I am happy, he thought again. Something is happening to me, to us, transmuting our shabby little love affair. Keep this mood, hold on to it. No slipping back.

The only sound all the way home was the bubbling of the stream beside their path. The house greeted them whitely. Moths fluttered away to the stars and the trees stood silent and black.

The front door creaked as they closed it, and they climbed the stairs with the air of conspirators. When they reached their room, they were laughing breathlessly at the thought of waking Jud and Prudie with such gentle noises.

She lit the candles and closed the windows to keep the moths out, took off the heavy coat, and shook out her hair. Oh yes, she was lovely tonight. He put his arms about her, his face still boyish in its laughter, and she laughed back at him, her mouth and teeth gleaming moist in the candlelight.

At this his smile faded and he kissed her.

"Ross," she said. "Dear Ross."

"I love you," he said, "and am your servant. Demelza, look at me. If I've done wrong in the past, give me leave to make amends."

So he found that what he had half despised was not despicable, that what had been for him the satisfaction of an appetite, a pleasant but commonplace adventure in disappointment, owned wayward and elusive depths he had not known before and carried the knowledge of beauty in its heart.

CHAPTER THREE

1

SEPTEMBER OF THAT YEAR WAS CLOUDED BY THE DEATH OF CHARLES. THE OLD man had grunted miserably on all through the summer, and the doctor had given him up a half-dozen times. Then one day, perversely, he collapsed just after Choake had made his most favourable report of the year, and died before he could be resummoned.

Ross went to the funeral, but neither Elizabeth nor Verity was there, both being ill. The funeral attracted a big attendance both of village and mining people and of the local gentry, for Charles had been looked on as the senior personage of the district and had been generally liked within the limits of his acquaintance.

Cousin William-Alfred took the service and, himself affected by the bereavement, preached a sermon which was widely agreed to be of outstanding quality. Its theme was "A Man of God." What did the phrase mean, he asked? It meant to nourish those attributes in which Christ himself had been so conspicuous: truth and honesty, purity of heart, humility, grace, and love. How many of us had such qualities? Could we look into our own hearts and see there the qualities necessary to make us men and women of God? A time such as this, when we mourned the passing of a great and good man, was a time for self-inspection and a renewed dedication. It was true to say that in the loss of our dear friend Charles Poldark we marked the passing of a man of God. His way had been upright; he had never spoken an ill word. From him you grew to expect only kindness and the courtesy of the true gentleman who knew no evil and looked for none in others. The steady, unselfish leadership of a man whose existence was an example to all.

After William-Alfred had been talking in this vein for five minutes, Ross heard a sniff in the pew beside him and saw Mrs. Henshawe dabbing unashamedly at her nose. Captain Henshawe too was blinking his blue eyes, and several others were weeping quietly. Yes, it was a "beautiful" sermon, tugging at the emotions and conjuring up pictures of greatness and peace. But were they talking about the decent peppery ordinary old man he knew, or had the subject strayed to the story of some saint of the past? Or were there two men being buried under the same name? One perhaps had shown himself to such as Ross, while the other had been reserved for the view of men of deep insight like William-Alfred. Ross tried to remember Charles before he was ill, Charles with his love of cockfighting and his hearty appetite, with his perpetual flatulence and passion for gin, with his occasional generosities and meannesses and faults and virtues, like most men. There was some mistake somewhere. Oh well, this was a special occasion… But Charles himself would surely have been amused. Or would he have shed a tear with the rest for the manner of man who had passed away?

William-Alfred was drawing to the end.

"My friends, we may fall far short of the example which is thus set before us. But in my Father's house are many mansions, and there shall be room for all that believe. Equality of life, equality of opportunity are not for this world. Blessed are the humble and meek, for they shall see God. And He in His infinite wisdom shall weigh us all. Blessed are the poor, for they shall enter into heaven because of their poverty. Blessed are the rich, for they shall enter into heaven because of their charity. So in the hereafter there shall be one mighty concourse of people, all provided for after their several needs, all rewarded according to their virtues, and all united in the one sublime privilege of praising and glorifying God. Amen."

There was a scraping of viols as the three musicians by the chancel steps prepared to strike up, the choir cleared their throats, and his son wakened Mr. Treneglos.

Ross accepted the invitation to return to Trenwith, hoping he might see Verity, but neither she nor Elizabeth came down. He did not stay longer than to drink a couple of glasses of canary, and then he made his excuses to Francis and walked home.

He was sorry he had not come straight back. The attitude of some of the mourners had a certain pained withdrawnness towards himself. Despite his own thoughts at the time of his marriage, he was unprepared for it, and he could have laughed at himself and at them.

Ruth Treneglos, née Teague. Mrs. Teague. Mrs. Chynoweth. Polly Choake. Quacking geese, with their trumpery social distinctions and their sham code of ethics! Even William-Alfred and his wife had been a little constrained. No doubt to them his marriage looked too much like the mere admission of the truth of an old scandal. Of course William-Alfred, in his well-intentioned way, took "the family" very seriously. Joshua had rightly called him its conscience. He liked to be consulted, no doubt.

Old Mr. Warleggan had been very distant, but that was more understandable. The episode of the courtroom rankled. So perhaps did Ross's refusal to put the mine business through their hands. George Warleggan was far too careful of his manners to show what he felt.

Well, well. The whole of their disapproval added together didn't matter an eyewink. Let them stew. As he reached his own land Ross's annoyance began to leave him at the prospect of seeing Demelza again.

2

In fact he was disappointed, for when he reached home Demelza had gone to Mellin Cottages, taking some extra food for Jinny and a little coat she had made for her week-old baby. Benjamin Ross, too, had been having trouble with his teeth and last month had had a convulsion. Ross had seen his two-and-a-half-year-old namesake recently and had been struck by the coincidence that Reuben's knife had left a scar on the child's face roughly similar to his own. He wondered if this would be remarked when the boy grew up.

He decided to walk over to Mellin now in the hope of meeting Demelza on the way back.

He met his wife two hundred yards from the cottages. As always it was a peculiar pleasure to see her face light up, and she came running and hopping to meet him.

"Ross! How nice. I didn't expect ee back yet."

"It was indifferent entertainment," he said, linking her arm. "I'm sure Charles would have been bored."

"Ssh!" She shook her head at him in reproof. "'Tis poor luck to joke about such things. Who was there? Tell me who was there."

He told her, pretending to be impatient but really enjoying her interest. "That's all. It was a sober crew. My wife should have been there to brighten it up."

"Was—was Elizabeth not there?" she asked.

"No. Nor Verity. They are both unwell. The bereavement, I expect. Francis was left to do the honours alone. And your invalids?"

"My invalids?"

"Jinny and the infant."

"Oh, they are well. A proper little girl. Jinny is well but very much down. She is listless-like and lacks poor Jim."

"And little Benjy Ross and his teeth. What is the matter with the boy: do they grow out of his ears?"

"He is much better, my love. I took some oil of valerian and told Jinny—told Jinny—What is the word?"

"Instructed?"

"No—"

"Prescribed?"

"Yes. I prescribed it for him like an apothecary. So many drops, so many times a day. And Jinny opened her blue eyes and said, yes, ma'am, and no, ma'am, just as if I was really a lady."

"So you are," said Ross.

She squeezed his arm. "So I am. I d' forget, Ross. Anybody you loved you would make a lady."

"Nonsense," said Ross. "The blame's entirely yours. Have they heard of Jim this month?"

"Not this month. You heard what they heard last month."

"That he was well, yes. For my part, I doubt it; but fine and good if it reassures them."

"Do ee think you could ask someone to go and see him?"

"I've already done so. But no report yet. It is true that Bodmin is the best of a bad lot, for what consolation that maybe."

"Ross, I been thinking—"

"What?"

"You told me I did ought to have someone else in to help in the house, to give me more time, like. Well, I thought to ask Jinny Carter."

"What, and have three infants crawling about the house?"

"No, no. Mrs. Zacky could look after Benjy and Mary; they could play with her own. Jinny could bring her mite and sit 'er in a box in the sun all day. She'd be no trouble."

"What does Jinny say?"

"I haven't asked her. I thought to see what you said first."

"Settle it between yourselves, my dear. I have no objection."

They reached the top of the hill by Wheal Grace, and Demelza broke away from him to pick some blackberries. She put two in her mouth and offered him the choice of a handful. He took one absently.

"I too have been thinking. A good flavour this year. I too have been thinking. Now that Charles is gone, Verity is much in need of a rest. It would give me much pleasure to have her here for a week or two, to recuperate from all her nursing."

They went down the hill. He waited for her to speak, but she did not. He glanced down at her. The vivacity had gone from her face and some of the colour.

"Well?"

"She wouldn't come—"

"Why do you say that?"

"All your family—they hate me."

"None of my family hate you. They don't know you. They may disapprove. But Verity is different."

"How can she be if she's one o' the family?"

"Well, she is. You don't know her."

There was silence for the rest of the walk home. At the door they parted, but he knew that the discussion was not finished. He knew Demelza well enough now to be sure that nothing but a clear-cut issue was ever satisfactory to her. Sure enough, when he went out to go to the mine she ran after him.

"Ross."

He stopped. "Well?"

She said: "They think—your family think you was mad to marry me. Don't spoil this first summer by asking one of 'em to stay here. You told me just now I was a lady. But I ain't. Not yet. I can't talk proper, and I can't eat proper, and I'm always getting cagged wi' dirt, and when I'm vexed I swear. Maybe I'll learn. If you'll learn me, I'll learn. I'll try all the time. Next year, maybe."

"Verity isn't like that," Ross said. "She sees deeper than that. She and I are much alike."

"Oh yes," said Demelza, nearly crying, "but she's a woman. You think I'm nice because you're a man. Tedn't that I'm suspicious of her. But she'll see all my faults and tell you about them and then you'll never think the same again."

"Walk with me up here," Ross said quietly.

She looked up into his eyes, trying to read his expression. After a moment she began to walk beside him and they climbed the field. At the gate he stopped and leaned his arms on it.

"Before I found you," he said, "when I came home from America things looked black for me. You know why, because I'd hoped to marry Elizabeth and returned to find her with other plans. That winter it was Verity alone who saved me from… Well, I was a fool to take it so to heart; nothing is really worth that; but I couldn't fight it at the time, and Verity came and kept me going. Three and four times a week all through that winter she came. I can't ever forget that. She gave me something to hold on to; that's hard to repay. For three years now I've neglected her shamefully, perhaps when she most needed me. She has preferred to stay indoors, not to be seen about; I have not had the same need of her; Charles was ill and she thought it her first duty to nurse him. But that can't go on, now Charles is dead. Francis tells me she's really ill. She must get away from that house for a change. The least I can do is to ask her here."

Demelza moodily rustled the dry stubble of barley stalks under her foot.

"But why has she need of *you?* If she is ill, she needs a surgeon, that's all. She'll be the better looked after at—at Trenwith."

"Do you remember when you first came here? A man used to call. Captain Blarney."

She looked at him with eyes in which the pupils had grown dark. "No."

"Verity and he were in love with each other. But Charles and Francis found that he had been married before; there were the strongest objections to his marrying Verity. Communication between him and Verity was forbidden and so they used to meet here secretly. Then one day Charles and Francis found them here and there was a violent quarrel and Captain Blarney went home to Falmouth and Verity has not seen him since."

"Oh," said Demelza moodily.

"Her sickness, you see, is one of the spirit. She may be ill other ways too, but can I deny her the help that she gave me? To find a change of company, to get away from brooding, that may be half the battle. You could help her so much if you tried."

"I could?"

"You could. She has so little interest in life, and you're so full of it. You have all the zest for living, and she none. We have to help her together, my dear. And for this I want your willing help, with no grudging."

On the gate she put her hand over his.

"Sometimes," she said, "I feel angry-like, and then I go all small and mean. But of course I'll do it, Ross. Anything you say."

CHAPTER FOUR

1

DEMELZA NIGHTLY PRAYED THAT VERITY WOULD NOT COME. When a reply was brought and she learned that her cousin-in-law had accepted the invitation and hoped to be well enough by next weekend, her heart turned over and climbed into her throat. She tried to hide her panic from Ross and to accept his amused assurances. During the rest of the week her fears found outlet in a frenzy of summer cleaning, so that not a room was left unscoured and Prudie moaned wild complaints each morning at the sight of her.

No amount of work could stave off Saturday's approach and with it Verity's. She could only hope that Aunt Agatha would have a fit or that she herself should go down with measles just in time.

Verity came shortly after midday, attended by Bartle carrying two valises strapped behind him.

Ross, who had not seen his cousin for some months, was shocked at the change. Her cheeks had sunk and the healthy open-air tan was gone. She looked forty instead of twenty-nine. The gleam of vitality and keen intelligence had gone out of her eyes. Only her voice was the same, and her disobedient hair.

Demelza's knees, which had wanted to give way earlier in the morning, were now as stiff and immovable as her lips. She stood at the door in her plain pink frock, trying not to look like a ramrod, while Ross helped his cousin from her horse and kissed her.

"Ross, how good to see you again! It's so kind of you to have me. And how well you look! The life is agreeing with you." She turned and smiled at Demelza. "I do wish I could have been at your wedding, my dear. It was one of my biggest disappointments."

Demelza let her cold cheek be kissed and stood aside to watch Verity and Ross enter the house. After a few moments she followed them into the parlour. This isn't my room now, she thought; not mine and Ross's; someone else has taken it away from us. In the middle of our bright summer.

Verity was slipping off her cloak. Demelza was interested to notice that she was very plainly dressed underneath. She wasn't beautiful like Elizabeth, but quite elderly and plain. And her mouth was like Ross's, and sometimes the tone of her voice.

"... at the end," Verity was saying, "I don't think Father minded so much. He was so very tired." She sighed. "Had he not gone so suddenly we would have summoned you. Oh well, that's over, now I feel only like rest." She smiled slightly. "I am afraid I shall not be a sportive guest, but the last thing I want is to put you or Demelza to any trouble. Do just as you have always done and leave me to fit in. That is what I want best."

Demelza racked her brains for the sentences she had prepared this morning. She twisted her fingers and got out:

"You would like something to drink, now, after your ride?"

"I have been recommended to take milk in the morning and porter at night. And I hate them both! But I had my milk before I left, so thank you, no, I'll stay dry."

"It's not like you to be ill," Ross said. "What ails you but fatigue? What does Choake say?"

"One month he bleeds me and the next he tells me I am suffering from anaemia. Then he gives me potions that make me sick and vomits that don't. I doubt if he knows as much as the old women at the fair."

"I knew an old woman once—" Demelza began impulsively, and then stopped. They both waited for her to go on.

"It don't matter," she said. "I'll go an' see if your room's ready."

She wondered if the lameness of the excuse was as plain to them as it was to her. But at least they raised no objection, so she gratefully escaped and went across to Joshua's old bedroom, which was to be Verity's. There she pulled back the coverlet and turned and stared at the two valises as if to see through them into their contents. She wondered how she would ever get through the next week.

2

All that evening and all the following day constraint was heavy on them, like an autumn fog hiding familiar landmarks. Demelza was the culprit but she couldn't help herself. She had become the intruder: two were company and three none. Ross and Verity had a good deal to say to each other, and he stayed in more than he would have done. Whenever Demelza entered the living-room their talk always broke. It was not that they had any secrets from her, but that the topic was outside her sphere and to continue it would be to ignore her.

It was always hard at meals to find a subject which would include Demelza. There was so much that would not: the doings of Elizabeth and Francis, the progress of Geoffrey Charles, news of common friends Demelza had never heard of. Ruth Treneglos was blossoming forth as the chatelaine of Mingoose. Mrs. Chynoweth, Elizabeth's mother, was troubled with her eyes and the doctors advised an operation. Cousin William-Alfred's second youngest had died of measles. Henry Fielding's new book was all the rage. These and many other items were pleasant to chat over with Ross but meant nothing to Ross's wife.

Verity, who was as susceptible as anyone, would have made her excuses and left on the third day if she had been sure that Demelza's stiffness was the outcome of dislike or jealousy. But Verity thought it arose from something else, and she hated the idea of leaving now with the knowledge that she could never return. She disliked equally the thought that she was coming between Ross and his young wife, but if she went now her name would be forever linked with this visit and she would never be mentioned between them. She was sorry she had come.

So she stayed on and hoped for an improvement without knowing how to bring it about.

Her first move was to stay in bed in the mornings and not get up until she was sure Ross was out of the house; then she would come on Demelza accidentally and talk to her or help her in the work she was doing. If this could be settled at all, then it must be settled between them while Ross was out of the way. She hoped that she and the other girl would lapse into companionship with nothing said. But after a couple of mornings she found her own casual manner becoming too noticeably deliberate.

Demelza tried to be kind, but she thought and spoke from behind a shield. Advances upon that sense of inferiority could easily be mistaken for patronage.

On Thursday morning Demelza had been out since dawn. Verity broke her fast in bed and rose at eleven. The day was fine but overcast and a small fire burned in the parlour, attracting as usual the patronage of Tabitha Bethia. Verity perched on the settle and shivered and began to stir the logs to make them blaze. She felt old and tired, and the mirror in her room showed a faint yellow tinge to her skin. It wasn't really that she cared whether she looked old or not these days... But she was always so listless, so full of aches, could do no more than half the work of a year ago. She slid farther into the corner of the settle. The pleasantest thing of all was to sit back as she was doing now, head against the velvet cover, to feel the warmth in her feet from the fire, to have nothing at all to do and no one to think of...

Having slept all night and been awake no more than three hours, she went off to sleep again, one slippered toe stretched towards the fire, one hand hanging over the wooden arm of the settle, Tabitha curled against her foot, purring lightly.

Demelza came in with an armful of beech leaves and wild rose hips.

Verity sat up.

"Oh, beg pardon," Demelza said, ready to go.

"Come in," Verity said in confusion. "I've no business to be sleeping at this hour. Please talk to me and help me wake."

Demelza smiled reservedly, put the armful of flowers on a chair. "Do you feel the draught from this window? You should have shut'n."

"No, no, please. I don't consider the sea air harmful. Let it be."

Demelza closed the window and pushed a hand through her ruffled hair.

"Ross'd never forgive me if you caught cold. These mallows is dead; their heads are all droopin'; I'll bury them." She picked up the jug and carried it from the room, returning with it freshly filled with water. She began to arrange the beech leaves. Verity watched her.

"You were always fond of flowers, weren't you? I remember Ross telling me that once."

Demelza looked up. "When did he tell ee that?" Verity smiled. "Years ago. Soon after you first came. I admired the flowers in here and he told me you brought in fresh every day."

Demelza flushed slightly. "All the same, you got to be careful," she said in a matter-of-fact voice. "Tedn't every flower that takes kindly to bein' put in a room. Some of them looks pretty but they fair stink when you pick them." She thrust in a spray or two of the rose hips. The beech leaves were just turning a delicate yellow and they toned with the yellow-orange-red of the hips. "I been trespassing today, picking these. Over as far as Bodrugan land." She stood back to look at the effect. "And sometimes flowers don't take kindly to one another, an' no matter 'ow you try to coax 'em they won't share the same jug."

Verity stirred in her seat. She must take the risk of a frontal attack. "I ought to thank you, my dear, for what you've done for Ross."

The other girl's body tautened a little, like a wire on the first hint of strain. "What he's done for me, more like."

"Yes, perhaps you're right," Verity agreed, some of the old spirit creeping into her voice. "I know he's—brought you up—all that. But you've—you seem to have made him fall in love with you, and that... has changed his whole life—"

Their eyes met. Demelza's were defensive and hostile, but also puzzled. She thought there was antagonism behind the words but couldn't make out where it lay.

"I don't know what you d' mean."

This was the final issue between them.

"You must know," Verity said, "that when he came home, he was in love with Elizabeth—my sister-in-law."

"I know that. You 'aven't any need to tell me that. I know it as well as you." Demelza turned to leave the room.

Verity got up. For this she had to stand. "Perhaps I've expressed myself badly since I came here. I want you to understand... Ever since he came back—ever since Ross came back and found Elizabeth promised to my brother I have been afraid that he would not—would not get over it as an ordinary man would get over it. We are strange that way, many of our family. We don't have it in us to make a compromise with events. After all, if part of you is—is wrenched away, then the rest is nothing. The rest is nothing—" She regained her voice and after a moment went on, "I have been afraid he would mope his life away, never find any real happiness, such as he might... We have always been closer than cousins. You see, I'm very fond of him."

Demelza was staring at her.

Verity went on: "When I heard he had married you I thought it was a make-shift. Something to console him. And I was glad even of that. Even a makeshift is so much better than a life that goes withered and dry. I was consoled to feel that he would have companionship, someone to bear his children and grow old with him. The rest didn't really matter so much."

Again she stopped, and Demelza was about to speak, but changed her mind. A dead mallow flower lay between them on the floor.

"But since I came here," Verity said, "I have seen it's no makeshift at all. It is real. That is what I want to thank you for. You're so lucky. I don't know how you've done it. And he is so lucky. He has lost the biggest thing in his life—and found it again in another person. That's all that matters. The greatest thing is to have someone who loves you and—and to love in return. People who haven't got it—or had it—don't believe that, but it's the truth. So long as life doesn't touch that you're safe against the rest—"

Her voice had again lost its tone, and she stopped to clear her throat.

"I've not come here to hate you," she said. "Nor to patronize you. There's *such* a change in Ross, and it is your doing. Do you think I care where you came from or what is your breeding or how you can curtsey? That's not all."

Demelza was staring again at the flowers.

"I've—often wanted to know how to curtsey," she said in a low voice. "Often I've wanted to know. I wish you would teach me—Verity."

Verity sat down again, desperately tired with the effort of what she had said. Near tears, she looked at her slippers.

"My dear, I am poor at it myself," she replied unsteadily.

"I'll get some more flowers," Demelza said, and fled from the room.

3

Ross had spent most of the day at the mine, and when he came home for a meal at five, Demelza had gone into Sawle with Prudie to buy rush-light and candles, and some fish for dinner tomorrow. She was late coming back on account of watching another catch of pilchards, so Ross and Verity had their meal alone. No reference was made to Demelza. Verity said that Francis still spent three or four nights a week in Truro playing whist and faro. This was bad enough in the winter months, but during the summer it was indefensible.

"I think," Verity said, "we are a peculiar family. Francis comes near to having all he desires, and now acts as if he cannot settle to anything but must rush off to the gaming tables and plunge further into debt. What is there in us, Ross, that makes us so uncomfortable to live with?"

"You malign us, my dear. It is only that, like most families, we are never all happy at one time."

"He is fretful and irritable," Verity complained. "Far worse than I. He takes no interference with his aims and is quickly angry. It's not a week since he and Aunt Agatha had a cursing match across the dinner table, and Mrs. Tabb listening open-mouthed."

"Aunt Agatha won?"

"Oh, without question. But it is such a bad example for the servants."

"And Elizabeth?"

"Sometimes she can persuade him and sometimes not. I don't think they get on very well. Perhaps I shouldn't say so, but that is my impression."

"Why should that be?"

"I don't know. She is devoted to the child, and he fond of him. Yet in a way—they say children cement a marriage. Yet it seems to me that they have not got on so well since Geoffrey Charles was born."

"There are no more coming?" Ross asked.

"None yet. Elizabeth has been ailing these last months."

There was silence for some time.

"Ross, I have been looking through the old library. In the part that has not been cleared there are bits and pieces of lumber which might be of use to you. And why do you not bring out your mother's spinet? It would go in that corner very nice and would enhance the room."

"It's out of repair and there is no one here to play it."

"It could be put *in* repair. And Prudie tells me that Demelza is always strumming on it. Besides, you may have children."

Ross looked up quickly.

"Yes. Maybe I will think it over."

Demelza came in at seven, full of the new catch which had been taken.

"The shoal was brought inshore on the tide and folk was going out knee-deep and catching 'em in buckets. Then they came in still farther and were wriggling 'pon the sand. It is not so big a harvest as the last; still, I am sorry there is no moon, for then we might have been enticed to go an' watch them again."

She seemed, Ross thought, at last less constricted, and he was thankful for the improvement. His discomfort during the last few days had been acute, and twice he had been on the point of saying something before them both, but now he was glad he had not. If they would but settle themselves like two cats in a basket, without outside interference, all might yet be well.

There was one question he intended to ask Demelza, but forgot to do so until they were in bed and Demelza, he thought, asleep. He made a note of it for some other date and was himself dozing off when the girl stirred beside him and sat up. He knew then at once that she had not been asleep.

"Ross," she said in a low voice, "tell me about Verity, would you? About Verity and Captain—Captain What's-his-name. What was it that 'appened? Did they quarrel, and why was it the—the others brokeen up?"

"I told you," Ross said. "Francis and her father disapproved. Go to sleep, child."

"No, no. Please. Ross, I want to know. I been thinking. You never told me what truly happened."

Ross put out an arm and pulled her down close beside him. "It's of no moment. I thought you were not interested in my family."

"I am in this. This is different. Tell me."

Ross sighed and yawned. "It doesn't please me to pander to your whims at this time of night. You are more inconsequent even than most women. It happened this way, love: Francis met Captain Blarney at Truro and invited him to Elizabeth's wedding. There he met Verity and an attachment sprang up—"

He did not enjoy resurrecting the dismal story. It was over and buried; nobody showed up well in it, and the retelling evoked memories of all the unhappiness and anger and self-criticism of those days. The episode had never been spoken of since: all that idiotic business of the duel, played out without any proper civilized sanctions in the heat of a common brawl... The party he had been going to at Ruth Teague's... One thing hung on another; and all that period of unhappiness and misunderstanding hung together. It was his marriage which had cut the strands and seemed to have given him a fresh, clean start.

"... so that brought it all to an end," he said. "Captain Blarney went off and we've heard nothing of him since."

There was a long silence, and he thought perhaps she had quietly fallen asleep while he spoke.

But then she stirred. "Oh, Ross, the very shame on you—" This in a troubled voice.

"Um?" he said, surprised. "What do you mean?"

She slipped away from his arm and sat up abruptly in the bed.

"Ross, how *could* you!"

"I want no riddles," he said. "Are you dreaming or talking sense?"

"You let 'em part like that. Verity goin' home to Trenwith. It would break 'er heart."

He began to grow angry. "D'you think I relished the adventure? You know what I feel for Verity. It was no pleasure to see her love affair go to pieces like my own."

"Nay, but you should've stopped un! You should have sided wi' her instead of wi' them."

"I sided with nobody! You don't know what you're talking about. Go to sleep."

"But siding wi' nobody *was* siding wi' them. Don't you see? You should have stopped the duel and stood up to them instead of letting 'em ride roughshod over all. If you'd helped Verity, then they needn't ever of parted, and—and—"

"No doubt," said Ross, "the matter seems simple enough to you. But since you know none of the people and weren't there at the time, your judgment may conceivably be at fault."

Sarcasm on his part was something she couldn't yet quite cope with. She groped for his hand and found it and put it against her cheek.

"Don't get teasy with me, Ross, I did want to know. And you d' look at it like a man would and I d' look at it like a woman. That's the difference. I can see what Verity would feel. I know what she would feel. To love someone and be loved by someone. And then to be quite alone—"

Ross's hand, from being quiescent, began slowly to stroke her face.

"Did I say you were the most inconsequent of women? It was an understatement. When I suggest Verity coming here you almost weep. And for half a week and more since she came you have been as stiff as an old gander. Now you choose this unseasonable hour to take Verity's side in a long-buried contention and to lecture me on my shortcomings. Go to sleep before I box your ears!"

Demelza pressed his hand against her mouth. "You have never hit me when I deserved it, so I am not scared now when I do not."

"That is the difference between dealing with a man and dealing with a woman."

"But a man," Demelza said, "even a kind one, can sometimes be cruel wi'out knowing it."

"And a woman," Ross said, pulling her down again, "never knows when a subject must be dropped."

She lay quiet against him, knowing a last word but not saying it.

CHAPTER FIVE

1

VERITY HAD KNOWN THAT NIGHT, FROM THE BOWL OF FRESHLY PICKED HAZEL leaves in her bedroom, that she had, with her halting self-exposure of the morning, at last got past Demelza's defences. But in reaching this tentative view she was underrating Demelza. The girl might lack subtlety, but there was nothing grudging in her decisions when she came to them. Nor did she lack the courage to own herself wrong.

Verity found herself suddenly in demand. Nothing more was said, but stiffness ripened into friendship in a day. Ross, unaware of causes, watched and wondered. Mealtimes, instead of being the chief ordeals of the day, were flowering with talk. The need for finding topics had quite gone. If Verity or Ross spoke of someone Demelza didn't know, she at once overflowed with questions and they told her. If someone very local was mentioned, Demelza, unasked, would explain to Verity. There was, too, more laughter than there had been at Nampara for years; sometimes it seemed not so much at the wit of the conversation as born of a relief common to them all. They laughed at Jud's bald crown and his bloodshot bulldog eyes, at Prudie's red nose and carpet slippers, at Tabitha Bethia's mangy coat and at the clumsy friendliness of the enormous Garrick. They laughed at each other and with each other, and sometimes at nothing at all.

In between times, usually when Ross was not there, Demelza and Verity would discuss improvements in the house or search the library and the unused rooms for odd bits of damask or velveteen to decorate or recover pieces of furniture. At first Verity had been chary of putting a strain on their new-grown friendship by offering suggestions, but when she found they were solicited, she entered into the spirit of the thing. At the beginning of the second week Ross came home and found the spinet back in the corner it had occupied in his mother's day, and the two women busy with its inside trying to repair it. Verity looked up, a faint pink flush on her sallow cheeks, and pushing a wisp of hair out of her eye, she explained breathlessly that they had found a nest of young mice under the bass strings.

"We were both too softhearted to kill them, so I brushed them into a pail and Demelza carried them out to the waste land on the other side of the stream."

"Like what you turn up under the plough," said Demelza, appearing, more tousled, from behind. "Little meaders. Bald an' pink an' scraggy and too small to run."

"Encouraging vermin," Ross said. "Who brought this spinet in here?"

"We did," said Verity. "Demelza did all the lifting."

"Dolts that you are," said Ross. "Why didn't you send for Jud and Cobbledick?"

"Oh, Jud," said Demelza. "He's not so strong as we, is he, Verity?"

"Not so strong as you are," said Verity. "Your wife is self-willed, Ross."

"You waste your breath in telling me the obvious," he replied, but went away content. Verity looked far better than a week ago. Demelza now was doing what he asked in good measure. It was what he had hoped for.

2

That night Ross woke just before dawn and found Demelza sitting up in bed. It was one of the rare wet spells of that splendid summer and autumn, and he could hear the rain splashing and bubbling on the windows.

"What is it?" he asked sleepily. "Something wrong?"

"I can't sleep," she said. "That's all."

"You won't sleep sitting up like that. Have you a pain?"

"Me? No. I been thinking."

"A bad habit. Take a nip of brandy and you'll settle off."

"I been thinking, Ross. Where is Captain Blarney now, Ross? Is 'e still over to Falmouth?"

"How do I know? I've not seen him these three years. Why must you plague me with these questions in the middle of the night?"

"Ross." She turned towards him eagerly in the half darkness. "I want ee to do something for me. I want you to go to Falmouth an' see if he's still there and see if he's still in love with Verity—"

He half lifted his head in astonishment.

"Begin all that again? Raise it afresh when she's just beginning to forget. I'd as soon raise the devil!"

"She hasn't forgotten nothing, Ross. She hasn't got over it. 'Tis there at the back just the same, like a sore place that won't heal."

"Keep your hands out of that," he warned soberly. "It doesn't concern you."

"It does concern me. I am grown fond of Verity—"

"Then show your fondness by not meddling. You don't understand the needless pain you would cause."

"Not if it brought them together, Ross."

"And what of the objections which broke up the attachment before? Have they vanished into thin air?"

"One of 'em has."

"What do you mean?"

"Verity's father."

"Well, by God!" Ross relaxed on his pillow and tried not to laugh at her impudence. "It may have occurred to you that I was not speaking of the objectors."

"About him drinkin'? I know it's bad. But you said he's given up."

"For the time. No doubt he has taken to it again. I should not blame him if he had."

"Then why not go an' see? Please, Ross. To please me."

"To please nobody," he said with irritation. "Verity would be the last person to wish it. The attachment is best broken. How should I feel if they came together through my contrivance and he treated her as he did his first wife?"

"He would not if he loved her. And Verity d' still love him. It would not stop me lovin' you if you had killed somebody."

"Um? Well, I've killed several as it happens. And as good men as myself, no doubt. But not a woman and in a drunken fit."

"I should not care if you had, so long as you loved me. An' Verity would take the risk, just as she would've done three years back if people 'adn't interfered. I can't bear, Ross, to feel she's so unhappy, down underneath, when we might do something to help. You wanted to help her. We could find out, Ross, wi'out telling her anything about it. Then we could decide, like."

"Once and for all," he said wearily, "I'll have nothing to do with the idea. You can't play fire-in-my-glove with people's lives. I'm too fond of Verity to wish to bring her all that pain back again."

She breathed a long breath into the darkness, and there was silence for some moments. "You can't," she said, "be very fond of Verity if you're afraid even to go to Falmouth and ask."

His anger bubbled over. "Damn you for an ignorant brat! We'll be arguing here till daylight. Am I to have no peace from your nagging?" He took her by the shoulders and pulled her back upon the pillow. She gave a gasp and was still.

Silence fell. The dripping window squares were just visible. After a while, uneasy at her quietness, he turned and looked at her face in the half dark. It looked pale, and she was biting her bottom lip.

"What's the matter?" he said. "What is to do now?"

"I believe," she said, "after all—I have a little pain."

He sat up. "Why didn't you tell me! Instead of sitting there prattling. Where is the pain?"

"In—my innerds. I don't rightly know. I feel a small bit queer. 'Tis nothing to alarm yourself."

He was out of bed and groping for a bottle of brandy. After a moment he came back with a mug.

"Drink this. Drink it down, right down. It will warm you if nothing more."

"I'm not cold, Ross," she said primly. She shuddered. "Ugh, 'tis stronger than I d' like it. More water would have made it very palatable, I b'lieve."

"You talk too much," he said. "It is enough to give anyone a pain. Damn me if I don't think it was moving that spinet." Alarm grew in him. "Have you no sense in your head?"

"I felt nothin' of it at the time."

"You will feel something from me if I know you have so much as touched the thing again. Where is the pain? Let me see."

"No, Ross. Tis nothin' I tell you. Not there, not there. Higher up. Leave me be. Get you back into bed and let us try to go to sleep."

"It will soon be time to rise," he said, but slowly doing as she suggested. They lay quiet for a while, watching the slow lightening of the room. Then she moved over into his arms.

"Better?" he asked.

"Yes, better. The brandy has lit a beacon inside me. Soon, mebbe, I shall be drunk and start tormentin' you."

"That would be no change. I wonder if you ate something bad. We cured the bacon ourselves, and the—"

"I think perhaps it was the spinet after all. But I'm well enough now. And sleepy—"

"Not too sleepy to hear what I have to say. I don't expect you to coddle yourself for anyone's satisfaction. But next time you have one of your moods and desire to do some fancy thing, remember that you have a selfish man to consider whose happiness is part of your own."

"Yes," she said. "I'll truly remember, Ross."

"The promise comes too easy. You'll forget it. Are you listening?"

"Yes, Ross."

"Well, then, I will promise *you* something. We spoke of chastisements the other night. Out of my love for you, and out of my own pure selfishness, I promise to beat you soundly the next time you do anything so foolish."

"But I won't do it again. I said I would not."

"Well, my promise stands too. It may be an added safeguard." He kissed her. She opened her eyes. "Do you want me to go to sleep?"

"Of course. And at once."

"Very well."

Silence fell within the room. Rain continued to beat on the knotted glass.

3

Verity's fortnight came to an end and she was persuaded to remain a third week. She seemed to have cast off the duties of Trenwith and to be finding her enjoyment here as he had hoped. Her gain in health was obvious. Mrs. Tabb would have to manage for another week. Trenwith could go hang.

During this week Ross was away two days in Truro for the first copper auction at which Wheal Leisure was represented. The copper they had to sell was divided into two lots, and both were bought by an agent for the South Wales Copper Smelting Co. at a total price of five hundred and ten guineas.

The next day Verity said to him:

"This money, when it is paid, Ross. I am very ignorant, but will some of it be yours? Will you have a little spare money then? Ten or twenty guineas perhaps?"

He stared at her. "Do you wish to buy lottery tickets?"

"The lottery is your own home," she said. "You have done wonders since you came back, with bits from the library, old pieces of cloth and the like, but apart from these curtains, I see very little that you've actually *bought*."

He stared round the parlour. There was a tactfully disguised shabbiness about it.

"Don't think I'm criticizing," Verity said. "I know how short of money you have been. I merely wondered if you could spare a little to renew things now. It would not be badly spent."

The copper company would pay in their draft at the end of the month; the venturers' meeting would follow; the profit would certainly be shared out: it was the way of such concerns.

"Yes," he said. "Personally I have no taste for fancy stuff, but perhaps we could ride in while you are still here and you could advise us on our purchases. That is, if you're well enough to make the distance."

Verity looked out of the window.

"It had occurred to me, Ross, that Demelza and I could ride in alone. We should not then take up your time."

"What, ride to Truro unescorted!" he exclaimed. "I shouldn't be easy for a moment."

"Oh, Jud could escort us as far as the town, if you could spare him. Then he could wait somewhere and return with us."

There was a pause. Ross came and stood beside her at the window. The rain of the last few days had freshened up the valley. Some of the trees were turning, but there was hardly a sign of yellow on the elms.

"The garden needs some renewal of stock also," he said. "Despite Demelza's efforts."

"Gardens are always straggly in the autumn," Verity said. "But you should order some sweetbriar and tansy. And I'll give you a cutting of herb of grace. It's pleasant to grow."

Ross put his hand on her shoulder. "How much do you want for your expedition?"

CHAPTER SIX

1

So on the first Wednesday in October Demelza and Verity rode into Truro to do some shopping, escorted, or rather followed—not from etiquette but because the track was too narrow to ride three abreast—by an interested but disgruntled Jud.

He was glad of the day off, but had taken some offence at Ross's threats as to what would happen if the two ladies returned to meet him and found him incapably drunk. It was, he felt, coarse and pointless to threaten the skin off his back for a crime he had no intention whatever of committing.

This was only the fourth time Demelza had been to Truro.

Underneath she was greatly excited, but once the journey was begun she tried to maintain an outward show of calm. Since she had nothing but her working clothes, Verity had lent her a grey riding habit, which suited her well enough. More than anything else it helped her to see herself as a lady and behave with the dignity of one. When they set off, she watched Verity and tried to copy her poise in the saddle and the straightness of her back.

It was cattle market day in the town, and as they came down a herd of young bullocks blocked the narrow street and Demelza had difficulty in holding Darkie, whose dislike of steers was deep set. Jud was too far away to be of use, but Verity edged her horse in front of the other animal. People stood to stare, but presently Darkie quieted and they were past.

"Silly old thing," Demelza said breathlessly. "She'll be sending me cat-in-the-pan over her tail one of these days." They crossed the bridge. "Oo, what a boilin' of people; us like a fair. Which way do we go?"

The time for one of the tin coinages was near, and at the end of the main street great piles of blocked tin had been set down ready for the day when the government stamp would be affixed. Weighing up to three hundredweight each, these great blocks were left untended, and glittered darkly in the sun. People milled around them; beggars stood in the gutter; the open market of Middle Row was doing a thriving trade; men and women stood in groups in the street and discussed the business of the day.

"Where are the stables?" asked Demelza. "We can't leave the horses here 'mong all these folk."

"At the back," said Verity. "Jud will take them round. We will meet you here at four, Jud."

The heavy rain of the past few days had dried the dust without leaving too much mud in its place, so that the streets were not unpleasant to walk in, and the little rivulets at the side bubbled youthfully to join their parent streams. Verity stopped to spend one and sixpence on a dozen sweet oranges, and then they entered Kenwyn Street, where the better shops were. This too was crowded with shoppers and street hawkers, though the throng was not so dense as about the markets.

Verity saw one or two people she knew, but to Demelza's relief did not stop to speak. Presently she led the way into a dark little shop, stacked almost to the ceiling with antique furniture and carpets and oil paintings and brassware. From the semi-darkness a little pockmarked man with a curled periwig shot out to greet his customers. One of his eyes was malformed by some accident or disease, giving him an odd look of duplicity, as if one part of him was withdrawn from the rest and taken with things the customer could not see. Demelza stared at him, fascinated.

Verity enquired for a small table, and they were led into a back room where a number of new and secondhand ones were stacked. Verity asked Demelza to choose one she liked, and after a good deal of discussion the matter was settled. Other things were bought. The little shopkeeper rushed downstairs for a special Indian screen he had to sell.

"How much has he given us to spend?" Demelza asked in a low voice while they waited.

"Forty guineas." Verity clinked her purse.

"Forty—Phoo! We're rich! We're— Don't forget the carpet."

"Not here. If we get one that is local made, we shall be sure of our values." Verity stared into a dark corner. "I cannot understand how you keep the time at Nampara. You need a clock."

"Oh, we d' go by the sun and the daylight. That never fails us. And Ross has his father's watch—when he recalls to wind it."

The shopkeeper popped up again.

"You have two agreeable-looking clocks there," Verity said. "Light another candle so that we can see them. What are their prices?"

2

Out in the street the two girls blinked a little in the sunshine. It was hard to tell which of them was enjoying this the more.

Verity said: "Now you need also bed linen, and curtains for two rooms and some new crockery and glassware."

"I chose that clock," Demelza said, "because it was such a jolly one. It ticked solemn enough like the other, but when it struck, I liked the way it struck. Whirr-r-r - bong, bong, bong, like an old friend telling you good morning. Where do they sell linen, Verity?"

Verity eyed her thoughtfully a moment.

"Before that, I think," she said, "we'll get a dress for you. We are only a few paces from my own dressmaker."

Demelza raised her eyebrows. "That isn't furniture."

"It is furnishings. Do you think the house should be decorated without its mistress?"

"Would it be proper to spend his money so wi'out his consent?"

"I think his consent may be taken for granted."

Demelza passed the tip of a red tongue round her lips but did not speak.

They had reached a door and a bow window four feet square screened with lace.

"This is the place," said Verity.

The younger girl looked at her uncertainly. "Would you do the choosin'?"

Inside was a plump little woman with steel spectacles. Why, Mistress Poldark! Such an honour after so long a time. Five years it must be. No, no, not perhaps quite that, but indeed a long time. Verity coloured and mentioned her father's illness. Yes, said the seamstress, she had heard that Mr. Poldark was mortal tedious sick. She hoped— Dear, said the seamstress. No, she hadn't heard; very sad! Well, but it was a pretty sight to see an old customer again.

"I'm not here now on my own account, but on my cousin's, Mistress Poldark of Nampara. On my advice she has come to you for a new outfit or two, and I'm sure you will give her the service you have always given me."

The shopkeeper blinked and beamed at Demelza, then adjusted her spectacles and curtsied. Demelza resisted the impulse to curtsey back.

"How do you do," she said.

"What we should like," Verity said, "is a view of some of your new materials and then we might discuss a simple morning dress and a riding habit something resembling the one she's now wearing."

"Indeed, yes. Do please take a seat, ma'am. And you also, ma'am. There, the chair is clean. I'll call my daughter."

Time passed.

"Yes," said Verity, "we'll take four yards of the long lawn for the riding habit shirts."

"That at two and six a yard, ma'am?"

"No, three and six. Then we shall need a half yard of corded muslin for ruffles. And a pair of the dark habit gloves. Now which hat shall it be, Cousin? The one with the feather?"

"That's too dear," said Demelza.

"The one with the feather. It is neat and not ostentatious. Now there's stockings to be considered—"

Time passed.

"And for an afternoon," said Verity, "I thought after this style. It is genteel and not fashionably exaggerated. The hoops must not be large. The dress, I thought, of that pale mauve silks with the front underskirt and bodice of the flowered apple-green, somewhat ruched. Sleeves, would you say, just over the elbow and flared a little with cream lace. Um—white fichu, of course, and a posy at the breast."

"Yes, Mistress Poldark, that will be most becoming. And a hat?"

"Oh, I shan't need'n," said Demelza.

"You are sure to sometime," said Verity. "A small black straw, I should say for the hat, with perhaps a touch of scarlet. Can you make us something after that style?"

"Oh, certainly. Just what I should've suggested meself. My daughter'll start right away on this tomorrow. Thank you. Most honoured we are, and 'ope we shall keep your patronage. Good day, ma'am. Good day, ma'am."

The better part of two hours had passed before they left the shop, both looking rather flushed and guilty as if they had been engaged in some not quite respectable pleasure.

The sun had gone from the narrow street and blazed in red reflection from the first-floor windows opposite. The crowds were no smaller, and a drunken song could be heard from a nearby gin shop.

Verity was a little thoughtful as they picked their way among some rubbish to cross the street.

"It will take us all our time to get the business done before four. And we do not want to be overtaken by darkness on the return. I think we should do well to leave the glass and linen today and go direct to buy the carpets."

Demelza looked at her. "Have you spent too many of your guineas on me?"

"Not too many, my dear… And besides, Ross will never notice whether the linen is new—"

3

They found Jud gloriously drunk.

Some part of Ross's threats had stayed with him through his carouse, and he was not on his back, but within those limits he had done well for himself.

An ostler had got him to the front of the Red Lion Inn. The three horses were tethered waiting, and he was quarrelling amiably with the man who had seen him this far.

When he saw the ladies coming, he bowed low in the manner of a Spanish grandee, clinging with one hand to the awning post outside the inn. But the bow was extravagant and his hat fell off and went floating down the rivulet which ran between the cobbles. He swore, unsettling the horses with the tone of his voice, and went after it; but his foot slipped and he sat down heavily in the street. A small boy returned his hat and was lectured for his trouble. The ostler helped the ladies to mount and then went to Jud's aid.

By this time a lot of people had paused to see them off. The ostler managed to get Jud to his feet and covered the tonsure and fringe with the damp hat.

"There, ole dear; stick it on yer 'ead. Ye'll need both 'ands for to hold yer old 'orse, ye will."

Jud instantly snatched off the hat again, cut to the quick.

"Maybe as you think," he said, "because as I've the misfortune of an accidental slip on a cow-flop therefore I has the inability of an unborn babe, which is what you think and no missment, that you think as I be open to be dressed and undressed, hatted and unhatted like a scarecrow in a field o' taties, because I've the misfortune of a slip on a cow-flop. Twould be far superior of you if you was to get down on yer bended knees wi' brush an' pan. Tedn't right to leave the streets before yer own front door befouled wi' cow-flops. Tedn't right. Tedn't tidy. Tedn't fair. Tedn't clean. Tedn't *good enough*."

"There, there now," said the ostler.

"'Is own front door," said Jud to the crowd. "Only 'is own front door. If every one of you was to clean before 'is own front door, *all* would be clean of cow-flops. The whole blathering town. Remember what the Good Book do say: 'Thou shalt not move thy neighbour's landmark.' Think on that, friends. 'Thou shalt not move thy neighbour's landmark.' Think on that and apply it to the poor dumb beasts. Never—"

"'Elp you on yer 'orse, shall I?" said the ostler.

"Never in all me days has I been so offensive," said Jud. "Hat put on me 'ead as if I was an unborn babe. An' wet at that! Wet wi' the scum of all Powder Street drippin' on me face. Enough to give me the death. Dripping on me 'ead: a chill you get, and *phit!* ye're gone. Clean yer own doorstep, friends, that's what I do say. Look to yourself, and then you'll never be in the place of this poor rat oo has to assault 'is best customers who is slipped in a cow-flop by danging a blatherin' wet hat on 'is 'ead from off of the foul stream that d' run before 'is own doorstep which should never 'appen, should never 'appen, dear friends, remember that." Jud now had his arm round the ostler's neck.

"Come along, we'll go without him," Verity said to Demelza, who had a hand up to her mouth and was tittering helplessly.

Another servant came out of the inn, and between them they led Jud to his horse.

"Pore lost soul," said Jud, stroking the ostler's cheek. "Pore lost wandering soul. Look at 'im, friends. Do 'e know he's lost? Do 'e know he's for the fires? Do 'e know the flesh'll sweal off of him like fat off of a goose? And for why? I'll tell ee for why. Because he's sold his soul to Old Scratch 'imself. And so've you all. So've you all what don't 'eed what the Good Book do say. 'Eathens! 'Eathens! 'Thou shalt not move thy neighbour's landmark. Thou shalt not—'"

At this point the two men put their hands under him and heaved him into the saddle. Then the ostler ran round to the other side as he began to slip off. A timely push and another hoist and he was firmly held, one man on either side. Old blind Ramoth stood it all without a twitch. Then they thrust one of Jud's feet deep in each stirrup and gave Ramoth a slap to tell him he should be going.

Over the bridge and all the way up the dusty hill out of the town, Jud stayed in the saddle as if glued to it, haranguing passers-by and telling them to repent before it was too late.

4

The girls rode home very slowly, drenched in a fiery sunset, with occasional snatches of song or a rolling curse to inform them that Jud had not yet fallen off.

They talked little at first, each woman taken with her own thoughts, and content with the excitements of the day. Their outing had given them a much closer understanding of one another.

As the sun went down behind St. Ann's, the whole sky flared into a vivid primrose and orange. Clouds which had moved up were caught in the blaze and twisted out of shape and daubed with wild colours. It was like a promise of the Second Coming, which Jud was just then loudly predicting in the far distance.

"Verity," Demelza said. "About those clothes."

"Yes?"

"One pound, eleven and six seems a wicked lot for a pair of stays."

"They're of good quality. They will last you some time."

"I've never had a proper pair of stays before. I was afraid they would want for me to take off my clothes. My inside clothes are *awful.*"

"I will loan you some of mine when you go in to be fitted."

"You'll come with me?"

"Yes. We can meet somewhere *en route.*"

"Why not stop at Nampara till then? Tis only another two weeks."

"My dear, I'm greatly flattered by your invitation, and thank you for it. But they'll need me at Trenwith. Perhaps I might visit you again in the spring?"

They rode on in silence.

"An' twenty-nine shillings for that riding hat. An' that handsome silk for the green-an'-purple gown. I feel we didn't ought to have spent the money on 'em."

"Your conscience is very restive."

"Well, an' for a reason. I should've told you before."

"Told me what?"

Demelza hesitated. "That mebbe my measuring won't be the same for long. Then I won't be able to wear 'em and they'll be wasted."

This took a moment to grasp, for she had spoken quickly. The track here became narrow and uneven, and the horses went into single file. When they were able to ride abreast again Verity said:

"My dear, do you mean—?"

"Yes."

"Oh, I'm indeed glad for you." Verity stumbled with words. "How happy you must be."

"Mind you," said Demelza, "I'm not positive certain. But things've stopped that belong to be as regular as clockwork with me, an' last Sunday night I was awake all night and feeling some queer. And then again this morning I was as sick as Garrick when he eats worms."

Verity laughed. "And you concern yourself over a few dresses! Ross—Ross will be delighted."

"Oh, I couldn't tell him yet. He's—strange that way. If he thought I was sickly, he'd make me sit still all day and twiddle my toes."

The brightest light had drained from the sky, leaving the clouds flushed with a rich plum-coloured afterglow. All the sparse countryside stood out in the warm light, the goats pasturing in numbers on the moorland, the scanty ricks of gathered corn, the wooden huts of the mines, the grey slate and cob cottages; the girls' faces under their wide hats were lit with it, the horses' noses gleamed.

The breeze had dropped and the evening was silent except for the sound of their own passing: the clicking of the horses' teeth upon the bits, the creak of saddle leather, the clop, clop of hoofs. A bit of a crescent moon hung in the sky, and Demelza bowed to it. Verity turned and looked back. Jud was a quarter of a mile away and Ramoth had stopped to crop a hedge. Jud was singing: "And for to fetch the summer home, the summer and the May -o."

They came to Bargus. Here in this corner of the dark and barren heath murderers and suicides were buried. The rope on the gibbet swung empty, and had done for a number of months, but the place was unhallowed and they were both glad to be past it before dusk began to fall.

Now they were on familiar ground the horses wanted to break into a trot, but the girls held them in so that Jud should not be left too far behind.

"I'm a bit afeared," Demelza said, speaking it seemed half to herself but aloud.

Verity looked at her and knew that it was not of ghosts or footpads she was thinking.

"I quite understand, my dear. But after all it will soon be over and—"

"Oh, not that," Demelza said. "Tesn't for me I'm afeared but for Ross. You see, he's not liked me for very long. Now I shall be ugly for months and months. Maybe when he sees me waddlin' about the house like an old duck he'll forget he ever liked me."

"You needn't be afraid of that. Ross never forgets anything. I think"—Verity stared into the gathering dusk—"think it is a characteristic of our family."

The last three miles were done in silence. The young moon was following the sun down. Soon it disappeared, leaving a ghostly smear of itself in the sky. Demelza watched the small bats hover and flicker in their path.

There was a sense of comfort in passing through the coppice about Wheal Maiden and turning into their own valley. Right and left were the new-built ricks of their own, two of wheat, one of oats; deep gold and pale gold they had been in this morning's sun. At the end of the valley the lights of Nampara were gleaming

Ross stood on the doorstep waiting to lift them down and welcome them in.

"Where's Jud?" he asked. "Has he—?"

"Up there," said Demelza. "Only just up there. He's washing his face in the stream."

CHAPTER SEVEN

1

AUTUMN LINGERED ON AS IF FOND OF ITS OWN PERFECTION. THE NOVEMBER gales did not develop, and leaves of the tall elms were drifting down the stream, yellow and brown and withered crimson, until Christmas. And life at Nampara drifted down the stream with the same undisturbed calm. They lived together, those dissimilar lovers, in harmony and good will, working and sleeping and eating, loving and laughing and agreeing, creating about themselves a fine shell of preoccupation which the outside world made no serious attempt to breach. The routine of their lives was part of their daily contentment.

Jinny Carter came to the home with a blue-eyed ginger-haired infant in a carrier over her shoulder. She worked well if silently, and the child was no trouble. They arrived each morning at seven, and at seven in the evening Jinny was to be seen with her bundle walking steadily back over the hill to Mellin. News of Jim was scanty. One day Jinny showed Ross an ill-spelt message she had received, written by someone in the same cell as Jim, telling her Jim was well enough and sending her his love. Ross knew that Jinny was living on her mother and sending her earnings to Jim as often as she could find a means. One never knew how much the gaoler pocketed; and it had taken all Mrs. Zacky's persuasion, and the claims of motherhood, to keep Jinny from walking the twenty-six miles to Bodmin, sleeping under a hedge, and walking back the following day.

Ross thought that after Christmas he would make the journey himself.

Demelza, freed of much drudgery but still eternally busy, found more time for her spinet playing. She could by now conjure some pleasant sounds from the instrument, and a few simple tunes that she knew well enough to sing she found she could also play. Ross said next year the spinet should be tuned and she should have lessons.

There was a surprise for the Nampara household on the twenty-first of December, when the boy Bartle arrived with a note from Francis, inviting Ross and Demelza to spend Christmas at Trenwith.

"There will be nobody but ourselves," Francis wrote, "that is, our household. Cousin W. A. is in Oxford, and Mr. and Mrs. Chynoweth are spending Christmas with her cousin, the Dean of Bodmin. I feel it a pity that our two houses should not similarly acknowledge their blood relationship. Also we have heard much from Verity of your wife (our new cousin) and would like to have her acquaintance. Come over in the afternoon of Christmas Eve and stay a few days."

Ross thought hard over the message before passing it on. The wording of the note was friendly and did not give the impression of having been incited by someone else, whether Verity or Elizabeth. He didn't wish to widen any breach which might still exist, and it seemed a pity to reject a move of friendship which was genuinely made, especially from the man who had been his boyhood friend.

Demelza's views were naturally different. Elizabeth was behind it; Elizabeth had invited them in order to examine her, Demelza, to see how she had developed as Ross's wife, to get Ross into an atmosphere where he would see what a mistake he had made in marrying a low-class girl, and humiliate her by a display of fine manners.

By this time, however, Ross had begun to see real advantages in going. He was not in the least ashamed of Demelza. The Trenwith Poldarks had never been sticklers for the *agréments,* and Demelza had a curious charm that all the tuition in the world could not bring. Knowing Elizabeth better, he had no thought that she would stoop to such a trivial act of enmity, and he wanted her to see that he had been content with no common substitute.

Demelza did not find this reassuring.

"No, Ross." She shook her head. "You go if you must. Not me. I aren't their sort. I'll be all right here."

"Naturally," said Ross, "we both stay or we both go. Bartle is still waiting, and I must give him a wedding present. While I go upstairs for my purse, make up your mind to be a dutiful cousin."

Demelza looked mutinous. "I don't want to be a dutiful cousin."

"A dutiful wife, then."

"But it would be something awful, Ross. Here I am Mistress Poldark. I can wind up the clock when I like. I can tease you and pull your hair, and shout and sing if I want, an' play on the old spinet. I share your bed, and in the mornings when I wake I puff out my chest and think big thoughts. But there—they are not all like Verity, you told me so yourself. They would quiz me and say 'dear, dear' and send me out to eat with Bartle and his new wife."

Ross looked at her sidelong. "They are so much better than you, you think?"

"No, I did not say so."

"You think I ought to be ashamed of you?"

In argument Ross always carried guns too big for her. She saw, she felt, but she could not reason it out to prove him wrong.

"Oh, Ross, they are your own kind," she said. "I am not."

"Your mother bore you in the same way as theirs," Ross said. "We all have similar motions, appetites, humours. My present humour is to take you to Trenwith for Christmas. It is little more than six months since you swore a solemn oath to obey me. What have you to say to that?"

"Nothing, Ross. Except that I don't want to go to Trenwith."

He laughed. Arguments between them usually ended in laughter nowadays; it was a signal grace leavening their companionship.

He went to the table. "I'll write a short note thanking them and saying we'll reply tomorrow."

The next day Demelza reluctantly gave way, as she usually did on important matters. Ross wrote to say they would come on Christmas Eve and spend Christmas Day at Trenwith. But unfortunately business at the mine would compel him to return that evening.

The invitation was accepted, so no offence could be taken; but if there had been anything halfhearted about it they would not be outstaying their welcome. Demelza would have a chance of meeting them as an equal, but the strain of best behaviour would not be prolonged.

Demelza had agreed because although Ross's arguments could not convince her, his persuasions she could seldom withstand. But she would much rather have gone to the mine barber and had six teeth pulled.

She was not really afraid of Francis or the old aunt; ever a quick learner, she had been gaining confidence all through the autumn. The bogy was Elizabeth. Elizabeth, Elizabeth, Elizabeth. On the eve of Christmas their footsteps beat out the name as they cut up across the fields behind the house and took the path along the cliffs.

Demelza glanced sidelong at her husband, who walked beside her with his long easy stride from which the last suggestion of a limp had now gone. She never really knew his thoughts; his deeper reflections were masked behind that strange unquiet face with its faint pale scar on one cheek like the brand mark of a spiritual injury he had suffered. She only knew that at present he was happy and that she was the condition of his happiness. She knew they were happy together, but she did not know how long such content could last; and she felt it in her heart that to consort with the woman he had once loved so deeply was flying in the face of fate.

The awful thought was that so much might depend on *her* behaviour during the next two days.

It was a bright day with a cold wind off the land. The sea was flat and green with a heavy ground swell. The long, even ridge of a wave would move slowly in, and then as it met the stiff south-easterly breeze its long top would begin to ruffle like the short feathers of an eider duck, growing more and more ruffled until the whole long ridge toppled slowly over and the wintry sun made a dozen rainbows in the mist flying up from its breaking.

All the way to Sawle Cove they were delayed by Garrick, who thought that Demelza could not be going out without him and was convinced that if he persisted long enough her better nature would come to see the matter as he did. Every few yards a sharp word of command would send his big lumpy body to the earth, where he would lie in complete and submissive collapse and only one reproachful bloodshot eye to prove that life still lingered; but a few more dozen paces would show that he was up and following them with slinking ungainly tread. Fortunately they met Mark Daniel, who was returning by the path they had come. Mark Daniel was standing no nonsense and was last seen marching in the direction of Nampara holding Garrick by one lopsided ear.

They crossed the sand and shingle of Sawle Cove, meeting one or two people who wished them an affable good day, and climbed the cliff hill at the other side. Before striking inland they paused for breath and to watch a flight of gannets diving for fish just off the shore. The gannets manoeuvred beyond the surf, their great stretch of white wings, brown-tipped, balancing them against the press of the wind; then they would dive plummet fashion, disappearing with a splash, to come up once in ten or twenty times with a small lance struggling in their long curved beaks.

"If I was a sand eel," said Demelza, "I should fair hate the sight of a gannet. See 'em fold their wings as they go in. When they come up without anything, don't they look innocent, as if they hadn't really meant it."

"We could do with some rain now," Ross said, staring at the sky. "The springs are low."

"Someday before I die, Ross, I should dearly like to go a journey on a ship. To France and Cherbourg and Madrid, and perhaps to America. I expect there are all sorts of funny birds out in the sea bigger than gannets. Why do you never talk about America, Ross?"

"The past is no good to anyone. It is only the present and the future that matter."

"Father knew a man who'd been to America. But he never talked of nothing else. Twas half a fairy story, I b'lieve."

"Francis was lucky," Ross said. "He spent a whole summer travelling Italy and the Continent. I thought I should like to travel. Then the war came and I went to America. When I returned, I wanted only my own corner of England. It's strange."

"Someday I should like to visit France."

"We could pay a visit to Roscoff or Cherbourg any time in one of the St. Ann's cutters. I have done it as a boy."

"I should rather go in a big ship," Demelza said. "An' not with the fear of being fired on by the revenue men."

They went on their way.

Verity was at the door of Trenwith House waiting to greet them. She ran forward to kiss Ross and then Demelza. Demelza held her tight for a moment, then took a deep breath and went in.

2

The first few minutes were trying for them all, but the trial passed. Happily both Demelza and the Trenwith household were on their best behaviour. Francis had a natural charm when he chose to exercise it, and Aunt Agatha, warmed by a tot of Jamaica rum and crowned with her second-best wig, was affable and coy. Elizabeth was smiling, her flower-like face more lovely for its delicate flush. Geoffrey Charles, aged three, came stumping forward in his velvet suit, to stand finger in mouth staring at the strangers.

Aunt Agatha caused some extra trouble at the outset by denying that she had ever been told of Ross's marriage and by demanding a full explanation. Then she wanted to know Demelza's maiden name.

"What?" she said. "Carkeek? Cardew? Carne? Carne, did you say? Where does she come from? Where do you come from, child?"

"Illuggan," said Demelza.

"Where? Oh, that's near the Bassetts' place, is it not? You'll know Sir Francis. Intelligent young fellow, they say, but overconcerned with social problems." Aunt Agatha stroked the whiskers on her chin. "Come here, bud. I don't bite. How old are you?"

Demelza allowed her hand to be taken. "Eighteen." She glanced at Ross.

"Hm. Nice age. Nice and sweet at that age." Aunt Agatha also glanced at Ross, her small eyes wicked among their sheaf of wrinkles. "Know how old I am?"

Demelza shook her head.

"I'm ninety-one. Last Thursday sennight."

"I didn't know you were as old as that," Francis said.

"It's not everything you know, my boy. Ninety-one last Thursday sennight. What d'you say to that, Ross?"

"Sweet at any age," Ross said in her ear.

Aunt Agatha grinned with pleasure. "You was always a bad boy. Like your father. Five generations of Poldarks I've seen. Nay, six. There was old Grannie Trenwith. I remember her well. She was a Rowe. Great Presbyterians they was. Her father, Owen, was a friend of Cromwell's; they say he was one of the fifty-nine that signed King Charles's death paper. They lost all their land at the Restoration. I remember her well. She died when I was ten. She used to tell me stories of the Plague. Not as she was ever in it."

"We had the Plague at Illuggan once, ma'am," Demelza said.

"Then there was Anna-Maria, my mother, who became a Poldark. She was an only child. I was old when she died. Charles Vivian Poldark she married. He was a roamer. An invalid out of the Navy from the battle of La Hogue before ever he met Mama, and he but five and twenty. That's his portrait, bud. The one with the little beard."

Demelza gazed.

"Then there was Claude Henry, my brother, who married Matilda Ellen Peter of Treviles. He died ten years before his mama. Vomiting and looseness was his trouble. That was your grandfather, Ross. You and Francis makes five, and little Geoffrey makes six. Six generations, and I've scarce been alive any time yet."

Demelza was at last allowed her hand back, and passed on to greet the staring child. Geoffrey Charles was a plump little boy, his face so smooth that one could not imagine it ever having creased into a thoroughgoing smile. A handsome child, as might be expected with such parents.

Ross's own sight of Elizabeth after six months had not been quite as casual or as unemotional as he had hoped and expected. He had hoped to find himself immune, as if his marriage and love for Demelza were the inoculation against some fever of the blood and this a deliberate contact on his part to prove the cure. But Demelza, he found, was not an inoculation, though she might be a separate fever. He wondered, just at that first greeting, whether after all Demelza's impulse to refuse the invitation had not perhaps been wiser than his own.

Their meeting, Elizabeth's and Demelza's, left him with a sense of dissatisfaction; their manner towards each other was so outwardly friendly and so inwardly wary. He did not know if their greeting deceived anyone else, but it certainly didn't deceive him. Naturalness just was not in it.

But Demelza and Verity had taken days to get on friendly terms. Women were like that: However charming taken singly, a first meeting with one of their own kind was an intuitive testing and searching.

Elizabeth had given them one of the best bedrooms, looking southwest towards the woods.

"'Tis a handsome house," said Demelza, dropping her cloak from her shoulders. With the first ordeal over she felt better. "Never have I seen the like. 'Tis like a church, that hall. And this bedroom. Look at the birds on the curtains; like missel thrushes, only the specks are the wrong colour. But, Ross, all those pictures hanging downstairs. I should be afeared of them in the dark. Are they all of your family, Ross?"

"I have been told so."

"It is more than I can understand that people should wish to have so many dead 'uns about them. When I am dead, Ross, I don't want to be hung up to dry like last week's bed linen. I don't want to stare down forever upon a lot of people I've never known at all, great-grandchildren and great-great-great-grandchildren. I'd much sooner be put away and forgot."

"This is the second time today you've spoken of dying," Ross said. "Do you feel unwell?"

"No, no; I am brave enough."

"Then oblige me by keeping to some more agreeable subject. What's this box?"

"That?" said Demelza. "Oh, that is something. I asked Jud to bring it over with our night rails."

"What is in it?"

"A dress."

"For you?"

"Yes, Ross."

"The riding habit you bought in Truro?"

"No, Ross, another. You would not like me to be shabby in front of all your great-grandmothers, would you?"

He laughed. "Is it a dress from the library you have adapted?"

"No… Verity and me bought this also in Truro at the same time."

"Did she pay for it?"

"No, Ross. It came out of the money you give us for furnishings."

"Deceit, bud. And you looking so innocent and guileless."

"You are stealin' Aunt Agatha's name for me."

"I think I like it. But I am just finding the worm in the bud. Deceit and duplicity. Still, I'm glad Verity did not pay. Let me see it."

"No, Ross. *No*, Ross! *No, Ross!*" Her voice rose to a shriek as she tried to prevent him from reaching the box. He got one hand to it, but she put her arms round his neck and hugged him to stop any further move. He lifted her up by the elbows and kissed her, then he smacked her twice on the seat and put her down.

"Where's your good behaviour, bud? They'll think I'm beating you."

"Which is the truth. Which is the truth." She slipped away from him and danced back with the box held behind her.

"Go down now, please, Ross! You was not to know anything about it! Maybe I'll not wear it, but I want to try it on and dinner is in an hour. Go down and talk to Aunt Agatha and count the whiskers on her chin."

"We're not attending a ball," he said. "This is just a family party; no need to flig yourself up for it."

"It is Christmas Eve. I asked Verity. She said it was right to change my clo'es."

"Oh, have it as you please. But mind you're ready by five. And," he added as an afterthought, "don't lace your stays too tight or you'll be incommoded. They feed you well, and I know your appetite."

With this he went out, and she was left to make her preparations alone.

She did not feel that she need heed Ross's final warning tonight at any rate. All day she had had recurring bouts of nausea. The Trenwith dinner was safe from her greed: all that was unsafe was the little she might force down. It would be too bad if she made a show of herself this evening. It would be tragic. She wondered if she had to get up from the table in a hurry where the nearest close-stool was.

She pulled her dress over her head, stepped out of her underskirt and stood for a moment in the small clothes Verity had lent her, staring at her reflection in the lovely clear mirror of the dressing-table. She had never before in her life seen herself so clearly and so entirely. This reflection was not too shameful, but she wondered how she had had the brazenness to move about and dress with Ross in the room when she was wearing the underclothes of her own and Prudie's devising. She would never wear them again.

She had heard it whispered that many good-class town women wore white stockings and no drawers. What with hooped skirts it was disgusting, and they deserved to catch their death.

She shivered. But soon she would be unsightly, however dressed. At least, she expected so. It was a surprise to her that so far there had been no change. Every morning she took a piece of string with a knot tied in it and measured herself. But, unbelievably enough, she seemed so far to have lost half an inch. Perhaps the knot had slipped.

A village upbringing had left little out in teaching her the ordinary facts of getting and begetting; yet when it came to herself she found gaps in her knowledge. Her mother had borne six other children, but she remembered so little of what had happened before she was eight.

She must ask Verity. This was now the usual resort for all problems which baffled her. She must ask Verity. It didn't occur to her that there were questions on which Verity might know less than herself.

CHAPTER EIGHT

DOWNSTAIRS IN THE LARGE PARLOUR ROSS FOUND ONLY ELIZABETH AND Geoffrey Charles. They were sitting in front of the fire. Geoffrey Charles was on his mother's knee, and Elizabeth was reading him a story.

Ross listened to the cool, cultured voice; there was pleasure for him in that. But she looked up, saw who it was, and stopped.

"'Gain, Mummie. Tell it again."

"In a little while, darling. I must have a rest. Here is your Uncle Ross, come to tell me a story for a change."

"I know no stories except true ones," Ross said. "And they are all sad."

"Not all, surely," said Elizabeth. "Your own must now be happy with so charming a wife."

Ross hesitated, uncertain whether he wished to discuss Demelza even with Elizabeth.

"I'm very glad that you like her."

"She's greatly changed since I saw her last, and that's not seven months ago, and I think she will change more yet. You must take her into society and bring her out."

"And risk the snubs of women like Mrs. Teague? Thank you, I'm well enough as I am."

"You're too sensitive. Besides, she may want to go out herself. Women have the courage for that sort of thing, and she is yet so young."

"It was with the greatest difficulty that I persuaded her to come here."

Elizabeth smiled down on her son's curly head. "That's understandable."

"Why?"

"Oh… it was meeting the family, wasn't it? And she is a little *gauche* yet. She would perhaps expect to find antagonisms."

"Mummie, 'gain. 'Gain, Mummie."

"Not yet. In a while."

"Man's got a mark on his face, Mummie."

"Hush, dear. You must not say such things."

"But he has. He *has*, Mummie!"

"And I've washed it and washed it and it won't come off," Ross assured him.

Thus addressed, Geoffrey Charles fell utterly silent.

"Verity has become very fond of her," Elizabeth said. "We must see more of you now, Ross, now that the ice is broken."

"What of your own affairs?" Ross said. "Baby Geoffrey is thriving, I see that."

Elizabeth put out her small slippered feet and allowed her son to slide from her lap to the floor. There he stood a second as if about to run off, but seeing Ross's eyes still on him was overcome with his new shyness and buried his face in his mother's skirt.

"Come, darling, don't be foolish. This is Uncle Ross; like Uncle Warleggan only more so. He is your true and only uncle and you mustn't be coy. Up, up, and say how d'you do."

But Geoffrey Charles would not move his head.

She said: "I haven't been too well in health, but we are all worried about my poor mother. She's greatly troubled with her eyes. Park the surgeon from Exeter is coming to examine her in the New Year. Dr. Choake and Dr. Pryce take a grave view of the disease."

"I'm sorry."

"They say it's a recurrent distemper of the eye. The treatment is most painful. They tie a silk kerchief about her throat and tighten it until she is nearly strangled and all the blood is forced into her head. Then they bleed her behind the ears. She has gone now to rest with her cousin at Bodmin. I am very worried."

Ross made a face. "My father had no trust in physicians. I hope you'll have good news."

There was silence. Elizabeth bent and whispered in Geoffrey's ear. There was no response for a moment, then with a sudden, peculiarly sly glance at Ross, he turned and ran from the room.

Elizabeth's eyes followed him. "Geoffrey is at an awkward age," she said. "He must be cured of his little whimsies." But she spoke in an indulgent voice.

"And Francis?"

An expression he had never seen before flitted across her face.

"Francis? Oh, we get along, thank you, Ross."

"The summer has gone so quick and I have intended to come and see you. Francis may have told you I spoke to him once."

"You have your own concerns to tend now."

"Not to the exclusion of all others."

"Well, we have kept our head above water through the summer." She said this in a tone that went with her expression. The personal pronoun might have referred to the finances of the house or to the fastnesses of her own spirit.

"I can't understand him," Ross said.

"We are as we are born. Francis was born a gambler, it seems. If he's not careful he'll have gamed away all that has come to him and die a pauper."

Every family, thought Ross, had its rakes and its spendthrifts; their blood was passed on with the rest, strange taints of impulse and perversity. It was the only explanation. Yet Joshua, even Joshua, who had been eccentric enough and roving in his eye for women, had had the sense to settle down when he got the woman he wanted and to remain so settled until nature took her from him.

"Where does he spend most of his time?"

"At the Warleggans' still. We used to have great fun until the stakes became too high. I have only been twice since Geoffrey was born. Now I'm not invited."

"But surely—"

"Oh yes, of course, if I asked Francis to take me. But he tells me that they're becoming more exclusively male. I would not enjoy them, he says."

She was staring down at the folds of her blue dress. This was a new Elizabeth who spoke so straightly, in such objective tones, as if painful experience had taught her the lesson of keeping life at a distance.

"Ross."

"Yes?"

"I think there is one way in which you might help me if you would—"

"Go on."

"There are stories concerning Francis. I have no means of knowing what truth there is in them. I could ask George Warleggan, but for a special reason don't wish to. I have no claim on you, you know that; but I should esteem it so highly if you were able to discover the truth."

Ross stared at her. He had been unwise to come here. He could not sit in calm intimacy with this woman without the return of old sensations.

"I'll do anything I can. I shall be pleased to do it. Unfortunately I don't move in the same set as Francis. My interests—"

"It could be arranged."

Ross looked at her quickly. "How?"

"I could get George Warleggan to invite you to one of his parties. George likes you."

"What's the extent of the rumours?"

"They say Francis is going with another woman. I don't know what truth there is in it, but it's plain I cannot suddenly choose to go to the parties myself. I cannot—*spy* on him."

Ross hesitated. Did she realize all she asked? She was of course reluctant to spy herself, but that would be his task in fact if not in name. And to what end? How could his intervention serve to underpin a marriage if the foundations of the marriage were already gone?

"Don't decide now, Ross," she said in a low voice. "Leave it. Think it over. I know I'm asking a great deal."

Her tone made him glance round, and Francis came in. Sitting in this big pleasant parlour, Ross thought, one would soon come to recognize the footstep of everyone in the house as it approached the door.

"A *tête-à-tête*?" Francis said, raising an eyebrow. "And not drinking, Ross? This is a poor hospitality we offer. Let me mix you an eggy-hot to keep away the chills of winter."

"Ross was telling me how well his mine is doing, Francis," Elizabeth said.

"Lord save us; such talk on Christmas Eve." Francis busied himself. "Come over in January—or maybe February—and tell us about it, Ross. But not now, I implore you. It would be dull to spend this evening comparing notes on copper assays."

Ross saw that he had been drinking, though the signs were very slight.

Elizabeth rose. "When cousins have been so long separated," she said pleasantly, "it's hard to find something to talk of. It would do us no harm, Francis, if we thought of Grambler a little more. I must see Geoffrey to bed." She left them.

Francis came across with the drink. He was wearing a dark green suit and the lace at the cuffs was soiled. Unusual in the immaculate Francis. No other sign of the rake's progress. Hair as carefully brushed, stock as neatly tied, manners of a greater elegance. There was an extra fullness of the face, which made him look older, and something superficial in his glance.

"Elizabeth makes life a mortal serious business," he remarked. "Aarf! as my old father would say."

"Elegance of expression is something I have always admired in you," said Ross.

Francis looked up and grinned. "No offence intended. We have been estranged too long. What's the good of choler in this world? If we took account of every grievance, we should only make more bad blood for the leeches. Drink about."

Ross drank about. "I have no grievances. The past is past and I'm content enough."

"So should you be," Francis said over the rim of his tankard. "I like your wife. From Verity's account I thought I should. She walks like a mettlesome colt. And after all, so long as her spirit be good, what does it matter whether she comes from Windsor Castle or Stippy-Stappy Lane?"

"You and I have much in common," Ross said.

"I used to think so." Francis stopped. "In sentiment or in circumstance, do you mean?"

"In sentiment I meant. Clearly in circumstances you have the advantage of me. The house and interests of our common ancestors; the wife, shall I put it, of our common choice; money to splash at the card table and the cockpit, a son and heir—"

"Stop," said Francis, "or you'll make me weep with envy at my own good fortune."

"I'd never thought it a conspicuous danger in your case, Francis."

Francis's forehead puckered in a frown. He set his tankard down. "No, nor in any other case neither. It's the custom of mankind to judge others in ignorance. They take it—"

"Then correct my ignorance."

Francis looked at him for a moment or two.

"Pour out my distempers on the eve of Christmas? God forbid. You would find it all so tedious, I assure you. Like Aunt Agatha talking of her kidneys. Finish your drink, man, and have another."

"Thanks," said Ross. "In truth, Francis—"

"In truth, Ross," Francis mocked from the shadows of the sideboard. "It is all as you say, is it not? A lovely wife, fair as an angel—indeed, perhaps more of an angel than a wife—the home of our ancestors, hung with their curious visages—oh yes, I saw Demelza admiring them open-mouthed—a handsome son brought up in the way he ought to go: honour thy father and be worshipped by thy mother that thy days may be long in the land which the Lord thy God giveth thee. And finally money to splash at the card table and the cockpit. Splash. I like the word. It has a pleasantly expansive sound. One is put in mind of the Prince of Wales dropping a couple of thousand guineas at White's."

"It's a relative word," Ross said evenly. "Like many others. If one is a country squire and lives in the western wilds, one may splash just as effectively with fifty guineas as George with two thousand."

Francis laughed as he came back. "You speak from experience. I'd forgotten. You have been the staid former so long I'd quite forgotten."

"Indeed," said Ross, "I should say that ours was far the greater hazard, not only in proportion but because we have no benevolent parliament to vote £160,000 to pay our debts or £10,000 a year to squander on the mistress of the moment."

"You're well informed on the business of the court."

"All news flies fast, whether it concerns a prince or a local squire."

Francis flushed. "What do you mean by that?"

Ross raised his mug. "That this drink's very warming to the vitals."

"It may disappoint you to know," said Francis, "that I'm not interested in what a set of braggarty, pockmarked old grannies are whispering over their turf fires. I go my own way and leave them to fetch up what poisonous gases they choose. We are none of us immune from their clackings. Look to your own house, Ross."

"You misunderstand me," said Ross. "I'm not concerned with gossip or the tales of idle women. But the interior of a debtors' prison is damp and smelly. No one would be the worse for your bearing that in mind before it is too late."

Frances lit up his long pipe and smoked for some seconds before saying anything more. He dropped a piece of smouldering wood back in the fire and put down the tongs.

"Elizabeth must have been pitching you a pretty story."

"I don't need her confidences for a pretty story which is known all over the district."

"The district knows my own affairs better than I do myself. Perhaps you'd advise me to a solution. Should I join the Methodies and be saved?"

"My dear man," Ross said, "I like you and have an interest in your welfare. But for all it will affect me you may find your way to the devil by the shortest route. Fortune can provide lands and family but it can't provide good sense. If you wish to throw away what you have, then throw it away and be damned."

Francis eyed him cynically for a moment, then put down his pipe and clapped a hand on his shoulder.

"Spoken like a Poldark. We have never been an agreeable family. Let us curse and quarrel in amity. Then we can get drunk in company. You and I together, and to hell with the creditors!"

Ross picked up his empty mug and regarded the bottom gravely. Francis's good temper under the quizzing struck a responsive chord. Disappointment, from whatever quarter it had come, had toughened his cousin; it had not changed the essential individual he had known and liked.

At that moment Bartle came in carrying two branching candlesticks. The yellow games flickered in the draught, and it was as if the firelight had suddenly grown to fill the room. Elizabeth's spinning wheel stood out in the corner, its bobbins shining. A linen doll lay on its back beside the sofa with stuffing hanging from its stomach. On a chair was a wicker basket with needlework and a frame with a half-finished sampler. The light of the candles was warm and friendly; with the curtains drawn there was a sense of cosiness and quiet affluence.

In the room were all the signs of feminine occupancy, and there had been about these few minutes of conversation an underlying maleness which drew the two men together by the bond of their larger, wider, more tolerant understanding. Between them was the freemasonry of their sex, a unity of blood, and the memory of old friendships.

It occurred to Ross in this moment that half of Elizabeth's worry might be the eternal feminine bogy of insecurity. Francis drank. Francis gambled and lost money. Francis had been seen about with another woman. Not an amiable story. But not an uncommon one. Inconceivable to Ross in this case, and for Elizabeth it had the proportions of a tragedy. But it was unwise to lose one's sense of perspective. Other men drank and gambled. Debts were fashionable. Other men found eyes to admire the beauty which was not theirs by right of marriage and to overlook the familiar beauty that was. It did not follow that Francis was taking the shortest route to perdition.

Anyway this was Christmas, and the day was intended to mark a family reunion, not to begin a new estrangement.

One could go no further. Let it rest. Ross thought of Demelza upstairs putting on her best and full of youth and good spirits. He hoped she was not going to overdo it. Fortunate that Verity had had the ordering. The thought of Demelza warmed his mind and lit it up, as the arrival of the candles had lit the room.

To the devil with vicarious worries. Christmas was no time for them. In January they could be revived, if they still had the power to vex and disturb.

CHAPTER NINE

D INNER BEGAN AT FIVE AND WENT ON UNTIL SEVEN-FORTY. IT WAS A MEAL worthy of the age, the house, and the season. Pea soup to begin, followed by a roast swan with sweet sauce; giblets, mutton steaks, a partridge pie, and four snipe. The second course was a plum pudding with brandy sauce, tarts, mince pies, custards, and cakes; all washed down with port wine and claret and madeira and home-brewed ale.

Ross felt that there was only one thing missing: Charles. The great paunch, the more or less subdued belches, the heavy good humour; at this moment the corporeal remains of that massive, mediocre, but not unkindly soul were rotting away and becoming one with the soil that had given it life and sustenance; the organic humours of which it was composed would soon be helping to feed the rank couch grass which overran the churchyard. But in this house from which he had spent few nights away in the course of his sixty-eight years, in this house remained some unspent aura of his presence more noticeable to Ross than the aura of all the portraits of forty-six ancestors.

One did not so much feel sorrow at his absence as a sense of the unfitness of his not being here.

For such a small party the dining hall was too gaunt and draughty; they used the winter parlour, which faced west and was panelled to the ceiling and was convenient for the kitchens. Chance stage-managed Demelza's arrival.

Verity had come to the large parlour to tell them that dinner was ready. Elizabeth was there and the four of them left the room smiling and chattering together. As they did so Demelza came down the stairs.

She was wearing the dress that had been made up from Verity's choice, the very pale mauve silk with the half-length sleeves, slightly hooped and pulled apart like a letter A at the front to show the flowered apple-green bodice and underskirt.

What Ross could not quite understand was her appearance, her manner. Natural that he should be pleased with her; she had never looked so charming before.

In her own queer way this evening she rivalled Elizabeth, who started any such competition with advantages of feature and colouring over almost all women. Some challenge born in the situation had brought out the best of Demelza's good looks, her fine dark eyes, her hair neatly dressed and tied, her very pale olive skin with the warm glow under it. Verity was openly proud of her.

At dinner she didn't burst her stays. In Ross's opinion she overdid her good behaviour by pecking at many things and always leaving the larger portion on her plate. She out-vied Elizabeth, who was always so small an eater; a suspicious person might have thought her to be mocking her hostess. Ross was amused. Tonight she was on her mettle.

A talkative girl at meals, full of questions and speculations, she took little part in the conversation at this meal, refused the burnt claret which the others drank and herself drank only the home-brewed ale. But she didn't look bored and her manner was always one of intelligent interest while Elizabeth spoke of people she did not know or gave some anecdote of Geoffrey Charles. When she was drawn in, she answered pleasantly and naturally and without affectation. Aunt Agatha's occasional broadsides didn't seem to disconcert her: she would look at Ross, who sat next to the old lady, and he would shout an answer. This put the onus on him of finding the right one.

Talk turned on whether there was truth in the rumour of another attempt on the King's life. The last such rumour had certainly been true, when Margaret Nicholson tried to stab him at a levée; Francis made some cynical comments on the good cloth used in the royal waistcoat. Elizabeth said she had been told the King's household servants had not been paid for twelve months.

They talked of France and the magnificence of the court there. Francis said he was surprised someone had not tried to sharpen a knife on Louis, who was far more deserving of one than Farmer George. The French Queen was trying to find a cure for all her ills in animal magnetism.

Verity said she thought she would try that for her catarrh, for she had been told to drink half a pint of sea water daily and she found she could not stomach it. Dr. Choake blamed all colds on the malignancy of the air; raw meat put on a pole turned bad in forty minutes, while similar meat kept in salt water remained fresh for a long time. Ross remarked that Choake was an old woman. Francis said perhaps there was literal truth in that statement, since Polly was so unfruitful. Elizabeth turned the conversation to her mother's eye trouble.

Francis drank ten glasses of port over the meal but showed little change. A difference, Ross thought, from the old days when he was always the first under the table. "Boy's no head for liquor," Charles would grumble. Ross glanced at Elizabeth, but her look was serene.

At fifteen minutes before eight the ladies rose and left the two men to drink brandy and smoke their pipes at the littered and derelict table. Between themselves they talked business, but the conversation had not been in progress many minutes when Mrs. Tabb appeared at the door.

"If you please, sir, visitors has just come."

"What?"

"Mr. George Warleggan and Mr. and Mrs. John Treneglos, sir."

Ross felt a spasm of annoyance at having this surprise sprung on him. He had no wish to meet the all-successful George tonight. And he felt sure Ruth would not have come had she known he and Demelza were here.

But Francis' surprise was genuine.

"Cock's life, so they come visiting on Christmas Eve, eh? What have you done with them, Emily?"

"They're in the big parlour, sir. Mistress Elizabeth said would you come soon and help entertain them, and they do not intend to stop long."

"Surely. We will go right away." Francis waved his glass. "Right away."

When Mrs. Tabb left he lit his pipe. "Imagine old George coming tonight. I thought he was spending Christmas at Cardew. A coincidence, what? And John and Ruth. You remember when we used to fight John and Richard, Ross?"

Ross did.

"George Warleggan," said Francis. "Great man. He'll own half Cornwall before he's done. He and his cousin own more than half of me already." He laughed. "The other half he wants but can't have. Some things just won't go on the table."

"His cousin?"

"Cary Warleggan, the banker."

"A pretty name. I've heard him called a moneylender."

"Tut! Would you insult the family?"

"The family grows too intrusive for my taste. I prefer a community run on simpler lines."

"They're the people of the future, Ross. Not the worn-out families like the Chynoweths and the Poldarks."

"It's not their vigour I query but their use of it. If a man has vitality let him increase his own soul, not set about owning other people's."

"That may be true of Cousin Cary, but it's a small matter hard on George."

"Finish your drink and we'll go," Ross said, thinking of Demelza with these new people to face.

"It is more than a little strange," said Francis. "Philosophers would no doubt hang some doxy name on it. But to me it seems just a plain perversity of life."

"What does?"

"Oh—" The other hesitated. "I don't know. We envy some other person for something he has got and we have not, although in truth it may be that he really hasn't it. Do I make myself clear? No, I thought not. Let's go and see George."

They rose from the ruins of the feast and walked through into the hall. As they crossed it, they heard shouts of laughter from the large parlour.

"Making a carnival of my house," said Francis. "Can this be George the elegant?"

"Long odds," said Ross, "on its being John the Master of Hounds."

They entered and found his guess a good one. John Treneglos was sitting at Elizabeth's hand spinning wheel. He was trying to work it. It seemed a simple enough action but in fact needed practice, which John Treneglos lacked.

He would get the wheel going nicely for some moments, but then his foot pressure on the treadle would be not quite even and the cranked arm would suddenly reverse itself and stop. While it was working right there was silence in the room, broken only by an interplay between Treneglos and Warleggan. But every time John went off his stroke there was a roar of laughter.

Treneglos was a powerful, clumsy man of thirty, with sandy hair, deep-set eyes, and freckled features. He was known as a fine horseman, a first-class shot, the best amateur wrestler in two counties, a dunce at any game needing mental effort, and something of a bully. This evening, though on a social call, he wore an old brown velvet riding coat and strong corduroy breeches. It was his boast that he never wore anything but riding breeches, even in bed.

Ross was surprised to see that Demelza was not in the room.

"You lose," said George Warleggan. "You lose. Five guineas are mine. Ho, Francis."

"One more try, damme. The first was a trial try. I'll not be beat by a comical contraption of this sort."

"Where is Demelza?" said Ross to Verity, who was standing by the door.

"Upstairs. She wished to be left alone for a few moments so I came down."

"You'll break it, John," said Elizabeth, smiling. "You're too heavy-footed."

"John!" said his wife. "Get up at once!"

But John had been merrying himself with good brandy and took no notice. Once more he got the wheel going, and it seemed that this time he had done the trick. But at the wrong moment he tried to increase the speed, and the cranked arm reversed and everything came to a jerking standstill. George uttered a cry of triumph and John Treneglos rose in disgust.

"Three more times and I should have mastered the pesty thing. You must give me a lesson, Elizabeth. Here, man, take your money. It's ill gotten and will stick in your crop."

"John is so excitable," said his wife. "I feared for your wheel. I think we are all a little foxed, and the Christmas spirit has done the rest."

If John Treneglos set no store by fashion, the same could not be said of the new Mrs. Treneglos. Ruth Teague, the drab little girl of the Easter Charity Ball, had shot ahead. An instinct in Ross had sensed at the ball that there was more in her than met the eye. She wore a blossom-coloured hoopless dress of Spitalfields silk with silver spangles at the waist and shoulders. An unsuitable dress for travelling the countryside, but no doubt her wardrobe was well stocked. John would have other calls on his pocket now besides his hunters. And John would not have things all his own way.

"Well, well, Captain Poldark," said Treneglos ironically. "We're neighbours, but this is how we meet. For all we see of you you might be Robinson Crusoe."

"Oh, but he has his Man Friday, dear," said Ruth gently.

"Who? Oh, you mean Jud," said Treneglos, blunting the edge of his wife's remark. "A hairless ape, that. He cheeked me once. Had he not been your servant I'd have give him a beating. And what of the mine? Old Father is cock-a-hoop and speaks of shovelling in the copper."

"Nothing ambitious," Ross said, "but gratifying so far as it goes."

"Egad," said George. "Must we talk business? Elizabeth, bring out your harp. Let us have a song."

"I have no voice," said Elizabeth, with her lovely slow smile. "If you have a mind to accompany me—"

"We'll all accompany you." George was deferential. "It would suit the night admirable."

Not for George the self-confident uncouthness of John Treneglos, who traced his ancestry back to Robert, Count of Mortain. It was hardly credible that a single generation divided a tough, gnarled old man who sat in a cottage in his shirt sleeves and chewed tobacco and could barely write his name from this cultured young man in a new-fashioned tight-cut pink coat with buff lapels. Only something of the blacksmith's grandson showed in the size of his features, in the full, tight, possessive lips, in the short neck above the heavy shoulders.

"Is Demelza coming down?" Ross asked Verity quietly. "She has not been overawed by these people?"

"No, I don't think she knows they're here."

"Let's have a hand of faro," said Francis. "I was damned unlucky on Saturday. Fortune cannot always be sulky."

But he was shouted down. Elizabeth must play the harp. They had come specially to hear Elizabeth play. Already George was moving the instrument out of its corner and John was bringing forward the chair she used. Elizabeth, protesting and smiling, was being persuaded. At that moment Demelza came in.

Demelza was feeling better. She had just lost the dinner she had eaten and the ale she had drunk. The occurrence itself had not been pleasant, but, like the old Roman senators, she was feeling the better for it. The demon nausea had gone with the food and all was well.

There was a moment's silence after she entered. It was noticeable then that the guests had been making most of the noise. Then Elizabeth said: "This is our new cousin, Demelza. Ross's wife."

Demelza was surprised at this influx of people whom she must now meet. She remembered Ruth Teague from seeing her once on a visit to Ross, and she had seen her husband twice out hunting: Squire Treneglos' eldest son, one of the big men of the neighbourhood. When she last saw them both she had been a long-legged untidy kitchen wench for whom neither of them would have spared a second glance. Or Ruth would not. By them and by George Warleggan, who from his dress she felt must be at least the son of a lord, she was overawed. But she was learning fast that people, even well-bred people like these, had a surprising tendency to take you at your own valuation.

"Damn it, Ross," Treneglos said. "Where have you been hiding this little blossom? It was ungrateful of you to be so close about it. Your servant, ma'am."

Since to reply "your servant, sir," was clearly wrong, besides being too near the truth, Demelza contented herself with a pleasant smile. She allowed herself to be introduced to the other two, then accepted a glass of port from Verity and gulped half of it down while they were looking the other way.

"So this is your wife, Ross," said Ruth sweetly. "Come and sit by me, my dear. Tell me all about yourself. All the county was talking of you in June."

"Yes," said Demelza. "People dearly love a gossip, don't they, ma'am?"

John roared and slapped his thigh.

"Quite right, mistress. Let's drink a toast: a merry Christmas to us all round and damnation to the gossips!"

"You're drunk, John," said Ruth severely. "You will not be able to sit your horse if we don't leave at once."

"First we must hear Elizabeth play," said George, who had been exchanging some close confidence with Elizabeth.

"Do you sing, Mistress Poldark?" asked John.

"Me?" said Demelza in surprise. "No. Only when I'm happy."

"Are we not all happy now?" asked John. "Christmastide. You must sing for us, ma'am."

"Does she sing, Ross?" Francis enquired.

Ross looked at Demelza, who shook her head vigorously.

"No," said Ross.

This denial seemed to carry no weight. Somebody must sing to them, and it looked as if it was going to be Demelza.

The girl emptied her wineglass hurriedly, and someone refilled it.

"I only sing by myself," she said. "I mean I don't rightly know proper tunes. Mistr—er— Elizabeth must play first. Later, mebbe—"

Elizabeth was very gently running her fingers up and down the harp. The faint rippling sound was a liquid accompaniment to the chatter.

"If you sing me a few bars," she said. "I think I could pick it up."

"No, no," said Demelza, backing away. "You first. You play first."

So presently Elizabeth played, and at once the company fell silent, even the tipsy John and the well-soaked Francis. They were all Cornish, and music meant something to them.

She played first a piece by Handel and then a short sonatina by Krumpholz. The plucked vibrating tones filled the room, and the only other sound was the murmur of burning wood from the fire. The candleglow fell on Elizabeth's young head and on her slim hands moving over the strings. The light made a halo of her hair. Behind her stood George Warleggan, stocky and polite and ruthless, his hands behind his back, his eyes fixed unwinkingly on the player.

Verity had subsided on a stool, a tray with glasses on the floor beside her. Against a background of blue moreen curtains, she sat with hands clasped about her knees, her head up and showing the line of her throat above its lace fichu. Her face in its repose reminded one of the younger Verity of four years ago. Next to her Francis lolled in a chair, his eyes half closed, but listening; and beside him Aunt Agatha chewed meditatively, a dribble of saliva at the corner of her mouth, listening too but hearing nothing. In her finery sharply different from the old lady, but having something strangely in common with her in the vitality of her manner, was Ruth Treneglos. One felt that she might be no beauty but that she too would take some killing off when the time came.

Next to her was Demelza, who had just finished her third glass of port and was feeling better every minute; and beyond her Ross stood, a little withdrawn, glancing now and then from one to another of the company with his unquiet eyes. John Treneglos was half listening to the music, half goggling at Demelza, who seemed to have a peculiar fascination for him.

The music came to a stop, and Elizabeth leaned back, smiling at Ross. Applause was on a quieter note than could have been expected ten minutes ago. The harp music had touched at something more fundamental than their high spirits. It had spoken not of Christmas jollity and fun but of love and sorrow, of human life, its strange beginning and its inevitable end.

"Superb!" declared George. "We were more than repaid for a ride twenty times as long. Elizabeth, you pluck at my heartstrings."

"Elizabeth," said Verity. "Play me that *canzonetta* as an encore, please. I love it."

"It is not good unless it is sung."

"Yes, yes, it is. Play it as you played it last Sunday night."

Silence fell again. Elizabeth played something very short by Mozart and then a canzonetta by Haydn.

There was silence when this was over before anyone spoke.

"It is my favourite," said Verity. "I cannot hear it often enough."

"They're all my favourites," said George. "And played like an angel. One more, I beg you."

"No," said Elizabeth, smiling. "It is Demelza's turn. She will sing for us now."

"After that I could not," said Demelza, whom the last piece and the strong wine had much affected. "I was praying to God you had forgotten me."

Everyone laughed.

"We must hear this and go," said Ruth with an eye on her husband. "Please, Mistress Poldark, overcome your modesty and satisfy us as to your attainments. We are all agog."

Demelza's eyes met those of the other girl and saw in them a challenge. She rose to it. The port had given her Dutch courage.

"Well—"

With mixed feelings Ross saw her walk across to the harp and sit down at the seat Elizabeth had left. She could not play a note on the instrument, but the instinct was sound which persuaded her to take up this position; the others were grouped round it to listen and she was saved the awkwardness of standing with nothing to do with her hands. But ten minutes ago was the time when she should have sung, when everyone was jolly and prepared to join in. Elizabeth's cultured, delicate playing had changed the atmosphere. The anticlimax would be certain.

Demelza settled herself comfortably, straightening her back, and plucked at a string with her finger. The note it gave out was pleasing and reassuring. Contrast with Elizabeth: gone was the halo and in its place the dark crown of humanity.

She looked at Ross; in her eyes was a demon of mischief. She began to sing.

Her slightly husky voice, almost contralto, an imperceptible fraction off the note, and sweet-toned, made no effort to impress by volume; rather, it seemed to confide as a personal message what it had to say.

> I d' pluck a fair rose for my love;
> I d' pluck a red rose blowing.
> Love's in my heart a-trying so to prove
> What your heart's knowing.
> I d' pluck a finger on a thorn,
> I d' pluck a finger bleeding.
> Red is my heart a-wounded and forlorn
> And your heart needing.
> I d' hold a finger to my tongue,
> I d' hold a finger waiting.
> My heart is sore until it joins in song
> Wi' your heart mating.

There was a moment's pause, and Demelza coughed to show that she had done. There came murmurs of praise, some of it merely polite but some of it spontaneous.

"Very charming," said Francis, through half-closed lids.

"Egad," said John Treneglos with a sigh. "I liked that."

"Egad," said Demelza, sparkling at him. "I was afeard you might not."

"A sharp answer, ma'am," said Treneglos. He was just beginning to realize why Ross had committed the solecism of marrying his kitchenmaid. "Have you any more of the same?"

"Songs or answers, sir?" asked Demelza.

"I have not heard that piece before," said Elizabeth. "I am much taken with it."

"Songs, I meant, chit," said Treneglos, putting his feet up. "I know you have the answers."

"John," said his wife. "It is time we were going."

"I am comfortable here. Thank you, Verity. A good body this port has, Francis. When did you get it?"

"Trencrom's firm. Their stuff has been less good of late. I must make a change."

"I bought some passable port the other day," said George. "Regrettably tax had been paid and it ran me in for near on three guineas for thirteen quart bottles."

Francis raised an ironical eyebrow. George was a good friend and an indulgent creditor, but he could not refrain from bringing into a conversation the price he had paid for things. It was almost the only sign left of his origins.

"How do you contrive for servants now, Elizabeth?" Ruth asked, her voice carrying. "I have the utmost difficulty. Mama was saying this morning that there was really no satisfying 'em. The young generation, she was saying, have such *ideas,* always wishing to rise above their station."

"One more song, Demelza please," Verity interposed. "What was that you were wont to play when I stayed with you? You remember, the seiner's song."

"I like them all," said John. "Damme, I had no idea we was in such gifted company."

Demelza drained her newly filled glass. Her fingers went over the strings of the harp and made a surprising sound.

"I have another," she said gently. She looked at Ross a moment, then at Treneglos from under her lashes. The wine she had drunk had lit up her eyes.

She began to sing, very low but very clear.

> I suspicioned she was pretty
> I suspicioned she was wed,
> My father told me twas against the law.
> I saw that she was coxy,
> No loving here by proxy,
> As pretty a piece of mischief as never I saw.
> With no intentions meaning
> I called at candleteening: All's fair they say in love as well as war.
> My good intentions dropped me,
> No father's warning stopped me,
> As pretty a piece of mischief as never I saw.

Here she paused, then opened her eyes for a second at John Treneglos before she sang the last verse.

> The nest was warm around us,
> No spouse came home and found us,
> Our youth it was as sweet as it was raw.
> And now the cuckoo's homing
> A-tired of his roaming.
> As pretty a piece of mischief as never I saw.

John Treneglos roared and slapped his thighs. Demelza helped herself to another glass of port.

"Bravo!" said George. "I like that song. It has a pleasant tripping sound. Well sung, indeed!"

Ruth rose. "Come, John. It will be tomorrow before we reach home."

"Nonsense, my dear." John tugged at the fob attached to his chronometer, but the watch would not come out of his deep pocket. "Has anyone the time? It cannot be ten yet."

"You did not like my song, ma'am?" Demelza asked, addressing Ruth.

Ruth's lips moved a fraction. "Indeed, yes. I found it most enlightening."

"It is the half after nine," said Warleggan.

"Indeed, ma'am," said Demelza. "I am surprised you d' need enlightening on such a matter."

Ruth went white at the nostrils. It is to be doubted whether Demelza understood the full flavour of her remark. But with five large glasses of port inside her, she was not given to weighing the pros and cons of a retort before she made it. She felt Ross come up behind her, his hand touch her arm.

"It was not of the matter I was speaking." Ruth's gaze went past her. "May I congratulate you, Ross, on a wife so very skilled in all the arts of entertainment."

"Not skilled," said Ross, squeezing Demelza's arm, "but a very quick learner."

"The choice of tutor means so much, does it not?"

"Oh yes," agreed Demelza. "Ross is so kind he could charm the sourest of us into a show o' manners."

Ruth patted her arm. She had the opening she wanted. "I don't think you are quite the best judge of that yet, my dear."

Demelza looked at her and nodded. "No. Mebbe I should have said all but the sourest."

Before the exchange became still more deadly, Verity interposed. The visitors were moving off. Even John was at last levered from his chair. They all drifted out into the hall.

Amid much laughter and last-minute talk, cloaks were put on and Ruth changed her delicate slippers for buckle riding shoes. Her new-fashioned riding cloak had to be admired. A full half hour passed while affectionate goodbyes and seasonal wishes were given and received, jokes made and replied to. At last, to the clop and clatter of hoofs, the party moved off down the drive, and the big door banged. The Poldarks were alone again.

CHAPTER TEN

———————⁓———————

ALL THINGS REVIEWED, IT HAD BEEN DEMELZA'S EVENING. SHE HAD COME through a searching test with quite remarkable success. The fact that the success was due partly to nausea at the dinner table and partly to five glasses of port at a crucial stage of the evening was known only to her and she kept it to herself.

As they said good night to their relatives two hours later and mounted the broad portrait-hung stairs, Ross was conscious of this new side of her nature which his wife had shown. All through the evening surprise had mingled with his inner amusement: Demelza's charm, almost beauty, in her new and fashionable dress; the impression she had created; her quiet unassuming dignity over the dinner, when he had expected her to be nervous and stiff or boisterous and hungry. Demelza among the unexpected arrivals, giving as good as she got without compromising her dignity, singing those saucy songs in her low, husky voice with its soft native burr. Demelza flirting with John Treneglos under Ruth's very nose—under Ross's own too for that matter.

Demelza being kept with difficulty and tact away from the port when the visitors had gone. (While they were at limited loo, which the girl could not play, he had watched her edge round the room and pour herself out a couple of glasses on the sly.) Demelza now mounting the broad stairs sedately beside him, erect and unruffled in her mauve and apple-green silk, from which emerged her strong slender neck and shoulders like the white inner heart of a flower.

Demelza more detached from him than he had ever known her. Tonight he had withdrawn from her, had seen her with a new eye. Here against the background, which was strange to her but which for him had the most definite of associations and standards, she had proved herself and was not found wanting. He was not sorry now that he had come. He remembered Elizabeth's words: "You must take her into society and bring her out." Even that might not be impossible if she wished it. A new life might be opening for them both. He felt pleased and stimulated and proud of the developing character of his young wife.

His young wife hiccupped as they reached their bedroom. She too was feeling different from what she had ever felt before. She felt like a jug of fermenting cider, full of bubbles and air, lightheaded, bilious, and as uninterested in sleep as Ross. She gazed round the handsome room with its cream-and-pink flock paper and its brocaded curtains.

"Ross," she said. "I wish those birds was not so spotty. Missel thrushes was never so spotty as they. If they wish to paint spots on birds on curtains, why don't they paint the spots the right colour? No bird ever had pink spots. Nor no bird was ever as spotty as they."

She leaned against Ross, who leaned back against the door he had just closed and patted her cheek.

"You're tipsy, child."

"Indeed I'm not." She regained her balance and walked with cool dignity across the room. She sat heavily in a chair before the fire and kicked off her shoes. Ross lit the rest of the candles from the one he carried and after an interval they burned up, lighting the room.

Demelza sat there, her arms behind her head, her toes stretched towards the fire while Ross slowly undressed. They exchanged a casual word from time to time, laughed together over Ross's account of Treneglos's antics with the spinning wheel; Demelza questioned him about Ruth, about the Teagues, about George Warleggan. Their voices were low and warm and confidential. This was the intimacy of pure companionship.

The house had fallen quiet about them. Although they were not sleepy, the pleasant warmth and comfort turned their senses imperceptibly towards sleep. Ross had a moment of unspoiled satisfaction. He received love and gave it in equal and generous measure. Their relationship at that moment had no flaw.

In Francis's dressing gown he sat down on the stool beside her chair and stretched his hands towards the glow of the fire.

There was silence.

Presently out of the fount of Demelza's content sprang an old resolve.

"Did I behave myself tonight, Ross?" she asked. "Did I behave as Mrs. Poldark should behave?"

"You misbehaved monstrously," he said, "and were a triumph."

"Don't tease. You think I have been a good wife?"

"Moderately good. Quite moderately good."

"Did I sing nice?"

"You were inspired."

Silence fell again.

"Ross."

"Yes, bud?"

"Bud again," she said. "Tonight I have been called both Bud and Blossom. I hope in a few years' time they will not start calling me Pod."

He laughed, silently but long.

"Ross," she said again, when he had at last done.

"Yes?"

"If I have been a good wife, then you must promise me somethin'."

"Very well," he said.

"You must promise me that sometime before—before Easter you will ride to Falmouth and seek Captain Blarney out and see if he still loves Verity."

There was a moment's pause.

"How am I to tell whom he loves?" Ross asked ironically. He was far too contented to argue with her.

"Ask him. You was his friend. He will not lie about a thing like that."

"And then?"

"If he still loves her, we can arrange for them to meet."

"And then?"

"Then we shan't need to do any more."

"You're very persistent, are you not?"

"Only because you're that stubborn."

"We cannot arrange people's lives for them."

Demelza hiccupped.

"You have no heart," she said. "That's what I can't fathom. You love me but you have no heart."

"I'm deeply fond of Verity, but—"

"Ah, your buts! You've no faith, Ross. You men don't understand. You don't know the teeniest thing about Verity! That you don't."

"Do you?"

"I don't need to. I know myself."

"Conceive the fact that there may be women unlike you."

"Tom—ti—pom!" said Demelza. "You don't scare me wi' your big words. I know Verity was not born to be an old maid, dryin' up and shrivellin' while she looks to someone else's house an' children. She'd rather take the risk of being wed to a man who couldn't contain his liquor." She bent forward and began to pull off her stockings.

He watched her. "You seem to have developed a whole philosophy since you married me, love."

"No I ain't—haven't," said Demelza. "But I know what love is."

The remark seemed to put the discussion on a different plane.

"Yes," he agreed soberly. "So do I."

A longer silence fell.

"If you love someone," said Demelza, "tesn't a few bruises on the back that are going to count. It's whether that other one loves you in return. If he do, then he can only hurt your body. He can't hurt your heart."

She rolled her stockings into a ball and leaned back in the chair again, wiggling her toes towards the fire. Ross picked up the poker and turned over the ash and embers until they broke into a blaze.

"So you'll go to Falmouth an' see?" she asked.

"I'll consider it," said Ross. "I'll consider it."

Having come this far, she was too wise to press further. Another and less elevated lesson she had learned in married life was that if she wheedled long enough and discreetly enough, she quite often got her own way in the end.

With ears grown more sharp to the smaller sounds, it seemed to them that the silence of the house was less complete than it had been a while ago. It had become the faint stirring silence of old timber and slate, old in the history of Poldarks and Trenwiths, people whose forgotten faces hung in the deserted hall, whose forgotten loves and hopes had drawn breath and flourished here. Jeffrey Trenwith, building this house in fire and faith; Claude, deeply involved in the Prayer Book Rebellion; Humphrey in his Elizabethan ruff; Charles Vivian Poldark, wounded and home from the sea; red-haired Anna-Maria; Presbyterian Joan; mixed policies and creeds; generations of children, instant with the joy of life, growing and learning and fading. The full silence of the old house was more potent than the empty silence of its youth. Panels still felt the brush of mouldered silk, boards still creaked under the pressure of the forgotten foot. For a time something stepped between the man and the girl sitting at the fire. They felt it and it left them apart from each other and alone with their thoughts.

But even the strength of the past could not just then break their companionship for long. Somehow, and because of the nature of their being, the old peculiar silence ceased to be a barrier and became a medium. They had been overawed by time. Then time again became their friend.

"Are you asleep?" Ross said.

"No," said Demelza.

Then she moved and put her finger on his arm.

He rose slowly and bent over her, took her face in his hands and kissed her on the eyes, the mouth, and the forehead. With a queer tigerish limpness she allowed him to do what he wanted.

And presently the white inner heart of the bud was free of its petals.

Only then did she put up her hands to his face and kiss him in return.

CHAPTER ELEVEN

They went home the following day after an early dinner, walking as they had come, by way of the cliff path and Sawle Village and Nampara Cove. They had said goodbye to their relatives, and were again alone, striding off over the heather-covered moor.

For a time they talked as they had talked last night, desultorily, confidentially, laughing together and silent. There had been rain this morning, heavy and windless, but it had stopped while they were at dinner and the sky had cleared. Now clouds had gathered again. There was a heavy ground swell.

Demelza was so glad that her ordeal was over, and decently even triumphantly over, that she took his arm and began to sing. She took big masculine strides to keep up with his, but every now and then would have to give a little skip to make good lost ground. She fitted these in with her song so that her voice gave an upward skip at the same time as her feet.

Before the sun set, the black day broke on the horizon and sea and land were flooded with light. At the sudden warmth under the lowering clouds, all the waves became disordered and ran in ragged confusion with heads tossing and glinting in the sun.

Demelza thought: I am nearer sure of him than I have ever been before. How ignorant I was that first June morning thinking everything was sure. Even that August night after the pilchards came, even then there had been nothing to compare me with. All last summer I told myself it was as certain as anything could be. I felt sure. But last night was different. After a whole seven hours in Elizabeth's company, he still wanted me at the end. After a talk all to themselves with her making eyes at him like a she-cat, he still came to me. Perhaps she isn't so bad. Perhaps she isn't such a cat. Perhaps I feel sorry for her. Why does Francis look so bored? Perhaps I feel sorry for her after all. Dear Verity helped. I hope my baby doesn't have codfish eyes like Geoffrey Charles. I believe I'm going thinner, not fatter. I hope nothing's wrong. I wish I didn't feel so sick. Ruth Treneglos is worse than Elizabeth. She didn't like me making up to her hare-and-hounds husband. As if I cared for him. Though I shouldn't like to meet him in a dark lane with nobody near. I think she was jealous of me in another way. Perhaps she wanted Ross to marry her. Anyway, I'm going home to *my* home, to bald Jud and fat Prudie and red-haired Jinny and long-legged Cobbledick, going home to get fat and ugly myself. And I don't care. Verity was right. He'll stick to me. Not because he ought to but because he wants to. Mustn't forget Verity. I'll scheme like a serpent. I would dearly love to go to one of George Warleggan's card parties. I wonder if I ever shall. I wonder if Prudie's remembered to meat the calves. I wonder if she burned the heavy cake. I wonder if it's going to rain. Dear life, I wonder if I'm going to be sick.

They reached Sawle, crossed the shingle bar, and climbed the hill at the other side.

"Are you tired?" Ross asked, as she seemed to lag.

"No, no." It was the first time he had ever asked that.

The sun had gone down now, and the brows of the sky were dark. After their brief carnival the waves had reassembled and rode in showing long, green caverns as they curved to break.

And Ross again knew himself to be happy—in a new and less ephemeral way than before. He was filled with a queer sense of enlightenment. It seemed to him that all his life had moved to this pinpoint of time down the scattered threads of twenty years; from his old childhood running thoughtless and barefoot in the sun on Hendrawna sands, from Demelza's birth in the squalor of a mining cottage, from the plains of Virginia and the trampled fairgrounds of Redruth, from the complex impulses which had governed Elizabeth's choice of Francis and from the simple philosophies of Demelza's own faith, all had been animated to a common end—and that end a moment of enlightenment and understanding and completion. Someone—a Latin poet—had defined eternity as no more than this: to hold and possess the whole fullness of life in one moment, here and now, past and present and to come.

He thought: if we could only *stop* life for a while I would stop here. Not when I get home, not leaving Trenwith, but here, here reaching the top of the hill out of Sawle, dusk wiping out the edges of the land and Demelza walking and humming at my side.

He knew of things plucking at his attention. All existence was a cycle of difficulties to be met and obstacles to be surmounted. But at this evening hour of Christmas Day, 1787, he was not concerned with the future, only the present.

He thought: I am not hungry or thirsty or lustful or envious; I am not perplexed or weary or ambitious or remorseful. Just ahead, in the immediate future, there is waiting an open door and a warm house, comfortable chairs and quietness and companionship. Let me hold it.

In the slow dusk they skirted Nampara Cove and began the last short climb beside the brook towards the house.

Demelza began to sing, mischievously and in a deep voice:

There was an old couple and they was poor, Tweedle, tweedle, go twee.

ABOUT THE AUTHOR

Winston Graham was the author of forty novels, including *The Walking Stick, Angell, Pearl and Little God, Stephanie,* and *Tremor.* His books have been widely translated and his famous Poldark series has been developed into two television series shown in twenty-four countries. A special two-hour television programme has been made of his eighth Poldark novel, *The Stranger from the Sea,* whilst a five-part television serial of his early novel *The Forgotten Story* won a silver medal at the New York Film Festival. Six of Winston Graham's books have been filmed for the big screen, the most notable being *Mamie,* directed by Alfred Hitchcock. Winston Graham was a Fellow of the Royal Society of Literature and in 1983 was awarded the OBE. He died in July 2003.

READING GROUP GUIDE

1. When Ross arrives home after years of fighting in America, he discovers that Elizabeth, the woman he loved, was engaged to marry his cousin Francis. This causes several confrontations, most notably the argument that Ross and Francis have down in the mine that nearly results in Francis drowning. Ross says that the incident had not only shown the extent of his anger, but its limitations as well. Do you think that Francis realized this? What do you think that Ross and Francis's reactions to this incident say about each man?

2. When Ross first returns to Nampara he finds Jud and Prudie drunk and the house and land in a terrible state of disrepair, yet he decides to keep Jud and Prudie on to bring the house back to working order. Does he keep them out of sentimentality or simply because it is easiest? How is he later rewarded by keeping rather lazy, but faithful, servants?

3. Ross seems to be more connected with the people who live on his land than many of the other members of his class are. Do you believe this is because of the way of life he saw in America, or is he inherently different from his peers?

4. Verity becomes romantically attached to Captain Blamey who, it is discovered, has a history of alcoholism and was involved with the death of his first wife. Verity claims that he is reformed, that he no longer drinks, and would not hurt her. Do you believe this is true? Are people capable of changing so drastically? Verity's relatives are violently opposed to the match. If you were in their position, would you be comfortable letting your child/sister marry a man in that situation?

5. Verity and Captain Blamey's romance ends abruptly after the duel between Captain Blamey and Francis. Demelza later tells Ross that this was at least partly

his fault. Do you agree that Ross should have done something to prevent the duel? Did he allow the duel to occur because he didn't approve of the match, or was there another reason?

6. Once Demelza grows into a young woman, rumors intensify that Ross is keeping her as a kitchen wench for his own lascivious purposes. He chooses to ignore the rumors, and seems to take it all fairly well, believing that the people who matter to him will know they are not true. How would you deal with unfounded but pervasive rumors about yourself? About someone you love?

7. Not long after Elizabeth give birth to Geoffrey Charles, Francis wants to be intimate but is rebuffed. "There was no one to tell him that he was wrong in being jealous of Ross. There was no one to tell him that another and more powerful rival had arisen. There was no one to warn him about Geoffrey Charles." Do you believe it is Geoffrey Charles, or Francis being jealous of Ross that drives Francis and Elizabeth apart?

8. Demelza is at first very nervous about meeting Verity and begs Ross not to invite her to the house. After a few days the two women bond and become fast friends. In what ways does Verity influence Demelza? In what ways does Demelza influence Verity?

9. At the Christmas party, Demelza surprises Ross by successfully navigating the social challenges of the evening. By the end of the night many people have changed their opinions of Demelza, and Demelza has changed her opinions of some people as well, particularly Elizabeth. Where she used to be intimidated and jealous of Elizabeth, she now feels sorry for her. Does Elizabeth deserve Demelza's pity? Have you ever been jealous of someone, but after getting to know them, discovered they were not as intimidating as they seemed?

10. Do you think that Ross and Demelza's marriage has a better chance of surviving than Francis and Elizabeth's despite the differences in their social class and backgrounds?

Demelza

A Novel of Cornwall, 1788–1790

Read on for an excerpt from *Demelza,* Book 2 in the Poldark series. Available from Sourcebooks in Spring 2010.

CHAPTER ONE

There could have been prophecy in the storm that blew up at the time of Julia's birth.

May month was not a time for heavy gales, but the climate of Cornwall is capricious as any child ever born. It had been a kindly enough spring, as kindly as the summer and winter that had gone before it; mild, soft, comfortable weather; and the land was already heavy with green things. Then May broke rainy and gusty, and the blossom suffered here and there and the hay leaned about looking for support.

On the night of the fifteenth Demelza felt her first pains. Even then for a while she gripped the bedpost and thought the matter all round before she said anything. All along she had viewed the coming ordeal with a calm and philosophical mind and had never troubled Ross with false alarms. She did not want to begin so late. Last evening she had been out in her beloved garden, digging round the young plants; then as it was going dark she had found a disgruntled hedgehog and had played with him, trying to persuade him to take some bread and milk, and had only come in reluctantly as the sky clouded and it went cold.

This now—this thing in the middle of the night—might yet be only the result of getting overtired.

But when it began to feel as if someone was kneeling on her backbone and trying to break it, she knew it was not.

She touched Ross's arm and he woke instantly.

"Well?"

"I think," she said, "I think you will have to fetch Prudie."

He sat up. "Why? What is it?"

"I have a pain."

"Where? Do you mean?"

"I have a pain," she said primly. "I think twould be as well to fetch Prudie."

He climbed quickly out of bed, and she listened to the scratch of flint and steel. After a moment the tinder caught and he lit a candle. The room flickered into view: heavy teak beams, the curtain over the door moving gently in the breeze, the low window seat hung with pink grogram, her shoes as she had kicked them off, one wooden sole upmost, Joshua's spyglass, Ross's pipe, Ross's book and a fly crawling.

He looked at her and at once knew the truth. She smiled a pallid apology. He went across to the table by the door and poured her a glass of brandy.

"Drink this. I will send Jud for Dr. Choake." He began to pull on his clothes, anyhow.

"No, no, Ross; do not send yet. It is the middle of the night. He will be asleep."

Whether Thomas Choake should be called in to her had been a dissension between them for some weeks. Demelza could not forget that twelve months ago she had been a maidservant and that Choake, though only a physician, owned a small estate which, even if it had been bought with his wife's money, put him on a level from which the likes of her would be seen as unimportant chattels. That was until Ross married her. Since then she had grown to her position. She could put on a show of refinement and good manners, and not at all a bad show at that; but a doctor was different. A doctor caught one at a disadvantage. If the pain was bad she would almost certainly swear in the old way she had learned from her father, not a few genteel "damn mes" and "by Gods," as anyone might excuse from a lady in trouble. To have a baby and be forced to act genteel at the same time was more than Demelza could look forward to.

Besides, she didn't want a man about. It wasn't decent. Her cousin-in-law, Elizabeth, had had him, but Elizabeth was an aristocrat born and bred, and they looked at things different. *She* would far rather have had old Aunt Betsy Triggs from Mellin, who sold pilchards and was a rare strong hand when it came to babies.

But Ross was the more determined and he had had his way. She was not unprepared for his curt, "Then he shall be woke," as he left the room.

"Ross!" She called him back. For the moment the pain had gone.

"Yes?" His strong, scarred, introspective face was half lit by the candle; the upgrowing dark hair was ruffled and hardly showed its hint of copper; his shirt was open at the throat. This man...aristocrat of them all, she thought...this man, so reserved and reserving, with whom she had shared rare intimacy.

"Would you?" she said. "Before you go..."

He came back to the bed. The emergency had come on him so quickly in his sleep that he had had no time yet to feel anything but alarm that her time was here and relief that it might soon be over. As he kissed her he saw the moisture on her face and a worm of fear and compassion moved in him. He took her face in his hands, pushed back the black hair, and stared a moment into the dark eyes of his young wife. They were not dancing and mischievous as they so often were, but there was no fear in them.

"I'll be back. In a moment I'll be back."

She made a gesture of dissent. "Don't come back, Ross. Go and tell Prudie, that's all. I'd rather—you didn't see me like this."

"And what of Verity? You specially wanted Verity here."

"Tell her in the morning. Tisn't fair to bring her out in the night air. Send for her in the morning."

He kissed her again.

"Tell me that you love me, Ross," she said.

He looked at her in surprise.

"You know I do!"

"And say you don't love Elizabeth."

"And I don't love Elizabeth." What else was he to say when he did not know the truth himself? He was not a man who spoke his inmost feelings easily, but now he saw himself powerless to help her, and only words of his and not actions would give her aid. "Nothing else matters but you," he said. "Remember that. All my relatives and friends—and Elizabeth, and this house and the mine...I'd throw them in the dust and you know it—and you know it. If you don't know it, then all these months I've failed and no words I can give you now will make it otherwise. I love you, Demelza, and we've had such happiness. And we're going to have it again. Take hold of that, my sweet. Hold it and keep it, for no one else can."

"I'll hold it, Ross," she said, content because the words had come.

He kissed her again and turned and lit more candles; took up one and went quickly out of the room, the hot grease running over his hand. The wind had dropped since yesterday; there was only a breeze. He did not know the time, but it felt about two.

He pushed open the door on the other side of the landing and went across to the bedroom where Jud and Prudie slept. The ill-fitting bedroom door opened with a long squeak which merged into Prudie's slow rasping snore. He grunted in disgust, for the hot, close, sweaty smell offended his nose. The night air might be dangerous, but they could surely open the window during the day and let this stink out.

He went across and parted the curtains and shook Jud by the shoulders. Jud's two great teeth showed like gravestones. He shook again, violently. Jud's nightcap came off and a spot of the candle grease fell on his bald patch. Jud woke. He began to curse; then he saw who it was and sat up rubbing his head.

"What's amiss?"

"Demelza is ill." How call her anything but Demelza to a man who had been here when she came as a tattered waif of thirteen? "I want you to go for Dr. Choake at once. And wake Prudie. She will be wanted too."

"What's amiss with her?"

"Her pains have begun."

"Oh, that. I thought ee said she were ill." Jud frowned at the piece of cooling tallow he had found on his head. "Prudie and me could manage that. Prudie d'know all that sort of panjandle. Tedn a 'ard thing to learn. Why, there's always such a dido about en I never can conceit. Tedn easy, mind, but once you've gotten the knack—"

"Get up."

Jud came out of bed, knowing the tone, and they woke Prudie. Her great shiny face peered through its tangle of greasy black hair as she wiped her nose on a corner of her night rail.

"Aw, my dear, I'll see to the mite. Poor maid." She began to fasten a pair of filthy stays over her shift. "I d'know how twas with my mother. She told me how twas when I was on the brew. Shifted I 'ad. Moved I 'ad. Twas a cruel chronic thing, they said. A weak, ailing little mouse, an' nobody believed I'd see the christening pot…"

"Go to her as soon as you can," Ross said. "I'll get Darkie from the stables. You won't want her saddled."

"Mebbe I can ride bare-ridged that far," Jud said grudgingly. "Though if onct you d'make a slip in the dark, like as not you're pitched off on yer 'ead, and then snap goes yer neck and where are you?"

Ross ran down the stairs. On his way out he looked in at the new clock they had bought for the parlour. It wanted ten minutes to three. Dawn would not be long. Things were so much worse by candlelight.

In the stable he delayed to saddle Darkie, telling his fumbling fingers that every woman went through this: it became a commonplace of their existence, pregnancies following each other like the summer seasons. But he would see Jud safely off; if the fool slipped he might be hours. He would have gone himself if he could have trusted the Paynters alone with Demelza.

At the front of the house Jud was fastening his breeches under the lilac tree.

"Don't know as I shall rightly see me way," he said. "Dark as a blathering sack, tis. By rights I should 'ave a lantern on a pole. A long pole as I could 'old out—"

"Get up or you'll have the pole across your head."

Jud mounted. "What's to say as he won't come?"

"Bring him," said Ross, and gave Darkie a slap across the haunches.

When Jud turned in at the gates of Fernmore, the house of Thomas Choake, he observed disdainfully that the building was little more than a farmhouse, though they put on airs as if it was Blenheim. He got down and rat-tatted at the door. The house was surrounded by big pine trees, and the rooks and jackdaws were already awake, flying round in circles and being noisy. Jud raised his head and sniffed. All yesterday they'd been unsettled at Nampara.

At the seventh knock a window screeched above the door, and a nightcap appeared like a cuckoo out of a clock.

"Well, man, well, man! What is it? What's the damnation noise?"

Jud knew by the voice and eyebrows that he had flushed the right bird.

"Cap'n Poldark sent me for to fetch ee," he said, mumbling. "Dem—um—Mistress Poldark's took bad and they d' need you."

"What Mistress Poldark, man? What Mistress Poldark?"

"Mistress Demelza Poldark. Over to Nampara. 'Er that be going to have 'er first."

"Well, what's wrong? Didn't they say what was to do?"

"Ais. Tes her time."

"Nonsense, fellow. I saw her last week and I told Captain Poldark that there would be nothing until June. Go tell them I stand by that opinion."

The window slammed.

Jud Paynter was a man much interested in the malign indifference of man and providence to his own needs, and interested in not much else; but sometimes an accident roused him for other ends. This was one of the accidents.

From feeling disgruntled at the simpering softness of Demelza and the misplaced harshness of Ross in turning him out on a bitter May morning without so much as a tot of rum, he came to reflect that Ross was his master and Demelza one of his own kind.

Three minutes later Dr Choake put out his head again.

"What is it, man? You'll have the door down!"

"I was told to fetch you."

"You insolent fellow! I'll have you thrashed for this!"

"Where's yer 'orse? I'll 'ave him out while you put yer drawers on."

The surgeon withdrew, Polly Choake's lisping voice could be heard in the background, and once her fluffy head passed the window. They were in consultation. Then Choake called down coldly:

"You must wait, fellow. We shall be with you in ten minutes."

Jud was sufficiently alive to the surgeon's peculiarities to know that by this Choake meant only himself.

Twenty-one minutes later, in icy silence, they set off. The rooks were still flying in circles and cawing, and at Sawle Church there was a great noise. Day was breaking. Streaks of watered green showed in the north-east, and the sky where the sun would rise was a bold, pale orange behind the black ribs of the night. A wild sunrise and a strangely quiet one. After the winds of the last days the calm was profound. As they passed Grambler Mine they overtook a party of balmaidens singing as they walked to work, their shrill fresh voices as sweet and young as the morning. Jud noticed that Will Nanfan's sheep were all gathered together in the most sheltered corner of the field.

Reflection on the quiet ride salved some of Dr. Choake's annoyance, for when they reached Nampara he did not complain, but greeted Ross stiffly and lumbered upstairs. There he found that the alarm was not a false one. He sat with Demelza for half an hour telling her to be brave and that there was nothing to be frightened of. Then, because she seemed constrained and was sweating a lot, he suspected a touch of fever and bled her to be on the safe side. This made her feel very ill, a result which pleased him for it proved, he said, that a toxic condition had existed and his treatment had brought on a normal and desirable intermission of the fever. If she took an infusion of bark once an hour it would prevent a renewal. Then he went home to breakfast.

Ross had been swilling himself under the pump trying to wash away the megrims of the night, and when he came through the house and saw a thickset figure riding up the valley he called sharply to Jinny Carter, who came every day to work in the house and had just arrived.

"Is that Dr. Choake?"

Jinny bent over her own child, which she brought on her back and kept in a basket in the kitchen. "Yes, sur. He d'say the baby won't be afore dinner at the early side, and he say he'll be back by nine or ten."

Ross turned away to hide his annoyance. Jinny looked at him with devoted eyes.

"Who helped you with your babies, Jinny?" he asked.

"Mother, sur."

"Will you go and get her, Jinny? I think I would trust your mother before that old fool."

She blushed with pleasure. "Yes, sur. I'll go right off. She'll be that glad to come." She started as if to go and then looked at her own baby.

"I'll see she comes to no harm," Ross said.

She glanced at him a moment and then snatched up her white bonnet and left the kitchen.

Ross walked into the low hall, stood at the foot of the stairs, disliked the silence, went into the parlour and poured himself a glass of brandy, watched Jinny's brisk figure dwindling towards Mellin, returned to the kitchen. Little Kate had not moved, but lay on her back kicking and crowing and laughing at him. This mite was nine months old and had never seen its father, who was serving a two-year sentence in Bodmin Gaol for poaching. Unlike the two eldest, who took after their father, little Kate was a true Martin: sandy hair, blue eyes, tiny freckles, already mottling the bridge of her button nose.

The fire had not been lighted this morning, and there was no sign of breakfast. Ross raked the ashes but they were dead; he picked up some kindling wood and set about lighting it, wondering irritably where Jud had gone. There must be hot water, he knew, and towels and basins; nothing was being prepared down here. Damn Choake for his impertinence, not even waiting to see him before he left.

Relations between the two men had been cool for some time. Ross disliked his inane wife, who had gossiped and whispered about Demelza; and when Ross disliked someone he found it hard to hide the fact. Now he fumed that he should be at the mercy of this obstinate stiff-necked unprogressive old fool who was the only physician within miles.

As the fire began to take Jud came in, and wind came with him and rushed round the kitchen.

"Thur's something blawing up," he said, eyeing Ross out of bloodshot eyes. "Seen the long black swell, 'ave ee?"

Ross nodded impatiently. There had been a heavy ground sea since afternoon yesterday.

"Well, tes breaking all ways. Scarcely ever did I see the like. It might be as someone was lashin' of un with a whip. The swell's nigh gone and the sea's all licky-white like Joe Trigg's beard."

"Keep your eye on Kate, Jud," Ross said. "Make some breakfast in the mean-time. I am going upstairs."

At the back of his mind Ross was aware of the sound of wind rushing about in the distance. Once when he glanced out of the bedroom window his eyes confirmed that the swell had in fact quite broken up and the sea was stippled with white-lipped waves which crossed and re-crossed each other in confusion, running heedlessly, colliding and breaking up into wisps of futile spray. The wind was as yet only gusty on the land, but here and there eddies rushed over the water, little winds, vicious and lost.

While he was there Demelza made a big effort to be normal, but he saw that she wished him gone. He could not help her.

Disconsolate, he went down again and was in time to greet Mrs. Zacky Martin, Jinny's mother. Flat-faced, competent, bespectacled, and sneezing, she came into the kitchen with a brood of five small children dragging at her heels, talking to them, chiding them, explaining to Ross that she had no one to trust them with—Jinny's two eldest and her three youngest— greeting Jud and asking after Prudie, commenting on the smell of frying pork, inquiring about the patient, saying she had a touch of ague herself but had taken a posset before leaving, rolling up her sleeves, telling Jinny to put the colewort and the motherwort on to brew, they being better than any doctor's nostrums for easing of the maid, and disappearing up the stairs before anyone else could speak.

There seemed to be a child on every chair in the kitchen. They sat like timid ninepins at a fair, waiting to be knocked off. Jud scratched his head and spat in the fire and swore.

Ross went back to the parlour. On the table was a bundle of crochet work that Demelza had been doing last night. A fashion paper which Verity had lent her lay beside it—something new and novel come to them from London; there had never been anything like it before. The room was a little dusty and unkempt.

It was fifteen minutes after six.

No birds singing this morning. A moment ago a ray of sunlight had fallen across the grass, but had been quickly put out. He stared at the elm trees, which were waving backwards and forwards as if with an earth tremor. The apple trees, more sheltered, were bending and turning up their leaves. The sky was heavy with racing clouds.

He picked up a book. His eyes scanned the page but took nothing in. The wind was beginning to roar down the valley. Mrs Zacky came in.

"Well?"

"She'm doing brave, Cap'n Ross. Prudie and me'll manage, don't ee worry an inch. Twill all be over long before ole Dr. Tommie d'come back."

Ross put down the book. "Are you sure?"

"Well, I've had eleven o' my own and there's three of Jinny's. And I helped wi' two of Betty Nanfan's twins and four of Sue Vìgus's, the first three out of wedlock." Mrs. Zacky hadn't fingers enough to count. 'This won't be easy, not like Jinny's was, but we'll do a proper job, never you fear. Now I'll go get the brandy an' give the maid a tot o' that t'ease her up."

The house suddenly shuddered under a gust of wind. Ross stood staring out at the wild day, anger with Choake rising in him and seeking outlet like a part of the storm. Common sense told him that Demelza would be all right, but that she should be denied the best attention was intolerable. It was Demelza who suffered there, with only two clumsy old women to help her.

He went out to the stables, hardly aware of the storm that was rising about them.

At the stable door he glanced over Hendrawna and saw that clouds of spray had begun to lift off the sea and drift away like sand before a sandstorm. Here and there the cliffs were smoking.

He had just got the stable door open when the wind took it out of his hand, slammed it shut and pushed him against the wall. He looked up and saw that it would not be possible to ride a horse in the gale.

He set off to walk. It was only a matter of two miles.

A hail of leaves and grass and dirt and small twigs met him as he turned the corner of the house. Behind him the wind was tearing off mouthfuls of sea and flinging them to join the clouds. At another time he would have been upset at the damage to his crops, but now that seemed a small matter. It was not so much a gale as a sudden storm, as if the forces of a gathering anger had been bottled up for a month and must be spent in an hour. The branch of an elm came down across the stream. He stumbled past it, wondering if he could make the brow of the hill.

In the ruined buildings of Wheal Maiden he sat and gasped and groped for breath and rubbed his bruised hand, and the wind blew bits of masonry from the gaunt old granite walls and screamed like a harlot through every slit and hole.

Once through the pine trees, he met the full force of the storm coming in across Grambler Plain, bringing with it a bombardment of rain and dirt and gravel. Here it seemed that all the loose soil was being ploughed up and all the fresh young leaves and all the other small substances of the earth were being blown right away. The clouds were low over his head, brown and racing, all the rain emptied out of them and flying like torn rags before the frown of God.

Down in Fernmore, Dr. Choake was beginning his breakfast.